THE
REGISTRATION

MADISON LAWSON

THE REGISTRATION

CamCat
Books

CamCat Publishing, LLC
Brentwood, Tennessee 37027
camcatpublishing.com

Hardcover ISBN 9780744307023
Paperback ISBN 9780744307030
Large-Print Paperback ISBN 9780744307047
eBook ISBN 9780744307061
Audiobook ISBN 9780744307092

Library of Congress Control Number: 2022936321

Book and cover design by Maryann Appel

5   3   1   2   4

For my dad, a miracle, superman, and proof that
good men and fantastic fathers exist.
I'll love you forever and I'll miss you always. Thank you.

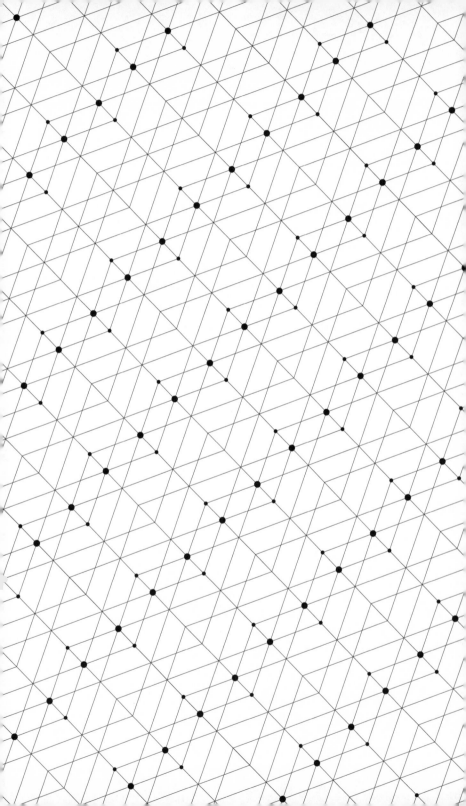

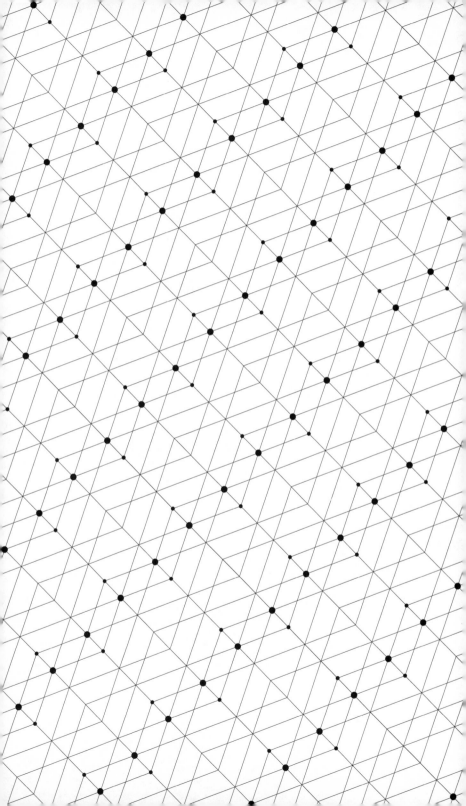

DAY 1 ————————————o

L ynell feels the sun cutting into her skin, a harsh reminder of her own mortality. She rolls forward onto her toes and holds her hand up against the sun. The motion puts an old scar on her forearm in her direct line of sight. Her stomach clenches and she steps back into the shade.

Dallas is busier today than on a usual Thursday. The first Thursday of the quarter, April 4th, brings promises of vengeance, clarity, relief, justice, and love.

It's Registration Day.

Lynell rests against the wall of the building and leans her head back. She flattens her palms against the hot stones, listening to the city's symphony. Hundreds of feet pound the pavement, and the streets are congested with honking cars and people on the phone.

Across the street, an old man walks out of the large glass door Lynell has been staring at for two hours. He folds a piece of paper and slides it into his back pocket. She wonders whom he just Registered. The odds suggest a wife or loved one in chronic pain, as mercy is the most common reason for using the Registration. But perhaps this man seeks justice. Lynell's high school history teacher used his Registration on a man who assaulted his daughter and got away with it. No jail time or community service.

But with the Registration, he found justice anyway.

A gunshot brutally pulls her out of her rumination. A young girl screams, and a few older kids jump or duck. Lynell, like most of the adults walking the streets, only flinches at the sound. While public Registrations aren't common, the first day is always the most violent.

She looks up to see a middle-aged man lying in a pool of his own blood and a woman, the same age, standing over him holding a small, smoking gun. Instantly, a pair of Elysian Regulators rush to her side. Lynell can't hear what they're saying, but after the woman holds up a piece of paper and the officers dig in the man's coat, they nod. A lengthy phone call later, the Regulators leave. If the Registration had been completed anywhere else, officers probably would have arrived first. But since she's right outside a Registration office, there are plenty of Regulators around to check the legitimacy of the completed Registration.

The woman kneels next to the man's side, back straight as she reaches toward his pocket. Two men a few feet away pull out their phones and start snapping photos before running off. Perhaps they're nothing more than curious bystanders, but the deep frowns on their faces tell a different story. Lynell would bet her own Registration that they're rebel vultures collecting gruesome images of any deaths they stumble across. Whatever remains of the revolutionists will flood the internet with photos of the worst completed Registrations to sway others to their cause. What they won't show are the grateful faces of those who will be Registered so they won't have to spend another day on a ventilator or suffering through chemo. They won't show the heartbroken women Registering the unnamed fetuses they carry with debilitating illnesses, or the poor teens ending a pregnancy they could never afford. They won't show people the government failed, like Lynell's old teacher or Lynell herself, who now must seek justice themselves.

With the Sanitary Crew yet to be dispatched, no one touches or moves the body. Pedestrians simply avoid stepping in the blood, continuing with their day.

Lynell turns away from the sight and stares at the tall glass doors again.

She takes a deep breath. Not for the first time, she considers going home and taking advantage of her day off. She has most of her life to Register. After all, she's always been told: "Never Register before you turn thirty.

Chances are, you'll need that Registration when you're fifty more than you think you need it when you're twenty."

But Lynell is twenty-four and she's been wanting to Register the same person for nearly two decades. She doesn't think she'll ever have a better use for this gift. And now, with the news that he's getting married at the end of the year to a woman with three daughters, Lynell knows time is running out. She needs to do it soon, if not for her own sanity, then for the safety of those girls.

She could still wait until next quarter's Registration, though.

Lynell looks at the scar on her arm. One of the oldest decorations to the canvas that is her body.

She pushes off the wall and walks across the street toward the glass doors. She's thankful Eric Elysian requested measures to make picketing and protesting outside Registration offices illegal, and grateful the government enforces them. She's not sure she would have been able to walk past a crowd of ignorant jerks calling her a murderer. Without the Registration, chaos, violence, and homelessness would have consumed their world. Without it, they would never know true love or have anything to test it with. It's the only thing that saved them after the devastating civil war that seemed to have no end. The entire country owes a lifelong debt to the Elysians for saving them. Lynell knows that.

The Registration is a product of the Elysians' private business, but they work so closely with the government that it's virtually an inalienable right. Well, an inalienable right that must be paid for. It's protected by both the Elysian corporation and, when necessary, the government's law enforcement. Eric Elysian, the current owner of the Registration, is practically one of the oligarchs himself.

In the past, before Lynell's time, the rulers of the United States were supposedly elected by the people. But really, they conned their way there. It wasn't a true democracy. Citizens fought back, demanding that their voices be heard. They wanted real power over their lives, laws, and money. They wanted to implement change. A civil war followed: brother fighting brother, sister denouncing sister, mothers, daughters, fathers, sons at each other's throats. In ninth grade, her school made all students watch a documentary about the war. It was bloody chaos with far too many points of contention between the two warring sides to find compromises.

Then Gideon Elysian showed up and proposed his idea to the few leaders still holding power on both sides of the war. The Registration would give individuals power over life and death while the government retained the authority to create laws and enforce them. For example, the death penalty would be abolished, which is what half the country wanted. But the other half, individuals who wished to sentence a felon to death, could use the Registration to execute their idea of rightful punishment. The war came to an end and, tired of fighting, the country settled into a precarious peace. The rest, as they say, is history. The country has since been ruled by oligarchs with the aid of the Elysians and their Registration. They keep the peace, ensure commerce, and everyone is happy because citizens have access to true justice and mercy with the Registration. No need for corrupt democracy or oppressive tyranny.

At first, when Gideon Elysian proposed and created the Registration almost seventy years ago, everyone—regardless of age, origin, color, title, or class—had the option to pay the fee to get one Registration. The Elysians worked closely with the oligarchs, ensuring laws were set in place to support it. The Registration entitles citizens to kill the person they Registered, no questions asked.

But there's a catch: you have to end that person's life within two weeks or your immunity is forfeited, as is your chance for another Registration. If you kill your Registree at any time other than the two weeks after Registering, you will be charged with murder.

After a few years of madness, the government added another law. Parents must pay the fee for their newborn, or that child will never be allowed to legally Register anyone.

That's why you need to know for certain. That's why you have to be sure that this is the person you want to Register. You can't waste such a gift.

Lynell has held onto her gift her entire life. Her mom didn't have that gift. If she did, their life would have been different. Her childhood would have been better. And Lynell wouldn't be using her own Registration right now.

Lynell looks at the scar again, thinks of those three young girls, takes a deep breath, and pulls open the large, glass door.

"Wait, please. Give her three more months. She may wake up!" A young girl, maybe twelve, yells at a boy only a few years older than her at the other end of the crowded room. They're easily the youngest people here, and Lynell's heart aches at what must have happened to them to cause the boy to use his Registration so early.

Most people in line are older, though there is a woman who looks close to Lynell's age holding two babies in her arms. A man halfway down the line leans on a cane, his legs shaking and his glasses balancing precariously on the edge of his nose.

It's a large room, probably twenty to twenty-five yards wide. The walls, floors and ceilings are white marble. There's no way to look outside or in. The only windows in the room are the eleven clerk stations where lines form to Register. Above each window are two letters. The first, on the far-left side, says A-B. The next says C-D. And so on. Some, such as X-Z, have much shorter lines. Lynell knows what to do: stand in the line coordinating with the last name of the person you intend to Register. She's walked inside the building and stood in line twice before, always chickening out at the last minute.

There are hundreds of people dispersed throughout the room. The young girl and boy stand behind a short, Black woman wearing a thin blue shawl in the U-W line.

With a deep breath, Lynell steps into the M-N line. There are probably thirty people ahead of her. Thirty people Registering. Thirty people being

Registered. Thirty deaths in the next fourteen days. Thirty moments when some lives end and others mark the new beginning they so desperately crave.

Lynell looks at her watch. It's almost 3:30 p.m., which means everyone in this time zone only has an hour and a half to Register before they must wait for July.

Lynell lowers her arm and sees a small scar peeking out from under the watch strap. Her stomach churning and heart palpating as if her own name were about to be Registered, she pulls down her sleeves. The unrelenting summer heat is no longer barreling down on her and the air-conditioned building starts cooling the sweat clinging to her skin.

She zips up her hoodie, tucks her fingers under the sleeves and pulls up the hood, as if to shield herself from the world.

She has no reason to hide. The Registration is good, pure, and just. People will not look down on her for Registering Alan.

She knows this, but she prays to remain unseen, nonetheless.

Sounds from the large building assault her ears as she rocks on her feet with her hands hiding in the pockets. Pens scratching on pages. Names spoken with a chilling finality. Crying. Whooping. Rustles of bags as people search for IDs. A cough from a small, frail, old woman clutching to her husband two lines over.

The line Lynell stands in moves forward. She looks at her watch again. 3:30.

Lynell watches the couple make it to their window. She listens as the man says he wants to Register his wife. She stands next to him, leaning on him for support, smiling up to him with so much gratefulness that Lynell wants to sob. That is what selfless love looks like, she thinks. Ending your best friend, your partner, your teammate's life because it is too unbearable to keep living. Because you love them enough to let them go.

The line moves. 3:33.

A small part of her hopes she won't reach the window before the clock strikes five o'clock and each window clangs shut. But when the queue is more than halfway done and her watch says 4:08, she knows she won't have that escape.

She starts shivering. The air-conditioning is blasting and she's standing directly under a vent. She glances up and a strand of deep brown hair breaks free from her bun. Huffing, she tucks it behind her ear and hunches her shoulders.

They move forward again. 4:11.

"I'd like to Register Michael Nancine," a stocky man with a shaved head says at the front of their line.

"Name?"

Lynell stops listening as the man starts feeding information to the Registration clerk. She wonders what Michael Nancine did. Does he know his days are numbered, that he probably won't live to see May? Does he feel regret for whatever propelled this man to Register him?

She knows Alan feels no regret. And that he's too arrogant to assume someone might waste their Registration on him. He doesn't truly know Lynell. He doesn't understand the effect of what he's done. And he doesn't care.

The line surges forward after Michael Nancine has successfully been Registered. Lynell flexes her fingers and moves her arm forward. As if in slow motion, she feels the friction as she pushes the sleeve back to read the watch again. She can feel every hair on her arm, the pain in her right ankle, the shortness of breath. The world loses focus, and she never notices the time at which she hears six words that make her spine shake with fear.

"I'm here to Register Lynell Mize."

Lynell smells unwashed feet, applesauce, and a sharply sweet peach perfume. But she hears nothing but the cough that comes from the man at the front of the line. She leans to the side so she can see his back, broad and covered in a simple gray T-shirt. It's stained with two small patches of sweat under his armpits. She sees him place his hands on the counter as he speaks to the woman behind the window. She watches the lady's mouth move as she asks for his name.

"Zachary Price."

Lynell feels her breath punch at her chest, forcing her to keep on living. She watches the back of the man's head as he accepts a form the lady slides under the window.

Confusion clouds her mind. Her hands feel numb. She turns around and stares at the woman in line behind her. She scowls at Lynell and looks down at her phone. The air-conditioning grows louder.

"Registree's date of birth?" Lynell hears the clerk ask.

Lynell hears the man's rumbling voice answer correctly. January 31st. Twenty-four years ago. He knows her birthday. He knows *her*.

Well enough to want to Register her. To waste his Registration on her.

Does she know him? Zachary Price. The name doesn't ring a bell. Who is he? Has she done something to him?

"Fill out this form. Be sure to include your social identification number at the bottom. Sign here, here, here, and here. Write the Reg—" Lynell checks out again, her ears filling with a deafening roar.

She looks down at her hands, sees them shaking, watches bulbs of sweat gather on the back.

She trips when the lady behind her shoves her.

"Make a little space," the lady behind her barks.

Lynell looks up and sees the man who Registered her turning towards the commotion. Before he can see her face and she his, Lynell turns away, breathing hard.

Zachary Price. She has never heard the name in her life. She's sure of it.

"What are—" the lady gasps as Lynell pushes her out of the way and starts for the door.

The world seems to tip as she grasps the handle.

I'm here to Register Lynell Mize.

Lynell shoves the door open and falls into the world outside.

A little boy turns to look at her, smiling wide to reveal two missing front teeth. He stops moving and Lynell trips over the tip of his shoe. She reaches out for a hold on something and the closest thing in her path is his shoulder.

The boy screams. His mom tugs him out of Lynell's grasp and starts yelling at her but the only thing she can hear is Zachary Price's voice.

I'm here to Register Lynell Mize.

The phrase repeats itself over and over in her mind. Screaming, whispering, echoing. Promising death. Making use of the gift of the Registration.

The gift that doesn't feel like a gift when you're on the other side.

I'm here to Register Lynell Mize.

She dares a look back and sees the door open. Without waiting to see who steps out, she takes off running. She pushes a man out of the way and dimly hears him shout at her. Then she stumbles over the legs of a homeless woman and lands hard on her elbows.

Pain shoots up her arms and the world returns to focus, filled with color that she didn't know had drained away. She blinks. Her ears ring and her mind seems to shake, unable to grasp the enormity of the situation she finds herself in. She smells trash and body odor. The homeless woman next to her is ranting about the Registration taking everything from her after her husband had been Registered and that the rebels are right and the Elysians are tyrants.

Lynell grunts and pushes herself up, trying desperately to ignore the pain in her arms. She twists her arm and sees blood dripping. When a drop splashes on the dirty pavement, it seems as if her heart has already been claimed by Price. She can feel his fist threatening to crush it.

Lynell stumbles back when someone runs into her. "Get out of the way, bit—" The shout is cut short when Lynell twists and slaps the man who was yelling at her. He blinks and scowls. His hands are curling into fists and his face turns red. Before he gets a chance to yell more or hit back, Lynell starts running.

She runs for six blocks before descending the steps to the subway. Her hands shake as she pulls her card out of her pocket and scans it so the doors will let her through. As soon as she reaches her train, she checks her watch. The train should arrive in seven minutes, which feels like enough time for Price to kill her three times over.

She glances around, trying to decipher each face to see if one of them could be the man planning to kill her. She looks for a gray T-shirt or recognition in the eyes of the many men crowding the underground train station.

She hides between a bench and a snack dispensary machine behind an exceptionally plump woman and lowers her head, looking at her feet, hoping to remain unnoticed.

As soon as the train arrives, she joins the crowd of people climbing on, not flinching at the skin-to-skin contact and putrid smells. She leans her head against one of the poles and takes several deep breaths to calm her racing heart.

It takes twelve minutes to arrive at her station. She stares at her watch, feeling the small hands mocking her as they tick away the seconds of her life.

"If someone is Registered, it's for a reason. It's never simply revenge or anger. The Registration is not subject to the fleeting quality of human emotions," her father said once. Well, according to her mom, anyway.

What would he say if he were here, watching Lynell run from a man who'd just Registered her? Who'd just promised the system that in fourteen days, Lynell Mize will be dead.

"Washington Station," the robotic voice shouts through the carriages.

Lynell leaves sweat behind on the pole when she exits the train. She looks both ways, making eye contact with no one. Her heartbeat continues to speed up as she takes the steps three at a time and exits the underground station. Her apartment is still a five-minute walk away, but she runs and makes it in two.

Price probably knows where she lives. He will have done his homework and likely knows everything about Lynell. He must know that her father was Registered twenty years ago. Must know that her mom married Alan a year later. Knows that she . . .

"SHIT!" Lynell shouts, despite her desire to stay unnoticed. Several people look her way and she smiles softly. "Sorry," she says, fishing her key out of her pocket and sliding it into the lock.

It doesn't turn. She pulls it out and tries again. Still, it doesn't turn, and Lynell begins pacing in front of the door. She's about to try one more time when she realizes the key isn't turning because the door is already unlocked.

He beat her here. She should leave. Go somewhere else. Go home. Leave the city. Hide for the next two weeks. Or perhaps she could go after Price herself and demand to know *why*. She could Register Alan and be sure to take him with her when she goes. She could write a letter to . . .

She shakes her head, stopping that line of thought. She probably just forgot to lock it after she left this morning. With a deep breath, she pushes the door open and disappears into the darkness of her apartment, only to be stopped by a tall man standing in front of her.

"Lynell."

She doesn't scream, but her entire body tenses up and her blood grows cold and her heart stops beating for a moment. She can't make out the man's face, but the stature is almost identical to Price.

The voice is familiar.

Too familiar.

"Lynell," he repeats. And suddenly Lynell wishes it were Price standing before her rather than the man she thought she'd never see again.

"What are you doing here, Daniel?" Lynell's body doesn't calm, but she does get enough energy to storm past him and into the apartment. She brushes his arm and feels his fingers graze her skin.

"I came to . . . Lynell, you have to listen to me. You need to leave town," he says, his voice shaking. Lynell spins around, almost bumping into her tattered green couch. The apartment is small. Lynell doesn't have much stuff and what she does have is old and worn.

"Why?" she demands, despite agreeing with Daniel.

"I can't tell you. But you have to trust me."

Lynell laughs and the sound is filled with so much venom she's surprised it doesn't kill her—or him—on the spot. "You promised me you would never say that again. You promised me you'd never come back into my life. Go home, Daniel."

"Lynell, please."

"Leave me alone!" she screams. The words bounce off the walls as Daniel blinks and takes a step back. He seems to just have taken in her state. Her damp clothes, tangled hair, and red eyes. She must look crazed.

"Leave me alone, please," she repeats, quieter this time. Lynell turns her back to Daniel and heads to her bedroom. She sets down her bag and pushes open the door.

She's digging through the bottom drawer of her dresser when she looks up to see him standing in the doorway, arms crossed. Lynell seethes, her teeth grinding together until her jaw hurts.

A small trickle of her fear instantly evaporates as she picks up the gun from the back of the dresser. She opens the barrel of the gun to find it's full, which is good since ammo is surprisingly hard to come by. Legally acquiring a gun is a long process and ammo is highly controlled: you have to provide a reason for every single bullet before purchasing them. As a result, very few Registrations are completed by using a gun.

Careful to keep the gun out of Daniel's vision, she tucks it in the waistband of her pants and stands up. She suddenly wishes she had kept her emergency bag in her bedroom, rather than under her desk at the office. Instead, she grabs a small bag and shoves in a change of clothes, a water bottle, and her wallet. She should probably get more, maybe a first aid kit and some food, but the gun is all she really came here for and now she needs to leave.

"Go home, Daniel," Lynell says, pushing past him to leave her bedroom. The weight of the gun suddenly disappears, and she whirls around.

"I thought you got rid of this," he says, holding the gun and examining it, as if the secrets of the Registration are etched into the metal.

"Give it back!" She reaches out, but he yanks it from her reach.

"Promise me you'll get out of town."

"Give it back or I'll call the cops, Daniel."

He raises an eyebrow. "Oh? So, this gun is legal?"

Lynell stops trying to reach for the weapon and crosses her arms. "What do you really want?"

"As thick as ever," he muses, lowering his arm and returning the gun within her reach. "I want you to leave town, Lynell."

She's about to tell him to go to hell but then wonders why he's so insistent on this. Does he know about the Registration? Does he know who Price is? "Where would you like me to go?" she asks.

He takes a deep breath and gives her the gun back. The feel of the cold metal is reassuring. His blue eyes meet her brown ones, and he sighs before saying, "As far away as possible."

Daniel, always prepared, had brought an extra change of clothes. He insists on following her to the station.

"Are you going to tell me why I should leave town?" Lynell asks, changing in her bedroom while Daniel waits outside. She pulls off her pants and shirt, replacing them with leggings, a T-shirt, black boots, and a deep red shawl tied around her waist while waiting for Daniel to reply. She's about to repeat her question when his answer comes.

"There's talk about some anti-Registration protests taking place all over the city. Businesses that support the Elysians will be targeted. You still work at that law firm?"

She does, and the office has been tagged by the rebels before. The firm's main purpose is to represent civil cases that are connected to the Registration. If someone sues a neighbor for property damage caused while completing their Registration, the defendant will likely hire someone from Lynell's firm. The lawyers are well-known for getting people off on a multitude of charges in the name of the Registration. Daniel's reasoning feels shallow. It's been several years since there were enough protests to cause real damage and even if something were to happen, Lynell could simply wait out the worst of it in her apartment.

"Back with the so-called freedom fighters, are you?" Lynell asks, instead of challenging him.

"It just might not be safe in town for a few days," he says, using his lying voice that Lynell would recognize anywhere. He's never been comfortable with dishonesty and all his lies have a truthful core. Maybe he really does want her to be safe. He just refuses to tell her what the danger is.

Or maybe he has no problem with lying to her anymore.

"Why do you care, Daniel?"

Daniel cuts her off with a chuckle. "You've always asked too many questions."

Lynell finishes lacing the boots and stands up, crossing her arms. "I think I'm entitled to a few questions. You show up after three years, demanding I leave town, and expect me to blindly obey? You—" She's about to throw a string of choice words in his direction when the look on his face causes the breath to stop in her throat.

His mouth is set in a tight, straight line. "You seem to have forgotten, Lynell." He turns around and picks up his bag. "You left me."

Lynell blinks, prepared to retaliate when he steps so close she can feel his breath.

Three years of guilt morphing into anger causes her hands to shake. She wants to scream about broken promises and broken hearts, but then he's reaching behind her and gathering up her hair.

"What are you doing?" she asks, trying to shrug him off.

"You'll want all this hair out of your way," he says, looking past her face to avoid making eye contact. His arms are on either side of her head and she feels heat radiating off them. She hisses as he tugs at her hair, pulling it through a hairband. "Sorry," he mutters before stepping back to admire his handiwork.

"I can put up my own damn hair."

Daniel shrugs, smiling sadly, before turning to the door. "We've already been here too long. Let's go."

Without further argument, Lynell grabs her small bag, turns off the lights behind her and walks out the door without so much as a backward glance. Daniel follows.

"I feel like we should be running," she says as they wait at a crosswalk.

"We should be as inconspicuous as possible," Daniel says, hooking his fingers through the straps of the backpack.

The light changes and they join the crowd of people leaving the city after they've finished their Registration. She wonders if there will be any fulfilled Registrations on the train station platform and desperately hopes not. She's not in the mood to see dead bodies left unattended.

Her body may add to their numbers soon enough.

Lynell speeds up her steps to keep up with Daniel's long strides. He smiles and nods at an old woman that passes them, always polite even during what may be the last moments of her life. Under the melting sun and surrounded by people, Lynell asks, "What's the plan here, Daniel? Why—"

He cuts her question short by grabbing her arm and pulling her to the edge of the walkway into the shade of the closest building. Someone bumps into her on the way, and her body freezes until she looks up and sees a man that is too old and short to be Price.

"We're Mark and Emily," he starts.

"Who?"

"A few days ago, I got us new IDs, complete with working social identification numbers and photos."

At that, Lynell's back straightens and she stares at Daniel, his words pulling her lips into a frown.

He got them both IDs days ago? That is far too much preparation for getting out of town to avoid a few protests.

"I had to use an old one of you, but it'll work," Daniel continues. "We are Mark and Emily Hunter and we've been married for two years."

"Convenient," she says, studying him with increased suspicion. Even as her brain tells her that these are too many coincidences, her body feels more relaxed in his presence. Her mind doesn't trust him and tells her to run. Her gut trusts him more than anyone else and begs her to stay.

Daniel ignores her and glances around them to be sure no one is listening. "I've got the IDs in the bag. I've also got us two tickets for a train that's going to leave without us if we don't start moving, like, now."

Lynell almost steps out of Daniel's orbit to flee but instead, she lets her ex pull her back into the flow of traffic. They quicken their pace toward the station, which is a twenty-minute walk away.

"You're coming with me?" She's not surprised that he's been planning to join. He was always good at that, revealing information to her slowly to keep from freaking her out. Maybe he's using that tactic against her now. Luring her into a trap disguised as safety. "Where are we going?" she asks, watching for any sign of guilt or dubious intentions in his face.

"North, to Chicago." Seeing her frown, he adds, "Not to my parents' place. I just wanted to get as far away as possible, and I have somewhere we can stay for a night before we keep moving."

He sounds sincere and it's enough to calm Lynell's suspicion for the moment. She nods, her mind too busy with her last memory of Chicago to properly respond. Her chest aches as she recalls grabbing hold of Daniel's arm and laying her head on his shoulder. She'd curled her feet up into the airplane seat while he chose an old movie to play, ignoring her protests. The air was cold, and she hadn't feared her stepfather in two years. Back then she had no idea what was coming, what would cause Daniel to leave her forever just a year later. She let herself stay in that moment, drinking water from a plastic cup and stealing Daniel's wine when she thought he wasn't looking. He smirked because of course he saw his twenty-year-old new wife drinking his wine and of course he didn't care because they might as well have been alone on the large plane. Lynell had felt untouchable.

Daniel's grip is no longer soothing, yet the touch is familiar enough to keep her from sinking into fear.

They make it to the station in fifteen minutes and Lynell follows Daniel through security, her heart beating faster than she thought was possible. She's thankful for the lack of metal detectors so her gun, tucked at the bottom of her bag, goes unnoticed.

Daniel digs two IDs out of his backpack and hands them to the guard with a big smile on his face and pulls her into his side. Lynell looks to the floor, certain her face is burning with the truth.

But then the guard says, "Have a good trip, Mr. and Mrs. Hunter," and he's waving them through. Daniel gives her shoulder a small squeeze and lets her go. Lynell lets out a breath.

It's not unheard of for people to try and run from their Registration, if they find out they're Registered, that is. Which is rare. Everyone knows the lists on the black market are fake. The Elysians made sure years ago that the Registration would be too heavily secured to be leaked. So, if they're lucky, people learn the old-fashioned way: word of mouth. If they don't find out soon enough to Register their would-be-killer in return, their only choice is to run. You can't fight back because assaulting or killing the person who Registered you isn't considered self-defense. That law took the longest for the government to pass, making it nearly impossible for a Registered person to defend themselves without being arrested on the grounds of assault.

Lynell has heard a handful of stories of people trying to survive the Registration. Most don't end with survival. The only two stories of people who have outrun the Registration are famous among the revolutionists, because rumor has it that the survivors became the first important rebels who fought against the Registration and government. Although they might have survived the Registration, they didn't survive the battle with the government forces.

"This way," Daniel says, pulling her to the right down another corridor. The white brick walls are covered in graffiti, posters, and a few screens. One flashes white before showing an image of Eric Elysian shaking hands with a congressman. The words "WE WORK TOGETHER FOR THE GOOD OF THE PEOPLE" cover the bottom half of the screen in big, block letters. The image flies to the left and an advertisement for a bank card takes its place.

A few feet down the corridor hangs a large poster featuring a new boarding school in West Texas. The poster claims to accept students of all religions and that 97 percent of their students go on to achieve a higher education degree. Lynell remembers begging her mom to send her to one of the popular boarding schools in the state, but they were too expensive.

Graffiti of crude drawings and names cover the poster, the most noticeable bright green words saying, "Brainwash your children!" and "Eric Elysian is a fraud!"

"Here we are," Daniel says when they reach the end of the corridor. They stop in front of platform seventeen and Daniel hands their tickets to the check-in lady. She slides them under a machine and after the *ding*, she hands them back, now covered in three blurred lines of ink.

"Welcome aboard," she says, handing a key and a receipt to Daniel. Lynell meets her eyes and wants to sink into the shadows.

"Thank you," Daniel says, then tugs Lynell down the hallway to the train.

They keep their two bags close instead of handing them to the baggage handler loading the undercarriage of the train. Daniel keeps hold of Lynell's hand as they board and walk through the train.

Her gaze darts around, jumping from face to face, half expecting that she'll see murder in one of them.

Most people aren't paying attention. They shove past each other to find their cabins, herd children onto seats in the public carriages, and push bags into overhead compartments.

It's Registration Day, the busiest day of each quarter for traveling, and no one knows that Lynell is standing there, expecting a bullet through her head at any moment.

"Come on," Daniel says.

She cowers away from the brush of a large man's shoulder and reaches over to grab Daniel's arm with her free hand. They force their way through the crowd until they are at the back of the car. Lynell sees two free seats and starts towards them, but Daniel pulls on her hand and shakes his head.

"What?" she asks.

"We're in Cabin F."

"We have our own room?" Lynell says, eyebrows shooting up.

Daniel smirks, showing off the small dimple in his cheek that she used to love so much. It makes her stomach clench. "You think I'm going to make my gorgeous wife travel coach?" He stares at her as if looking for a response. When he finds none, he shrugs. "Plus, they were the only tickets left at the last minute."

They head down three more cars before they reach the one with their room. Daniel lets go of Lynell's hand to fish the key out of his pocket. She takes her moment of freedom to run her fingers through her hair and down her face.

"Here we are," Daniel says, pushing the door open. It creaks and shudders, banging against the inside wall when pushed all the way open. Daniel tosses the bag on the bed as he walks in.

The bed is barely the size of a full and fills up most of the room. On its right is a small wardrobe built into the wall, and next to it a single chair and the door leading to the small bathroom. Daniel falls back onto the bed and threads his fingers together behind his head, Lynell hovering in the doorway.

"Well, you going to come in?"

"It's tiny," she says.

"At least it's private."

"There's one bed." The realization that she'll have to sleep next to Daniel if she wants to sleep at all sends a flush to her cheeks. Hoping he doesn't notice, she shuts the door and locks it, dropping her bag.

"It's a twenty-four-hour train ride, Lyn. You'll be thankful for the bed soon."

"Don't call me that," she says, dropping into the chair.

Daniel angles his head so he can get a better look at her. "Why can't I call you Lyn?"

"Because I'm Emily, remember?"

"When we're in public, not in a private room where no one can hear us." As if to prove his point, Daniel makes a wide gesture with his arm to encompass their room. The train isn't moving, people are still boarding, and if Lynell strains, she can hear another couple in their car talking and laughing loudly. "What's the real reason?"

"No one calls me Lyn," she says. The only people who ever called her Lyn were Daniel and her mom.

"I used to exclusively call you Lyn."

"'Used to,'" she says. "Past tense, Daniel. If I remember correctly, you stopped calling me 'Lyn' the day you made the promise you broke today."

"What promise?"

"We don't have to do this," she says, resting her head against the wall.

Daniel sits up and throws his legs over the side of the bed, so their knees are mere inches apart. "Do what? Have a conversation?"

"Dig up everything that happened. We broke up, but we're here now, so can we leave it at that? Just for today?"

Daniel sighs and looks down, picking at a stain on his pants. The silence stretches on for so long that the train whistles and lurches before he speaks again. The movement thrusts Lynell back and she grasps the arms of the chair to steady herself.

"I didn't mean it. What I said that day," Daniel whispers.

Lynell stands and turns away from him, attempting to put as much distance between them as possible in such a cramped space. "Seriously, Daniel. Leave the past where it belongs. I don't want to bring it all back up when I don't even have a future."

She realizes her mistake as soon as the words escape her mouth. He doesn't know that a stranger Registered her. He can't know unless Price isn't a stranger to him. Unless he knows about Price's plan. Knew about it even before Price Registered her.

She hadn't considered the possibility. That Daniel was somehow involved in her being Registered. But it makes sense. That could be the real reason he insisted she leave without telling her why. To keep her safe without revealing he knew this was going to happen. But why would he know? Was it his idea?

Daniel hates the Registration, he always has. He hated it enough to join the rebels although it was so unlikely they'd succeed. She can't imagine him ever being involved with someone Registering her.

She knows she hurt him. But did she hurt him enough to make him bend his morals?

The train lurches and Lynell loses her balance, causing her to fall onto the bed. Lynell instantly rolls to the head of the bed and pulls her knees up.

"What do you mean, you won't have a future?" Daniel asks.

He might not know. Maybe he really is worried about riots. Maybe that's all.

Somehow, she doesn't believe that. He won't answer her questions, but maybe his horrible poker face will give him away.

"I heard someone Register me," she says, studying him closely.

Daniel falls onto his back, hands covering his face in a clear sign of guilt.

Her hands curl into fists. "What do you know about this?" Lynell asks, pulling long breaths through her nose to keep the anger from rising.

"I don't know what you heard but . . . wait." He removes his hands and sits up again, turning to look at Lynell. "How did you hear him Register you?"

Lynell blinks at him. "I . . ."

"Lynell."

"I was there when he did . . . I was in line." She looks down, resting her forehead on her knees.

"In line . . . doing what?" When Lynell doesn't answer, Daniel surges forward and grabs her shoulders. She looks up, and Daniel's nose is close to touching her own. His face is wild with emotion. "Lyn, what were you doing there?"

She leans back and rubs the palms of her hands against her legs. "I was going to Register Alan."

Daniel's mouth drops open and he shakes his head, pulling his hands away from her. "What?"

Her mouth feels dry. "I was . . ." The words don't come. What is there to say?

"How, Lynell? You only get one Registration."

"Daniel . . ." she reaches out to touch him, but he pulls away, standing quickly and starting to pace the tiny compartment. "Daniel . . . please." She leans forward on the bed, and he turns to her, eyes so wide she recoils, afraid he's going to attack.

"How were you going to Register Alan? You already used your Registration."

His voice is low and steady, and she wishes he were screaming, not looking at her with this cold, calculating expression. She turns away, unable to hold his stare.

"Lynell."

After a long moment and a deep breath, she looks up, meets Daniel's eyes, and mutters, "I didn't do it. I never used my Registration."

DAY 2 ———————

"**W**ed. That's twenty-one points. And incredibly relevant," Lynell had said, smirking at her new husband. Her face was resting against her hand, elbow propped on the pillow. The windows were open, allowing a perfect view to the city beyond.

"What? That's at most seven points." Daniel reached out to stop Lynell from adding twenty-one to her score on the little scratch paper the hotel provided in their bedside table, along with a bible and a room service menu.

Lynell pulled the pen out of his reach. "Not when it's on a triple word score," she replied and pushed the "W" tile back to reveal the star beneath.

Daniel grumbled, "Fine," as Lynell proceeded to write down the number. Before she could, he pushed the board aside and threw his leg over her torso, straddling her. Lynell laughed and ran her fingers through Daniel's dark hair that was messier than usual after hours spent in bed. He leaned his head into her touch, eyes fluttering closed.

"You're like a dog," she said.

Daniel kicked his leg out behind him and stuck out his tongue, panting. Lynell hit his shoulder, yelling "Stop!" through her laughter. He did and reached back to shove the near full Scrabble board off the bed to join the covers and sheets that had long ago been discarded on the floor.

Daniel leaned on his forearms, placed on either side of Lynell's head. His hair fell in curls around his face as he stared down at her, his entire face smiling. Lips, eyes, even his ears seemed to be filled with the joy and love found in that smile. Even several months into their relationship, Lynell couldn't get enough of him. Of his smile or his blue eyes that were darker on the edges and grew cooler and lighter as they reached his pupils.

Lynell reached up and wrapped her arms around his neck, pulling him down to meet her in a kiss.

"Have I told you today how lucky I am to be in love with you?" Daniel said, words brushing her lips.

"In every way imaginable," Lynell replied.

"Good." He kissed her again. "Because you deserve to hear that." His long, dark lashes fluttered closed and grazed her cheeks as he moved his lips along her skin.

"I love you," Lynell said. She brushed a thumb over his lower lip, red and swollen. Her hands roamed, as if of their own accord, over his broad shoulders and down his arms that were mapped with rippling muscles and prominent veins. Her hands made their way to his wrists, which she grabbed before leaning up to kiss him again. He moved one hand to tangle in her hair.

Day two of marriage with the greatest man to ever live. Lynell's heart swelled, threatening to swallow her whole and erase every negative memory and emotion she'd ever had.

She knew with every fiber of her being that she loved Daniel Carter more than she should be allowed to love anyone or anything, and she never wanted to know a life without him again.

———————

The lack of movement wakes Lynell up. She squeezes her eyes tight, desperately trying to hold onto the dream. When the last strand of memory floats away, she allows her eyes to open, and reality returns.

She turns to see Daniel sprawled out next to her on the bed, on top of the sheets. He's still wearing yesterday's clothes, hugging the pillow close to his face, mouth slightly open. He seems peaceful and relaxed, a jarring contrast to the tension and anger oozing from his every fiber last night. Remorse tugs at Lynell's heart. If she'd never tried to Register Alan, she wouldn't have been there when Price was. She wouldn't have heard him Register her. She wouldn't have run.

Or she still would have. Because Daniel would have found her.

But if she hadn't heard Price, then Daniel wouldn't have found out that she hadn't yet used her Registration. And last night wouldn't have happened.

Seeing him sit at the edge of the bed, still as a statue and hands curled into fists, while Lynell told him the truth, broke her heart. He wouldn't let her touch him. He wouldn't look at her. When she'd finished her story, her entire body was shaking. For a moment, she imagined Daniel holding her like he used to. Her body yearned for it.

Instead of giving him details, she filled in gaps with "I don't know's" and "I'm sorry's" that all fell flat.

Daniel was broken.

She'd broken him.

Lynell gently climbs off the bed and goes to the bathroom. She stares at the cloudy mirror.

Her hair has partly escaped her ponytail and is tangled in knots. Leftover makeup cracks in the corners of her eyes and a film has gathered at the corners of her lips. She turns on the tap and splashes her face with cold water, wishing for a shower. Thankfully, she packed her toothbrush and hairbrush and makes quick work on her appearance until she's presentable.

The clock in their cabin reads 6:00 a.m., which means they've been traveling for ten hours. Only fourteen more. Then twelve more days of surviving.

Lynell bends down, going through the bag Daniel had packed. There are two IDs, a plastic bag filled with more money than Lynell has seen in over a year, two books, rope, a small first aid kit, some protein bars, and three bottles of water. She huffs and grabs a protein bar when her stomach growls.

"They serve breakfast."

Lynell jumps and turns around, dropping the bar. Daniel is sitting up, staring at her with dark shadows under his eyes.

"Oh . . ."

"It's included. Save that for when we really need it," he says, each word clipped.

"Okay." Lynell returns the bar to the bag.

"I'll go get breakfast and bring it back to the room. Just let me piss first. Don't let anyone in the room while I'm gone. And keep your gun close."

"Okay," she repeats, the air taut with tension.

Daniel climbs out of bed, stretches, and ruffles his hair.

"Daniel . . ."

"Not now, Lynell. I'm just exhausted."

She nods, and he brushes past her to get to the bathroom. Her skin tingles from the near touch. Her chest tightens, and she climbs back into bed, suddenly feeling sick. As the train starts moving again, she lies on her side, facing the wall and pulling her legs into her chest.

Over the last few years, she trained herself not to think of Daniel or remember what she left behind. But now that he's so close, the memories are flooding back. Worse, the way she felt with him—safe and happy— threatens to drown her.

Daniel doesn't say anything when he leaves the room. She hears the lock click into place behind him. She rolls over, stares at the ceiling, and covers her face with her hands, stifling a scream.

How could she have been so stupid? How could she let that slip?

She never wanted to hurt Daniel. The only way she could get through the past few years was to force her guilt to turn into anger. Hurting him once was enough to nearly break her. And now she's done it again.

Zachary Price may as well find her now and end it. If she was half the person her father had been, she would welcome it. Maybe he would tell her why he Registered her before killing her. Maybe she really deserves this. Daniel probably thinks she does.

Accepting it would be easier than trying to outrun it. She can't fight it without risking arrest for hurting or killing Price.

The Elysians didn't create the system and the government didn't pass laws to allow it for no reason. It's designed to work. To help natural selection keep their world alive and running. To keep the peace and avoid another civil war. The Registration is a compromise most people can agree upon.

And yet, now that Lynell is at the receiving end, she's fighting it.

Fifteen minutes later the lock clicks and the doorknob turns. Only as the door starts opening does she realize she left the gun in her bag on the other side of the room. There's a moment of panic before Daniel's face emerges. He glances at her, eyes still full of sleep, and sets the tray he's holding on the edge of the bed.

Lynell sits forward, glancing down at the contents.

There are two muffins, three small packages of jelly, a plate of watery scrambled eggs and bacon, and two cups of yogurt. There are also three cups, two with coffee and one with juice. Lynell reaches out for one of the muffins and sinks her teeth into it, instantly feeling more relaxed.

She looks up to find Daniel staring at her from his seat on the chair. Maybe he's changing his mind about helping her run.

She swallows and watches Daniel's jaw flex. "Are you going to have some?" she asks before wiping her mouth and taking the paper off the muffin.

"In a bit." Daniel drops his face into his hands, rubbing his temples.

What was left unsaid last night hangs in the air and Lynell expects Daniel to bring it up again at any moment. When he doesn't, she returns to breakfast. Eating quickly, she goes through her half of everything and lies back down on the bed, covering her full belly with her hands.

Finally, the chair scrapes along the ground and she looks down to see Daniel grabbing a piece of bacon. She lets him eat in silence for a while before sitting up.

"What's going on, Daniel?"

His eyes stay glued to the tray on the foot of the bed as he eats. "Lyn . . ."

She moves to her feet and leans forward until they're so close that she can feel his breath and see the hair on his tan arms stand on edge. "I'm on this stupid train. I'm going to Chicago with you. I think I should know what's going on. I think I deserve to know why someone would Register me."

"Do you?" he asks, looking up. Their eyes meet, and Lynell almost can't feel the movement of the train. "Do you deserve to know?"

She leans back, sitting on her feet. "I don't know what you want me to say."

He shakes his head. "Nothing. There's nothing else to say. What's done is done." He shrugs and some of the tension leaves his voice with his next words. "And, besides," he reaches out and grabs the muffin. "Right now, we need to focus on keeping you alive for the next thirteen days."

Lynell flicks away a muffin crumb. "Don't you think knowing why I'm in someone's crosshairs would help?"

Daniel offers a small smile and a breath of a chuckle. "No. I think you knowing things is dangerous."

"Hey!" she shouts, shoving his shoulder. The moment gives her a sense of déjà vu to a happier time when teasing each other was second nature.

"Just don't do anything stupid. And don't trust anyone that's not me."

They sit in the room for a few hours before deciding to stretch their legs and explore the train. Lynell is on alert the entire time, her hand gripping tightly onto Daniel's. He'd probably prefer not to touch, but she's too anxious not to. Each car with private rooms looks the same, with four doors to rooms on the left and a small hallway connecting the cars on the right. There are two dining cars, one at the end of the train and one in the middle. They walk through ten public cars, and dozens of people scowl at them from their uncomfortable seats. Lynell tries not to make eye contact with anyone but fails multiple times over when she can't stop studying their faces. When noon approaches and service personnel begin delivering lunch to the individual cabins, they return to their room in silence. They eat as the train moves along, jostling them and causing soup to spill on the way to their mouths. When finished, Lynell places the empty trays outside their room, and Daniel lies back on the bed, instantly falling asleep.

Lynell sits on the corner of the bed, watching him. His chest rises slowly, and his eyelids flutter, as if his dreams are trying to wake him. Every once in a while, his arms clench, and Lynell has to control the desire to lie next to him and pull him close to her chest. She remembers the nightmares he used to have three years ago, courtesy of the fruitless battles he fought. He'd wake up with sweat coating his skin and breaths tearing at his lungs. She'd grab his shoulders and rub her hands along his arms, promising that he was okay, that they were safe. The worst nightmare he ever had ended with him giving Lynell a black eye in his sleep. He was horrified. Hated himself, wouldn't let her touch him for hours, as if his skin was poison to her.

He never touched her like that when he was awake. He couldn't control his dreams, but he usually calmed down with a gentle touch of her hands. And yet, twice she'd been injured because of his dreams. After spending his first two years of adulthood fighting, it was a marvel he didn't have more nightmares. Lynell wanted to be there for him and try to understand his trauma, but she also couldn't ignore the trickle of anxiety in her gut.

He thrashes in his sleep and Lynell hugs her knees to her chest, wishing she could take his pain away. Especially the pain she caused.

―――――

"Lynell . . . baby . . . wake up. Lynell. Wake up!"

Lynell moans and rubs her eyes. She sees Daniel sitting at the head of the bed, staring at her. His eyes are wide, and his hands are held out in front of him, palms facing out. She frowns, about to ask what's wrong when he looks past her. She turns and her heart stops. A man stands in the doorway with two guns pointed at Daniel and Lynell.

Lynell gasps and pushes up from the edge of the bed, toward where Daniel is sitting up front.

"Don't move," the man says. His voice is low and smooth. She recognizes it instantly. Zachary Price.

Lynell freezes, her hand halfway to Daniel's leg. She looks up at Price's face, feeling her own drain of color.

His features are soft, though his nose is long, and his brows are bushy. He's got slicked back, dark brown hair, and a bit of chest hair is visible at the top of his V-neck T-shirt. He's staring at her, eyes hard, and both guns are steady in the air. Lynell mimics Daniel, holding her hands up palms out.

"Get off the bed slowly. Keep your hands up," Price orders. Both Lynell and Daniel start moving and Price steps forward. "Just Lynell."

Daniel stops, one leg hanging off the bed. "Zach," he says, with so much familiarity in his voice that Lynell whips around to stare at him. His face drops, and he avoids her gaze. "You don't need to do this."

"Shut the hell up, Danny. What are you even doing here?" All the calm seems to slip from Price's words. The gun trained on Daniel shakes and Lynell glances between them, horror filling her veins.

They know each other. So well that they have nicknames. Price meets Daniel's eyes, and they seem to have a silent conversation. Lynell feels her heart banging against her ribs and her head echoes with the sound of Price's voice. She can't pull her eyes from the gun a foot from her face.

"You're not going to shoot me," Daniel says, lowering his other foot to the ground.

Price takes another step forward, shoving one of the guns in Daniel's face. "You don't know that. I could. There's a silencer on this gun so no one would know."

"You didn't Register me. You'd go to jail."

"You know I wouldn't."

Daniel grimaces. "Zach. Put the guns down," he says as he slowly starts to stand.

Price quickly takes a step back, shoves one of his guns in his pants, grabs Lynell's arm, and pulls her flush against his chest. Lynell gasps, her hands instantly going up to grab Price's forearm. Daniel jumps up, but Price holds the gun against Lynell's temple, and Daniel freezes. He glares at Price, his teeth bared.

The gun feels like it's burning a hole where it's pushed against her skin. She closes her eyes and takes a deep breath, trying to calm her heart.

You can never outrun your Registration.

She'd barely made it 24 hours.

"Let her go," Daniel growls.

Price shakes his head, and Lynell feels the motion against her back. "I can't, you know that. Why are you fighting this, Danny?"

Lynell opens her eyes to see a flash of anger go through Daniel's eyes and his hands curl into fists. "You know why."

"The Registration is fair and good." Lynell can hear a tinge of regret and disbelief in Price's words. "You know this."

"Don't quote that bullshit to me, Zach."

Price doesn't answer, and Lynell keeps her eyes trained on Daniel, trying to communicate with him that it's okay. She's okay. If it's her time, it's her time. She deserves it.

Price takes a step back, pulling Lynell with him. "Don't follow me, Danny. Go home."

"Zach!"

Lynell stumbles as he pulls her, keeping her grip tight on his arm. The door to the room closes behind them and Price lets go, pushing Lynell forward. He keeps the gun against the middle of her back. "Walk," he says.

She starts moving and glances back when the door opens again.

"Zach, leave her!" Daniel yells. "I swear if you hurt her . . ."

"What? You'll Register me?" Price says, a distasteful mockery in his voice. "You know you can't."

Lynell meets Daniel's eyes again just in time to see him mouth, "*I love you.*"

"Excuse me," a conductor says as Price is elbowing his way through the line of passengers getting off at this stop. "No need to push. There's plenty of time to—" He stops as he notices the gun in Lynell's back and then looks at Price.

Price instantly pulls a piece of paper and an ID out of his pocket and hands it over. "I've Registered her."

Dozens of eyes turn to them. A mother shields her son's face from the scene. Lynell wants to scream for help, to run, to drop to her knees. But Price is completely within his legal rights and no one can do anything for her. The conductor glances at the paper, then at Lynell, trying to match her face with the picture on the Registration form. Then he looks at Price and his eyes widen. He even offers an awkward tilt of his head.

"I apologize," the conductor says, terror in his voice.

Lynell glances at Price. He seems uncomfortable and rips the papers out of the man's hands.

When the conductor speaks again, he doesn't meet Price's eyes. "I'm sorry but if you'll please wait until you are off the train, our cleaning crew just disembarked."

"Of course," Price says. "Thank you."

"How thoughtful of you," Lynell hisses, "to wait to kill me until we are off this lovely train."

He pushes Lynell again and mutters, "Move."

"Please, follow me." The conductor takes them past the other passengers trying to get off the train.

Lynell turns as much as she dares, wondering if Daniel will come to her rescue. He clearly knows Price and knew he Registered her. Did he change his mind last minute and come to warn her? Or did he never want this? Or was he acting when Price appeared out of nowhere? Maybe what Lynell told him last night angered him enough to call Price and tell him where he could find her.

Lynell steps off the train first. The platform is bright with tiles and busy with people rushing from train to train. The far wall of the station is a blue and yellow mural with the words "WELCOME TO ST. LOUIS" written in large bubble letters.

"Aren't you going to kill me now?" Lynell asks as they approach the edge of the platform, where the crowd is thinnest.

"Not quite yet," Price says, guiding her toward the exit. They weave through hundreds of people. Lynell has trouble keeping herself from desperately reaching out and grabbing a stranger.

"Where are we going?"

"Back to Dallas."

"Why? What's the point in waiting?" she asks.

"Stop asking questions," Price says, pulling his phone from his pocket. He lets go of her arm to tap on his phone while they walk, but he remains close enough that she wouldn't be able to take two steps before he could grab her. They step outside and the air slaps her in the face. It's refreshing, probably fifteen degrees cooler than Texas. The sun is still bright and Lynell squints.

"How do you know Daniel? You're not going to hurt him, are you?" Lynell asks as they turn left down the sidewalk. Whether he was involved with Price's decision to Register her or not, he clearly doesn't want her to die. He tried to save her.

She looks at Price, seeing a muscle tense in his jaw. "Danny has nothing to do with this," he says.

Lynell tries to ignore the rush of relief. "And what is this?"

"Stop asking questions," he repeats. "We'll fly back to Dallas tomorrow. You'll get your answers then," Price says. A wave of relief washes over her. The word "tomorrow" holds the promise that she won't die today.

He steps forward, carefully leading her along, so he doesn't hurt her again. They stop under a sign that says "PICKUPS" and he pulls his phone out again. Lynell glimpses the screen and sees a small cartoon car driving down the street toward a flashing circle. He must have ordered them a car.

Price is wearing a small black watch, and the blank face on the front flashes bright red. He lowers his hand, tucking his phone back into his pocket. A minute later, a small black car arrives, and Price opens the door, pushing Lynell in first.

"Good afternoon," the driver says, looking through the rearview mirror. He has a foreign accent and Lynell wonders what made him move here. Acquiring citizenship has gotten more complicated every year and new citizens can never Register anyone, but they can be Registered. It doesn't make for a very appealing immigration. "Château Hotel?" the driver asks. Price nods, and Lynell fixes her eyes on him.

"Stop staring," he says.

Lynell doesn't look away. "Were you hired?" she asks. She's heard of people selling their Registration for hundreds of thousands to a few million dollars. It's like being a legal hitman just once in your life. But only the richest can afford it and she can't think of anyone powerful enough to care about wanting her dead. "If so, you don't have to kill me. I can disappear. Pretend to be dead."

Price scoffs, glancing at her. "That's not an option. And if you try to run again, you'll be putting Daniel's life in danger."

"You said you wouldn't hurt him." Worried that her fear will just spur him to use Daniel as bait, she clears her throat and says, "It's not like I'd care. We—"

"Don't take me for an idiot," Price interrupts. "Is it just a coincidence that he took you out of the state the day I Registered you? He was ready to attack me on that train. You were in bed together. You . . ." Price's voice seems thick and Lynell looks at him with her eyebrows furrowed. "You'll care what happens to him. You can't outrun the Registration, but you can keep him from being killed, and I know you want that."

Lynell wants to argue with him but doesn't want to give him the satisfaction. Also, her throat feels tight and she's not sure she could get the words out anyway. So, they endure silence for the rest of the drive until they stop in front of the hotel. Before they climb out, Price taps a bank card against the transaction machine reader on the back of the driver's seat. It blinks green, indicating he has successfully paid, and they head to the hotel, where Price checks them in at the front desk.

"Have a good night, Mr. and Mrs. Price," the lady at the front desk says with a smile.

Lynell feels bile rise in her throat. "We aren't—" she starts. Price grabs her wrist.

"Thank you," he says, smiling. He accepts the key card and they follow the receptionist's directions toward the stairwell and elevator.

The hallway is brightly lit. Generic paintings hang on the walls every few feet, and an alcove across from the elevators sports two chairs and a small bookshelf. Lynell steps to it, scanning the books lining the shelf.

She pulls a booklet from the top shelf. It's only about six inches long and has thin pages bound together with a silicon spiral. It's similar to the pamphlets many free clinics, poorer public schools, and a few independent stores display in Dallas.

She remembers stealing one that said "Leave Home, Find Peace" on the front as a kid, hoping it would teach her how to escape Alan. Instead, it was all about moving on as an adult after you've moved out of your parents' house.

"Finding Peace" included working a job or volunteering somewhere that benefits society. Reading that booklet at night after Alan passed out was the first time Lynell learned about vigilante Registration. The booklet's author started a nonprofit that walked victims through using their Registration for justice, connected them with therapists, and even suggested alternatives to Registering someone if the crime they had committed didn't call for death.

If, however, Registration was the best action, or if several victims wanted justice if a crime had not been met with a just sentence, say, if a violent sex offender or a child-killer was back out in the streets in no time, then the nonprofit helped victims decide who would Register the offender and provide support before and after.

Back then, Lynell called the number listed for the nonprofit with a friend's phone only to be told that they never advise children to use their Registration.

"Half of those booklets are paid for by Eric Elysian," Price says. Lynell jumps, having forgotten he was standing behind her.

"I always wondered why a booklet supporting the Registration would be at stores clearly geared toward anti-Registration rebels," Lynell says. "My mom took me to an arts and craft store once and their most prominent displays were clearly against the Elysians, but there was a shelf full of pro-Registration booklets right by the front door."

"Shop owners are paid to display them."

Lynell picks up a booklet that says, "A Fetus Isn't Human" on the front. It only takes a quick glance inside to know it's all about how Registrations shouldn't apply to pregnancies and women should be allowed to terminate several pregnancies without using their single Registration. That is one of the strongest arguments among the rebels, that abortions should be legal, should be a woman's choice, and that forcing women to use their one Registration for an abortion is the government's way of taking power back. That was also the deciding argument for Daniel to join the rebels: not that abortion was always the best choice to make, but that people should be *allowed* to choose.

"What about the pamphlets that are clearly against the Registration?" she asks. "Why does Eric Elysian allow their distribution?"

Price shrugs. "As much as I'm sure he would like to be, Eric Elysian is not the king of this country. He can't change the laws. And besides, the freedom of speech is still a highly regarded value."

Lynell puts the booklet back and turns to Price. "You seem to know a lot about him."

"Doesn't everyone?"

Lynell doesn't argue as she follows Price to the elevators. They head to a large room on the sixth floor with two beds against the far wall and a table between them.

It's not even five o'clock yet, but Price sits on the bed. "We're having dinner delivered. Might as well get comfortable."

Lynell frowns, glancing around the room. She feels the absence of Daniel like the loss of a limb. She climbs under the covers of the free bed and lies on her side, staring at Price.

He pulls a book out of his bag and scoots back, lying with one hand stretched behind his head and the other holding his book in front of his face.

"You're staring again," Price says, looking over at Lynell.

She huffs and moves to her back. "Excuse me if I want to get a good look at the person who is going to kill me tomorrow."

"Don't be so self-righteous. You were also going to Register someone yesterday," Price says, lowering his open book to his chest.

"Yeah, well . . . I never got the chance." She doesn't bother asking how he knew that. It wouldn't surprise her if he saw her at the office and let her run for the fun of it. Like playing with your food.

"You can't judge me for doing something you were planning to do yourself."

"Not judging," Lynell says, turning her head. She meets Price's eyes and suddenly feels like she may have met him before after all. "But I know why I was going to Register Alan. I had a good reason. Why did you Register me?"

"You think you're above reproach?"

"Maybe not, but I want to know why you'd want to Register me."

"Are you ever going to stop talking?" Price sighs.

"I imagine sometime tomorrow I will."

"Ever the sense of humor, you have. Just like your—" Price stops talking and clears his throat.

Lynell sits up, ready to ask him what he was going to say, but one look from him arrests all words in her throat.

"You can have whatever you want to eat tonight," he says, rolling over to pull a menu out of the drawer in the nightstand between the two beds. He throws the thick black envelope to her and returns to his spot on the bed. "We'll order in an hour."

"My last meal . . ." she mutters under her breath, flipping open the menu.

"Hardly. I'm sure there will be time for meals tomorrow. Now shut up so I can finish reading this chapter." He returns to the book but pauses again when his watch flashes three times, bright white and blinding. Lynell frowns when he groans and takes it off, dumping it in the drawer between them.

Fighting the urge to ask him about it, she says, "Not a talker, are you?" She pulls off her shoes, scanning the dinner items. "Conversation is good, you know. Healthy for the soul."

He doesn't respond, so Lynell rolls her eyes and focuses on the menu. But she continues to occasionally glance at Price. When it's finally time to order, she relays what she wants, "Roasted Free Range Chicken with fries," and devours the food when it arrives an hour later. She licks ketchup off her fingers and catches Price looking at her with a small frown.

"Excuse my manners," she says. "Fries are my favorite." Price smirks. "Care to watch a movie?" Lynell pulls the remote out of the drawer between the beds and turns on the TV. She quickly finds one of the old classics, settling into the bed to watch it.

"Do you care at all?" Price asks a few minutes later.

Lynell looks over at him. "About what?"

"That you're here. That I'm here. That I'll . . . Aren't you scared?"

She shrugs. "Yeah. But it is what it is. And it's not like I don't dese—" the words fizzle in her throat. "You must have a reason," she says instead. "And you say I'll learn it. That's enough for now. I'm not going to spend my last night in fear. I've had far too much of that for one short lifetime."

Price doesn't answer.

And true to her word, despite being stuck in a room by herself with the man who will take her life, Lynell falls asleep quickly and easily that night, tumbling into a memory.

DAY 3 ———————————————o

L ynell hears Price order coffee and waffles to be delivered to the room and cracks one eye open to check the time. The clock's light is blinding and when she sees it isn't even seven a.m., she pulls a pillow over her head and burrows deeper into the covers. She's not sure how much time passes before room service knocks and Price carries the food inside. Lynell lowers the pillow, blinks against the sunlight, and rolls over.

"You're awake," Price says. It sounds like he's speaking around a mouthful of waffles. "You want some breakfast?"

She lies still, the blanket shielding her body from the stranger who slept in the bed next to her all night. She smells the waffles and . . . bacon? The scent taunts her, but she can't get her limbs to move.

Don't give him the satisfaction, she thinks. Having a second meal with him borders on intimate, and she has no desire for intimacy with the man who Registered her.

"They're decent waffles," Price says. His fork clinks against the metal plate and the sound grates in Lynell's ears. She lifts the blanket so it covers her head. "You should try them," he continues. "They even gave us a bowl of berries."

She feels her bed dip and when he starts talking, Lynell realizes Price has sat down.

"You're going to get hungry on the plane and I'm not getting you any-thing."

"I have money," Lynell says, her voice muffled. *And I might as well spend it.*

"Suit yourself." He stands. "Our flight doesn't leave for three more hours, though, so you're probably going to get hungry before," he says.

Lynell ignores him in favor of trying to fall back asleep. But Price cuts his waffles loudly and hums while he eats, as if her comfort is the last thing on his mind.

When her sheet is ripped back and the cold air assaults an exposed sliver of skin between her pants and shirt, she sits up with a shout.

"Hey!"

He's holding the sheets in one hand and a plate in another. He smirks at her and drops the plate next to her on the bed. The waffle flops on the plate and one edge hits her leg. "It's time to eat and get up, Lynell. Stop moping."

"Moping?" Lynell swings her legs over the edge of the bed and grabs the waffle in her fist. "You think I'm moping?" She stands up and throws the waffle at Price. He holds his hands up but doesn't block fast enough, and the waffle hits him in the middle of the face. "I'm not moping, you arrogant shit. I'm just not playing your little game. I won't be the food you play with before your feast." Her face heats up as she yells, but Price just blinks at her, his hands loose at his side. "Screw you, Zachary Price. I'm taking a shower." She turns and heads to the bathroom, slamming the door behind her before turning on the water.

When she's finished, Price knocks on the door. "Leaving in an hour, Lynell. Be ready."

Lynell returns to the bedroom where Price is perched at the edge of her bed. She lies back down and rests her hands over her rumbling stomach, taking deep, steadying breaths.

"Do you agree?" Lynell asks after deciding the silence is more uncomfortable than it's worth. "That the Registration is a way of life and we should respect it?" She sits up, looking at Price with an eyebrow raised. He doesn't answer but shifts from foot to foot, avoiding her eyes. "I do," she continues.

"It's not always perfect but it does more good than bad, I think. But maybe I'm wrong. Maybe I'm brainwashed? That's what the rebels say. I don't know. But let me tell you, being on this end, despite the crap pile of a life I'm living, gives you a different perspective. Suddenly, the Registration doesn't seem as fair." She lies back down and closes her eyes, thinking about Daniel's look of betrayal and anger when she came home all those years ago. "It seems like I should have respected life more. Made amends."

Price doesn't respond. Lynell can hear the tick of the watch he must have put back on that morning. The thin black fancy one he keeps glancing at every time it flashes a different color, most often red.

"It's time to go," he says with a sigh.

Price carries their bags, and she follows him. She feels every breath she takes and every hair on her body. While Price checks them out, Lynell watches a woman struggling to stuff clothes in a bag while her young child waves a set of keys in the air.

The child throws the keys across the lobby.

"Carla!" the woman shouts. Lynell can hear the exhaustion in her voice. Before she can stand to retrieve the keys, Lynell steps forward.

"I got it," she says, heading to the bench on the side of the lobby where the keys slid beneath. Lynell has to kneel and lean down to reach the keys and when she returns, the woman is grinning, and the child is reaching up for the keys. "How old is she?" Lynell asks.

"Almost two," the woman says.

Lynell smiles and waves at Carla. "Good morning, Carla." The little girl hides behind her mom's legs but waves gently even as she does.

"Sorry, she's a bit shy."

"It's fine," Lynell stands, crossing her arms. "She's gorgeous."

"Thank you."

Before Lynell can reply, she hears Price thanking the receptionist and turns just in time for him to grab her arm and say, "Making friends?"

Lynell nods, glaring at him in a silent challenge to forbid her from being kind to strangers.

Price holds out his hand and the woman takes it, shaking it respectfully before pulling away and grabbing her daughter's hand. "Thanks for keeping my wife company, but we really must be going."

"Good to meet you," Lynell says before Price tugs her away from the woman. "Have a good day, Carla."

"Bye!" the little girl shouts. Lynell's chest tightens.

Price ordered another car that's already waiting outside when they leave the hotel.

"Today then?" she asks five minutes into the drive.

"Hmm?" he mutters, staring at his phone.

"You're doing it today? Completing the Registration?"

He shrugs, his fingers dancing along the screen of his phone.

Lynell reaches over and tugs the phone out of Price's hand. "Can you at least pretend to care about this?" she asks, voice harsher than she thought capable. She'd assumed her anger would fade into acceptance and resignation.

Price curls his hands into fists. "Give me back my phone, Lynell."

"One question," she says, holding the phone behind her head.

Price looks like he could strangle her. "Excuse me?"

She puffs out her chest and meets his gaze with as much confidence as she can muster. "I'll give you back your phone if you answer one of my questions truthfully."

"You're joking, right?" He looks from her to the phone before making a lunge for it. She dodges and pulls a leg up onto the seat between them.

"No, I'm not," she says. Price looks murderous, and she begins to wonder what could be on his phone that would get him to react like this. Answers to her questions maybe? Messages to the person who hired him?

Messages from Daniel?

Price sits back. "One question."

Lynell grins and relaxes some. She purses her lips, considering all her options.

"Any day now."

Lynell scowls. "Fine." She fully intends to ask why he Registered her, but before she can stop herself, a different question escapes. "How do you know Daniel Carter?" She blinks at her own question, internally kicking herself.

It doesn't matter how her Registerer and her ex know each other. It *shouldn't* matter. And yet, it does.

Price has the nerve to chuckle. He shakes his head and rubs his eyes with his fingertips.

"What?" Lynell says, defensive.

"You're sitting in a car with the man who Registered you, you have no idea when exactly in the next twelve days or how or where your life will end, and the most pressing question on your mind is *that?*" He looks at her with so much amusement in his eyes that Lynell shoves him before crossing her arms.

"Yes. And you have to answer."

He's still smiling when he says, "You really are something, Lynell Mize."

"Answer the question."

"Phone first," he says, holding out his hand.

"No."

He lifts an eyebrow.

"You called him Danny. He called you Zach. You know each other. And he just let you . . ." she takes a deep breath and steadies her gaze on the man across from her. "Tell me."

He sighs and pulls his hand back. "Fine. We met at a pub two years ago. Danny was there, drinking alone, and we just got to talking. He honestly seemed confused about why he was there. We drank a bit too much and I apparently complained about my father a lot, because Danny said, 'Let's go teach him a lesson.'" Price shrugs, smiling at the memory. "So, we stole a bottle of brandy, went to my father's office, trashed the place, and ended up on the roof. I was able to remotely turn off any security cameras, so my father never found out who ransacked his place. Been great friends ever since."

He stops talking, staring at Lynell expectantly. She blinks, frowns, and tries to picture the event. Daniel has never been a big drinker. Or partier. Daniel is safe, secure, and predictable. He always said he had enough excitement when he fought with the rebels before they were quickly subdued by the Elysians.

"I'll be boring as long as I'm here for you," he'd said.

How did he end up with a guy like this?

She stares at Price until the car comes to a halt and the driver leans back, shouting that they've arrived. This car doesn't have a machine to pay at the back, so Price hands his bank card to the driver. He taps it against the machine built into the dashboard of the car and hands it back when it shines green.

"Thanks," Price says to the driver. Then he turns to Lynell. "Now can I have my phone back?"

Lynell returns the small device to Price who instantly starts typing. He doesn't look up from the screen as he climbs out of the car.

So Daniel knew. He had to have known, but Lynell refuses to believe it was his idea. Either Price decided to get revenge for his friend by registering the horrible ex or this is unrelated to her marriage with Daniel.

Suddenly her door opens, and she's yanked from her thoughts and the car by Price's strong hand.

"Come on. We've got a plane to catch."

"No need to be so forceful," she says, climbing out of the car and pushing Price's hand off.

She's never been to St. Louis, but the airport is small compared to the Dallas and Chicago airports. Even still, it's crowded, and the security lines are completely full. Traveling during the Registration is always more difficult. The rules are slightly different, with weapons being allowed onboard and more paperwork to check.

She follows him into the bustling airport, ignoring the way he glances at her every few seconds. It takes forty minutes to reach the top of the security line, where Price has to go to the furthest booth to check in his weapon.

Lynell probably shouldn't be surprised that Price owns a weapon, but she is. Acquiring a legal weapon like a gun is difficult, and the fact that Price has one makes him that much more mysterious. He must be rich. Or well connected. Or both. The security guard checks to make sure the gun isn't loaded before returning it. Price has to sign a paper saying he won't complete his Registration on the aircraft, or his immunity will be forfeited. Lynell didn't even know there were limits on where a Registration could be completed, except that it can't be in another country.

"Don't try anything," Price hisses in her ear before heading through the metal detector and agreeing to a pat-down.

She hadn't planned on it. Not in a crowded airport with officers every ten feet. But then she thinks of Daniel and those last three words he mouthed.

After he left her three years ago, she was certain he'd never forgive her, never love her again. But she was wrong. What else was she wrong about? Lynell realizes she can't find peace in her Registration until she has some answers.

She goes through the security calmly and when Price reaches out to grab her arm after she makes it through, she grabs his hand instead. He's about to pull away when she laces her fingers between his and starts walking toward their gate.

"What are you doing?" he whispers in her ear.

She just winks at him and subtly guides them into a crowd.

A bump. "Excuse me." A suitcase grazes her leg. A mom yells at her children. Shoving. A man speaks over a loud intercom.

Lynell takes the moment to carefully pull his phone from his back pocket and drop it to the ground.

Thankfully, he feels the drop of his phone and mutters a curse as he lets go of Lynell's hand to reach down and retrieve the phone.

Her heart pounds in her ears. She takes multiple large steps forward, through the crowd, and into a store. She hides behind a bookcase and feels the back of her hands become slick with sweat. She grabs a book, opens it and rests her hot forehead against the pages. Price doesn't shout for her, but she sees him run past the store, grab a girl with similar brown hair as hers and turn her around. She yells, and while Price is apologizing, Lynell returns the book to the shelf and slides out of the store, heading back in the direction they came.

An old man sets his bag down and walks to a counter. Lynell grabs the bag and keeps walking. Two gates down, a woman takes off her sweater, drapes it over her seat, and walks to the trash can. Lynell grabs the sweater and pulls it on over her shoulders, quickening her pace. She turns a corner, leans against the wall and opens the bag. There's a beanie inside she pulls over her head before zipping up the bag, sliding it into the middle of the aisle, and continuing her trek through the airport.

"Lynell Mize, please check in at Gate A12," someone says over the speaker.

Lynell needs to leave the airport. She stops and glances around. A security guard catches her eyes and starts toward her. She pulls the beanie lower and sees a sign that points her to the exit.

Before she makes it three steps, a hand curls around her arm and jerks her back. She shouts in protest and turns to yell at Price, fully expecting him to be fuming at her. All the hope she'd felt drips from her body, and rage fizzles at the edge of her mind.

The grip on her arm is harder than Price has ever held her. "Hey! Will you—"

The words catch in her throat when she makes eye contact with an older man. His face is carved with wrinkles and there's a scar across his nose. He sneers and she gets a whiff of his breath that makes her stomach curl in on itself.

"I've been looking for you for almost three days. You're a hard girl to get ahold of," he says. His voice is gritty, and he pulls her closer. "Then that dumbass found you first and he doesn't even know how to get information without getting soft and letting the contact guilt him into releasing her. Figures he wouldn't be able to separate personal life from the job at hand."

Lynell's breaths are quick and short and her heart beats faster. She can't even comprehend what he's said about Price or the fact that he called her a "contact." What the heck is a "contact?" His hold on her arm is too painful and the fear building in her chest is even more overwhelming than when she heard Price Register her. She claws at his hand and glances around for help desperately. A guard starts toward them.

"Let go of me! Help!" she shouts, pulling away from the man. She turns to the guard. "Help!"

The man pulls a paper and ID out and shoves them in the guard's face.

No. No, no, no, no. Lynell looks from the stranger to the paper to the guard, her world melting in front of her.

"You Lynell Mize?" the guard asks. The question is rhetorical. He can surely tell from the paper and her photo displayed on the front that the Registration is legal.

"I've Registered her," the man confirms. His grip somehow gets tighter and Lynell gasps. Her legs give out from under her and she falls to her knees, which forces her arm into a weird angle and sends pain dancing through her arm.

"Well, keep it civil or take it outside," the guard says.

Wait, Lynell wants to yell. *Can't you see he's hurting me?* But the air seems taken from her lungs and she can't gather the energy to say anything.

"Get up," the man orders, pulling at Lynell's arm.

She moves to her feet and sways, taking a deep breath. She half-heartedly tries to tug her arm out of his grip again.

"Who—?" she gasps.

"Shut up." He pulls her against his chest, lets go of her arms, and grabs both of her shoulders. "Tell me the code."

She blinks at him. "What?"

He shakes her. "Don't play dumb. Tell me the code and I'll kill you faster."

Lynell looks around. A few rubberneckers have turned to watch the scene with wide, curious eyes. One man even walks closer, his lips twitching into a sick grin as he pulls out a phone and starts taking pictures. Most everyone else has turned away, ignoring just another Registration.

"I don't know what co—"

He pulls a hand back and slaps her in the face with so much force that she is thrown back and hits the ground with a loud *crack*. She blinks and opens her eyes to see the world swirl and distort, as if falling down a drain and into a dream.

"Hey!" the guard shouts. "Take it outside!"

The man grabs her arms and yanks her back to her feet and flush against his chest. She winces, turning her head to the side so his hot breath brushes over her cheek.

"It's pointless trying to fight. If I don't get it out of you, the next one will. You can't keep the code a secret forever."

Her brain tumbles as she tries to figure out the meaning of his words. At her silence, his lips peel back to reveal crooked, off-white teeth.

"Tell me, you stupid bi—"

All at once, his grip on her is removed and Lynell steps back, too stunned to run again. Her arm throbs and she coughs, blinking at the sight of Price tackling the man to the ground. Several more bystanders have gotten their phones out, and Lynell looks at them without truly seeing anyone. The two men grapple on the floor and Lynell's breaths are coming faster and faster until she begins to feel lightheaded. A group of Elysian Regulators runs over, one knocking into her. She doesn't fight it as she falls to the floor, everything going black.

The bed is soft, holding her gently like a concerned lover. Her limbs are heavy and too comfortable to even think about moving them. There's still a dull pain in the back of her head, but she almost doesn't notice it amongst the flurry of thoughts.

She opens her eyes and instantly closes them again against the light.

"You're awake," someone says.

Lynell moans and blinks again. The light assaults her eyes like tiny arrows until her vision can adjust. She sits up, looking at Price, who's sitting on a bed a foot away. He's watching her with more concern than she expected.

"You okay?"

Lynell lifts her hand and rubs her forehead. She stretches her head from side to side until her neck gives a small crack. There's an ice pack next to her on the bed and she frowns at it, looking back to Price.

"What the—"

"Why did you run away?" Price interrupts.

She blinks and looks at him again. He shakes his head, stands up, and starts pacing. "You're more of an idiot than I expected. He could have broken your arm. You're lucky you got out of that with just a black eye and a few bruises. Maybe a small concussion." Lynell's lips part like she wants to argue or ask questions, but words don't form. She must be in shock.

"I was going to take you back to Dallas and now we have to stay at this shitty motel for another night. If you would've just stayed with me then that lumbering idiot never would've gotten close to you. Shit, Lynell! Couldn't you just . . . listen to me?"

"Who . . ." she starts, but he turns around and squats next to her.

"Do you want to die? Because it seems like you do." He stands again, shaking his hands out at his side. "God!" he shouts. She flinches at the exclamation, and he gives her an almost apologetic look. "No one prepared me for such a difficult—"

"Price."

He stops pacing and turns to her. "What?"

Lynell turns, dropping her legs over the side of the bed. Whatever bruises she has must be deep because the movement causes a slight spike of pain. She grits her teeth and Price walks closer, settling his hand on her shoulder to steady her.

"Careful," he mutters. His voice is filled with so much concern, and she can't understand why he cares. Not after Registering her.

"What happened? Who was that? He said . . ." she swallows and finishes, words quieter now. "He said he Registered me."

"I think his name is Jered or something stupid. I knocked him out. The Regulators were ready to arrest me, but I explained that you were my Registration, and you know how they get, protect a man's Registration or some shit like that. You fainted. I had to carry you. I'm sure Jered will come looking for us soon, but I can handle him."

"For how long?"

"A few hours. It's almost seven."

She blinks. *Hours.* This isn't the first time she's fainted from a panic attack, but she always wakes up after just a few seconds. "What's going on?"

He shakes his head. "I can't . . ."

"Price."

"Stop, Lynell. I can't say. Not now. Not until I get you to Dallas. God, why couldn't you just stay with me? The others won't be patient or gentle with you. They're brutes, Lynell. They just want to win."

"They? Win what?" Her throat burns, but she's desperate for answers.

"The reward. There are at least ten people after it. They Registered you and they won't stop looking for you. Whoever gets you first has the best chance of getting the reward. You've got to stay with me."

Reward. Who would care enough about her to offer a reward for Registering and capturing her? Selling your Registration is rare enough, but the only people who have ever had a bounty on their head were dangerous criminals.

"Why should I stay with you?" she asks. "You Registered me, too."

Price frowns and drops to the bed next to her. "Yeah."

"Why?"

Price turns to her and cocks his head. His eyes are glassy and he reaches out to tuck a strand of hair behind her ear. "Because my d—I had to. I didn't have a—I didn't want one of them to—" He pulls his hand down his face, shaking his head before saying, "I don't know, Lynell. But you've got to trust me."

She scoffs.

"Seriously. Right now, we need to get you to Dallas. Promise me you won't run away again."

"Price."

"And call me Zach. I hate it when you call me Price."

"Why?"

He shakes his head and drops his hands into his lap. He looks at them as if they're covered in blood. "Soon, Lynell. I swear. But just . . . promise me."

"Price . . ."

"Lynell," he turns to her again, eyes so full of pleading that, for a moment, Lynell falters and forgets that this man will kill her in less than two weeks. She sees so much of her own fear in his eyes that a small part of her wants to reach out and give him a hug.

But mostly, she wants to slap him and demand answers.

She makes a compromise with herself and grits her teeth before saying, "Zach."

He grins. "I wish you weren't who you are, Lynell. But you are. And I am who I am. This is our situation, and we have to deal with it as best we can." She's about to ask more questions, but Price leans forward, grabs a pill and a cup from the bedside table, and hands them to her. "Go to sleep. Tomorrow, we're going home."

DAY 4

Nightmares wake her up and cling to her all morning. She ignores Price when he asks what's wrong but takes the pain meds he offers as she heads for the bathroom. With no shower, Lynell settles for splashing water on her face and taking deep, calming breaths. She leans over the sink and gently places two fingers under the cut on her cheekbone. Color is just beginning to form around the wound, and she knows in a few hours it will be a proper black eye.

She's no stranger to cuts and bruises. She's even had her fair share of broken bones. But something about seeing her reflection this morning makes her feel small and insignificant. Soon, she'll just be another casualty of the Registration.

Not a victim.

Those who are Registered are never referred to as victims. Eric Elysian once said, *"The real victims were the citizens oppressed and practically enslaved by the government before the civil war. But you are no longer a victim. You are free. You have power and a choice. You have the Registration."*

She once watched that speech four times in a row, trying to convince herself to take a stand against Alan so she would no longer be victimized.

But she didn't. And now she'll never have the chance again.

"Just ordered a car. They're seven minutes away," Price says when she emerges from the bathroom, hair in a loose bun to ease the growing headache.

Lynell nods and grabs one of the plastic cups sitting next to an empty ice bucket. She fills it with water from the bathroom, ignoring how cloudy it is before downing all of it. It's not like she'll be alive long enough to worry about getting sick from unfiltered water.

The car is waiting at the curb and the driver, an older man who grew up here, talks nonstop during the drive. He tells them about all six of his children, that his oldest is planning to run for office.

"She has a bit of a crush on Elysian's son. Can't remember his name. The guy's never in the spotlight, not like his dad. Well, my girl is going to change that. They'll be a power couple. The Elysian kid with the Registration and my girl in the government. Think of what they'll do together!"

Lynell never gets a word in, much less to tell the guy that the current leaders have already done quite a lot together.

Price keeps his face down and eyes staring at the phone in his lap, as if unwilling to even look at the man, much less speak to him.

"Traffic ahead," the driver calls back. "Might be an extra few minutes."

Lynell looks out the window as they turn onto what looks to be the main road downtown. She cranes her neck to try and get a better look at the Gateway Arch that dominates the skyline. A few minutes later, they drive past the cause of traffic.

The open space and green lawns under the arch are crawling with people sitting, standing, walking, and chanting. Many are holding signs that all say a variation of the same thing: "End the Registration."

"REGISTER THE ELYSIANS"

"MURDER IS MURDER LEGAL OR NOT"

"LEGAL ≠ MORAL"

"ERIC ELYSIAN IS A BASTARD"

"REGISTRATION IS NOT CHOICE"

"I didn't realize there were still so many rebels," she says, almost to herself.

"There's always more during the two-week Registration period. After, people seem to go about their lives and forget," Price replies.

She can't go about her life. Can't forget. Only eleven days left. "If they only care when it's relevant, do they really care?"

Price scoffs. "That is the question, isn't it?"

Lynell turns away from the window and frowns at him.

"Maybe they have a point," Lynell says, but she doesn't believe her own words. She sympathizes with the rebels, more so after meeting Daniel, but if she had to pick a side, she'd never turn against the Registration. It's the only thing offering a shred of freedom from people like Alan.

"They're fanatics. Radicals. Rebels," Price says, his voice laced with disdain. He looks up, focusing on Lynell. "They forget that there is no perfect world. Overturning the Registration, or this government, would leave a huge empty space anything could fill. What comes next could be worse."

"Wouldn't the revolutionists be prepared to fill that empty space?" Lynell asks. Daniel explained once how the rebels planned to overthrow the government right after succeeding in their main goal of ending the Registration. He said they wanted to get rid of the oligarchy and replace it with a system that gives individuals more of a say.

"Destabilizing the current system would leave us vulnerable to foreign powers," Price says, looking through the back window where the protest is now growing small as they drive away. "The West Mediterranean Federation may try to conquer us, and they're a dictatorship governed by brutal force."

Brutal force? Wasn't that also an accurate description of the Registration? Lynell doesn't have the energy to argue.

As they reach the airport, Price pulls a hat over Lynell's head, tucking all the hair underneath.

"You're not going to run away from me this time, are you?" he asks while he tugs the hat down.

"No point, is there?"

His lips press together, as if the statement offends him.

The security line is shorter this time, but it still takes half an hour to get through.

"Don't know why they allow weapons during Registration season," Lynell mutters as the security guard inspects Price's gun.

"To limit hindrances for completing Registrations," Price says, after thanking the man and sliding his gun back into the bag.

"Then why allow everyone? Why not just people who have Registered that quarter?"

Price grabs her right hand after they pass through the metal detectors and leads her in the direction of their gate. "Simplicity's sake?"

"Yeah," Lynell fills her voice with sarcasm, practically feeling it drip from each word. "Because everything about the Registration is so simple."

To Lynell's surprise, Price laughs.

When they reach their gate, Lynell sits in the corner and rests her head against the wall. Price pulls two protein bars from his bag, handing one to Lynell. Her stomach rumbles painfully at the sight and she takes it without comment.

A loudspeaker crackles on and then a woman's crisp, clear voice begins to speak. "Good morning, passengers."

Leaning forward and glancing to her right, Lynell can see a tall, curvy woman with unblemished brown skin and pink hair braided in an intricate crown on top of her head speaking into a microphone.

"This is the pre-boarding announcement for flight 89B to Dallas. We are now inviting those passengers with small children, and any passengers requiring special assistance, to board at this time. Have your boarding pass and identification ready. Regular boarding will begin in approximately ten minutes' time. Please remember that the use of weapons is prohibited on the aircraft. No Registrations may be completed on this or any flight for health and sanitation reasons. Noncompliance with this will result in prosecution despite any Registration immunities. Thank you."

The speaker clicks off and Lynell leans back, closing her eyes. When the woman calls for group five to board, Price nudges her calf with his foot.

"That's us," he says.

Lynell nods and follows Price to join the queue.

The flight attendant smiles at her, and to her own surprise, Lynell manages to smile back. Lynell sees the woman look at the bruise forming around Lynell's eye and cheek, but she doesn't say anything other than, "Have a good flight."

Price nods and ushers them both into the tube leading them to the plane. The air is stuffy and Lynell feels herself getting light-headed. She grasps Price's hand to steady herself.

"You okay?" he asks.

"Yeah."

They finally reach their row and she sinks into the window seat. Price sits next to her and places his hand over her forehead.

"You're burning up," he says, concern lacing his voice. "Here," he rummages in his bag before pulling out two pills.

"Will they knock me out?" Lynell asks.

"Shouldn't. Though sleeping now wouldn't be a bad thing. It's a two-hour flight."

Lynell shakes her head. "I don't trust you, Price."

"Zach," he says.

"It's not happening."

"Well, I'm napping. I didn't get much sleep last night and we'll need the energy today. Wake me if anything interesting happens." He crosses his arms, settles his head against the seat, and closes his eyes.

Lynell glares and buckles her seat belt, then stares out the window, watching the baggage handlers throw suitcases from a large metal container onto a conveyor leading up to the cargo hold.

When the plane takes off, Lynell is pushed further into her seat. Almost half an hour later, the flight attendants walk down the aisles with two carts, one with drinks and one with snacks.

"Anything to drink?" The attendant's bright red hair is pulled into a bun.

"Some tea, please. And he'll have red wine," she says, gesturing to Price, who is still sound asleep. She lowers both of their tray tables and accepts the drinks with a smile. She places the wine on his and the tea on her own. When the next cart comes, Lynell gets a cookie for herself and pretzels for Price. He continues to sleep as she eats the pretzels first then the cookies. She downs the wine quickly before sipping on the tea.

Over an hour into the flight, Lynell looks up and sees a skinny man with a patchy beard staring at her. Her face heats up and she becomes keenly aware of her body's every inch. She looks down, out the window, and runs her fingers through her hair.

She counts to ten before looking up again. He's still staring.

She mimics him, filling her own stare with as much venom as she can manage. He grins. Lynell seethes.

"Want a picture?" she asks, loudly enough for him to hear. Several other people turn to look at her, but she doesn't remove her gaze from him.

He tilts his head, unbuckles, and stands. Lynell almost shakes Price awake but instead sits straighter and keeps her eyes trained on the man as he walks over. He sits in the empty aisle seat in their row.

"Picture won't work. I need you," he says. His voice is low, and Lynell sees Price twitch but not stir. "You don't even realize what's happening, do you?"

Lynell frowns. "I know more than you think," she lies.

"Oh?" he perks up. "So, you know about the code?"

"Yes."

He raises his eyebrows and leans forward, gaze searching hers. After a few seconds, he sits back. "No, you don't. Which is probably good. If you did, you'd die faster. But we all need it, and you're the one who has it. So at least you'll be alive until one of us gets it."

"Won't be you."

"If not me, then one of my colleagues. If none of them, Zach here will." He looks down at Price, his face full of hatred. "If he wants it, he'll get it. You'll give it to him no problem." He looks back up at Lynell. "And you'll even think that you're doing the right thing. That you can trust the idiot. But after you hand it over, you know what he'll do?"

Lynell pushes her mouth into a thin line. She feels the truth of his words and each syllable like a needle in her skin. She doesn't want to agree with him. She doesn't want to think that one day she may trust Price or give him anything he wants.

"He'll kill you. And if there's anyone you love, he'll kill them too. But we've been watching you for a year now. A sad life. No husband. No kids. No family. At least, none that you love." The man leans forward, his smile widening. "Your mother, once. But she's gone. Daddy's gone. Alan is still here, isn't he?" He tilts his head. "You'd want us to kill him, though. So, I think we won't. I think we'll let that bastard roam free. Marry new women and have more stepdaughters to—" he suddenly stops talking and at first Lynell thinks her anger took over and she'd punched him like she desperately wanted to.

Then she sees Price's arms around the man's neck, his eyes bulging. The man is turned at an awkward angle, so his head is almost in Price's lap. The move was quiet and none of the passengers are looking yet, but they're bound to take notice soon.

"You talk too much, Markus," Price says. "It's going to get you Registered one day."

Markus struggles in Price's grip and his face starts to turn purple.

"Didn't he tell you not to Register Lynell? You won't win and you're just in the way. You're not a Researcher, Markus. You never will be. Poor thing, you're just a nuisance allowed to stick around because my father says so." Price leans closer to Markus and whispers in his ear. "If you so much as look in Lynell's direction again, I will rip you apart. You'll never even get a taste of the reward." Price sits up, and Lynell thinks if he doesn't let go of Markus soon, he'll pass out. "I'm going to let go in five seconds. Return to your seat, face forward, and when the plane lands, go home and forget any of this happened. Okay?"

With limited movement, Markus gives a weak nod.

"Good." Price lets go, and Markus takes a deep breath that pulls a few eyes toward them. He holds onto his neck for a moment, still sucking air in, as if Price is going to cut his oxygen off again. He glares at Price and Lynell one more time, then returns to his seat, looking straight ahead.

"Next time, wake me up," Price says, his voice like a growl.

"Sorry . . ." she mutters, wanting to ask him a million questions but sensing that now is definitely not the time.

"It's fine." Price is steadily looking at his hands in his lap and his voice seems exhausted. The plane shakes with turbulence and Lynell grasps the arms of her seat.

He'll kill you.

And anyone she may love, Markus said. She can't help but think of Daniel.

"I'm sorry," Price says after a long stretch of silence.

Lynell looks up to see him staring at her. "What?"

"For . . . for seeing you as nothing but a means to an end. And for—" he stops and swallows, averting his gaze. "For wanting to Register you."

"But not for Registering me?"

Price shakes his head. "That couldn't have been avoided. But everything else wasn't necessary. Kidnapping you, holding you at gunpoint. This," he reaches up and gently touches her black eye. "I'm sorry."

Lynell pushes his hand away. "How is Daniel involved?" she asks.

Price laughs. "He's not. That man is pure through and through. He'd never be involved with the likes of us."

"Who is 'us'?"

His eyes flick to the side and he licks his bottom lip. When it's clear he doesn't intend to answer the question, she asks, "If Daniel isn't involved, then how did he know?"

That, apparently, Price has no trouble sharing. "I told him."

"You did? Why?" Lynell tries to snub the anxious curiosity in her gut, but it burns, threatening to overtake her.

"I honestly don't know. Moment of weakness? Second-guessing? Pride? Did I want his help, or did I want him to see how cool—how important I am?" Price shrugs and gives a self-deprecating chuckle. He looks back at her then, squinting as if to study her. "I don't know who I am. Damn," he shakes his head. "That sounds so lame, but it's true."

"You don't know who you are," she says, each word monotone and face void of emotion. "That's a copout. Who are you, anyway? And who are all the other men Registering me?"

Price seems to struggle with himself for a moment before saying, "We all work for the same guy."

"Who?"

He shakes his head.

"And this guy is the one who wanted me Registered?"

He nods.

"Is he why we're going back to Dallas? You're taking me to him?"

Price nods again.

"Did you forget how to speak?"

He laughs and shakes his head. Lynell notices Markus flinch at the laughter, but he doesn't turn around.

He must be terrified of Price. If these violent men are scared of Price, then Lynell wonders why her own fear seems to be dissolving.

"Why didn't he just do it himself?" Lynell asks. The idea of a man so powerful he can make others use their Registration on *her* makes frost fill her chest.

Price reaches forward and grabs all the trash on her tray table. "Didn't want to leave me anything?" He raises an eyebrow. "It's fine. We'll be in Dallas any minute now and I bet there will be a full dinner ready for us." Price winks at Lynell.

Lynell scowls, but before she can reply, the pilot's voice echoes through the plane, letting them know that they've started the descent.

Lynell watches Markus leave the plane in a hurry. Price doesn't move from his seat until everyone else has disembarked, then he grabs Lynell's hand

and leads her down the aisle. She's annoyed to realize that his grip around her arm is more calming than it is unnerving.

Maybe Markus was wrong. Maybe Price won't kill her. Maybe once the guy who sent him gets what he wants, Price will help her make it through the rest of the Registration period alive. After today, there will only be ten more days left to survive.

It's pointless to hope, she knows. She's barely survived the first four days. There's no way she'll make it ten more.

When they walk into baggage claim, she sees a man in a pitch-black suit, black sunglasses, and a white hat holding a sign that reads "E. ZACH." Price stops in front of the man, yanking Lynell to a halt.

"Hey, Zimmer," he says with a nod.

"Sir," the man responds. He lowers the sign and grabs Price's bag.

Lynell frowns, looking from this man—Zimmer—back up at Price, who just shrugs and pulls her along to follow the man outside. They don't have to walk far. Right outside the door is a black hatchback with tinted windows. It shines in the daylight and even though Lynell doesn't know much about cars, she can tell this one is probably expensive. Next to the passenger's seat stands a tall man with muscles bigger than his black shirt can handle. He's in simple black pants, and two holsters hang around his arms, both of which are holding guns. Lynell stops walking and sucks in a breath, fear lancing through her body.

Price grabs her hand and turns to face her. "It's okay. He's here to protect us and only protect. He didn't Register you," he says, calmly and quietly so the other two men can't hear him. Lynell searches his gaze but finds no trace of a lie. Not that she's confident she would know if he were lying, but it's enough to make her nod.

The large man doesn't look at her as he opens the door. Price thanks him and climbs in. Lynell pauses to study his face. It's covered in tiny scars, as are his arms.

"Coming?" Price asks from inside the car. His eyes are glinting, as if he's proud of her reaction to their entourage.

She clears her throat and follows him into the car. Zimmer and the large man follow, closing and locking the doors behind them. No music plays as Zimmer drives, and the car moves almost silently, so Lynell is left to stew in her thoughts.

She tries to ignore how Price's posture straightens and his hands regularly curl in and out of fists as they drive. She looks at the two men in the front, who both stare forward with unwavering attention, backs rigid. The large man's hands rest on his thighs, eerily close to his guns. Zimmer's hands gently curl around the steering wheel, and he drives with more caution than is necessary. They take a turn and Lynell sways, her heartbeat speeding up.

"Where are we going?" she whispers to Price.

"You'll see," he whispers back. He reaches up and rubs his neck. Lynell notices tiny beads of sweat covering the back of his hands. His nervous unease does nothing to calm Lynell and it feels as if all the veins in her body are on fire, vibrating with the need to get out of the car and run.

Lynell's not sure how long they've been on the road. There is a lot of traffic, but Zimmer never gets closer than ten feet to the cars in front of him.

It's as if they're carrying the president.

She turns back to Price. "Who are you?" she asks.

He laughs. "The question is, who are *you*?"

The car pulls to a stop. Price blows out a large breath, rubs his hands together and through his hair, and looks at Lynell. "Ready?"

"For what?" But he doesn't answer.

The house is so grand Lynell feels like a speck on its sparkly clean surface.

There are four large, cream-white pillars in the front, framing the porch where two more large and muscular men stand. Each man holds three guns, two in holsters and one grasped in hand. Price leads her out of the car and holds her sweaty hand with his own as they walk, and if she wasn't too preoccupied with what lies ahead, she'd find the mixture of sweat gross. Zimmer walks in front of them and the bodyguard behind.

The house is a blend of white, cream, and gold. The window rails and weatherstripping are gold, giving them an untouchable look. The corners of the house are round and there's a chimney on the far-left side.

Neither guard looks at them as they walk to the front door. Lynell attempts to ignore her surroundings, watching her feet as they climb the steps, to keep her anxiety at bay. The door is flung open before Zimmer even reaches it.

Lynell looks up and sees a man standing on the threshold, smiling. He's wearing a blue suit with golden vertical lines, a gold pocket square, and a dark yellow tie. His hair is dark brown with flecks of gray and slicked back. Lynell notices the lack of guns and the way his clothes seem to pull tight around his midsection, as if struggling to hold in a gut that wasn't always that round.

Lynell knows this man. She's seen him before. The eerie familiarity makes her body feel cold but she can't place him. It's as if his name is right in front of her eyes but blurred just enough so she can't read it.

"Zachary, my boy!" he says, holding his arms out. He sounds happy, despite the deep frown. "That took a while."

Price lets go of Lynell's hand and steps in front of the man. Price is probably four inches taller but still dips his head in a near bow. "I know, sir. I would say I was sorry, but it was quite an impossible job."

The man—*how* does she know him?—scowls before grabbing his belly and leaning forward with a deep laugh. "Trained for twenty-eight years and you find Registering and bringing Lynell home an impossible job? One you weren't even hired to do, mind you."

Lynell perks up at that bit of news. Price wasn't supposed to Register her.

Price shrugs. "You're the one who gave an incentive no one could ignore. Which, I might add, was more hindering than it was helpful."

"Was it?"

"Yes."

"Well," the man sighs loudly and claps his hands together. Lynell flinches. "I guess you better come in. You both look in need of a shower and a nice meal." For the first time, he turns his attention to Lynell. "Then, I suppose we should talk, darling."

Darling?

The only other person to ever call her darling was her mother.

"You must have many questions," the man says.

An understatement, Lynell thinks, but her throat is too dry to form words.

"Come in, come in." He turns to the side, extending an arm. Price walks over the threshold without grabbing her hand, which forces her to walk into the unfamiliar house alone.

The inside is just as grand. There's a large front entrance hall and a curved staircase on the left. What looks to be a dining room is located to the right, and the left opens into a sitting room with at least two couches and four armchairs.

"I hope my son has been pleasant company," the man says, looking back at Lynell.

She freezes.

Son?

She looks at Price. He stares at his feet, a blush tinting his cheeks.

"He can be quite the charmer when he wants to be," the man says, dropping his hand on Price's shoulder. Despite being taller and stronger and younger than the other man, Price still looks small standing next to his father.

His father.

Price doesn't just work for this man who wants her dead so badly. He's this man's *son.*

Lynell tries to swallow, but her mouth is so dry there's barely any saliva. Her chest is tight with fear and the need to know who this man is.

"Showers first, I think. Zachary will show you to your room, Lynell. You'll find a shower and a set of fresh clothes on the bed," Price's father says.

She wants to ask why they're getting showers and dinner. Why he cares about her cleanliness or comfort when they're just going to kill her. Lynell steals a glance at Price, whose jaw is set firmly.

"I would advise against trying to escape. My guards are armed and stationed strategically in anticipation of your arrival. Though they have been instructed not to kill you, I have given them the liberty to do what they need to keep you detained." He says it with a sick amount of joy in his voice, and Lynell fights the desire to run. "Up you go! Dinner is almost ready, and I don't want to eat it cold if it can be avoided."

Price waves her forward. They walk up the staircase in silence and Lynell looks around with wide eyes. Everything is a subtle cream color with gold and red accents. A large chandelier hangs from the ceiling and muted red rugs lead up the stairs and along the hallways. Whoever this guy is, he clearly can't help but show off.

Price turns left, and as soon as they are out of sight, Lynell lets out a heavy breath.

"So . . ." Lynell says, voice cracking. "I just met your *dad*."

Price grimaces. "Uh, yeah."

"Which means you grew up here." She almost groans at the juvenile statement when there is so much more to be asked.

Price grins. "Kind of. I stayed at the nanny's house most of the time. With a whole gaggle of personal guards. Dad spared no expense at keeping me safe, even if he didn't put in the effort himself." He shrugs and turns them into the third room on the right. "All comes with the territory, I guess."

Lynell wants to ask what territory that is but stops short at the room they entered. It's beautiful. The bed is huge with a blush-pink canopy. The vanity matches the color. A tall wardrobe made of dark wood sits in one corner. A pink dress, a pair of gold heels, and a gold hat are displayed on the bed. Recessed overhead lighting bathes the room in a bright light, but there are no windows.

There is nothing that's loose and could easily be picked up, like a lamp or potted plant.

"What . . ." she mutters.

"Yeah. Dad is serious about his standards. He may not expect you to be alive in a few more days, but until then, you'll be who he thinks you should be."

The words cut deep as she steps into the room and up to the bed. "And who does he think I should be?" she asks, curling her fingers around the dress. The silk is cool and fluid under her touch.

"You'll get your answers at dinner," Price says. He sounds tired, like walking into his childhood home sucked all of his energy. "Bathroom is through that door." He points to the only door in the room other than the one they just walked through. "I'm across the hall. Listen . . ." He steps closer. "You're going to learn a lot at dinner but promise me one thing—whatever you find out, remember that it doesn't change who you are. I thought I knew you but I . . . I didn't . . . know that you are—"

"What the hell does that mean?" Lynell asks, turning to face him. "Why can't you just tell me what's going on instead of playing some stupid game?"

Price gives a small smile and shrugs. "Stay in here after you're dressed, and I'll come get you."

Lynell frowns but nods. He turns and closes the door behind him. The air weighs down on Lynell and she leans her head against the bedpost. She closes her eyes and tries to summon tears. None come, though, so she takes a deep breath and heads to shower.

The first thing she notices in the bathroom is not the grandeur or large tub, it's the toilet.

There are no lids, neither on the tank nor the toilet itself.

When she notices that there's also no mirror, it dawns on her that anything that could be used as a weapon was removed from the room. She can't decide if she's annoyed that they stripped her of anything she could use to defend herself or pleased that they think she is capable of using a toilet lid to escape. She turns on the shower, not even processing the perfect water pressure. When she's finished, she wraps a towel around her and opens the door. Price is sitting on the bed, facing away.

"What the hell—" she gasps, gripping the towel tighter.

"Sorry," he says. He doesn't turn around, which she's grateful for. "I have to escort you downstairs and I'd rather wait in here so no one else comes in. I'll face this way while you dress."

"Price!"

"Lynell, we need to hurry. He won't be happy if we're late for dinner."

She grits her teeth but speeds up anyway. Carefully, she pulls the dress over her head and straightens it before sitting on the bed to put on the shoes.

"You can turn around," she mutters. Price does, and she can tell he approves of what he sees. He's wearing a suit the same blue color as his father's, but with no stripes, tie, or pocket square. "Do I have to wear this stupid hat?"

Price laughs. "Unless you want to put my dad in a temper."

Lynell grabs the hat and puts it on. It sits at an angle on her head, the stiff brim twice the size of a normal hat.

"Okay, let's go." He heads for the door and pulls it open, gesturing her through. "Remember what I said," he says before they descend the stairs. "Deep down you are who you are, no matter what you hear tonight."

Lynell nods. She can hear her heartbeat in her ears.

Price leads them into the dining room where his father is already sitting at the head of a very long table. There are three guards in the room, two covering the exits. Price's father stands up and gestures for them to approach the chairs on either side of him. Two men step forward and pull out the chairs before retreating.

Lynell gulps as Zach separates from her to approach his seat on the far side of the table next to his father.

"I'm so glad you two can finally join me," Price's dad says. Mr. Price, at least Lynell assumes that's his name, clasps his hands together and his face forms an odd grimace of a smile. "We have much to discuss. But first, I'm sure you're hungry."

Lynell keeps her eyes trained on Zach, who nods.

"Great! The chef has prepared salmon, so please sit and enjoy!"

Both men sit and Lynell follows their lead, pulling her chair closer to the table. She stares down at her plate, her mouth watering. There's a large piece of salmon on a bed of avocado. Asparagus and potatoes round out the offerings, and a glass of wine sits in front of her plate. She goes for that first, not even waiting to see what the men do before downing the entire glass.

Mr. Price laughs. "Nervous? Don't worry, darling. I suspect you'll finish the day safely in that beautiful bed upstairs."

Not much reassured, Lynell digs into the food, too hungry to even consider not eating out of protest.

They eat in silence and when the last plate—Zach's—is cleaned, a young woman enters the room and gathers their dishes before disappearing.

"All right, now that we're all full, let's talk."

Lynell leans forward, meeting the man's deep brown eyes. Her legs are numb with fear, but the promise of answers keeps her from shaking. Or puking.

"Lynell, I think first it's time you know my name." He sits up straighter. "I am Eric Elysian."

Realization slams into her like an ice waterfall.

That's why he seemed familiar. She sees him on a poster or on TV or on her phone every single day. How she didn't recognize him sooner, she'll never know.

Elysian. She's sitting at the dining room table of THE Eric Elysian. Eric Elysian knows who she is. Why on earth would Eric Elysian want to Register her, of all people?

She looks to Price as another realization dawns on her. If Eric Elysian is Price's father, then that means Price is not Price. Price is Elysian.

She gasps.

"My family has given so much to this country since the civil war," Price's father, Mr. Elysian she now knows, hums in satisfaction. "You'd be surprised how many people forgot how bad it was before the war ended, when the government controlled everything, and citizens had no power or control and murder and mayhem filled the streets with innocent blood."

He sits back and claps a hand on his son's shoulder. "The man you know as Zachary Price is my son, Zachary Elysian. Price is the name he uses in public. Even the system knows him as Zachary Price. Though, of course, Zachary Price can no more be Registered than Zachary Elysian can. It's to keep him safe, to guard his identity."

Lynell turns to Zach, searching for eye contact, but he's staring at the table.

The Elysians are practically royals, though technically businessmen. Their Regulators keep order during Registration season. They hold the power everyone craves while staying out of the government. They're the only people in the country who can't be Registered. And, of course, they're filthy rich.

"For almost seventy years, the Registration has been in place, working perfectly. Keeps our population in check and solves dozens of problems, like abortion. Half the country wanted it to be illegal. Imagine that! Forcing women to have a baby no matter the situation, no matter the danger to mom or baby. And the other half wanted it legal. Women free to end any pregnancy at any time, to kill as many unborn babies as they wanted, no repercussions."

Lynell stares at her plate, her hands gripped tightly together under the table as Elysian's words wash over her.

"They couldn't find a middle ground, and that's just one issue that drove this country to civil war. With the Registration, the issue is solved. End a pregnancy if you want, but after that, take measures to keep from getting pregnant again. All birth control is already free but did you also know that anyone using the Registration on a pregnancy must learn about all other options beforehand?"

She did know that. Schools teach that and give out birth control to anyone who wants it—no questions asked.

"Our desire is to give citizens the power to make choices without permitting chaos."

Elysian pushes his chest out and lifts his chin as he talks.

Lynell has heard all of this before: in school, on TV, in pamphlets, and in magazines. But something about hearing it straight from the lips of the man himself as he sits a foot away makes everything seem grander.

"Before our time, our country was practically drowning due to uncontrollable population growth. Not enough room for all the elders and terminally ill who needed full-time care. No homes for all the unwanted children. People had to rely on the justice system, which often failed them. Guilty people got off and no one could do anything about it. You had no right to claim your own justice from another. The death penalty issue split the country apart in every election cycle. Now, taking a life in the name of justice is in the hands of individual citizens. Use your Registration to end the life of a heinous criminal, someone who has done you wrong, and rid the world of one evil, or trust the system to keep them locked up. It's your choice."

Lynell looks up at Eric, who is smiling wide.

"Our country was deteriorating under the civil war and my family came up with the perfect solution: a self-regulatory system—the Registration."

He pauses, waiting for the effect of his words to sink in.

"Now, you're probably wondering where you come in."

Lynell fights the urge to nod vigorously.

"You, Lynell, are much more important than you'll ever know. And you have information that you may not even realize you have."

Lynell frowns.

"I wonder what you would say if I told you that I need a secret code, a very important cipher, to keep the Registration running smoothly and the country from falling back into lawless turmoil," Eric Elysian says, leaning across the table so he's much closer to her.

She thinks about what those men said. They wanted some sort of code from her.

Eric Elysian smiles. "I see the recognition in your eyes. You know about this code, don't you?"

Lynell sucks her cheeks into her teeth, biting down. She can't help but flick her eyes away from the man in front of her.

"You do!" he snaps loudly. "I need that code and you have it in your head."

Lynell looks back at him, suddenly finding her voice. "I have no idea what you're talking about. I don't have a code. I'd never even heard of it until one of your men attacked me." Her mind tumbles over itself, digging through his words and every corner of her memory in a desperate search for anything that could be considered a code. But she doesn't even know what it would be or how or why she would know it. She doesn't know why Eric Elysian thinks she has any information he doesn't. She has no idea why she would have anything to do with the operations of the Registration.

She turns to Price—*Zach*—looking for a clue as to what to say. All she sees in his eyes is sadness and resignation, as if this was the moment he's been dreading.

"Ah, but you do," Eric Elysian says. "When you were a child, barely four, I believe, your father was killed."

Lynell's attention snaps back to him. "How did you know that?"

Eric smirks. "I know a lot about you. I know, for example, that your father wrote you a letter before he died."

All the food she just ate is no longer settling easily in her stomach. How would Eric Elysian know her father? Much less know that he wrote a letter to her, a letter she read so often her mom suggested she memorize it. Her father was no one. Just a nameless, faceless man who, if her mother could be believed, loved her but never got to know her. "Why do you care?" she asks. "I didn't even know the man, so why would a letter he wrote to his bastard child matter to *you*, one of the most powerful men in the country?"

Mr. Elysian drags his finger along the top of his wine glass, his eyes firmly trained on her. "You may not have known him, but I did. I knew your father well."

"What?" Lynell gasps. She grips her dress under the table, body tensing with the shock of it.

He was a king, her mom used to say, but Lynell had long since decided that her mom had made that up to comfort a scared and abandoned child.

But if Eric Elysian, the closest thing to a king this country ever had, *knew* her father, then maybe her mom was not so wrong after all.

Eric nods. "Yes, your dad and I were quite close once. And I would bet anything he secretly hid the code inside the contents of the letter he wrote you all those years ago."

"What, no, he—" Lynell begins.

Eric leans back in his chair, holding up his hand. "I know without a shadow of a doubt that your father had this key. He was the only person who did, and not only that, he also knew he was going to die soon. He would never let such important information die with him. And the only person he would entrust it to is you."

Lynell is already shaking her head. "I was a child. And he didn't know me. Why would he trust me with anything?"

"Because you are his child. It is tradition to pass it down through the family. Your father got the code from his father." Eric taps the table in a rhythmic pattern, starting with his pointer finger and ending with his pinky. The sound grates on Lynell's nerves.

The palms of her hands are clammy, so she rubs them against the dress, trying to dry off any sweat. "You're telling me that this man had information so important that you, of all people, want it and he—what? He wrote a letter to a child he didn't know so he could hide some code, hoping I would one day decipher it and know what to do with it?" Something about the preposterous idea fills her with some much-needed confidence. She sits up taller and meets Eric's stare.

"I'm aware it sounds unbelievable—"

"Try batshit insane," Lynell interrupts. Zach chokes and she looks over to see him scratching his head. His silence is just as loud as Eric's voice. He knew about all of this. This is why he Registered her. Why he kidnapped her and threatened Daniel.

Because of some idiotic claim his father made that can't possibly be true.

"Can we just agree that while it sounds far-fetched, I knew your father better than you?" Eric asks.

A long moment stretches between them. Lynell wants to yell, "No," and run out of the house. But she's surrounded by big men with muscles and weapons and she knows she would never reach the door.

"He was a strong and mighty king with a million lives in his hand," her mom had said.

Could it be true that this mighty king knew Eric Elysian? Why would a man so close to such power leave the woman he loved and his daughter in squalor? If her father knew Eric Elysian, why did she have to grow up with Alan?

"So, if your father did leave the code, and I'm certain he did, I could decipher it if I had the letter. But, unfortunately . . ."

"I burned it . . ." Lynell mutters.

Eric spreads his hands wide. "And herein lies our issue. I need you to recreate the letter for me."

"I haven't read it in years," she says but even as she does, she starts reciting the words in her mind: *Little Lynell, I am sorry I will not see you grow.* She imagines her father writing each word, knowing his days are numbered. *That is my greatest regret in life. I will not get to see you fall in love, create your own words, or discover the world. I will not know your heart or the way your face ages.* Did he hide something else, something bigger in that letter? Did he want to leave her with something that could possibly change her life? *Please don't be angry with me for leaving. I promise I mean only to protect you.*

Because it probably would change her life. Whatever the code is and whatever it does, it has to be something huge if Eric Elysian is going through so much trouble to just have a *chance* of deciphering it. *Perhaps one day you'll realize why.*

She shakes her head. No, it can't be true. If it is true, then not only did her father fail her but she is going to fail him because she knows nothing about any code. Whatever he thought she could do when he left her that code, she can't do it.

"You were a young girl suffering from an unkind stepfather and little joy. I bet you dreamt of your father. I bet you created an idealized version and all you had to connect with him was that letter. I bet you read it all the time. A daughter longing for a father will do anything to feel close to him."

Lynell blinks and her throat starts tightening around a knot. "I . . ."

Eric smiles. "I see the truth in your eyes. He was the one source of light in your dingy, horrible life. You probably even memorized the words."

She can't stop herself from looking away or keep her mouth from opening slightly in surprise.

This man seems to see right through her.

Eric gives a little holler, as if he's just won a game of cards. "I knew you wouldn't disappoint me, Lynell." He leans forward again, his voice falling so the next words are almost a whisper. "Now, I need the contents of that letter. And you will give me what I need."

Eric Elysian, a stranger, seems to know her better than anyone. Growing up scared even in her own home, that letter was the only proof that Lynell had a father who loved her once, even if he was gone and dead now. Reading the letter kept her going. The dream that she would one day find the hope and love and life her father wanted for her got her out of bed in the morning.

And now a stranger wants her to hand it over? She doesn't care who he is or that he could have her killed without even lifting a hand. She doesn't care if he knew her father or if what he claims is true. Lynell will not hand over the very thing that was her lifeline for years without a damn good reason.

"What makes you so sure?" she sneers at the owner of the Registration. "You had me Registered by multiple people. You dragged me from my life. Why would I give you anything?" She practically spits the last words.

Her change in demeanor doesn't faze Eric at all. His smile stays in place. "Because you have no other choice. Just like your dad didn't when I stood by him, holding a gun to his temple."

And with that one comment, her newfound bravery melts away.

He didn't just know her father.

He *killed* her father. The rebels have always said that the Elysians are the reason so many people have lost their loved ones. They villainize Eric

Elysian, saying that he's behind so many unnecessary deaths. And he freely admits that what they say is true. Eric Elysian, the leader of the Registration, the man everyone knows and some adore and others hate, murdered her father.

"I didn't know Eli had a daughter." Eric Elysian picks up his wine and takes a sip, continuing as if he didn't just casually confess to killing her father. "Your father was a rebellious son."

Eli. Her dad's name was Eli. She never knew.

"And his rebellion landed him a child." He tilts the cup in Lynell's direction. "You. But I didn't know before I pulled that trigger. Didn't know he wrote a letter to a child he'd never know. Had I known you existed, I would not have killed him. I swear . . ." He trails off, casting his eyes downward.

She wants to throw the wine in his face. He won't convince her that he cares about her. That he wouldn't have taken her parent from her if he'd known. Maybe the rebels are right. Maybe Eric Elysian is a monster.

Eric Elysian's face falls and his eyes start to water. His voice breaks as he speaks. "I loved my brother, but I had to stop him from ruining everything our father created. Please believe me when I say I didn't know about you. I never want to hurt my own family. He should have told me," he nearly begs. "You and your mother could have come to live with us. With Eli. You all could have been a family. Happy and safe and healthy. With me and my son. We would have found a way."

Family. Eric Elysian killed his own brother. His brother was Eli. Eli was her father. This would have been her family, if Eli hadn't left her mother. If Eric hadn't killed him. If everything had been different.

Lynell was lying on her stomach on her childhood bed, an old, crinkled paper held tightly between her small fists. Alan had been gone all day. Lynell didn't miss him when he was gone. Not anymore. Not since he'd become so unpredictable.

"You're reading that old letter again?" Elizabeth asked, standing in the doorway. Lynell jumped, stuffed the page under her pillow, and sat up. Her mom chuckled, stepped in and closed the door behind her. "You should memorize it."

Her mom sat next to her and pulled the letter out from under her pillow. She held it in trembling hands as her eyes scanned it. Lynell watched, biting her lip, trying to fight the urge to take it back.

"'Know that your father will always love you,'" Elizabeth read. "He did, honey." She sighed and set the page down, leaning over to kiss the top of Lynell's head. "I can't believe he's been gone for almost five years." She squeezed Lynell's shoulders and said, "Or that you're going to be nine tomorrow."

Lynell grinned and her mom pulled away, touching the corner of the paper. "Have I ever told you about how I met your father?"

Lynell shook her head. Elizabeth frowned and leaned back on Lynell's bed. She patted the blanket next to her and Lynell crawled to join her.

"You know he was a king."

Lynell nodded. That, she'd heard before. The older she got the less she believed that her father had a royal bloodline.

Elizabeth continued, stretching her arm out in front to mime her story. "He was a strong and mighty king with a million lives in his hand. But how did I meet him, such a powerful man?" Elizabeth looked down at Lynell and tapped her nose. "Scrabble."

Lynell frowned, her nose crinkling. "The game?"

Elizabeth nodded. "I was at this little coffee shop playing Scrabble with a friend, but she had to leave. So, your father, the king, came over and said, 'Mind if I have this game?'" She smiled in reminiscence. "I said yes. We played five games. I kept winning and he refused to stop playing until he'd win a game. Hours later, he still hadn't won, and he insisted we meet again. I think at that point it was less about the game and more about just being together. We met again the very next day. Thus, began our romance."

Elizabeth reached down and grabbed the letter, holding it up.

"His dad taught him how to play Scrabble. Taught him so well that he had never lost a game. Until he met me." Elizabeth winked at Lynell and handed her the letter. She stood up and sighed. "We'll go for ice cream tomorrow. Just the two of us, for your birthday. And after that, I'll teach you how to play Scrabble. Who knows? One day you may meet your own king for a game."

DΛY 5—————————————————

"You knew the whole time?" Lynell asks, throwing a pillow at Zach. He dodges it, closing the door behind him. She'd barely slept the night before, despite the fluffy pillows and a comforter enveloping her and trying to lull her to sleep. But she'd fought them, giving precedence to her reeling mind.

The news she'd heard at dinner, the revelation of Zach's true identity, her father's true identity, her true identity, kept her awake and staring at the canopy with red eyes.

Elysians. Close to royalty. Creators of the Registration.

She'd tossed and turned in bed until Zach quietly opened the door and she sat up, meeting his eyes. It was only 6 a.m., but she could tell he hadn't slept either.

Lynell throws another pillow. He catches it and gently sets it on the ground.

"You knew, and you didn't tell me!"

"Lynell, please." He holds his hands up as if trying to calm a wild animal. "The guards . . ."

"Will what? Knock me out? So, what!" Her voice rises and she leans forward, moving closer to Zach, her posture that of an animal ready to pounce. "They can't kill me, can they? Or you, dear *cousin.*" The word instantly drains all energy from her, and she sinks back, face in her hands.

"I'm sorry . . ."

"You knew we're family." She spits the words at him. "You knew who I was. And you didn't think to tell me? You were totally fine to Register me? Your—" She shakes her head, unable to finish.

He reaches out and places his hands on her knees. "I didn't know. I mean, shit, I did, but... I didn't know *you*." He's looking at her with so much regret that she fights the urge to push him away. "I didn't know how kind you'd be. How strong and—"

"Why does that matter? I could have been a weak bitch and I'd still be your cousin. I'd still be human."

Zach stands, shaking his head. "You don't understand. You didn't grow up here."

"No, I didn't," she says, climbing off the bed. "I grew up under one roof with an abusive alcoholic and a last name that was forced on me. I grew up with a mom who tried to hide her pain with drugs and couldn't even Register the man that hit us because she was never blessed with a Registration. I grew up thinking my father walked out on us, but now I hear he was killed by his own brother. Killed, not Registered. Because if he was an Elysian, he couldn't be Registered, right? Which means it was cold-blooded murder. By the same man who had his own son, my cousin, Register me, kidnap me, drag me across the country, make me believe he cared about me, just to get the information he needed out of me before he had me killed!" As she speaks, Lynell steps toward Zach until he's standing with his back against the wall. When he has nowhere left to retreat, she hits his chest. She takes a deep breath, closing her eyes momentarily before meeting his again. "That's what *I* understand, *Price*. Do you?"

There's clear pain and regret in his face but she's too heated to care. She wants to give him his own black eye.

"I don't," he says. He steps off the wall, shaking his head. "I don't understand what you've been through. But you're not the only one who got screwed by heritage. My father never hit me, but as soon as I could walk, he dumped me with nannies. Shipped me off to month-long training camps where they taught me how to turn off emotions and gain power, how to..."

He takes a deep breath before continuing. "He used me. I am nothing but a tool to him. I may never understand what you have gone through, Lynell. But you'll never understand what I've gone through either."

"Poor little rich boy! You're nothing but a cliché!" Lynell grinds her teeth and curls her hands into fists. "I don't give a flying fuck, Zach. You knew I existed, didn't you?"

"Not always—"

"Did you know I existed?" she interrupts.

He sighs. "Yes. I knew someplace, somewhere, Eli Elysian had a daughter."

"And when your father gave you this . . ." she throws her hands out, "job, you knew who I was, didn't you?"

"He didn't give me this job," Zach says, plainly.

Lynell's jaw aches with tension. "Explain."

He sighs and lowers his head. "He was offering a reward to his men to bring you to him. Alive, but not unharmed. They had freedom to do whatever it took to get you here, no questions asked. These men are brutes. I had to find you myself to protect you."

"By Registering me?"

He bites his lip and offers a reluctant nod. "You were going to get to this house one way or another and I was your safest option."

"Why?" Lynell asks.

He blinks. "Why what?"

"Why do I need to be here? What was in that damn letter?"

"*My* father thinks that's where *your* father has hidden the code. Dad has access to the software of the Registration, but unfortunately, it's . . . in a different programming language. And this code, for lack of a better word, will translate the entire thing."

"That doesn't make any sense," Lynell says.

"This code would give him access to the Registration." Zach gestures while he talks, only occasionally flicking his eyes in Lynell's direction.

"He's Eric Elysian," Lynell says in a matter-of-fact tone. "He owns the Registration. He has access to everything."

Zach is already shaking his head. "No, he doesn't. There are aspects that only someone with this code can access and manipulate."

"Why didn't he have it in the first place? Why did Eli have it but not his brother?" Lynell asks, crossing her arms.

Zach sighs and sinks onto the edge of the bed. "My dad looked for it for years after he killed Eli, your dad. Then, one day he found out about your mom. At first, he thought she was just one of Eli's flings. But then he found a letter Eli wrote to your mom." Zach must see the shock on Lynell's face, and he sighs. "Yes, he wrote to both of you. From what I gather, he told your mom he was going to be a servant rather than a king. He mentioned that the secret was in the letter he wrote to their daughter. To you."

"So my mom knew about the code?"

Zach shrugs. "Most likely. It would have ensured that the code didn't get overlooked. That someone knew there was an important message in that letter. I'm sure he also warned her to never speak his name again. For her safety. And yours."

"Our safety?"

"Being an Elysian isn't safe. Why do you think we have so many guards? We can't be Registered, but we can be killed. The rebels already tried to do that in their little uprising a few years ago."

The uprising Daniel was a part of, Lynell thinks. Daniel joined a group fighting against a man who is now his friend.

"By leaving you and practically erasing himself from your life, Eli was trying to keep you safe. I guess he took the whole 'if you love someone, let them go' to a whole new extreme." He grins, trying to infuse some levity into the conversation.

Lynell doesn't return the smile. "It didn't work."

"I guess not."

Family has never kept her safe. Family has only ever caused her pain. And now family was going to kill her. She plops down on the bed, dropping her face into her hands. She wants to cry. Her throat is tight and her head is hot with the need to shed tears.

But none fall.

Zach scoots closer to her on the bed and wraps his arm around her shoulders. She leans into him, allowing him to rub her back. Her heart seems to instantly recognize him as family and craves his comfort and touch. But her body still hates him and recoils in fear.

"What happens if I tell your dad what the letter said?" she asks.

He shrugs. "He figures out the code."

"What does the code do?"

"I don't know if . . ." Zach says, looking away from her.

"You don't know shit, but you're going to tell me anyway. It's the least you can do," Lynell says, leaving their embrace and moving away from Zach.

Zach sighs and stares at the ground as he talks. "The code does two things. First, it proves your legitimacy."

"How does it do that?"

"Well, I mean, not technically," Zach says, scoffing. "The rule was to only give the code to legitimate Elysian children, so no one else except a few trusted employees would know the code. Gideon Elysian, Eli and Eric's father, was a selfish man and a bit of an elitist."

Gideon, the original creator of the Registration. Something connects in Lynell's brain and she gasps. "Wait. Their father, so . . ."

Zach nods. "Our grandfather, which, incidentally, is what I used to call him. 'Grandfather Elysian.' Cozy, right?" He laughs again and stands, walking around the room as he speaks.

"Good old grandpa preached that the Registration is good and just but made sure no one in his family could ever be Registered. I mean, in a screwed up way, he *really* valued family. Thought himself royalty and, therefore, only his legitimate heirs should be able to inherit the dynasty. Here's the catch. His two sons, our fathers, had different moms. Your dad's mom was Gideon's wife. My dad's mom was a mistress." Zach finally meets Lynell's eyes.

"So that means I'm . . ."

"The legitimate heir, yes. But my father didn't know that. Eli was a bit of a playboy and no one knew he was married. So at first you were considered illegitimate. Nothing to worry about. Just a bastard."

Lynell frowns and crosses her legs, watching Zach talk with a tilted head. He occasionally looks around, as if to make sure they are not being overheard. "But I'm not?"

Zach nods. "My father found a marriage license dated a month before your assumed conception. It shouldn't have mattered, but a few of the rebels were starting to spread rumors that my father was a bastard and hence not the heir to the Registration. There wasn't much traction to it, but Dad freaks out any time there's a threat to his control. So, when he found out about you, he panicked. If anyone figured out who you are, then maybe you'd one day take control of the Registration. You're legitimate. He's not."

"But if I could possibly . . . 'take his throne,'" she says, making air quotes, "why not just have me killed?" Lynell asks, leaning forward so her chin is resting in her hand.

"He *needs* the code."

"And after he gets it . . ."

"You'll have to go."

Lynell flinches at the words. "What's the second thing the code does?" Zach is quiet for a moment and Lynell glowers. "Price."

He grimaces. "You know the Registration is well protected."

Lynell shrugs.

"There is one database where every Registration is filed," Zach explains. "Only those Registrations in that database are legit. There are multiple digital barriers and only a handful of people can access it. That's because in the beginning, people would hack it to add a name to the list or take their own name off. Some would hack it and sell parts of the list, or fake lists, to the public. So, Grandfather hired a whole team of people to make the Registration impenetrable." Lynell watches Zach get up and pace as he explains.

"The Registration laws prescribe that the system and all its defenses are updated annually, which also effectively changes the 'language,'" he makes air quotes, "it's written in. Which is why the Registration works so well and has never been hacked. It's perhaps the most complex software system there is. But Grandfather, always thinking ahead, built in an exit strategy. To be sure he would always have sole control over the Registration, he created a code."

Zach sits facing Lynell and sets a pillow in his lap.

"Think of the Registration database as a large house. Every room is locked, and to get to the center of the house, where the lists are, whether to add a name illegally or take one off or release all the stored information to the public, you must unlock every door in the building. But each door has its own key which is held by only one person. Most of those people are either dead, don't know what key they hold, or have lost the key. It's pretty much impossible to get to that center room. Unless . . ." He pauses and raises an eyebrow, as if expecting Lynell to finish his sentence. She doesn't.

"Unless you have the master key," Price finishes.

Lynell frowns and stands, stretching her legs and pacing the room. "And that's what your father wants?" she says, pulling at an earlobe in thought, a habit she picked up from her mom. "Gain access to and release all stored information?"

Zach sighs. "No. Because this would cause utter chaos. It works so well right now because it's controlled. You get one Registration. Once you use it, that's it. Two weeks and then no other chance. It's safe and anonymous. No one knows they've been Registered unless . . . well, they're standing right there." He gives her a sheepish look and she rolls her eyes.

"Right, anyway," he clears his throat. "Registrations can't be seen or changed. All the restrictions are in place so no one can use the Registration to their advantage. But if those restrictions were gone, if it was no longer anonymous and anyone could access the database then . . ."

"There wouldn't be any controlling it," Lynell says.

Zach nods. "Exactly. Everyone would have access. People would give themselves more Registrations. People would erase Registrations. It would be the end of the Registration. And chaos would reign."

"If using the code destroys everything, why does Eric want it so badly?"

"He's a businessman. He wants to grow his business."

"I don't follow."

"He's been slowly raising the price of the Registration. But he wants more. Sell more than one Registration to people who can afford it. Take it away from those he wants to pressure. This power would grant him control over the oligarchs so he can force any law he wants into effect. Bottom line, he wants more money and more power, and he thinks the code is the only, or the easiest, way to get it."

"And the only place the code exists is my letter?"

Zach nods and throws the pillow back on the bed. "Pretty much. Your father obeyed Grandfather in one thing—only let the code be known by the true heir. I was just a kid when Uncle Eli died, but I remember him. He started sympathizing with the rebels. He was questioning the Registration, and I think Dad was worried Eli would use the code to destroy the Registration."

A dim numbing fills Lynell's feet and climbs up her legs at Zach's words.

She'd always thought her father supported the Registration. Her mom had said as much. And his letter had told her to use it wisely.

"My father thought getting rid of his brother would eliminate the only real threat to the Registration. Now that he knows about you and that your father passed the code on to you, he will pressure you for the code and then get rid of you," Zach says, keeping his eyes locked on Lynell's.

She swallows and forces herself to ask, "And who'll do it?"

"Do what?"

"Get rid of me?" The words come out strong, despite the helplessness Lynell feels at the prospect of her impending death. Less than ten days from now.

Zach runs his hand through his hair, quickly averting his gaze. "He picked me. Wants me to prove my loyalty or some shit. Loyalty to him or the family or the company. Sometimes I don't know the difference."

"What if there isn't a difference? What if being an Elysian means un-wavering loyalty to the Registration? No matter what?"

Zach stares at her.

"What if I prove to your father that I'm loyal to him and the Registration? That I'm not a threat? Would he let me live?" Lynell asks.

Zach shrugs. "Maybe. But I doubt it."

Lynell nods. "Well, in that case, if someone has to do it, I'd rather it be you." She forces a smile. Then, with an idea forming, she perks up. "If I'm Eli's daughter, then I'm an Elysian. I can't be Registered."

"I wish that were the case," Zach says with a sigh. "But you weren't, uh, claimed by him at birth. You're in the system as Elizabeth's daughter. Our grandfather kept himself, his wife, Eli, and Eric off the Registration when he created it. Then Dad did the same when I was born. But the real protection is our status. Regulators and government officers know us and protect us. Nobody will touch us."

A sour taste fills Lynell's mouth at the unjust privilege, but also at the sick desire to have it. The protection of status, wealth, power, and a name.

"Okay," she says, clearing her throat. "I don't think I can give him the code."

"Ah, but you will."

Lynell and Zach both jump at the words and turn to face Eric Elysian. Eric stands in the doorway with two guards behind him. He looks between his son and his niece. His clothes are much calmer than yesterday. A light black suit with no tie. His hair is undone, showing off loose curls.

"Lynell, I'm not evil," Eric says, walking into the room, his hands behind his back. "You're an Elysian. You're my niece and I care about you."

Lynell scoffs.

"Be a part of this family. Share in its privilege. Its wealth. You can. All you need to do is share the letter with me, and together we will make this world a better place." He's smiling, and for a moment, Lynell thinks he's being sincere. "Or deny us. Deny your blood right and your name. Become my problem and live in fear. It's up to you, Lynell. Just know that I am very good at solving problems."

Lynell feels Zach step closer to her, between her and his father.

Some tension slips from her muscles.

Eric places his hand on Zach's shoulder, yet his eyes remain trained on Lynell. "I'm not threatening you, Lynell. I'm offering you a choice." He turns and heads to the door, pulling Zach with him. "I suggest you make the right one."

⌐┬─┬─┬┐

The door to her room is unlocked, but there are two guards stationed outside and Lynell stays in the bedroom, pacing.

Little Lynell,

I am sorry I will not see you grow. That is my greatest regret in life. I will not get to see you fall in love, create your own words, or discover the world. I will not know your heart or the way your face ages.

Please don't be angry with me for leaving. I promise I mean only to protect you. Perhaps one day you'll realize why. Your mother— your dear mother—opened my eyes to a world I never thought was possible. And until my dying breath, I will do everything in my power to make that world reality. If I am killed in the attempt, do not be angry. Know that I left with hope for the future. A future that is not defined by the past.

You, too, are not defined by your past, Little Lynell. You are not defined by the choices of your absent father or unknown grandfather. Someday it may seem like that. I hope not. It is my dream for you that you are not defined by things outside your control, but by your own heart. Your own choices.

It is okay to resent me, but please also hear me. Learn from me. Do not take for granted what you have. Never forget that you are loved. Use your Registration wisely. Cherish life and the privilege of choice.

If I fail to create the future your mother helped me see, perhaps you will succeed. Don't settle for what has always been. Demand better. Be better.

Know the worth of love, Lynell. Of joy. Of forgiveness. Know the worth and double it. Live it. Hope for more. Do not transpose your values. Know that your father will always love you. Know that I would change anything to get to see you once more. I love you so much. You are strong, kind, joyful, wise, and so full of patience. Never lose that.

Love,

Dad

She recites the letter in her head, trying to decipher where a code could be hidden in the words her father wrote two decades ago.

Love

Joy.

Forgiveness.

Live.

Hope.

Value.

Strong, kind, wise, and patient.

She says these words over and over like a mantra. She rearranges letters in her mind's eye trying to form a new word, but nothing she comes up with makes sense. She tries to imagine her father writing the words. How long did he spend writing the letter, hiding the code in the words? Did he know his brother was plotting his murder?

Lynell tugs at her hair in frustration and lies down on the bed, squeezing her eyes shut as she thinks. She could give the letter to Eric with the stipulation that she be involved in deciding what to do with it. If Zach was right, then using the code was a bad idea. It could ruin their country. But Daniel would want them to, she thinks. He would probably support ending the Registration no matter the consequences.

If she doesn't survive, what kind of world does she want to leave behind? She wishes her parents were alive so she could ask them. What would her mom say? And her father? As an Elysian, her father should, in theory, want to protect the Registration at all costs. But if Zach was right and he was questioning that, then maybe she should too? The possibility that things could be worse, that thousands could die, is too big a risk. If nothing changes, then nothing can get worse. If Eric tries to change things, even if he thinks he can do so without threatening the Registration and his power, then things could get far worse. His thirst for power may blind him to the dangers. Maybe she should give him a fake letter. Change some words. But maybe he knows how to figure out the code and he just needs the right words. Maybe he would know the letter is wrong. The door opens and Lynell flinches, turning to face it. Two guards are standing there, Zach between them. He looks at her quickly before looking away.

"Let's go," he says.

"Where are we going?"

"Downstairs. Lunch." Zach's words are brisk.

"What's going on?"

"Dad likes to have the family together for lunch. Says it keeps you focused on what really matters." He turns and walks out the door. The glares from the guards propel Lynell forward to follow him.

He leads them to the dining room, and she sits in the same chair as the night before and looks around.

"He'll be here," Zach says, probably noticing her search for Eric. "Work keeps him late sometimes."

Lynell meets Zach's eyes. "You really eat with him often?"

Zach shrugs. "He's my dad. He's not all bad."

Lynell narrows her eyes. "I'm assuming that if I don't give him the letter, it won't look pretty for me."

At that, the doors open and Eric walks in, smiling and holding two plates. He sets one in front of Lynell and the other in front of his chair. She watches Eric, noticing how he seems to occupy all the space around him. Behind him comes a young lady with Zach's plates and the drinks. Lynell looks down at her plate, filled with a toasted sandwich and salad.

"Sorry to keep you waiting," he says. "Meeting ran long. How was your morning? Were you able to explore?" he asks Lynell.

"I didn't know I was allowed."

Eric leans forward and gives her an exasperated look. "Of course, you're allowed. This could be your house as much as Zach's."

"But I'm a prisoner." She crosses her arms and leans back in her chair.

"More like a guest I'm not sure I can trust. Please try to understand where I'm coming from," Eric says. He reaches out and grabs the salad dressing from the middle of the table. He pours a generous amount over his salad as he talks. "Even though I'd like you to be a member of this family, unfortunately, I don't know you. You could betray me at any moment. You are not loyal to the Elysian name like Zach here."

Zach avoids his father's eyes and picks up his sandwich.

"And you have important information," Eric continues. "All I'm asking is that you share it."

Lynell frowns, grabbing her fork. "I don't know you either. All I know is you had me Registered and kidnapped because I'm your brother's daughter."

"Don't you want to know your real family?"

"You don't want me in your family. You want me dead."

He shakes his head. "That's not true."

Lynell glances at Zach, who's slowly chewing and staring at the table. "Why should I give you the letter?"

Eric shoves some lettuce in his mouth, studying Lynell while he chews. He swallows and grabs his water. "Because I'm the owner of the Registration and your uncle. Your last surviving relative, along with my son." He claps Zach's shoulder, who straightens and nods.

"I don't know if I can trust you with the code." She looks over to see Zach widen his eyes and give a small shake of his head. "I don't even know what it does," she adds, which makes Zach relax.

"Would it help if I told you?" Zach looks incredulously at his father.

"Yes," Lynell says.

Eric nods.

"I'll give you today and tomorrow. Show me I can trust you. See the family you could have. The family you've always wanted." He pauses as if he could see the shock of yearning flash through Lynell's body. "You really can choose us, Lynell. You don't have to die this week."

"But I have to give you the letter and denounce my claim," she says.

Eric smiles and nods. "Give me the letter and denounce your claim."

Lynell's mother wasn't around much in those last few years of her life. When she was, she was usually drunk or sleeping. But sometimes, she'd sit with Lynell in her locked bedroom in the hopes that Alan would leave them alone.

"Why are you married to him?" Lynell asked one night. She was fourteen and her mom had been married to Alan for almost nine years.

Elizabeth picked up a Scrabble piece and slid it across the board, finishing the word "GOAT" she'd created out of the "A" in "MAGIC." "Uhm," she said, leaning back on her ankles. They were sitting on the floor of Lynell's room, the Scrabble board set up in front of them. Elizabeth rubbed her nose and pushed her lips to the side, sniffing.

"Mom . . ." Lynell said. "Why are we staying with him?"

"Honey, he wasn't always bad. When we first met ten years ago, he—"

"It doesn't matter, Mom," Lynell interrupted. "He's bad now. And you're not . . . you're not the same with him."

Elizabeth looked down at the board. "It's your turn."

"Mom."

"There's a perfect 'E' here." Elizabeth pointed to the bottom of the board but Lynell grabbed her hand, causing her mom to meet her gaze.

"Mom. Please."

Elizabeth sighed, folding her other hand over Lynell's. She let go and reached down, touching the top of the first word played, "LOVE."

"The beautiful thing about Scrabble is it connects," she said. "Connects words and people. Connected your father and me. That's how we fell in love, you know. He said I was the only person to ever defeat him in Scrabble since his father."

"I know, Mom," Lynell said, frustrated at hearing the same sentimental story over and over again.

"Let me finish." Elizabeth reached out and tucked a piece of Lynell's deep brown hair behind her ear. "You got this hair from him, your father. Mine was always bright blonde. Your father, though . . . they all had dark hair. Him, his dad. You. Fit for a king, for a queen," she said, holding the back of Lynell's head and smiling down at her. "I loved him so much. Every day I'm thankful for this beautiful game that brought us together, because together we made you." Elizabeth grabbed the "L" tile from the word "LOVE" and placed it in the center of Lynell's hand. "Scrabble is a game of connections. Connected me with your dad and him with his father. Connects letters to numbers. Take the word 'love' for instance." She tapped the "L" in Lynell's hand and smiled. Lynell watched with a deep frown but curled her fingers around the tile as her mom talked. "Alone, it is just a word. With Scrabble, you add the numbers together and get seven. If you're lucky, maybe more."

The softness of her mom's smile made Lynell's frustration melt away.

"We let words define us every day, Lynell. 'Mother,' 'daughter,' 'pretty,' 'angry.' They create us. With this game, we create the words. We hold the key to everything. The code to unlocking whole worlds."

DAY 6 ———————————————————————o

"**D**ad says a good start to proving your loyalty would be showing up to family meals."

Lynell groans and opens one eye. Zach is standing at the end of her bed, holding two plates in front of him. He looks fresher today, though there are small bags under his eyes.

He's wearing a button-up and jeans, hair brushed to one side with a slight gleam to it, like Daniel's used to get when he soaked it with styling gel. He offers a hesitant smile.

"Forgive me, but I wasn't hungry at dinner. Lunch was just too rich."

"You hardly touched your sandwich."

Lynell rolls her eyes. "It was a metaphor. And besides, I needed to think." She covers her face with the duvet, trying to shut out the day. She feels Zach sit on the edge of the bed and tug the blanket away.

"You told the guard who woke you for breakfast to, and I quote, 'get the hell out of my room if you value your left testicle.'" Zach chuckles and Lynell can't help but smile.

"I'm not allowed to sleep in? Who eats breakfast at six-thirty?"

"Working men."

"Is this you working?" Lynell asks, raising an eyebrow.

"What can I say? There are benefits to working with your family." He holds one plate close enough for Lynell to glimpse the corner of crisp bacon and a biscuit.

She sits up, accepts the plate and goes straight for the biscuit. She eats half of it in one bite and scowls at Zach when he laughs.

Sitting at the end of the bed against the post, Zach dips his bacon in ketchup before popping it in his mouth.

When half her eggs are gone, Lynell lowers the plate to her lap and picks dead skin off her lip. "Should I do it? Give it to him?"

"I don't know," Zach whispers.

She pauses, considering how much she trusts Zach. "What if I gave him a fake letter?" she asks, picking up her last piece of bacon.

"He'd know."

"How?"

Zach shrugs. "Or he'd find out and you'd regret it." They sit in silence, each slowly eating through their eggs.

"Will he let me live?"

"I hope so."

"Do you think so?"

Lynell studies him. She sees his father in the shape of his face, nose, and thick eyebrows. But his eyes are starkly different. Dark green like a solid emerald gemstone. They must be from his mom. A spark of jealousy ignites when she thinks of her own eyes, which Elizabeth always said look exactly like her father's. That just means they look like Eric's, too.

Lynell sets her plate down, appetite gone.

"He may. Let you live," Zach says.

Lynell shakes her head. "But can I take the chance? Is the slim possibility of living worth giving him the chance of gaining even more power?"

"Please, Lynell?"

She sets her jaw, glaring at Zach. She understands why he wants her to do it. Why he wants her to give Eric the letter in the hopes of living, actually being a part of their family.

Family.

Her heart burns with the desire for a family. And when she looks up at Zach, she thinks this might be a decent one.

But then she thinks of Eric. How his solution to getting her and the letter is Registration by multiple men. He would have her killed for the chance of even more power and money.

"I can't," she says. "I'm sorry, Zach. I can't."

It looks like he wants to convince her but then he just nods, averting his gaze as he speaks. "I always knew you were good." His lips form a small, sad smile when he looks back to her. "You're good."

He grabs their plates, gets off the bed, and quietly leaves the room.

<hr />

Lynell takes a shower, pulls on a flower dress from the closet and opens the door to leave her bedroom. Two guards look at her. One is dark and all hard lines. The other is short with hair pulled into a bun and a patchy beard that covers his chin and neck. A long scar seems to cut his chin in half, extending from his cheek down his jaw.

"Good morning," she tells them. They respond with silent stares. "Am I allowed to leave my room?"

The taller, darker man nods. "Of course," he says, unimpressed.

"Feel free to join me," she says, pulling the door shut behind her. Neither man says anything, but both follow closely as she heads down the hallway. She glances back every couple of seconds, their silent yet intrusive presence unnerving.

Half the doors on the floor are locked. The others lead to bathrooms, empty bedrooms, and one closet filled with winter coats. She considers grabbing a hanger as a makeshift weapon, but they're plastic, and the guards are watching her every move.

Next, she goes downstairs and checks out the dining room, the empty kitchen that still smells like bacon, and the TV room with a flat-screen on the far wall. She walks faster, wanting to leave the guards behind. But they keep up effortlessly. Gritting her teeth, Lynell throws open a pair of double doors to find a large parlor that faces the front lawn of the house. She walks past two couches and three chairs to stand in front of a fireplace currently void of a crackling fire. One wall is covered in bookshelves and the other is mostly windows, blinds open, filling the room with promising natural light.

Lynell picks a book off the shelf and sits in the chair closest to the fireplace.

"Do you like it here?" She's not sure who she's asking. The guards? The fire? Herself?

A guard answers. "Yes, ma'am."

Lynell turns to them. It seems the shorter one answered, and she narrows her eyes. "Are you lying to me?"

He doesn't answer immediately. But when the other man glances at him, the shorter one clears his throat. "No, ma'am. Of course not."

Lynell hums in thought and turns back to the fireplace. "I've wanted a family my entire life," she says. "A good one. Filled with safety and love." There's no answer.

Lynell settles into the chair and continues to watch the fireplace, the book lying untouched in her lap.

Hours go by. She doesn't move until the doors open again. Zach walks in, frowning.

"There you are."

Lynell nods. "Here I am."

"Want to join us for lunch?"

Lynell shrugs and stands. "Might as well." She leaves the book in her chair and follows Zach back to the dining room, where Eric is already waiting.

"So glad you could join us," Eric says, giving Lynell a wide smile. "I hear you've been doing some exploring?"

Lynell just stares at him.

"I hope you've liked what you've seen so far. If you'd like company, I'm sure Zach would love to join you."

The conversation progresses and miraculously, nobody brings up the letter. Lynell barely speaks, and though Eric seems irritated, he doesn't comment on her silence.

When they finish, Eric stands and gives Lynell a nod. "Thank you for having lunch with us, Lynell. Remember, you have the rest of today to consider my offer. I hope you choose us." And with that, he leaves the dining room.

Lynell looks up at Zach. She feels detached from her situation. "Choose you?" she asks.

Zach sighs. "Choose good."

There's one more floor for Lynell to explore. It's mostly offices and a locked security room. Lynell peers through the little window in the door to glimpse some screens showing the front of the house, the yard, the dining room, and the staircase. She's sure there are a dozen more screens showing every inch of the house. Probably even her bedroom.

There are two doors that seem to go to stairwells, but both are locked. Lynell returns upstairs and heads to the backyard, which is huge and surrounded by a tall fence. Four more guards stand watch, and Lynell gives each a nod.

The dress hugs her legs as she walks, wind making the fabric dance. Green grass folds under her feet and the sun licks her skin. She wishes she could feel its promise of life. But she can only think of her death.

Fake letter. He finds out and tortures the real one out of her. Death.

Real letter. He doesn't need her anymore and she's a threat whether or not she denounces her claim. Death.

No letter. Death. Probably a very painful death.

Choose good. Never done that.

She's always chosen fear. Done whatever it took to save her own skin. Even with Daniel, she could never fully let go of the fear that he might hurt her. And all too easily she gave in to the fear that she would hurt him. She sacrificed something beautiful so she could keep gripping the fear close to her chest.

The only words her father ever spoke to her were in that letter. Somehow, she doesn't think he would want her to give Eric anything.

You are strong, kind, joyful, wise, and so full of patience. Never lose that.

Lynell turns her face up to the sun and knows what she has to do. It's not just her own life at stake anymore. That code in the wrong hands could destroy the country. Even if Eric finds a way to use it without destroying the Registration, he could change so much. The Registration her grandfather created to give every citizen the opportunity for equal power would be unrecognizable. He could change it to be nothing more than a path for the rich and powerful to legally kill whomever they want. Everyone else would be disposable.

And there are still people Lynell wants to keep safe.

"You didn't come to dinner."

Lynell is sitting in her chair by the fire in the parlor. She's reading an old book she's never seen before. *To Kill a Mockingbird.* At the sound of Eric's voice, ice fills her body.

"I wasn't hungry," she says.

His footsteps are quiet on the carpet in the room. He pulls a chair up to the fire and sits next to her.

"I understand this must be difficult," he says.

"No, you don't."

"I'm sorry?"

Lynell looks at Eric. In any other setting, he would just be a normal middle-aged guy. But she knows better.

"I've dreamt of a family my entire life."

"And I'm offering you one," Eric says.

She shakes her head. "You're offering a name. Survival. But at a certain point, surviving just feels like you are dying bit by bit."

"That's a bit dramatic." Eric is grinning, like she amuses him.

"What would you do with it? The code."

"The right thing."

He looks sincere. Lynell looks for his invisible shield and thinks he might have lowered it for her. He truly thinks using the code, having that kind of control, would be the right thing.

And somehow, that's one of the most terrifying things Lynell has learned.

"Are you going to accept my offer?" he asks.

She takes another look at her book, then shakes her head. "No."

The silence is like poison to her heart.

"You understand that if you turn me down, you become my enemy? You have the choice right now. Pick us, your family. Or make us your enemy. Live here as one of us or become a prisoner."

One last time, she considers. She thinks of her father. Of Daniel. Of Zach.

Choose good.

She shakes her head. "I can't."

Out of the corner of her eye, she sees disappointment flash across Eric's face. He sighs and stands. "I wish it could be different, I really do." Then he gestures to his guards and hands are grabbing Lynell. Her eyes go wide and she struggles automatically. But there are too many of them and they're too strong.

Lynell watches Eric turn away as she's dragged from the room.

⁃⁃⁃⁃⁃⁃⁃

They take her down the previously locked staircases. She fights and yells, calling for Zach. But he's nowhere to be seen, and struggling against the guards is pointless.

When they get to the bottom level, Lynell is led down a hallway with no windows. It's cold. The lights are dim, barely bright enough to see five feet ahead. It smells of rubbing alcohol and cleaning supplies. Every few feet are doors set in the steel wall. A dungeon. She almost wants to laugh. For a second, she'd considered making the house above a possible home, not knowing what horrors lie below the floorboards.

She's dragged past doors and taken to a small, bright room at the back. Against one wall is a small, bent, wired skeleton of a bed with no blanket or mattress. A single chair stands in the middle of the room. There's a bucket in the corner that looks nailed to the floor and the walls are chipped concrete that look cold to the touch.

The guards lead her to the chair, and she sits without being prompted. Without another word, both guards walk away from her and stand in the corners of the room.

The door opens and Lynell snaps her attention forward. Eric stands there, looking at her in what can only be described as devastation.

He sighs and walks toward her. "I can get you a pen and paper. I imagine writing the letter down would be easier than simply reciting it."

"If you think I'm telling you anything you want to know, you're an idiot." The words escape without consideration of the consequences.

"One more chance," Eric says, squatting in front of her. "I don't usually give second chances, much less as many as I've given you."

There's a fire behind the façade of kindness. She recognizes it like she recognizes her own.

"You don't deserve my father's words," she says.

Eric straightens, his back going rigid and hands curling into fists. "You are so like him. The bastard thought he owned the world, that he could get away with anything." He pauses and takes a deep breath.

"Technically," Lynell says, folding her arms and glaring at her uncle, "you're the bastard."

It was clearly the wrong thing to say. Eric's face falls and his lips tremble in anger. He takes a step closer and she barely has time to blink before his hand is flying through the air. Lynell falls from the force of the slap. She catches herself with her right hand and lands on her shoulder, sending a spark of pain down her arm.

"Your father was a coward and a cheat. He didn't deserve the Elysian name. And neither do you," Eric says, standing over her.

Lynell's body pulses with anger. A desperate need to defend the father she never knew, the father who never knew her but still loved her, fills her veins. She pushes herself to her feet so she can look Eric in the eyes.

And then she spits in his face.

His eyes widen, and he curses. She sees movement on both of her sides from guards stepping closer to her.

Then everything goes dark.

DAY 7 ———————————————————————

Pain pulses through her.

She opens her eyes and sees nothing.

Everything is still dark.

She panics and moves to sit up.

Her arms yank against restraints around her shoulders and wrists. Her injured shoulder shoots agony through her body, threatening to knock her out again.

She takes a few controlled breaths, eyes prickling with tears.

She moves her legs and finds them held down by restraints too. Her back aches against steel rods, and she guesses she's tied to the bed frame.

It's cold. Goosebumps flourish over her body. She moves and metal rubs directly against her skin.

She's naked.

Panic takes over every cell. She starts writhing. The pain overwhelms her. Every inch of her body feels raw. She feels dizzy, disconnected from herself.

She screams.

"You asked for this, Lynell," a voice says. She thinks it's coming over a speaker. It fills her up from the inside.

"You can make it all go away. Just give me the letter," Eric says. His voice is low and fighting anger.

Lynell blinks. She cries. She screams and lashes against the restraints.

Blood trickles down her face, her arms, and her legs under the restraints. Then she sees a man walk into the room, grinning.

She shakes her head, tugging against the restraints as the guy comes to her with a knife. He pulls the flat side of the blade up her body without breaking the skin, leaving a track of cold fear behind. Until he gets to her left arm. Then he turns it, so the sharp end pierces her wrist and drags down the back of her hand.

She screams. For how long, she doesn't know. She can feel the sound scraping against her throat. The oxygen escapes her lungs, her vision falters. She doesn't think it's her voice anymore.

She passes out.

Water fills her nose and wakes her up. She chokes and jerks to sit up and expel it and take a deep breath, but the restraints are still in place. She gasps, sucking in water which only causes her to cough and splutter and tug at the restraints again.

Her eyes fly open and she gags, staring up into the blinding light above the bed frame she's bound to. Panic overwhelms her, and the edges of her vision blur before she's finally able to suck in a decent breath. It feels like hours before she calms and sinks back into the metal frame. She closes her eyes and pulls in haggard breaths, her lungs burning.

"Ready to give us the letter?"

She turns her head and pulls her eyes open to stare at Eric. He's sitting in the chair, one leg crossed over the other. His hands are folded gracefully in his lap and he eyes her with disinterest.

A guard comes into her vision, clad in black. She looks up to see his face, calm and expressionless. He looks at her and his lips quirk into a smile before he drops a metal bucket. It clatters against the ground and rolls away. Lynell flinches at the sound, which just causes her naked body to rub against the tight restraints again.

"We let you sleep late. It's almost noon, you know," Eric says. He leans forward, and a single strand of hair falls away from its gelled companions. He pushes it back and tilts his head. He looks at her as if she's an experiment, nothing more than a specimen in a dirty lab. "I trust you slept well."

Lynell looks away from Eric and stares at the ceiling. She doesn't want him to see the nightmare in her eyes. The way her body slipped in and out of consciousness, trying to forget where she is.

"Zach is on an errand for me or I'm sure he'd want to say hi," Eric continues. Lynell hears the chair scrape against the metal floor, and she fights another flinch.

Then she feels something on her arm, and she turns away from Eric to see the guard drying all the water off her skin. He starts on her arms then moves to her face, stomach, and chest. Lynell's not sure if they're doing this to clean her, torture her, intimidate her, or all three.

Eric walks as the guard cleans her, and when he comes into her view, leaning over her, she closes her eyes. "I hope it's okay we removed your clothes. I figured you would be more comfortable like this. Don't worry, we've treated you with the utmost respect."

Lynell wants to argue, scream at Eric to look at the slices on her left hand and arm. But she manages to keep her mouth shut and hears the guard toss the rag away and walk off.

"Maybe they went too far earlier, with the knife. But I wanted to give you a glimpse of what you're facing." Eric must be leaning close to her because his breath brushes her face. She turns away only for his fingers to grip her chin and pull her back toward him. She keeps her eyes squeezed shut. "I'm not Alan. I gave you a choice. I will give you the option to defend yourself and your dignity. But in the end, I'll take whatever measures necessary. Are we clear?"

Lynell opens her eyes, glaring at him. He smiles in response and lets go of her face. He steps back, and she watches him pace. Out of the corner of her eye she sees the guard setting up some sort of machine, untangling wires and organizing them carefully.

"I'm sorry about your current situation. But we had no choice but to restrain you, which I'm sure you understand." He looks at her periodically as he walks, his hands still firmly held behind his back. "Zach threw a fit that rivaled his tantrums as a child. He wanted me to spare you and take you back up to your room, but you understand why I can't do that. You give me no reason to trust you. Chance after chance and you still disappoint me. So, this is where we are. I'm going to leave, but know there's a monitor on your heart." He steps closer as he says this, gesturing to the guard.

Lynell turns to see him holding two wires with small, silver circles on the ends. He sticks them on her chest, working quickly while Eric talks. "It will keep track of your heart rate. If it slows too much, signaling sleep, then it will send a vicious shock through your body. It is very painful, I've been told. So, I advise against sleeping."

The guard attaches five more wires to her throat, chest, and below her ribs. Lynell's eyes burn and she looks down to try and get a glimpse of the heart monitor, catching sight of her body for the first time. Blood and bruises paint her skin, but she can't lift her head enough to see how bad the damage is.

Eric steps closer to the door, the guard following behind, and places his hand on the handle. "Someone will be back to question you soon. Take this time to truly think about your position here." Eric sighs and drops his head, shaking it slightly. "I honestly did hope it wouldn't get here. I wanted to trust you, Lynell." Eric looks up and shrugs. "I still hope you'll surprise me."

Eric knocks on the door and as it opens, he glances back at Lynell one more time. "Think hard, Lynell. Make the right decision."

Then they leave, and Lynell is alone.

Lynell manages to keep herself awake by detailing everything that has happened in the last six days. She spends hours remembering every second of her time with Daniel. She thinks about the way he mouthed, "I love you!" before Zach took her away.

She tries to remember the way the train rocked or the look of fear on Daniel's face six days ago.

Six days ago. She's been running for seven days.

Halfway. She's managed to stay alive halfway through the fourteen days in which Zach and the others could complete their Registration.

She should be proud of that. Maybe it's enough. Maybe she can give up now. When she feels exhaustion threatening to take over, she rubs her arms against the restraints which is enough pain to keep her awake but not enough to make her pass out.

She prays.

She can't remember the last time she prayed. Living under Alan's roof made her believe nothing could really be out there.

Somehow, being tied to this bedpost makes her anxious for the belief in a god. Buddha, Zeus, Mohammed, Allah, Jesus, Brahma. She asks each of them by name to take away the pain, to let her stand up, to let her go home, to tell her it's okay to give the letter to Eric.

Nobody answers, and she's still connected to the flat, metal cage when she hears the door unlock and the knob turn. Skin prickling, fear spiking, heart racing, Lynell looks up and sees Zach enter the room and close the door behind him. Her eyes go wide.

"Zach," she breathes, ecstatic to see him.

"You stayed awake," Zach says.

His words are loud and bounce off Lynell's bare skin, leaving unseen bruises. She watches him pick up the chair, confusion filling her mind.

"Zach, please help me. You told me to choose—" she stops short at the look on his face. He's leaning over the chair with his back to the door. He narrows his eyes, which are bright red, and shakes his head.

She swallows and rolls her lips between her teeth. Zach places the chair next to her and sits, leaning forward on his knees.

She feels his warmth and her body strains to reach for it, but the restraints keep her from moving. He sighs, and his breath hits her face. She closes her eyes and takes a breath.

"You're doing good, Lynell," Zach says. His voice is low but she's under no impression that they aren't being listened to.

A knot of unshed tears forms in her throat.

"Forget what I said," he says, each word tight and terrified. "Just give me the letter. Please. There's still time."

He doesn't mean it, Lynell thinks. *He's just scared.* But the effort to convince herself falls flat.

She wants to give in.

To give it to him.

He clears his throat and stands from the chair, causing it to drag along the floor. Lynell flinches at the sound, her eyes springing open. "Please, Lynell. We don't have to go through this."

"We?" Lynell says. Zach sighs and pulls a hand down his face. It's clear now that he's not here to save her. He told her to choose good, knowing that would land her here. Anger fills her body and fuels her words, strengthening her resolve. "I forgot, this is so hard and painful for you, *Price*." She spits the name, hating how it tastes in her mouth. "I forgot that you're also tied naked to a table. I forgot that you have a black eye and a busted face. I forgot that you were Registered and kidnapped by your cousin. I'm so sorry for being so insensitive to your feelings. I can't believe I—"

"Enough!" Zach shouts, cutting her off. He turns and punches one of the walls, making Lynell jump enough to send a new wave of pain through her body. The edge of her vision blurs and she feels dizzy until a shock hits her, starting at her chest and traveling to her fingers and toes. She shouts in pain, her eyes snapping wide open and her limbs stiffening. She gasps, her back arching as far as the restraints will allow. The shocks continue through her body until she's breathless and the world is blurry.

Her scream reverberates off the walls in the small room even after she has fallen silent. Her eyes water and she gasps, trying to fight off the agony.

"Are you okay?" Zach asks, his voice quiet.

Lynell squeezes her eyes shut and takes several deep, leveled breaths. When she gathers enough courage to speak, she breathes, "Fuck you."

Zach sighs and steps closer to her. She opens her eyes and notices him looking down at her. "It's me or someone else, Lynell. And trust me, you want it to be me."

Her chest tightens, her bottom lip quivers, and her nostrils flare. "Fine. Do your worst."

"The letter, Lynell."

"Screw you."

She glares at him, blood dripping down her chin. Her body continues to tremble from the after-effects of the shock. She feels limp, ready to pass out at any moment.

Then Zach has the nerve to grin. He stands closer to her and mouths, "You're good."

Despite the fury filling her stare, a tear falls down her face.

"Okay. We'll start simple," Zach says, turning away from her. She watches him walk to the door, knock, and leave. It's only a few moments before he's back. Two other men follow him, each holding a bucket.

Zach takes the device off her chest and doesn't meet her gaze as he drapes a rag over her face.

She panics, jerks away from him, the pull against the restraints painful. She tries to speak, but the rag dips between her lips and before she can make a sound, Zach starts pouring.

She's heard of waterboarding, of course, but couldn't be prepared for it. It takes three pours to empty the bucket. The relief between each pour makes the next one worse. When he's done, he removes the rag and she coughs, wheezes, and screams. Her lungs burn and her heart races.

The other three men stay in the room. They watch with hungry eyes as Zach undoes all the restraints and pulls her gently to the ground. His touch, so careful and tender, is a sharp contrast to what he's doing to her. When Zach lets go of her, Lynell attempts pushing herself up to stand, but her arms are too weak. She slips on the wet floor and falls, hitting her chin hard.

Zach grabs her under her arms. His chin rests on her shoulder and he whispers. "Hang in there. I have a plan," before pulling her over to the buckets.

She blinks, trying to decide if she heard his words correctly. How is torturing her a plan? How can he tell her to hang in there?

She looks up at the buckets, one steaming and the other filled with ice water. Zach holds her head under the hot water for so long that she starts clawing at the edges of the bucket. She reaches up to try and grab him, but his arms are too strong, and she's kept under the water until she's sure she's about to die.

Then at the last minute, just as she starts to feel consciousness slip away, he pulls her out of the water. She has just enough time to take a breath before she's plunged into the other bucket filled with ice water.

And repeat.

Until she can't take it anymore and she sucks in a lungful of the hot water and finally, mercifully, passes out.

<hr />

She wakes on the bed again and hears the door open. Expecting to see Zach and prepared to demand answers, she looks up but instead finds herself looking at Eric. Biting back a scowl, Lynell lowers her head and closes her eyes.

"Zach went easy on you," Eric says.

Lynell would scoff if she could.

"Just a bit of waterboarding. I'll have to send Reggie in next. He has an affinity for fire. But his favorite toy is Arnold." Lynell winces and opens her eyes when a few items fall to the ground. Eric pulls the chair closer to her and sits, leaning forward. "Arnold is his rat. He's not a good owner, barely feeds the thing. But Reggie seems fond of putting Arnold in a metal bowl held against a stomach."

Eric's hand is suddenly resting on Lynell's bare stomach and her eyes snap open. She cowers away from the hand, but Eric just keeps it pressing down.

His eyes twinkle as he smiles at her.

"He heats up the bowl. It takes Arnold a bit of time before he realizes he's too hot. Then, he needs to get away from the heat. And he can't eat his way out of the metal bowl. So . . ." Eric takes his hand off Lynell's stomach. "He goes the only way he can. Right. Down." The tip of a knife returns to the spot above Lynell's belly button where Eric's hand had been moments previously. "Through you." He pushes the knife just enough to pierce the skin before pulling it away.

Lynell grits her teeth and keeps her eyes trained on Eric, trying to ignore the new pain.

"I really don't want you to have to meet Arnold, though. So, I'm going to give Zach one more shot. But . . . that'll have to wait for tomorrow. It's late. Almost ten o'clock, and he needs his sleep. We all do." Eric stands up and leans over Lynell. "As a gesture of good faith, I'll let you off the bed," he says, standing to undo the restraints. "Then maybe you'll realize I'm not a villain."

Lynell's stomach tightens as Eric leans closer to her. She keeps her mouth clenched shut and her eyes trained on his.

"If Zach refuses to try again, you may have to meet Arnold," Eric says as he undoes the last restraint on her foot. "Or worse, one of my men who has appreciated the fact that you've laid here willing and naked for so long." Eric pats Lynell's cheek, causing her face to heat up with fresh anger.

He steps away and heads for the door as he says, "I hope you'll have a change of heart tomorrow."

She leans in the corner of the room, inspecting her throbbing feet. She's not sure when, but at some point, two of her toes were broken. There are also wounds on her wrists, ankles, thighs, and neck where the restraints used to be. Her hair is still wet.

She's freezing. Hungry. Thirsty. In pain.

Terrified. Breaking.

She counts the seconds between each drop of water falling from her hair and hitting the floor.

One second.

Don't give them the letter. Don't give in.

Three seconds.

Stay strong. Stay alive. Don't let them break you.

Four.

Don't let them see the fear.

Two.

Don't think about what's next.

She sees Eric in her mind, leaning over her and promising her future forms of torture. She sees him telling her about Reggie and Arnold. About his men. And she knows her own thoughts are empty. She's not going to last.

You made it through years of Alan. You made it this long. You can do this.

She shivers from the cold and holds her knees close to her chest. Her skin erupts in goosebumps and she shakes her head. She's going to give him the letter. She knows it. She's already reciting it in her head.

Don't give up.

DAY 8—————————

Lynell was riding her bike under a thicket of trees in the park. The wind tugged at her hair, tangling it behind her. Her shirt was fluttering around her waist and she stood up on the pedals, grinning. When she broke free from the shade of the trees, the sun rested gently on her face and she leaned back, closing her eyes for a minute to revel in the feeling on her skin.

She never saw him coming. Her bike slammed into his, and she flew over the handlebars, landing half on the sidewalk and half on the grass in front of him.

"Oh, my god!" a man yelled.

Pain slipped into her left side, and she looked down to see a deep scrape along her fingers and the back of her hand. She hissed, inspecting the wound closely.

When he dropped his bike and stepped toward her, she visibly flinched and crawled away from him.

Their eyes met, and her mind battled between fear and . . . curiosity? Attraction?

"Are you okay?" he asked, kneeling next to her. She cowered away from him, cradling her hand against her chest. "I'm so sorry, I didn't see you." He was looking at her closely, his eyes wide.

They were so blue. So full of empathy. So kind.

The fear started receding, but even still, she yanked her arm out of his grasp when he reached out, saying, "Let me see that."

At her movement, he quickly pulled his hand back and leaned away from her, tilting his head. "I'm sorry. I didn't mean to get in your way."

Finally, she found her voice. "No, it's okay. It was my fault. I wasn't looking . . ." Her voice trailed off. Admitting that she was riding her bike with her eyes closed seemed stupid.

He chuckled and dropped to the grass next to her. Their bikes were still blocking the sidewalk but neither one of them made a move to fix that. "You were going fast. Running from something?" he joked.

Yes. Lynell laughed quietly. "No. Just enjoying the weather. I was being reckless." She studied his face closer. He was young, couldn't be much older than her. His hair was a lighter brown than hers and pulled into a small bun. He had a week's worth of stubble lining his jaw. There was a small scar through his right eyebrow, which gave him the look of a young adult novel villain. Or an incredibly handsome, rugged hero. She wondered if he fought in the recent battles between rebels and government forces. If he fought, was he on the right side? Or was he with the guerrilla group who fooled themselves into thinking they could overthrow the government and end the Registration?

They were quiet for too long before Lynell got ahold of herself. "I'm sorry," she said again. "Are you okay? Your bike?"

He chuckled again, tugging a handful of grass free and setting the blades loose in the wind. "I'm fine. Not a scratch on me." He held out his arms as proof. "You caught the front of my tire." He leaned forward and gently touched the wheel in question. "Seems fine though. Even if it wasn't, it wouldn't be a big deal. I own a bike shop, so I could fix it for free."

Lynell smiled. "You own a bike shop?"

He nodded. "Yeah. Half bike shop, half coffee shop. It just opened a few months ago. Over on Main Street."

"That's awesome," Lynell said. The stinging in her hand grew stronger and she tried to hide the pain in her face. But he must have noticed because he sighed.

"Can I please take a look at that?"

Lynell almost refused point-blank. But the way he looked at her calmed any nerves, and she extended her hand. When he took her wrist with one hand and cradled her palm with the other, she sucked in a breath. Not from any pain, but the contact.

His hands were large and rough and warm. They had the potential to be dangerous, but he was holding her so gently, almost as if not touching her at all. But he was, and she didn't want to recoil. His fingertips danced over her skin, and the touch warmed her all the way to her toes.

"None of the scratches seem too deep," he said, letting go. "But they could get infected. I'd like to clean them and get your hand wrapped up as quickly as possible."

Lynell held her hand close to her chest. Her eyes flicked down to his lips.

"My shop is just on the other side of the park. A fifteen-minute walk. I've got a first aid kit."

She didn't say anything at first. His words didn't even register in her mind. Then she sucked in a breath. He was inviting her back to his shop. This stranger was trying to get her to go with him, completely unguarded and vulnerable.

And she was going to agree.

She nodded and a grin split his face. He quickly stood up, wiped the dirt and grass from his pants, and held out a hand. She looked up at him before placing her right one in his.

He guided both their bikes down the sidewalk, and Lynell walked next to him, smiling as he spoke. He told her all about opening the shop with his partner, a young man who fought with him. She noticed he didn't give a clue as to the side they fought on.

After the rebellion was squashed, he moved to Dallas to care for his sick mom. His partner had studied business and marketing in college before they met.

"He's a good guy. Takes care of the boring financial side, leaving me with the coffee and bikes."

"That's awesome," Lynell said as they pulled in front of the shop. It was cute, split between the bikes and the coffee. It was packed with people, but the man led her around back.

"Do you mind coming into my office?" he asked, fishing some keys out of a jacket pocket. "That's where the first aid kit is." He unlocked the door and guided the bikes inside before turning back to Lynell. He glanced at her for a moment, and she tried to school her features into a comfortable position that didn't give away her fear. "I'll leave the door open," he said.

Lynell took a deep breath. "Yeah, of course."

He grinned again and held the door open for her to walk through. "Cool. Hey, I never got your name, by the way."

They held eye contact as Lynell smiled and said, "Lynell."

"Nice to meet you, Lynell. I'm Daniel."

Lynell tries desperately to hold onto the dream. Or memory. It clings to the front of her mind, about to float away. She wants to grasp onto it. Wants to remember the moments that came after meeting Daniel. The years. She wants to feel his lips again. Wants him to hold her. To nurse her back to health. She's waking up and she knows Daniel won't be there. She keeps her eyes resolutely shut, hoping to return to the dream.

Then her eyes fly open as pain attacks her. Reggie stands above her from where she's lying on the ground, bending her pointer finger on her left hand back. She stares up at him, tears pricking at her eyes as the hurt overtakes her. The finger snaps, Reggie laughs, and Lynell screams, curling away from him.

He lets go and Lynell cradles her arm to her chest.

She gasps for breath but loses it when Reggie grabs another finger. Black spots splatter in front of her eyes when he breaks it, too.

Reggie's grip moves to her hair. She claws at his hands as he pulls her up to her knees.

"Guess what I brought with me this morning," he whispers, his breath brushing against her ear.

Lynell's eyes are wide with fear when she looks to the center of the room to find a silver metal bowl, a blow torch, and a small glass cage that holds a patchy rat.

"Say hi to Arnold. He's very excited to meet you. Hasn't had any action in a few months."

Lynell's breath quickens, watching the rat scurrying around the cage. Reggie tugs at her hair and she shrieks again.

"I said, say hi," he growls.

She squeezes her eyes shut and uses her last drop of energy to fight against Reggie's hold, which causes his grip to tighten and fill her with more pain.

"Before we begin, would you like to give me the letter?" Reggie asks.

Yes. I'll tell you anything. But no words leave her throat.

Reggie chuckles and yanks her head back before pulling her toward the bed. She kicks and claws at his arms as he lifts her onto the bed. Her mind wants to shut down from the pain and Arnold is staring at her with eager, beady, rat eyes and the terror is too much to handle, and—

The door swings open. Reggie pauses and drops Lynell onto the bed. It creaks and groans under her weight.

"What are you—" Reggie cuts off and Lynell flinches at the sound of something large slamming into him. He crumples in front of her and she blinks at his body.

Blood trickles from a large gash on his head.

Zach stands, half facing Lynell and half facing the door. He's holding a gun out and he looks at her quickly before turning his attention to the door. "Hurry," he says.

Lynell looks to a large metal pipe that's just clattered to the ground. Then her eyes follow a pair of legs until landing on the last face she would have expected.

Daniel crouches in front of Lynell, cradling her face in his hands.

"Lynell. Oh, my god. It's okay. I got you. You're safe. You're okay," he says, pulling her against him.

Her head falls against his chest as she's lifted from the bed. The world falls into darkness again.

It was the third anniversary of the day they met and Daniel had just surprised her with two tickets to Chicago. They hadn't been since their honeymoon.

"I don't deserve you, Daniel Carter," she had said, straddling him on the couch and smiling down at him.

"You, Lynell Mize-Carter, deserve the entire world." He tucked a strand of hair behind her ear and gazed at her with so much love that she thought she would explode under his gaze. "And every minute of every day I can't believe my own luck that you settled for me."

"Settled?" she said, laughing. "You're my world."

He grinned. "I'm so thankful you suck at biking and have the attention span of a squirrel."

She playfully smacked his shoulder. "I still have a scar from that crash," she said.

Daniel threaded his fingers through hers and ran his thumb over the back of her left hand, where the scar in question sat prominently. He then pulled her hand to his face and kissed it, watching her as he did.

Her knees went weak and she leaned in, catching his lips with her own. "I love that scar, and I love you. I will always love you," he said, holding her close.

His arms are still around her. His hands are still just as reassuring. His chest is still just as strong.

"It's okay, Lyn. I got you. You're okay," he says over and over, whispering it into her ears. She grips his shirt and feels his chest moving as he runs.

Take me back.

"We are going to get you out of here."

Lynell's eyes flick open and she finds herself staring at Daniel's chest. She lifts her head slightly to look over his shoulder and sees Zach following them with his gun held out. He glances over his shoulder before looking forward again. Their eyes meet and Lynell tenses. The broken fingers throb and fear thrums through her body. She whimpers and curls further into Daniel, shaking.

"Shh, it's okay," he says, taking a turn. He starts up some steps, jostling Lynell as he takes them two at a time.

She keeps her eyes trained on Zach. "Danny . . ." she moans.

"I got you."

"Zach . . . No. Please," she mutters. She thinks of full-length sentences she'd like to say, but the words don't form. Her brain teeters on the edge of unconsciousness.

"He helped me get you," Daniel says. "He—" he stops short as a gunshot explodes next to them. He slams his back into a wall and pulls Lynell close. She squeezes her eyes shut and focuses on Daniel's arms holding her securely. There's screaming and more gunshots and a splatter of something like bits of rock hits her face. Her eyes fly open and she turns to see what's happening, but Daniel's hand settles behind her head, pulling her to his chest again. "No, don't move."

Lynell struggles against his grip and turns just enough to catch Zach run past them, gun raised.

"Stand down!" he yells. A few more gunshots before they stop, and silence enters the stairwell. Lynell hears her breath like a beacon.

"Zach?" Daniel asks, quietly.

"Clear," he replies.

Daniel lets out a deep sigh and pushes off the wall. He climbs two more flights before Zach opens a door and shepherds them through.

"Go right and stay close to the wall," he says.

Daniel obeys, and as he moves, his grip loosening, Lynell is able to lean out enough to watch their progress. She doesn't recognize the hallway they're running down. It's small and bleak. They pass a door and Lynell flinches, half expecting someone to burst out and start shooting. She cradles her left hand between her body and Daniel's, gritting her teeth together. Daniel's deep breaths brush her forehead and her short dream about their morning in Chicago passes through her mind.

"Danny . . ." she mutters.

"Shh. Don't talk. We're almost there." His voice is filled with anxiety and fear. It hurts Lynell to hear it and she wonders how she ever made it three years without him. "Stay with me."

He's sweating. Lynell lifts her right hand up and gently places it around the back of his neck, holding herself close.

"Okay," Zach says. "The gym is through this door. The exit should only have one guard." Lynell blinks over at her cousin and watches him slowly open a door, revealing a dark gym beyond. Zach enters before Daniel, his gun extended. "Clear," he says after circling the room. He motions Daniel to run forward. "Through that door," he says, pointing to the other side of the room.

"Almost there," Daniel says.

The walk across the room is never-ending. Lynell doesn't know how her heart doesn't run out of steam or fail from fright.

Then Daniel is pushing open the door without waiting for Zach and Lynell feels the sun on her face. The relief she feels is so intense she's breathless.

"Hello, Daniel, is it?"

Lynell gasps at the sound of Eric's voice. She looks at her uncle standing in front of them in the garden. His arms are crossed behind him and he's flanked by four men, all of whom have massive guns trained on her and Daniel. She's distantly aware that she's still naked and now under the eyes of her cousin, her uncle, her ex, and four strangers.

Lynell swallows, breath evading her. She tries to find Zach but fails. There's a flicker of anger in her chest when she realizes he's probably still inside, maybe running away. Then she remembers his words. "I have a plan."

This must have been it. *Some plan.*

"I would ask how you got in undetected," Eric says, taking a step forward. "But I assume it was my defiant son. You wouldn't have made it this far without him. So, where is he?"

Daniel shakes his head and steps back but pauses when a guard shouts and aims his guns more forcibly. His arms shake with the strain of holding her for so long and she wants to tell him to put her down, but she doesn't trust that her legs won't fall out from under her.

"I was under the impression you meant nothing to each other after the separation," Eric says, gesturing at Daniel and Lynell. "Seems my son lied, betrayed the family, and disgraced the Elysian name."

"You disgrace it enough with your cowardice and violence."

Lynell jumps at the sound coming from behind them. Eric's eyes move above Daniel's shoulder where the voice came from. She raises her head to see Zach there, holding his own gun out. It's trained on his father, not any of the four guards. In a second that seems to both stretch for an eternity and end in a blink, three things happen.

Eric begins yelling, the sound ricocheting off each wound on Lynell's body. "Zachary, how dare you—"

Zach pulls his trigger and Eric jerks, blood spreading along his leg.

And Daniel is yanked backward, into the building once more.

The second ends as Zach bangs the door shut just as the shooting begins. Zach shouts, locks the door, and turns back to them, blood oozing from his shoulder. The rest of the bullets thud against the door and walls.

"Zach—" Daniel starts, but Zach just grabs him and pulls him across the gym, causing Lynell to jostle in Daniel's arms.

"It won't hold long," Zach says. His words fly out fast and Lynell barely processes them, though Daniel is nodding along. "I'll lead them this way. There's another exit. You go back. Right. Down. Right. Run."

"But—"

"There's no time, *go!*" Zach yells, and instantly turns and starts running down a different hallway.

Daniel doesn't hesitate and goes down the direction they came, and just as he turns right, Lynell hears the door of the gym splinter and burst open.

Daniel's breathing quickens as he opens a door to reveal a set of stairs. They reach the bottom and see two doors, one that goes left and the other right.

Daniel turns right and pushes open the door, revealing a tunnel.

"Tricky bastard," he mutters before he takes off running. Each step is accompanied by a small splash, and a few times Lynell thinks she can feel a few drops of something wet hit her.

The door closes, trapping them in darkness. Lynell's chest feels tight and panic fills her bones, but she focuses on matching her breaths with Daniel's. He doesn't stop running, even as his breathing turns to ragged gasps and his legs shake from exertion.

Lynell tries to keep track of how long they run, but she feels her mind slipping slowly and it's all she can do to stay conscious.

Daniel stops running at the sight of a small sliver of light and mutters, "Shit."

Lynell looks forward. There's a ladder that extends up to a hatch. "It's okay," she mutters. "I can climb."

"Are you sure?" Daniel asks.

"I have to. Put me down." She lets go of his neck and extends her legs. Daniel slowly lowers her, and her feet touch a stone floor covered in a thin layer of liquid. Just as she shivers, Daniel pulls his shirt off and holds it out. She nods and Daniel pulls it over her head and helps her guide her arms into the sleeves, taking care to work the shirt around her hand without touching her two broken fingers. Daniel holds his hands on either side of her hips to keep her from falling. She sways, sight going in and out of focus as she reaches out for the first rung of the ladder with her right hand. Her fingers curl around the bar and she holds on with all her strength as she raises her foot to the rung. Her leg shakes as she puts all her weight on it and she almost falls back, but Daniel keeps his hands against her back.

"You got this," Daniel says.

Lynell nods to herself and starts climbing, careful to only use the unbroken fingers on her left hand. The strain is too close to her fingers, and pounding reverberations of pain flow through her arm. Daniel follows close behind. When she reaches the top, he presses his chest to her back and opens the hatch. Lynell squints against the light as she climbs out, rolls onto her back, and takes a deep breath. Daniel follows close behind and closes the hatch. He drops next to her on the patch of grass and cradles her face with his hands.

"Lyn. Baby. Are you okay?"

She blinks and smiles slightly. "You saved me."

Daniel lets out a choked laugh. "Yeah. But we have to go, Lynell. We can't stay here."

Lynell starts to sit, shaking as she does.

"It's okay. I got you." Daniel snakes his arms under her knees and her back again, lifting her up. "And I'm not letting go." He holds her close. "Ever again."

Daniel starts running and Lynell looks behind them in the direction they came. She can't even see the Elysian house anymore or hear any signs of their escape. But she knows they're coming. She knows they'll probably never stop coming.

"We're so young," Lynell said, sitting on the toilet of their small apartment. Daniel knelt in front of her, holding onto her wrists. "We're too young." She looked down at their hands, at what she held.

"Yeah, we're young," Daniel said. He lifted one hand and placed the palm under her jaw. "But we're together. In love."

Lynell scoffed and shook her head, looking up at the ceiling. "That's not enough, Danny."

"It is. It can be! Lynell . . ." he moved his hand to the back of her neck and guided her face toward his. He stood up slightly so he could place his forehead against hers. "It can be enough, baby."

Lynell sniffed again, curling her hands into tighter fists. She shook her head, feeling the familiar panic building in her toes and filling her body.

"It's enough, Lynell. We're enough. *You're* enough." He said it all with their faces pushed together, watching her closely. He gently gripped her neck, his fingers mixing into her hair.

"I'm not." Her voice broke as she spoke, and she pulled her head away from Daniel's. "I'm broken."

"No . . ."

She nodded and stood. She began pacing the small bathroom, noticing every out-of-place detail. The toothpaste with a missing cap. The wad of hair that missed the wastebasket and had been sitting on the ground for at least a week. The thin layer of grime on their bathtub. Three hair bands littered the floor.

"You're not," Daniel said. She felt him watching her.

Her skin prickled, and her eyes filled with tears. She leaned down and grabbed two of the hair bands and tossed them in the trash. "It's too messy. I'm too messy. Not clean. Not good. Not safe. Not enough." She muttered the words under her breath, expecting a hand to fly in her direction at any moment, to connect with her face and send sparks blossoming behind her eyelids.

"Stop it, Lynell," Daniel said. Three years into their relationship and he'd come to know the beginning signs of her panic attacks. He stopped in front of her and grabbed her shoulders, dipping his head so she was forced to look him in the eyes. "Take a breath."

She stared at him, feeling her heart fill up her throat, threatening to break free.

"I can't do it, Danny."

He gave her a pained smile. "You can."

Lynell cautiously sits up, trying to keep the pain an arm's length away. The movement from the car rhythmically sends bouncing waves of hurt through her body.

"Careful," Daniel says, handing her a thin blanket. She covers her legs, jaw clenching at the motion. "Try to lie down. Don't move too much."

Lynell obeys, keeping her eyes trained on the side of Daniel's face. "How . . ." she says. Her voice is hot and dry in her throat.

"A rental car," Daniel says, saving her from having to finish the question. "Zach got it with cash after he called me. Gave me the keys when we met up. I guess in case . . ." he trails off, his voice wavering.

"Where are we going?" she asks.

He shakes his head. "I don't know. You need a hospital, but they'll look for us there. They'll look for us at every hotel and motel within driving distance. They'll get in contact with everyone we know. I don't think they have the power to freeze our accounts, but who knows? They'll definitely be able to trace any activity on our cards. Lynell, I don't . . . I don't know what we're up against." He speaks so quickly that Lynell has trouble following him.

"Slow down," she says, sitting up to rest her right hand on his shoulder.

Daniel tilts his head to rest a cheek against her hand. "Yeah . . . sorry. By the way, there's a change of clothes in the back. I'll help you get dressed when we stop."

Lynell nods. "Thanks . . . What about Deandra's house?" she asks, thinking of Daniel's older sister. "She's still here, in Dallas."

Daniel shakes his head. "I called her yesterday, told her to leave the city. The country, even. As soon as they realize we're still in touch, they are going after her. I told her to go get dad and take him back to England."

"One of the girls from book club might—"

"They'll know everyone in your life, Lyn. Any place that may be a safe haven for us will be watched."

"What about someone they wouldn't think of? Someone who'd let us crash at their place without calling the cops?" Lynell asks. She thinks of people he may have known back in his days as a rebel.

Daniel shakes his head. "The last rebel safe house I knew of was raided a few months ago. I've lost contact with everyone else. Plus, I don't know how much of what I told Zach passed on to his father."

"We could go to my office."

"They'll check there. They'll check everywhere. I even called Sarah. Zach told me you two still talked. I was worried they'd suspect her of helping you because she's your . . ."

"Only friend," Lynell finishes.

Daniel clears his throat. "Anyway, I told her to leave for a bit. She took a bit more convincing than Dee and Dad, but she's gone. Went to visit her parents in Canada, I think." Daniel trails off, glancing behind him through the back window before changing lanes. "Maybe a motel . . . but they'll check everywhere," he says, mostly to himself. "And we'd have to use cash. I don't have much cash on me."

Lynell gets her first good look at his face when he turns.

Stubble is already turning into a beard and his normally well-maintained hair is tangled and greasy. Deep bags are under his bleary eyes and his lips look chapped. She wonders how long it's been since he got a decent night's sleep. He must have been worried sick, awake all night, and fearing the worst since Zach took her from him six days ago.

"We could find somewhere to hide out. Like a cafe or homeless shelter," Lynell suggests.

Daniel shakes his head. "I don't want too many eyes on us. We need somewhere private where we can clean you up and you can rest."

"We could break into someone's garage."

"What if someone sees us? I don't want to risk the cops being called," Daniel says, giving a frustrated groan.

And at that moment, she realizes the best option they have is one she never wanted to ever consider. But they need to get somewhere safe, if not for her sake, then for Daniel's. She takes a deep breath, counts to ten, and returns to those years she spent in the dark, teaching herself to compartmentalize and control the fear.

"There is one place we could go," she says, so quietly that for a moment she thinks Daniel might not have heard her.

But then he glances at her and asks, "Where?"

"The one place they'll never expect us to go. They'll never bother to look at . . ." She looks at the two broken fingers as she talks, her stomach turning at the awkward angles.

"Where?" he asks, and his voice fills with so much hope that it gives her the strength to continue.

"Alan's."

The moment stretches on for so long Lynell thinks she passed out. But the throbbing pain in her hand and the way Daniel looks at her, worry etched in the new wrinkles on his face, tells her otherwise.

"Lynell—"

She can tell he's about to object, so before she loses her nerve, she interrupts him. "Listen, it's our best shot. They know what he is. What he did to me. They'll never in a million years expect me to willingly return there. And if they believe you love me, they'd never expect you to ever take me there. And it's not like Alan would have any idea where I might go, so I can't imagine that they'd ever bother to even ask him about me. He lives a few miles outside the city limits. It's a good idea, Danny. You know that." She says it all quickly and takes a deep breath, relaxing against the seat when she's done. The effort it took to say it all seems to squeeze her dry.

"I don't know, baby . . ."

"Do it," she says, pushing as much assurance into her voice as she can muster.

Daniel looks back at her, his eyes swimming, before he finally sighs and nods. She gives him the address, knowing Alan hasn't moved in the last six years and hoping his fiancée and her daughters haven't moved in yet. Fear and dread fill her as Daniel throws on his blinker and makes his way to the closest exit. Alan is bad, but he's never tortured her or kept her in a dungeon. Right now, he is the lesser of two evils.

"You've never met him," she says when she notices Daniel's tightened grip on the steering wheel. He nods at her words but doesn't say anything. "What time is it?" she asks.

"Almost one p.m."

"He may already be drunk," she says.

"Lynell . . ."

"You can't do anything stupid, Danny," she says, foreseeing a problem in their plan. "If he calls the cops, or if you guys get in a fight and get seriously injured, then we lose this."

Daniel nods and a moment of silence glides over them before he takes another deep breath. "How am I supposed to just . . . look at him?"

"You won't have to for long. He'll leave if we give him money and point him to a bar. It won't be suspicious. He used to disappear for days at a time."

"I love you, Lyn."

"I know." He looks back and she meets his eyes. "For the first time in his miserable life, Alan can actually be of use to me. Maybe even save my life."

"I saved your life," Daniel bites back and immediately winces at his own words. "I'm sorry." He shakes his head and runs a hand through his hair. "I just can't stand the idea of you being near that bastard again."

Lynell sighs. "It's a good plan." The only plan.

Daniel nods. "You always were too smart for your own good."

She starts to laugh but then the car hits a pothole, jostling her slightly. Her laugh turns into a groan, and Daniel mutters apologies, turning back to the road.

"I'll go in first," he says a few minutes later. "I'll take care of Alan and then come get you." At Lynell's expression, he quickly amends his statement. "I won't kill him or hurt him too badly or do anything that may call attention to us, I promise."

"Offer him money in exchange for the house for a night. He never turns down free cash."

"I don't have much."

"Give him the car."

"Lynell, it's . . ."

"It'll work," she says.

"Then you'll have to see him," Daniel counters, chancing a glance at her again.

"If I'm not passed out by then, I—" she stops talking, hissing at another wave of pain through her body, this time originating in her feet. Nausea hits and she has to take a deep breath to fight it off.

"Are you okay?" Daniel asks.

Lynell grits her teeth and nods.

"We're almost there," he says, and the car accelerates.

Unconsciousness pulls at the edges of her mind.

Her plan was to leave while he was at work. She had a small suitcase packed and placed the long letter she'd spent two hours writing that morning on Daniel's pillow. She'd made dinner for every night that week. Everything was ready and all she had to do was . . . leave.

She stood in front of the couch, her bag at her feet, and stared at the front door, trying to work up the courage to leave.

She took a deep breath and picked up her suitcase, heading for the door. It opened before she reached it.

"Hey, baby," he said as he stepped inside. He leaned in, pressing a kiss to her cheek. He smelled so good, like winter and trees and new books. "I needed to get out of the office for a bit and I thought we could grab lunch."

"Danny . . ." she muttered, trying to hide her suitcase behind her back.

"Work is insane today," he said. He kicked the door shut behind him and walked into the house. "I swear, my boss *likes* seeing us frazzled."

Lynell turned as he walked past her, her mind clouded by the shock of being caught before she could leave.

Daniel took off his coat and draped it over the couch. "When I get that promotion, everyone is getting a raise." He turned to her, smiling as he looked at her face. Then his eyes traveled down to the suitcase in her hand and the smile melted.

"What are you doing?" He took a step forward, his eyes jumping from the suitcase to her feet to her face and around the house, as if looking for an answer. "Where are you going?" Fear filled his eyes. "Lyn . . ."

Lynell's lips quivered. She managed to keep herself from crying, but her voice was still thick when she said, "I'm sorry, Danny. I can't do it."

"What are you talking about? Baby . . . sit down and we can talk." He rushed to her side and grabbed her hands. The suitcase dropped to the floor.

She shook her head and looked away. "I can't. I'm sorry. There never was a chance that I would. You know that."

He placed his hands on the sides of her face. "You can do this. We can do this." The panic was evident in his voice. "Please, Lyn."

"I'll come back, I promise. I'll be back. In . . . in less than two weeks. I'll come back."

Realization dawned on Daniel's face and he took a step back. "You can't."

Lynell dropped her eyes. "I'm so sorry, Danny. But this is best. For everyone."

"No, it's not!" Daniel yelled, causing Lynell to flinch. "You can't do this! This isn't just your decision."

"It is. It has to be." Lynell was begging him now. Begging him to forgive her for doing something she hadn't yet done.

"But you're good. I'm good. This is a home of love, Lyn. Not hate."

"That won't be enough. I'm . . ." She searched desperately for the right word before whispering, "broken."

"Fine then!" he yelled. "Be broken. But don't break me just because you're scared." His voice lowered and filled with venom that struck Lynell in the middle of the chest.

She sucked in a breath, sobs building in her throat.

A long moment of silence passed before Lynell nodded. "I'm sorry, really. But I have to. I'll be back."

"Don't bother."

"Daniel . . ."

"If you leave, leave. Stay gone. Don't come back."

Lynell reached for his arm and he yanked it away. Her vision started to blur. "Danny, please."

"If you're going to go, then go." His voice cracked.

Lynell closed her eyes and took a deep breath before nodding again. She looked at Daniel, but he was staring at the floor, facing away from her. Lynell bit her lip until she tasted blood then leaned down, picked up her suitcase, and walked to the door.

"I love you, Daniel Carter. And I will come back."

She left.

They drive through a neighborhood of two-story houses with immaculate lawns and nice cars sitting in the driveways. Even a boat is parked in the circular driveway of one house. Lynell remembers the school bus stopping at the corner of the street to pick up the few children in the neighborhood whose parents didn't drive them to school. She would stare out the window and imagine a life here. A life just three blocks away from her house but so out of reach it seemed like a different galaxy.

Daniel stops before turning to the next road.

"We're almost there," he says, unnecessarily. "It's not too late to change your mind."

It had been a good day. Alan was gone and Lynell was playing Scrabble with her mom for hours. They always did when they had the house to themselves. "The only chance we get to create the words and the words don't create us," Elizabeth would say. Then Alan came home, earlier than expected, pissed for a reason Lynell would never know, and stormed into the living room, approaching them, rage in his eyes. Before her mom had a chance to calm him down or put the game away, Alan grabbed it and threw it at the wall before disappearing into his room.

Lynell drags herself out of the memory and shakes her head. She's not scared anymore.

She won't be scared anymore.

"It'll be fine," she says.

"It will."

The car turns, slows, and comes to a stop. Daniel takes a deep breath and Lynell sits up enough to see through the window.

A small, deep red house with a connecting garage and a neglected garden. A door that Lynell knows is decked in a dozen different locks. There's no car in the driveway, which she doesn't find surprising. Alan's shit car must either be hiding in the garage, or he finally totaled it.

Her heart stutters, and her breath stops in her throat. Daniel turns in his seat and grabs her right hand.

"I'm here and I'm not leaving," he says, squeezing her hand. "You're not alone." He presses his palm against her cheek, and she leans into it, letting out a shaky breath.

She'd screamed and dodged Alan's fist as he shouted at her in a drunken rage. She was sixteen and her own rage was starting to outgrow her fear. She ran from her small bedroom and made it to the living room, where she saw a bottle opener with a screw on one end. Alan was stumbling from behind her, yelling and screaming. She grabbed the corkscrew and turned but he reached her first and when he pushed her, the corkscrew dug into the couch.

"This isn't forever. Just until we figure out what to do next," Daniel reassures her with his hands still holding her face. She blinks until he comes back into focus. "Let me get your clothes," he says, before smiling and climbing out of the car. She hears him open the trunk before returning with a large, light sweater and some baggy sweatpants. "I think Zach was going for easy and comfortable."

"It's perfect," Lynell says, accepting Daniel's help to sit up slightly. Daniel helps her pull his shirt off, stretching the sleeve so no part touches her injured hand. She blushes despite him carrying her earlier, naked and vulnerable, and despite their three years together.

Putting the sweater on is more difficult, and she bites her lip hard to keep from yelping at the pain. "Sorry," he mutters. She waves her good hand in the air and tugs the hem of the sweater down before helping him guide her legs through the pant legs. When they're finished, Daniel climbs out of the car and looks toward the house. "Well, I'll be back." He moves to turn back but Lynell grabs his hand. "What?"

"Take me with you."

"Lynell . . ."

"He's going to take the car, so I'll have to see him anyway. Trust me. I need to go with you."

Daniel stares at her, ready to argue. She rubs the inside of his wrist with her thumb. She nods, trying to convince him and herself that she can handle this.

Finally, Daniel concedes. "Okay," he says before helping her out. She winces as he picks her up and sets her on the ground. Her legs shake and she has to lean against him, but she can walk.

The front door has never looked so far away.

She'd drawn the purple, uneven face on the kitchen door when she was eight. She knew she shouldn't, knew she would get punished, knew the smiling face was a lie, but she'd done it. She'd done it out of spite, because when her mom bought her a coloring book, Alan had complained that she was too old, so he set it on fire. So, Lynell decided to make the walls her coloring book. When Alan caught her—she'd expected no less—he hit the back of her legs hard, took away all her markers and pens and pencils, and made her stand in the doorway of the kitchen for six hours, missing lunch and dinner, watching him eat despite her mom's teary-eyed pleas.

Lynell forces her posture to straighten and pulls a deep breath through her nose. It causes a twinging ache in her chest and she blows it out through her mouth. Daniel looks down at her. His dark eyebrows hug closer to his eyes in a silent question.

She nods.

He knocks on Alan's door.

Silence.

Lynell glances at Daniel and back at the door. Her skin crawls with anticipation and she grasps hold of his arm for balance. He places his hand on her back, a steady anchor to reality. She has to fight to stay present, to keep herself from falling into nightmares of the past that lie just beyond this door.

Daniel knocks again. Finally, from behind the door, Lynell hears a crash. She tenses, and Daniel wraps his arm further around her waist, holding her close.

"Who the hell—" someone yells, followed by another crash and a series of curses. "What do you want?" The door swings open to reveal a middle-aged man with a large gut hanging over tattered jeans. His hair is a deep brown and falls unevenly under his ears. He sneers at them with yellow teeth under an upturned nose. Lynell has a very foggy memory from a dozen years ago when he was a decent looking man with a flat stomach and white teeth. Looking at him now, she wonders if that version of him ever existed.

Lynell lifts her chin and says, "Alan."

He frowns, studying her face. Then his lips break into a wide smile showing off every yellow tooth. He laughs and says, "Awe, little Linnie came home at last! What's up with your face?" His words tie together in a slight slur, but he's not swaying.

So, not pissed drunk yet.

"Alan," Daniel says, stepping forward and gently pulling Lynell back. She wants to argue, but the movement causes her vision to go blurry for a moment and she has to catch her breath to stay on her feet. "I'm Daniel and—"

"I don't give a damn who you are," Alan interrupts.

Daniel's grip on Lynell's side tightens in response and she sucks in a breath, which causes him to instantly let go and return his hand to her back.

"Lynell and I need somewhere to stay for a few days, and your place is our best option. Therefore, we are going to stay here."

Alan glares at him. "Excuse you. You have no right to—"

"I think the childhood Lynell had to endure gives us the right to a simple favor," Daniel says.

Alan stands taller and the fat on his cheeks shakes with the anger that's building. Lynell can see the warning signs in the way his lip curls and his hands roll into fists. But before he can keep talking, or throw a punch, Daniel reaches forward and pushes the door open wider.

"You are going to help us and you're not going to complain about it. I would prefer to go about this without violence or threats. Really, I'd prefer if you helped because it is the right thing to do, but sadly, I know better. So, you're going to do this because you'll get something valuable in return."

Alan continues to fume but with the mention of something valuable, he deflates enough to allow Daniel to continue.

He holds up the car keys and Alan's eyes zoom in on them. "The car is brand new, filled with gas, and ready to go. Take it and leave the house to us for a few days. We'll cause no damage."

Alan reaches out for the keys, and Lynell notices his fingernails are short and jagged. She remembers the days when she prayed his nails were short because the longer they were, the more it hurt when he slapped her.

Daniel pulls the keys out of Alan's reach.

"What are you playing at, boy?" Alan growls.

"You can't tell anyone you've seen us."

Alan laughs. "Like I'd want to be associated with the likes of you."

"I mean it, Alan. I'm not afraid of hurting you." Daniel leans in, causing Lynell to move with him. "And I still have my Registration left. Not saving it for anyone special. If you tell anyone we're here or if you ever lay another filthy hand on Lynell, I will use it. For you."

Alan's eyes narrow before he snags the keys out of Daniel's hand. "Don't trash my house."

"Wouldn't dream of it."

Alan turns his attention to Lynell. "My dear little Linnie, this is who you left home for? That's sad, even for you."

Daniel bristles next to her, but she gives his arm a quick squeeze, trying to communicate to let her speak.

"Don't call me that," she says, the words nearly spitting from her mouth. "I'm not yours. I left home because you were sucking the life out of me. Because every day I woke up under your damn roof, every minute I spent here, I wanted to slit my wrists. And yours. I left because you made my life hell and I wanted something more. A life worth living. Daniel found a place in my life but it's just that—*my* life. And you will never be a part of it again."

Daniel rubs her back once and Alan frowns. He takes a step toward her, but she doesn't move, even when Daniel grips her side again. "Harsh words from a coward coming to me for help."

"A coward would never willingly return to this hellhole," she replies.

"Think you ought to be a little nicer to the man with the home you want to use," he says, leaning close enough for her to smell the beer and cigarette smoke that permanently taint his breath.

"Take the car and leave, Alan," she says. The effort of standing tall is beginning to take its toll on her.

Alan lifts his hand and pulls a dirty finger across her jaw. She flinches and loses her balance but before she can fall, Daniel grabs her, holds her up, and pushes Alan back with his other hand.

"Go now," Daniel says. "Or I will kill you right now, Registration be damned."

Alan doesn't say anything else. He turns back into the house, grabs a wallet, a beer, and a jacket, and returns to the door where Lynell is holding on to the wall.

"Looks like you'll be dead before I get back, anyway," Alan says, looking Lynell up and down. "I guess I'm not the only one who saw what you are and what you're good for, you pathetic piece of—" His words are cut off by Daniel's fist slamming into his temple.

Alan crumples to the ground with an angry shout. He looks up at Daniel, who stands over him, breathing hard. Lynell grabs his bicep and whispers, "Daniel," before he steps back.

"Leave, Alan. Now," Daniel says.

Alan sends them another string of curses before he turns and heads to the car. Daniel watches him climb in and drive away before he grabs Lynell's hand.

"You okay?" he asks, leading her into the house.

She nods, despite memories assaulting her from every angle. A red and brown plaid couch with sunken seats sits on the far wall. There's still a frayed tear on the left armrest. She scans the rest of the room, noting the empty bottles and only a handful of takeout containers. The whole place is cleaner than she expected, which is probably due to the woman he's with, even if she doesn't live here yet.

The face she drew on the door all those years ago is gone, as are several notches and cracks on the wall.

She feels Daniel watching her as she crosses the room, carpet flattening under her feet. A magazine with a picture of a young movie star sits on top of the coffee table. She picks it up and fans the pages. Never before has she seen a magazine in this house. Maybe Alan truly loves this new woman.

Lynell drops the magazine back on the table and sits on the couch, pulling her legs up and resting her chin on her knees.

Daniel sits next to her, rubbing her back. "We can leave."

"No, we can't. We don't have a car. Or anywhere to go. I really am okay, Daniel. I'm just . . ." She shivers, and Daniel shushes her, running his hands through her hair.

"It's okay, you don't need to explain. I know." Lynell looks up at him and sees the tension in his jaw and glistening in his eyes. She lifts her right hand up to his face and he covers her hand with his. "You shouldn't be the one comforting me," he whispers.

"I'm familiar with the demons that live here. I know how they work. You're fresh meat," she says.

Daniel presses his mouth into a thin line and takes a deep breath. "I'm going to raid the house for some first aid supplies."

"Good luck."

Daniel nods and stands, rubbing his nose. He walks over to the door and locks each individual lock saying, "We can't leave any of those injuries untreated. You need a doctor."

"We can't go to the hospital."

"I know," Daniel says. "I'll do what I can. But I was thinking, what if I called my great-uncle? He used to be a doctor. He's retired now, and we haven't talked in a couple of years, but we aren't on bad terms. I don't think they'll think of him, but he could come help."

"What if they're watching him? He'd lead them straight here. He's related to you, however distant. And, by extension, to me." Lynell's throat starts to burn. "You'll have to do the best you can with what we can find here."

Daniel scowls but concedes. "I'll be back."

When he's gone, Lynell turns and lies down on the couch, head on the armrest. She stares at the conventional white ceiling that used to be popcorn. Before she can wonder what else has changed, she closes her eyes, hoping to imagine herself anywhere except this house.

But then she returns to the bed frame in the Elysian basement and her chest tightens. Her eyes fly open with a gasp. She mutters a string of curses, forcing her eyes to stay open. To keep any other memories at bay, she focuses on her breathing, counting to five between each breath.

"It's a miracle," Daniel says. Lynell lifts her head and sees him walking toward her holding a red toolbox.

"A first aid kit?"

Daniel nods, sinking onto the couch. He puts the toolbox on the coffee table and unlatches it. Lynell leans forward to watch as he sorts through the kit.

"His new fiancée must have brought it over here," she says. There are bandages, gauze pads, medical tape, band-aids, hydrogen peroxide, antibiotics, and even painkillers. "Will you get me some water from the kitchen?" she asks, gesturing to the door next to the TV across the room.

Daniel nods, hurrying away. She opens the painkillers and drops three pills in the palm of her hand. She hears Daniel open and close cupboards and the sink turn on.

Then he returns and hands the plastic cup to her. She tosses the pills in her mouth and follows them with a gulp of water.

"Okay," Daniel says, squatting next to her. He lifts up her shirt and presses his hands against her stomach. Lynell tenses and grits her teeth as he gently cleans the cut. "This needs stitches," he says. "But the bandage will do for now." He places a gauze pad over the wound and secures it with some medical tape. She tugs her shirt down as he digs in the kit again.

"I'm never leaving you again," he says, cleaning her lip, chin, and the small cut on her temple.

Lynell feels her throat tighten and her eyes heat up. "Danny . . ."

He shakes his head, applying healing gel to the wounds on her wrists and neck before wrapping them, too. "What happened?" he asks.

She doesn't want to explain the details. He moves to her ankles and feet next, making her flinch when he touches the arch of her foot.

"Lynell."

"Eric Elysian," she says. Daniel doesn't react, which means he probably knew who was behind it. Or Zach told him. "My uncle."

She hopes Zach explained it all, but from the look on Daniel's face, she assumes he didn't.

"Elysian?" he repeats. She nods and he sucks his cheeks in between his teeth the way he used to when thinking too hard. Then he pulls some splints from the kit and says, "I think you'll have to explain that to me."

He gently grabs her left hand but before he does anything he says, "I need to look up how to do this. The fingers are broken, I need to set them properly."

"Alan should have a computer in his bedroom," Lynell says, pointing him in the right direction. Daniel nods and heads to the bedroom. He's gone for several long minutes during which Lynell takes deep breaths, trying to prepare herself.

"Alan is shameless," Daniel says, walking back into the living room. "The things I saw just from the browser already open." He gives an over-dramatic shiver and gently picks up her hand at the wrist. "This will hurt."

She holds her breath as he touches the two fingers. Thankfully, they're next to each other, so he only has to set them once. They're both swollen, bruises already forming. "Here, bite down on this. Google said it'll stimulate nerves to help with the pain since we don't have any anesthesia," Daniel says, handing her a folded rag.

She places it between her teeth and as soon as Daniel grabs her middle finger, which is bent at an odd angle, she bites down so hard that her jaw aches. "It looks like it's broken at the knuckle," he says. "I'm going to try and pop it back in place. It's going to hurt badly." He looks up at her, an apology in his eyes. "Ready?"

She doesn't finish nodding before he pulls hard on the finger. Lynell doesn't hear the accompanying pop when the knuckle fits back in place. All she hears is the roaring in her ears as she screams, the rag muffling the sound. Her scream still fills the room and her chest heaves with heavy breaths as tears spill from her eyes. Daniel's lips are moving, but she can't make out any words. Crushing agony continues to flash through her body while Daniel positions two splints wrapped in gauze on either side of the fingers and one between them.

Her screams quiet into a whimper as Daniel starts wrapping the fingers, loose enough to allow for further swelling but tight enough to keep them in place. The pressure lifts from her chest and turns to a thick fog that obscures her vision. She squeezes her eyes shut, floating in the fog until Daniel finishes and lets go of her hand.

"Are you okay?" he asks.

She opens her eyes and lets out a breath, nodding.

Daniel wipes a bead of sweat off her temple and asks, "What happened, baby?"

"I declined his offer," she says, breathing hard. "To give him what he wanted. To be a part of his family."

Daniel grinds his teeth together.

Lynell is careful to keep the pain from her voice while explaining. "A few punches and cuts. Waterboarding. Broke my fingers."

Daniel closes his eyes. Lynell swipes her thumb over the inside of his wrist and he opens his eyes, meeting her gaze. "Who?" he asks.

"Some guy named Reggie." She pauses and looks away from him. "And Zach."

Daniel lets go of her hand and stands up, turning away from her. He starts pacing and tugs on a few strands of his hair.

"Danny..."

He spins. His face is red, and his voice rises as he says, "He told me he was forced to hurt you, but he refused to give any details. Just that it was the best thing for you, the only thing really, and that I needed to come soon because he wouldn't have much time. He said he was too easy on you but he was under so much—" he shouts, and his face drains of color. "I can't believe..."

"Daniel, come here," Lynell says, holding her hand out.

He hesitates for a moment before walking over. "I'm so sorry."

She nods, and he leans down to kiss her forehead. "It's okay. He saved me... you saved me from something much worse."

Daniel rests his head against the edge of the couch. Lynell runs her right hand through his hair.

"Make sure everything is cleaned and dressed so nothing gets infected. Then I'll be okay, Danny. I will."

He raises his head and nods at her. His voice shakes when he says, "You always are." He slides his fingers between hers. "If there's anything you know how to do, it's surviving."

She smiles and keeps her response locked away in her mind. *Surviving isn't living.* No one can simply *survive* forever.

"You need to rest," Daniel says.

Lynell vaguely feels herself nod. "My old bedroom . . ." She wonders if Alan ever changed it. Daniel scoops her up and follows her directions down the hallway. The bedroom is smaller than she remembers, and while the bones are the same, with the full-sized bed in the corner and the pink dresser missing one drawer on the other side, it's different. The walls are now baby blue instead of cream, and the small desk her mom found on the curb outside one of the nice houses a few neighborhoods over is no longer next to the door. Instead, there's a crib with several stuffed animals lined up in it. Maybe it belongs to Alan's future stepdaughters. If so, they already have more toys in this house than Lynell ever had.

Daniel pulls back the covers of the bed and gently places her down. "I'll go get water." He's not gone long and when he returns, she drinks half the cup of water before setting it on the bedside table. "I'll be sure to wake you up in a few hours when you can take more painkillers," he says, as she lies down, pulling up the blanket.

The bed is far more comfortable than she remembers. Her consciousness starts slipping away, but she pulls her eyes open to look at Daniel. "Don't leave me," she says.

Daniel smiles and climbs in bed next to her, holding her close. He kisses the side of her head. "Never."

DAY 9 ————————

D aniel wakes Lynell up twice to give her painkillers. Each time, she watches him leave the room before sleep tugs her back under.

When she wakes in the morning, Daniel's lying on the bed, head propped on his arm so he can look down at her. "Here." He reaches over her to the bedside table and grabs two more pills and a glass of water. After she swallows them, he kisses her forehead and climbs off the bed. "How did you sleep?"

Lynell sits up, wincing, and leans her head back. She considers telling him about her dream, another from the early days of their relationship, but she can't bear to see the hurt in his eyes. "Fine," she says.

His lips twitch into half a frown, as if sensing a lie. "Good," he says. "Want any breakfast? I found some frozen waffles and a few eggs."

Lynell nods and pushes off the blanket. She studies her body, getting her first good look at the damage. There are bruises littering her legs and both ankles are wrapped. She lifts her shirt and prods the bandage on her midsection. Then she looks at her hand, completely covered in a bandage. All the wounds, small and large, throb, as if reminding her of their existence.

"I'm so sorry." Daniel tucks a strand of her hair behind her ear. "I'm sorry I didn't come sooner. And that I didn't realize what Zach was going to do."

"Daniel . . ." Lynell whispers.

"I'm sorry I didn't keep you safe. I—"

"Danny. Stop." She lays her hand on the back of his neck, but his eyes stay trained down. "None of this is your fault. You saved me. You always save me."

He meets her eyes and reaches up, wrapping her good hand in his. His lips part slightly as he searches her eyes. Lynell smiles and it's all Daniel seems to need before his lips are pressing on hers for the first time in over three years.

It's gentle and calm. Lynell can tell Daniel is holding back, for fear of hurting her broken body. Even the tender kiss irritates the cut on her lip. Lynell grips his shirt at his chest and when he leans forward and deepens the kiss, she gasps.

He pulls away and looks down at her hand and back up to her face, eyes wide. "Are you okay?"

She smiles. "Yes. Yes. You didn't hurt me." When he doesn't look convinced, she pushes her lips against his for a second and rests her forehead against his. "You didn't hurt me."

Daniel closes his eyes and sighs, shaking his head.

Lynell moves her hand up to his chin and tilts her head. "Hey . . ." she mutters. Daniel opens his eyes and meets hers. "You didn't, I promise."

Daniel sighs and pulls his hand down his face before standing from the bed.

"What? Where—"

"I'll be back. I'm going to make breakfast." Before Lynell can argue, Daniel rushes from the room, leaving Lynell feeling cold, alone, and unsure how their moment of intimacy plummeted so quickly.

He did hurt her. But not today. Three years ago, when he told her to leave. Leave and not come back. That devastated her. Broke her.

A war between guilt, grief, and anger rages in her chest. Lynell looks up, staring at the stupid water stain in the corner of the ceiling that's been there for almost two decades. She remembers leaving this house six years ago, positive she would never return. She'd been terrified of facing the world alone but determined to do it, to be free of this hell.

And now she's back. With the man who watched her heal. Who helped her heal.

She reaches up, touching her cheeks to find them wet with tears. She wipes them away and lowers her fingers to her lips. She can still feel the kiss.

If she can return to this house, then she and Daniel can return to who they used to be. Lynell *wants* to return with him.

Lynell drops her hand and climbs off the bed. She heads straight to the kitchen, taking steadying breaths to push away the tears and prepare herself for the upcoming conversation.

Daniel turns from his spot in front of the microwave. "Hey," he says. The word is soft, unsure, and Lynell wants to pull him into a deep kiss to wipe away all his uncertainties.

"We need to talk." Daniel opens the microwave but leaves the plate inside. "Okay," he says. It's the same "okay" he uses when he knows exactly where the conversation is going and is strapping in for the ride.

"Okay," she repeats. "You think you hurt me."

"I didn't mean physically."

"I know," Lynell says, nodding.

Daniel scratches his chin and looks down, shifting from foot to foot. "Lyn, I—"

"Wait," Lynell steps forward, and Daniel looks up at her. "Can I talk?"

He sighs, his Adam's apple bobbing as he says, "Of course."

"When you said you didn't think you'd be able to forgive me for what I did . . ." Daniel opens his mouth to respond but Lynell holds up her hand. He stops and frowns, leaning against the kitchen counter. She takes a deep breath, her eyes locked with his. "When you told me ending it was best for both of us, because I would be happier with someone . . ." Her voice is steady while she speaks, filled with relief for voicing the thoughts that have been stuck in her mind for so long. "Someone who didn't want to scream and cry and hit something every time he looked at me . . . I was devastated but I understood. I know I hurt you. But you came back to me. To save my life, even after what I did." She swallows, and her voice is strong as she asks, "Why?"

Daniel steps toward Lynell. "Lynell, when you left, everything about my life crashed around me. I didn't know if I would ever heal. I . . ." He clears his throat. "I made some awful decisions. Drank until I thought I could forget." He reaches out and grabs her hand. Lynell meets his eyes. "I never forgot, Lyn. I never forgot you or how much I love you. But," he says, dropping her hand and taking a step back, "I also never forgot her. Or the idea of her."

Daniel closes his eyes, and she allows him a moment to gather himself before continuing, this time with a shaky voice. "I'm sorry. I was so angry. I know I said some horrible things."

"Danny." Lynell's voice cracks as she reaches for his hand. Thankfully, he lets her take it.

"Lyn." He places his free hand against her face. "I didn't think I'd be able to stay with you after, but I thought about you every day. When Zach told me he was going to Register you, the moment he told me your life was in danger, the grief and anger I'd felt because you . . ." His voice trails off. "The anger just disappeared. I couldn't stand the thought of never seeing you again. No matter what you did, I never stopped loving you."

Lynell sobs and curls into Daniel's chest. He holds her close, rubbing her back. He kisses the top of her head, and she grips his shirt. "I'm so sorry," she says through tears.

"I know. Me too." He runs his hand over her hair. "But we're here now."

They stand in the kitchen, locked in each other's arms. Daniel rests his chin on top of her head, and Lynell shakes with the relief of finally having him against her again. The smell of waffles surrounds them. Only when Daniel decides the waffles need to come out of the microwave does he let go of her. Lynell stands still when he turns and removes the plate, watching him move. He places it on the counter and turns back to her. They lock eyes and Daniel leans in, capturing her lips in another short kiss.

"Danny . . ." she whispers. Their lips brush with the word and she feels him smile slightly before stepping back.

"Yeah?" he says, dropping his hands.

"Her name is Anna."

Daniel blinks. His voice is rough when he says, "What?"

She sniffs and nods. "Anna Elizabeth Carter." She whispers the name, feels it in her mouth like a promise of grace, of a life she could have again.

Daniel's hands clench into fists and Lynell watches him take three deep breaths, nod, and rub his eyes before he looks back up at her. "Anna."

"Anna."

His mouth opens, and he takes a step forward. "You named her after my mother?"

She nods. "Anna for your mom, and Elizabeth for mine. She was born two years ago at 3:02 a.m. on the fifth of February."

Daniel gasps and drops into a squat. Lynell lowers herself to her knees and drapes her right arm around him. He buries his face into her chest.

"She weighed six pounds and three ounces," Lynell continues. "She . . ." Lynell chokes over her words. "She has your eyes, Danny. She's beautiful."

It's a punch when Daniel lets out the sob. He shakes and Lynell feels small as his tears splash onto her shirt. When he finally calms down enough to get a decent breath, he mutters, "I wish I'd been there."

Lynell closes her eyes and nods, her chin grazing his hair. "I know."

"I wish I could have held her," he says, voice growing in strength.

"I know."

"I wish I could have seen her take her first steps."

She runs her hand through his hair. "Me too."

He leans back and stares at her, eyes red. "Have you seen her?"

Lynell rubs her nose, wiping the snot away with her sleeve. "Not since she was born."

Daniel drops to his butt and stares with his mouth hanging open. "She . . . she doesn't know us."

Shaking her head, Lynell pulls her knees up to her chest.

"Every day I wanted to call you and tell you about her. Tell you I had her. I think about her every day, wishing I could see her face, hear her laugh, hold her hand. I hate what I did. I regret keeping her from you. But I couldn't stand the thought of hurting her. All I could think about was . . . was my life here." She gestures around her, looking at the dirty kitchen with the grime on the walls and empty bottles littering the countertops. She looks at Daniel, whose face has fallen, watching her with complete attention. "I didn't think I'd be a good mom. I was so scared of seeing Anna feel pain, fear, and hopelessness. I didn't want to ruin her."

"Lyn . . ." Daniel reaches forward and grabs her hand.

He doesn't look at her as she speaks, and with each word, she feels herself breaking open. "I don't know where she is. It was a closed adoption." Lynell chews on her cheek and forces the words. "I made the biggest mistake of my life, and I can never take it back. I understand if you can't forgive me. If you don't love me anymore." Lynell removes her hand from Daniel. He looks up quickly and shakes his head.

"Lyn . . ." Still sitting on the kitchen floor, Daniel pulls Lynell forward so she's sitting between his legs. "I don't love you despite the mistakes you've made. I love you with your mistakes. Yes, I'm heartbroken. I hate that I don't know Anna." Lynell tenses and Daniel runs his fingers through her hair, kissing her forehead. "And I have to be honest, I am a little angry. Angry that you let me think that you Registered our unborn child. But mostly, I'm sad. I'm sad that I don't know her, never will."

She lets him hold her and caress her hair and kiss her head.

"But I do love you. Very much."

They sit there until she hears his stomach growl and the pain in her hand becomes too much to ignore. He stands, helping her to her feet.

"I don't deserve you," Lynell says, watching him grab a half-empty bottle of honey that's already starting to crystallize from the back of a cupboard.

Daniel smiles at her and sets the honey down. He turns, pecks her lips, and says, "I'm no more than a man who wants a chance to love you more every day." He steps behind her and grabs a bottle from the counter, dumping two pills onto his hand. "Now take these so that chance becomes real," he says with a wink.

Lynell grins and accepts the pills, swallowing them without any water. She grabs a small waffle, leans against the counter, and eats it while staring at Daniel. She remembers the first time she slept at his apartment over five years ago. She'd woken up to the smell of chocolate chip pancakes and bacon and found Daniel standing in the kitchen in nothing but boxers with messy hair. He'd still had long hair back then, and she'd found the way it was still tangled, not brushed, endearing.

Daniel splits the waffles between two plates and squeezes honey over each. They take them to her bedroom and eat them sitting on the bed. Then she fishes out a cheesy young adult novel from under the bed and reads it to him while he rests his head in her lap.

After lunch—peanut butter and jelly sandwiches—Daniel changes her bandages and lies next to her on the bed. He holds her close, telling the story of when he first fell in love with her. She's heard it a thousand times, but it still calms her nerves.

"It was the first time you asked for my help," he says, tracing her jaw with his thumb. "It was stupid. You couldn't reach the plug behind your computer desk, remember? I was in the kitchen checking on the chicken, and you called me, 'Danny I can't get the stupid plug in, will you do it?' Your hair was coming out of its ponytail and you were wearing one of my sweaters and only one sock. We'd never slept together, and you'd told me about your childhood about two weeks earlier. You told me you still didn't feel safe around men and never wanted to depend on someone else. So when you asked for my help, for something so small, I knew I loved you."

Daniel says it all quietly while playing with Lynell's hair. She readjusts herself to lie on her back, her head resting on his stomach. The words propel her into the memory of that day, only three months into their relationship. She wouldn't realize she loved him until almost two months later.

"Most people are products of their environment. But you, Lynell Mize, never knew the love you deserved. The system failed your family. Failed you. And yet you're strong, resilient, and kind. You amaze me not because you're a product of your environment, but because you overcame it. You don't need help from anyone but you're not afraid to ask for it. That's why I love you."

Lynell sits up and turns in the bed, holding herself up with her right hand against Daniel's chest. She smiles and leans down to kiss him.

Halfway through the kiss, there's a knock at the door.

Lynell pulls away and pushes against the wall, her eyes wide. Daniel holds a finger up to his lips and slowly stands from the bed. He takes a step and freezes when someone yells.

"Alan Mize!"

Lynell climbs off the bed and steps in front of Daniel. He grabs her arm and shakes his head, but she pulls free and leaves the bedroom, pausing when the guest knocks again.

"Alan Mize! It's the RRD! Please open the door. We have some questions."

Lynell looks back at Daniel who frowns and mouths, "The Registration Regulation Department?" She nods.

Eric must have sent them.

They knock again, and Lynell takes another step, leaning forward so she can hear better. Daniel follows her, keeping a tight grip on her wrist.

"Mr. Mize, this won't take long," the man calls. "We just have some questions about your stepdaughter, Lynell Mize."

Lynell quietly steps through the living room. Daniel tugs her away from the front door. "Is there another way out?" he whispers.

She nods and leads him into the room across from hers.

The knocks are louder this time, followed by, "Mr. Mize, we have a warrant to search the property if you do not cooperate."

They rush through Alan's bedroom. The bed has a single ruffled sheet hanging off the edge of the bed. There are two pillows and the bedside table holds empty pill bottles, a bra, and lipstick. They cross the room, and Lynell carefully pushes aside a curtain to reveal two glass doors. She peers through into the fenced-in backyard just as the men at the front door announce they're coming in if Alan won't answer the door.

"Hurry," Daniel whispers.

Lynell pauses. "What if it's a trap?"

"We can't stay here."

"We could—" She's cut off by the sound of the front door crashing and boots entering the house. Without another thought, she opens the door and they run outside.

"Clear!" a man yells from inside the house.

Lynell glances back and stumbles when Daniel tugs on her. She spins forward and jumps over a dead plant, wincing at the pain blossoming from her bare feet. The air is warm, causing her skin to heat up under the afternoon sun. Daniel breathes hard, glancing around the small backyard. They reach the fence quickly and Daniel yanks at the gate's old lock before pushing it open. Lynell looks behind them again but doesn't see any men pouring out the back door, so she follows Daniel and closes the gate behind them.

"Where now?" he asks, turning into the back alley between the rows of houses. Lynell takes a breath and nods to the left.

"That way will take us further into the neighborhood. Right will spit us out into the front yard and the main road."

"Found something!" a man yells from behind them.

Not wanting to stick around to discover what "something" is, whether it's her pills or Daniel's shoes or their empty plates still sitting on the floor by her bed, Lynell starts running on the balls of her feet. Years of sneaking out of the house at night trained her to run quietly and Daniel follows close behind. Lynell leads them through the neighborhood until she can no longer handle the pain. They slow to a quick walk, Daniel looking back every few minutes to be sure they aren't being followed. Lynell holds her side, taking long breaths before she stops completely.

"Are you okay?" Daniel asks, touching her back when she leans forward.

She nods. "This alley comes out on another street," she says, gesturing forward. "We're at the end of the neighborhood." She stands up and looks at Daniel, her eyes wide. "There's nowhere else to go."

"We can . . ."

"No, Danny. There's nowhere else. We're stuck. What are we going to do? Hide forever? Never stop running? They're not going to stop."

"Lynell, take a breath. We'll figure something out."

"How?"

Daniel looks around and wipes sweat off his forehead. "We'll try to get in touch with Zach. He helped me save you once. Maybe he'll do it again."

Lynell frowns. She wants to argue, remembering the Registration, kidnapping, and waterboarding. But then she thinks of Zach's despair at her situation. Zach kidnapped her but kept her safe from the other brutes. He tortured her, but far more gently than Reggie. He took her to Eric Elysian's house, but he also helped her get out. And then it dawns on her.

"Danny . . ." she whispers. "He could be dead." The words punch her with an overwhelming sense of loss. "Even if he survived the shoot-out, his father may have killed him because he helped me."

"Maybe." Daniel glances back and Lynell can tell he's only doing it so he doesn't have to look her in the eyes. "Maybe not. And if he's alive, he may be our only chance."

"How are we supposed to get in touch with him?"

"Same way I did the first time." He holds up his wrist to show her a thin black watch she hadn't paid much attention to. But as she looks at it, she notices it's the same watch Zach wore and checked every few minutes when he first took her. The one that constantly flashed different colors. Daniel smirks as he tilts the watch so it's facing him.

"What? Your watch?" Lynell asks.

He nods, his tongue peeking out between his teeth as he taps on the watch until the face shines. "Zach has the brother watch. He got them for us a year ago before we, uh . . ." Daniel chuckles and the sound makes Lynell roll her eyes. "We were messing with some friends. The watches will flash certain colors based on a code we came up with. I tap here." He turns so Lynell can see his finger clicking the screen above the number seven. "And his watch face will flash red. Basically, it means 'emergency, abort.' But, coupled with a tap above the twelve, which will make his watch turn off completely, it means 'emergency, meet me now.' Or, 'call me.'" He taps the two numbers while explaining it.

"We don't have our phones."

"It's okay. If he can, he'll get me another message through the watch," Daniel says, staring at it as he speaks.

A horn honks in the distance, and they both jump. Lynell rushes up the concrete alley and pushes herself against the closest fence.

"We need to find a place to wait and rest." Daniel sighs and squats in front of Lynell, letting his head hang forward. He looks up, and Lynell sees fear lacing the lines on his face. "If Zach's gone, we'll figure something else out. Preferably not out in the open where anyone can see us."

Lynell looks down at him before sitting against the fence. She leans her head back and closes her eyes. "I don't know where else to go." A few seconds of silence follow before Lynell opens her eyes and sits forward, turning to Daniel. "All these houses have doors to the back yards."

Daniel frowns. "We break into someone's house?"

Lynell shakes her head and stands, glancing down the alleyway. "We find one that's for sale. An empty one."

———

After arguing about the best way to do it, Daniel wanting Lynell to stay behind and Lynell refusing to split up, they end up heading to the sidewalk together. Daniel glances up and down the road before leading them forward. Their walk is brisk, and soon Lynell is breathing hard, sweat gathering on the back of her neck and the cut on her midsection throbbing. Each time a car drives past them, they turn and pretend to walk up the sidewalk to the closest house, Lynell sure to keep her bandaged hand out of view.

A few houses have signs in the front yards, either bragging about the many successes of their children or making political statements. The most popular sign seems to be in support of someone running to be a school district trustee. A few houses support the newest oligarch family and there are even a couple that say the Elysians should be official members of the oligarch.

That makes Lynell want to vomit. A year ago, she might have agreed with the statement. After all, the Elysians have nearly as much power as the oligarchs without being tethered to the government. Having them be official members of the government would make the Elysians accountable to the checks and balances that are in place. Although Lynell never wanted the Registration to end, she didn't want it to be a product owned by a private company. Instead, she'd hoped it could be a public service for the people. She'd always hoped that rebel supporters and Registration supporters could find some sort of compromise based on that premise.

Now, she's not so sure. She's not so sure about anything. None of the solutions feel like solutions. Every option seems like a different form of the same bad ending: people will be Registered and killed, and not all of them, she now knows, deserve it.

They enter two more neighborhoods before finally finding a house with a sale sign out front. Daniel heads up alone and knocks once, waiting for a reply. Nothing comes, and he rings the doorbell. Nothing. He returns to Lynell, eyebrows raised. "Ready to squat?"

"If you are," she replies before they head around the back of the house and through the gate. The back door is locked and after searching for a key in vain, Daniel grips the doorknob, turns it as hard as he can, and slams his shoulder into it. It flies open with a loud crash and Daniel stumbles in after it. Lynell jumps and looks behind them, fully expecting an alarm to go off.

When nothing happens, Daniel reaches out and pulls her into the house, closing the splintered door behind them.

The house is large, completely empty, and so quiet Lynell can hear her labored breathing.

"Welcome home," Daniel says after checking each room and returning to Lynell.

"It's beautiful," she says, looking up at the large ceiling. The living room has a brick fireplace, wood floors, and a window seat. The kitchen is large with an island and marble countertops.

"The water is on," Daniel says, checking the kitchen sink.

"It's stifling hot in here," Lynell says. She finds the thermostat and taps it, pushes the knob, and scans the edges, but can't turn it on. Daniel comes up behind her, tries, and also fails. Lynell shrugs. "No air for us, I guess."

"We'll open a window."

"Do you think that's smart?" she asks.

"Just the windows to the backyard. No one will notice."

After Daniel opens the windows that can't be seen from the street, he pulls off his shirt and holds it under the faucet.

"What are you doing?" Lynell says, reaching out to stop him from turning on the water. "That's your only shirt."

"Yes, but you can't get too hot. I don't want you getting a fever or infection. We don't have the medication."

"Danny . . ."

"I'm hot anyway," he says, turning on the faucet. He soaks his shirt before ringing it out and turning to Lynell. "You should take this off." He tugs at the bottom of her shirt. "And sleep with this covering you." He holds up his wet shirt.

"You're just trying to get me naked."

"Maybe." He shrugs with a smile. Lynell rolls her eyes, but she does as he says, handing him her shirt after she pulls it off. "Let's stay in here tonight," Daniel says, taking her to the living room. "We can see the front door and have quick access to the back. Not to mention the two open windows."

Lynell nods and sits in the corner close to one of the windows. She looks out to see the sky already growing dark. "What time is it?" she asks.

Daniel looks at his watch. "Eight." He sits next to her and rolls up her shirt. He puts it in his lap and gestures to it, saying "Lie down."

"What about you?"

"I'll keep watch for a while. I can sleep sitting up."

Lynell rests in his lap and drapes his cold, wet shirt over her chest. The initial touch makes her tense but her body doesn't take long to acclimate and relax. "What if he never replies?" she asks.

He pushes hair off her forehead. "Then we'll come up with a new plan."

Lynell absentmindedly pushes at her cuticles. "I started trusting him," she says, her voice a whisper. "Despite everything, before I even knew Zach was my cousin, I started trusting him. How crazy does that make me?"

He smirks and she can see the amusement in his eyes as he looks down at her. "I'd say only a little crazy."

She flicks his arm and he laughs, catching her hand in his.

"Not crazy at all, actually. He's got that personable way about him. I didn't know who he was when we first met either, but I instantly liked him. He was charming, seemed trustworthy. He would act cagey any time I brought up his family or childhood, and I knew he was hiding something. It wasn't until someone recognized him at a coffee shop that I found out who he was."

Lynell imagines Daniel, the man who fought with the rebels, standing next to his new friend while someone fawns over meeting *the* Zachary Elysian. "Were you pissed?" she asks.

Daniel shakes his head. "I already knew at that point that he was pro-Registration. We had a few arguments about it but mostly just avoided the topic. Except this one time I went on a bit of a rant about Eric Elysian and how he doesn't have a soul and Zach just laughed and said, 'I imagine it's hard to have a soul when you see firsthand how dark a soul can get.'" Daniel starts running his fingers through Lynell's hair while he talks. His eyes train forward, probably getting lost in the memories. "After I found out who he was, I apologized for calling his father evil. He told me I was right, and he was glad I was honest with him."

"You told him that you hate his family and all they stand for?"

"Of course," Daniel says. "That's when our pranks started. He supports the Registration, but he doesn't like his father. So, we started causing trouble. He got to act out his daddy issues and I got to relive my rebel days. It worked, somehow."

"The rebel and the Registration kid. It's like *Romeo and Juliet*," Lynell says.

Daniel laughs. "Except Zach isn't the Elysian I'm in love with."

Lynell looks away from Daniel and mutters, more to herself than him, "And he's not the one who's going to die at the end of the play."

"Hey." Daniel shifts so he can lean down and press a kiss to her forehead. "I'm not letting them hurt you again."

"You may not be able to prevent it."

"Well, I sure as hell will do everything in my power to try." He sighs and combs her hair with his fingers. "If he doesn't reply, then we'll come up with a new plan. But first, you need to outlive the fourteen days of the Registration."

"Five more," she says.

He nods. "Five more."

"I never told you why I was Registered," she says.

"I don't care."

He knows who she is, and she wants to tell him everything, tell him about the code and the letter and ask him what he thinks she should do.

Maybe she should just give Eric the letter and be done with it. But if she gives it to him, she'll die. She's positive his offer, if it ever was legit, no longer stands. She's proven her disloyalty to him and is now a threat as the only legitimate heir. That's when it hits her and she gasps.

"What?" Daniel asks, jumping as she sits up. She turns to him, eyes wide. "What is it?" he says, looking back to the front door.

Lynell shakes her head. "Anna . . ."

He frowns and relaxes, turning back to her. "Lynell, you don't need to—"

"No. It's not that." Lynell drops her face into her hands, her teeth gritting and eyes burning. Finally, she looks up at Daniel again. "Danny, they want to kill me not just because I'm another Elysian, but because I'm the legitimate heir to the Registration. They think I'm the only one." Confusion plays on Daniel's face.

"Danny, if Eric finds out Anna exists. That you and I were married when she was born. That she's a legitimate heir—"

"He'll go after her, too." Daniel finishes her sentence.

Lynell nods.

DAY 10

Daniel sends the same message to Zach every half hour. Lynell stays up with him, staring at the face of his watch for any sign that Zach is there, alive, and listening. She leans against him, paces the room, rests her head in his lap, curls into a ball on the floor. Daniel rubs her back when he can and his eyes flick from the watch to Lynell. At two a.m., she lets out a loud, wide yawn.

"Go to sleep," Daniel says. Lynell starts to shake her head, pacing from one end of the room to the other. Daniel stands and grazes his fingers across her shoulder blades. "Lynell, you need some rest. You're running on adrenaline and your body needs time to heal."

"How am I supposed to sleep when at any moment Eric could find out about Anna?" She sighs when his hand retreats and his eyebrows furrow. "I'm sorry. I'm just . . . angry with myself. For not considering this sooner. For getting you into this. For . . ." she trails off, all that she's angry about swimming in her mind.

"How many people know you gave birth to her?" Daniel asks.

Lynell considers the question. She hadn't told anyone she was pregnant, apart from Daniel. "Uhm, a bunch of nuns. I went to the Registration office that day but when I got to the front of the line, I couldn't do it. I couldn't go home either, because you and I, we . . ." She glances at Daniel, who nods, ". . . so I went to a church. I figured it was the best place to figure out what to do."

"And?" Daniel prompts, and Lynell sees pain in the way his cheeks fill with color.

"I stayed there all day. At some point, a priest approached me and asked if I was okay and I lost it. I couldn't stop crying long enough to tell him who I was or what I was doing, so he took me to this place for young girls like me run by nuns." Lynell stops talking to take a breath and turns away from Daniel. She walks across the room and runs her hands through her hair, remembering that first night in the house as if it was yesterday. "No one asked me questions," she says, her memories of being led to a room full of other girls and onto a cot with soft sheets and a thin pillow so vivid it was almost physical. "It was a halfway house managed by the nunnery. All the girls were either homeless or drug addicts or," she scoffs, "disgraced pregnant women." She turns, her eyes softening at the sight of him standing, arms at his side, drinking in her story. "They let me stay until I had Anna. I helped around the house, went grocery shopping, and went to church with them. I gave them a fake name and they only asked questions once, but I didn't want to tell them anything and they dropped it."

"You stayed there the whole time?"

She nods. "Almost eight months. After Anna was born, I stayed for a few more weeks to heal; it was a hard delivery. I felt safe there. Taken care of."

"What happened to—"

"Anna?" Lynell interrupts. Daniel nods.

"The nuns let me name her and say goodbye, but then they took her away. They already had a family lined up to take her. They told me she'd be safe."

Lynell stops, trapped in her memory.

"I'm sure she was. And still is," Daniel says. "So, no one but the nuns and the other girls in the house knows about Anna?"

Lynell shrugs, reluctantly remembering that the perceived safety of the nunnery was long past. "I went out a couple of times when I was obviously pregnant, so people could have seen me, I guess. But for all intents and purposes, yeah, only the nuns and a few of the girls. There were about fifteen of us during those last four months. But no one knew my real name. Oh, and the priest that took me there."

Daniel nods, resting his chin between his thumb and forefinger. "Okay, so . . ." he moves so his forehead is in his hand and takes a deep breath. "So, no one really knows that Lynell Mize—Lynell Carter," he corrects himself, and Lynell sucks in a breath. She hasn't heard that name in three years and didn't think she ever would again. "No one knows that you had a baby?" he asks, staring at the ceiling and crossing his arms.

Lynell shakes her head. "I don't think so." Despite the early hours of the morning, she hears horns honking outside and grits her teeth. She rubs her right hand up her left arm, trying to stave off anxiety.

"Closed adoption, right?"

Lynell nods and doesn't miss the fact that Daniel hasn't looked at her in a while. "Yeah. I don't know them; they don't know me."

"It'll be nearly impossible to track her down."

"And once we do, she's not legally ours anymore."

Daniel swallows. "Well, considering the circumstances, that seems like a good thing."

Lynell presses her fingernails into the palm of her hand and watches him breathe, willing him to look at her.

"We have to trust that she's safe for now," he says quietly, finally meeting her gaze. "That her identity is unknown. And until we are led to believe otherwise, let's assume she's not in immediate danger."

"We still need to find her," she says, begging Daniel to join her in her fear. But he takes a step forward and it's obvious he already has. Despite his calm tone, Daniel's hands are shaking, his eyes are wide, and his lips are quivering slightly.

"We have to pretend she doesn't exist," he says, and his voice finally breaks. "I want to find our daughter, but right now, the best we can do to keep her safe is pretend she doesn't exist. We can't tip off Eric in any way."

"Daniel." Lynell rushes toward him and throws her arms around his neck, carefully holding her left hand away to keep from aggravating the injuries. He drops his head into the crook between her neck and shoulder, shuddering out a jagged breath. His hands are rough against her back, but she missed the sensation so much she doesn't care.

"They won't find her," he says. "They can't find her."

———

She wakes up in the corner of the room, her head lying on her rolled-up shirt. Goosebumps travel up her arms and she drags Daniel's shirt, still wet but no longer cold, off and replaces it with her own.

"Daniel?" she says. She clears her throat and climbs to her feet. Light streams through the open windows and she squints as she steps forward. "Daniel?" she repeats, her chest feeling tight when there's no answer.

"Danny!" she yells, anxiety spiking and no longer caring if neighbors hear. She runs through the bedrooms and bathrooms, each one empty. She slaps the wall before dropping her forehead against it, teeth grinding together to keep from screaming. The house feels like it's melting around her, sticking to her skin and keeping her locked inside. She pushes off the wall, wipes her forehead and leaves the bedroom.

Muttering a curse under her breath, she strides for the still-splintered back door. She yanks it open and flinches when sunlight slaps her face and black spots disturb her vision. She closes her eyes and takes a moment to gather courage before heading into the backyard.

The gate opens when she's halfway across the yard. Her original instinct to run falls away when she sees Daniel closing the gate behind him, his shoulders slumped forward. He's wearing a large black T-shirt she doesn't recognize and holding a bag.

"Daniel, what the hell?" she hisses.

Daniel spins and frowns at her. He rushes forward and grabs her arm, pulling her back inside. "What are you doing?" he says.

When they close the door behind them, Lynell yanks her arm out of his grasp. "I woke up and you were gone! I didn't know where you were."

He sets the bag down and sighs. "You were asleep. I thought I'd be back before you woke up. It's just seven." Daniel leans down and fishes through the bag. He grabs a bottle of pills and hands them up to Lynell. "I went back to Alan's," he says.

"What?" She gasps. "Someone could've seen you. They could have people watching the house!"

"They didn't." Daniel holds up his hands and shrugs. "You needed pain-killers, and we need clothes and food. I didn't have any more money and the house is close, so I chanced it."

"You chanced it?"

"I watched the house for half an hour before I went in. No one saw me."

Lynell looks down at a bottle of pills, the pain maximizing now that she realizes there's a form of relief just moments away. She looks back to Daniel, who watches her with tired, glassy eyes. "You didn't sleep at all," she says.

He shakes his head. "I was keeping a lookout and trying to contact Zach and then at five-thirty, I decided I could pretend to be on a run and go back to the house. I'm sorry you woke up alone."

She stares at him through her eyelashes before sighing. "You need to sleep for a few hours. Teach me how to use the watch and I'll stay up."

"No, I'll—"

"Daniel Carter, if you don't sleep, then you'll pass out and be useless to me."

He laughs. "Fine." He picks up the bag and takes out four bottles of water, a bag of crackers, a can of beans, half a loaf of bread, an old apple, chips, two towels, one of Lynell's old T-shirts, and two sweaters, one of hers from high school and one of Alan's.

"How did you fit so much in that bag?" Lynell asks, squatting next to Daniel and grabbing the old T-shirt and shoes. The shirt is thin and gray with a badger on the front, her high school mascot. She remembers when they gave them out at school; she was so excited, up until Alan yelled at her for buying something she didn't need. He wouldn't listen to her explain it was free.

"Magic," Daniel says, wiggling his fingers in the air. Lynell grins, pushing her shoulder against his. She pulls off her dirty shirt and replaces it with the new one. It's stiff from years of sitting in a drawer but still feels much cleaner. Daniel hands her the apple and tells her to eat it. "I had one on the walk over," he says when she argues about him needing it too. Lynell concedes and sinks her teeth into the sweet fruit. She finishes the entire thing while Daniel walks her through using the watch to contact Zach. "Make sense?" he asks, fastening the watch onto her wrist.

She nods. "Yeah. Seems simple enough."

"If he replies, wake me up."

"Of course."

Daniel sighs and leans forward until their faces are an inch apart. Lynell stares at his eyes as they flick between hers and her mouth. "I love you," he whispers. She knows he's waiting for her to say it back. She wants to, she feels it, but no words escape. These words would give him hope for a future together.

But she can't give him that hope. She can't bear to think of a future with him. To imagine a life together. Because there is no future. Not for her. She'll be dead before the week is over. And even if she survives, how could she selfishly accept the love of this incredible man, when she took away his family? Anna deserves a father like Daniel. Daniel deserves a daughter and a family. Lynell doesn't deserve either.

"I know you love me, too," Daniel says, his hand cupping her cheek. She leans into it but keeps her eyes closed. "I want you to love me." His thumb rubs her cheekbone and her eyes burn. His lips meet hers and she relaxes them, moving into the kiss despite the shame and regret warring in her mind. When he pulls away, she opens her eyes and sees him still staring at her, lips tilted up in a hint of a smile. "You don't have to be afraid of this. Of us."

"I'm not," she says. "I haven't been in years."

He tilts his head. "Then what are you afraid of?"

She looks down and shrugs. "Everything else."

Daniel runs his hand through her hair, and he pulls her in for a hug. "It's okay. I am too." They embrace for several long minutes before Lynell pulls away.

"Sleep. I'll wake you up if anything happens."

Daniel nods and lies back, closing his eyes. Lynell drinks an entire bottle of water, downs as many pills as she's allowed and uses the bathroom twice. She sends messages to Zach through the watch every fifteen minutes and tries not to remember the past ten days, or really the past three years. She thinks about Anna and what she may look like now. What kind of life she may have. She wonders if her second birthday two months ago was fun. What kind of cake did she have? Did she smile and laugh? Can she talk yet? Lynell sits with her head against the wall, staring at the ceiling.

Lynell looks down at her watch to check the time. Almost one o'clock. Daniel's been asleep for a good five hours and there's still no word from Zach.

She thinks about her father's letter, reciting it quietly over and over, trying to decipher a code. She tries putting together the first letter of every word, then the first word of every sentence.

The watch buzzes.

Lynell jerks and stares down at the face of the watch.

It's flashing. Black. Red. White. Black. Red. White. Black. Red. White. With each flash, it buzzes. Lynell spins around, her heart thudding in her throat.

"Daniel!" she yells. He jumps, sitting up quickly and rushing to her side.

"What? Are you okay?" He reaches her with three long strides and grabs her shoulders, letting go when she winces.

"The watch," she says, holding up her hand. It continues flashing and buzzing, and Daniel grabs her wrist and hand, watching the pattern. "It just started," she explains.

Daniel stays quiet, eyes glued to the screen. It keeps going for a minute before it stays black.

"What—"

"Shh," Daniel cuts her off, never pulling his eyes from the watch. Then, after ten seconds of silence, it gives a high pitch ding and "5:00 p.m." flashes on the screen and instantly disappears. Daniel lets go of Lynell's arm and looks at her, a smile spreading across his face. "It's Zach," he says.

Lynell stares at him. "Are you sure?"

He nods. "Unless someone else figured out our code." He takes the watch off Lynell's wrist and pulls it on his own. "The three colors stand for location, safety, and success. Back in the day, it was more for fun, so the last color was just to communicate if the prank had been pulled off. White means yes, black means no. I'm not sure what he means in this situation, but I'm going to guess that he succeeded in helping us escape? Or maybe in killing Eric. I'm not sure, but it was white and that's encouraging."

"What about the black and red?" Lynell asks.

"We had a ton of potential meeting locations and we assigned a color to each one. Black is this little warehouse off Forney Street. It used to be a women's clothing store, but it closed about five years ago. I have no idea if it's still empty or not."

"How far away is it?"

Daniel frowns, eyebrows scrunching together in thought. "Probably twenty miles."

"We don't have a car."

"We can take the bus. Or I might remember how to hotwire a car." Lynell raises her eyebrows at him and Daniel shrugs. "Zach and I got into a lot of trouble. He hated his life with his dad and wanted to be the idiot he never got to be as a teenager and I—" Daniel clears his throat and stops talking. Lynell imagines he probably wanted to do anything, no matter how reckless, to get his mind off all he'd lost.

"Right, okay," Lynell says, saving him from having to finish the sentence. "So, that explains the black and white. What about the red? Doesn't sound good."

Daniel shakes his head. "It's not. Red is the most severe form of danger. We never used it. Back then it pretty much meant, 'Dad found out, he's pissed, we're both dead.' If he ever sent a red, it basically meant to stay away until Zach could calm down his dad. Now, it could mean anything. I think he's just trying to tell me it's dangerous. To be careful."

Lynell frowns. "Of course, it's dangerous. Does he think I don't know that?"

Daniel sighs and pulls Lynell against his chest. She falls silent and he rubs her back. "We'll be okay."

"At least he's alive," Lynell says, stepping out of Daniel's arms.

"He's alive," Daniel says. "And willing to help us."

They have a plan. A flimsy one that could go wrong in a dozen ways, as Lynell points out multiple times, but a plan nonetheless. They gather their stuff, pull on their shoes, and leave the house through the back door, taking the alley to the closest street. Lynell walks with her shoulders slumped forward and her head down, one hand in Daniel's. She holds the injured hand close to her chest, her broken fingers aching.

They follow the sidewalk for fifteen minutes before they get out of the neighborhood. Lynell's skin prickles, every single nerve on edge. Her hand sweats in Daniel's, and her head thuds with pain. The sun feels unnaturally hot, and each car that flies by makes her jump.

"Breathe," Daniel mutters, squeezing her hand.

She clenches her eyes shut and nods.

They keep walking. Past a dozen fast-food restaurants, three gas stations, a tattoo parlor, a grocery store, a convenience store, a laundromat, and a Registration office. Lynell flinches and almost turns to run the other way, but Daniel keeps his hold on her hand tight and pulls her quickly past it, talking loudly. "I mean, come on, Emily, you have to admit that your parents can be a bit overwhelming."

Lynell gives him a confused look, but he winks at her and squeezes her hand once. She gives him a weak smile and says, "Yeah, but only because they care, Mark." She emphasizes the name, remembering how prepared he'd been ten days ago.

Daniel responds, talking about an imaginary dinner with Sherri and Robert, Lynell's fake parents. He gives the story so much detail that he manages to pull her attention away from the Registration office now a block behind them. He's in the middle of describing how they should decorate "Little Jeremiah's" bedroom when he raises his hand and a taxi pulls up next to them.

They stop walking and Lynell's eyes go wide. She stares at him, and he turns to her and whispers, "It's okay. Stay calm and remember the plan."

Lynell nods and Daniel opens the back door of the cab. She climbs in first and Daniel follows.

"Where to?" the driver asks, turning back to look at them. Lynell watches his eyes flick down to her hand, up at her black eye, and over at Daniel, who's clean and unharmed. He frowns and Lynell shifts in her seat, wanting to scream that Daniel would never touch her, but instead she flicks her eyes away, putting both hands in her lap.

Daniel gives the driver the address, his voice rougher than it was only moments before. The driver hesitates before he turns forward and starts driving. Lynell closes her eyes and sucks in a breath. She counts to ten before letting it out, opening her eyes and turning to Daniel.

"You know I hate going to see your brother," she mutters under her breath.

Daniel shifts in his seat and looks out the window. "Yeah, Em. I know."

Lynell lets the silence settle for a moment and the driver reaches forward, turning the volume up a few notches. Spanish music with a quick beat fills the car, and she curls her right hand into a fist, nerves shaking.

"We never go see my sister," she says, raising her voice just enough so the driver can still hear them over the music. She sees him purse his lips and look through the side mirror before merging onto the highway.

Daniel takes an overdramatic breath and turns to her. For a moment she sees amusement in his face before he hardens his expression. "That's because your sister is certifiably insane."

"She's not." Lynell fights the urge to look back at the driver. They planned for a twenty-five-minute drive, so she has time to escalate the fake argument and watch for a reaction.

"She is. She's crazy. Everyone in your family is crazy," Daniel says.

Lynell wants to agree, feeling the truth of his statement in every wound on her body. Every scar that she continues to hide. Instead, she grits her teeth and says, "Well, I'm so sorry that you married into such a crazy family."

"I am too," he says, biting the end of his words.

Lynell glances forward and sees how the driver's shoulders tense. "It's not like you ever try, Mark. You could make an effort with them."

The irony in their fight is not lost on her. She could cry or laugh or scream. She lets the emotions fester, needing the conversation to sound as real as possible. Daniel doesn't reply immediately, and the song changes. Lynell focuses on the piano and violin before Daniel finally replies.

"You want me to make an effort? Fine. I bet your sister would love me to make more of an effort."

"What's that supposed to mean?" Lynell slightly raises her voice. The clock shows they've been in the car for nearly ten minutes but the way her back aches and hands shake, it seems like an hour.

"You know what it means. Your sister has been dying to get with me since we got married. Is that what you want? For me to screw your sister?"

The argument is escalating too quickly and Lynell raises her eyebrows at Daniel. There's a quick smirk that instantly turns into a frown while Daniel glances ahead at the driver, as if prompting her to respond so the driver doesn't get suspicious.

"This again, Mark? You can't threaten to sleep with my sister every time we get in an argument."

"Then stop complaining about my family when yours is insane!" Daniel flinches at his own words and admiration for him swells in Lynell's chest. She can see how much he hates what he's saying, even if it's fake, in the way his eyes blink and flick from side to side, not wanting to land on Lynell's for too long.

"Go ahead and do it. See if I care. It's not like I can't do the exact same. I bet your brother would love a piece of this."

Daniel's lips tighten like he's fighting a smile. It's a moment before he's able to respond. "Well, then it's a good thing we're heading there right now, isn't it?"

"Yeah. Maybe you don't even have to come in. You want me to spend time with him so much? Just stay in the cab. Give us a good three minutes. If he's anything like you, we won't need much longer."

Daniel's eyes widen and he drops his face into his hands. He's completely silent but the way his back shakes, Lynell can tell he's laughing. Finally, he lifts his face again and it's so red, Lynell wants to let out her own laugh.

When he speaks, he sounds so angry she might have been convinced he was never laughing if he didn't finish the sentence with a wink.

"Oh, that's rich, Emily. Three minutes is all it'll take for him to decide he doesn't want crazy."

The argument continues, steadily getting louder until the taxi exits and takes two turns. They've been in the car for twenty-two minutes, and Daniel reaches over and grabs her knee in the middle of saying, "And don't get me started on last Thanksgiving. Who tries to microwave a turkey?"

Wrap up, the squeeze to her leg says. She nods and yells, "At least my mom can make a turkey! Yours just knows how to make weak men who can't satisfy a woman!"

A flash of amusement in his eyes before he throws his hands in the air. "I'm done, Emily! I can't stand being married to someone so crazy!"

"Then leave!"

"Oh, just jump out of a moving car?"

"Please, be my guest! I won't stop you."

"Fine. You know what? Fine. Sir." Daniel leans forward between the seats, and the driver, who has steadily looked more and more uncomfortable, flinches away from him. "Please pull over. I can't stand being in the car with someone so insane one minute longer."

"Sorry, we aren't at your destination yet," the driver says, glancing between Daniel and the road.

"I don't care! Stop the car and let him out," Lynell shouts.

"Please, for the love of the Registration, stop this car before I lose it!" Daniel yells. The driver jumps, and Lynell feels bad, even though this was their only choice.

"I don't think I can just stop here," the driver says, though the car starts to slow down.

"He needs to get out now . . . or he may get violent," Lynell says, hating every syllable as it leaves her mouth. "Please, just stop the car."

He does, and Daniel huffs and says "Have a good life," before climbing out of the car. He starts walking away and Lynell pauses, pivoting back to the driver.

"Are you okay?" he asks, turning in his seat.

Lynell frowns, wishing she could pull tears to the surface. "I . . ." she mutters. The driver's face is full of concern. "I'm sorry, I can't." She gets out of the car, chasing after Daniel. The cabbie hollers after her, clearly angry about not being paid.

"Mark!" she screams. "Mark, wait!" She runs without looking back at the car. The driver shouts again and honks the horn. Daniel quickens his pace and when Lynell reaches him, she tugs at his arm, struggling to keep up. "Mark, let's talk about this!"

"There's nothing to talk about. I'm done!" He turns so they head down a side street away from the cab. He chances a look back before adding, "I can't believe you."

"Mark, please," Lynell says, trying to make it sound like a sob. The driver calls for them to stop once more before giving up and speeding away. Lynell and Daniel turn down another street and look back, verifying that the taxi has left.

"I think we did it," Lynell mutters.

Daniel grabs her hand and pulls her forward and between two buildings. A few minutes later, they stop talking and he pulls her into a hug. "I hated that," he mutters.

"Me too," Lynell says, her voice muffled against his chest.

He lets her go and she steps back, their eyes meeting for a moment before they both start laughing.

"Microwaving a turkey?" Lynell gasps between laughs.

"Three minutes? Harsh!"

She shrugs. "At least we aren't Mark and Emily. They sound like they have major problems."

"Oh, yeah." He chuckles. "Like we don't have any." The mood sobers, and Daniel locks their hands together, looking at his watch. "It's almost four o'clock. The warehouse is still about a fifteen-minute walk. We better get going."

Lynell nods and Daniel turns, but she tugs on his hand. "Wait." He looks back at her, eyebrows raised in question before she stands on her toes and captures his lips in a deep kiss. She pulls away and breathlessly says, "I'd rather have Daniel Carter than Mark any day." She gives him another quick kiss before standing back. "Lead the way, Mr. Longer-Than-Three-Minutes."

Daniel smiles and adjusts the bag on his shoulder before starting the walk.

"No one knows about the warehouse except Zach and I," he says. "We picked it at random and only met there once."

Lynell nods, trying to ride the high for as long as she can before feeling it fall away into fear, anxiety, and pain. They stop once for Daniel to fish out two pills and a water bottle, which they split. It's 4:20 when Daniel stops walking. Lynell looks up at the large building across the street. It appears empty and abandoned, with only two cars out front, one of which has no tires.

"Let's stay here and watch," Daniel says.

They sit against the graffiti-covered wall of a closed gas station across from the warehouse. The overhanging ceiling and multiple old gas stalls, one of them with an old, vandalized car sitting next to it, keeps them hidden from any prying eyes. The wall reads, "BLEED THE REGISTRATION," which makes Lynell scoff. It's not the most creative phrase, but common for graffiti. She'd never given it much thought before, knowing it would be painted over within hours, but now she wonders about the artists. Did they fight with Daniel? If they knew who she was, would they hate her as much as Eric? Would she want them to or would she actually join them in their rebellion?

For the first time in her life, she's not sure which side she's on.

There's more graffiti on the abandoned car: "REGISTER THE ELYSIANS," accompanied with an image of Eric being hung by the neck. A month ago, she would've thought it was good that Elysians couldn't be Registered, that they deserved protection from rebels who threatened their power.

Now, everything has changed. Through no fault of her own, the Registration has turned against her. It's personal. A threat. Unjust.

Almost twenty minutes pass in silence before Daniel sits up quickly. Lynell follows his gaze to the warehouse across the street to see a black car driving in. She pulls her knees to her chest and tries to hide in the shadows.

"It's Zach!" Daniel says. He starts to run out of their hiding place before Lynell reaches up and grabs his hand.

"Lynell, it's Zach."

Lynell pulls him down and shakes her head. "Look."

The doors of the car open, and Eric Elysian steps out into the sunlight.

Eric is walking with a cane now, probably courtesy of Zach's bullet. Two guards get out of the car and flank him, guns held across their chests. They survey the area, never more than three steps away from Eric.

"Lynell," Daniel hisses in her ear. His impatient tone tells her it's not the first time he's tried to get her attention. "Lynell." He whispers her name so quietly it lingers with the wind.

She turns to look at him, her eyes wide, and her lips parted in dull shock. Each breath she takes sounds like a bullhorn in her ears.

"Eric..."

Daniel nods, his eyes growing wider. He covers her mouth with his hand and holds a finger to his lips. "We need to go," he whispers.

Lynell shakes her head with Daniel's hand still clamped over her mouth.

"Yes," he says.

She closes her eyes and takes a quiet breath through her nose. She repeats this two more times until her mind feels free from the dense fog that rolled in with Eric's car. She reaches up and pulls Daniel's hand away from her mouth.

"He'll never stop," she whispers.

Daniel narrows his eyes and turns back to look at Eric across the street. Lynell follows his gaze and watches Eric pace in front of the warehouse, looking around corners and leaning heavily on the cane. Soon, they'll move to the areas around the warehouse and that'll mean the gas station currently acting as Lynell and Daniel's refuge.

She's basically dead already.

But Daniel doesn't have to be.

"Lynell, let's go," Daniel whispers, grabbing her arm again.

"He'll find me," she says, voice still low, "no matter where I go."

Realization dawns and Daniel's eyes widen. He shakes his head. "Lyn, no."

"I'm as good as dead. You don't have to die, too."

"Baby, please."

Lynell's eyes water and her lips tremble. "Find Anna."

"Lyn," Daniel hisses as Lynell stands up, face emerging from the shadows of the gas station.

She glares, watching as Eric taps his cane on the ground impatiently. Daniel grabs her wrist. She glances back at him, taking the moment to memorize every feature of his face. The way his dark hair refuses to all go in one direction. The way the outer edges of his blue eyes fade to gray and how the skin underneath is almost a permanent shadow, evidence of his selfless, busy way of life. His long chin, and the small mole hiding under his jaw.

The wrinkles on the corners of his mouth, proving to the world that Daniel Carter loves to smile.

Lynell feels her entire body ache with love. She leans down and gives him a quick kiss.

"I love you," she says.

When she pulls away, she can see the fear edged in the corner of Daniel's eyes. The way his grip on her wrist tightens and his head shakes ever so slightly. The words, the ones she hasn't said in three years, hang in the air between them. An unfair proclamation for her to make after all that's happened, all she's done. And especially knowing what she's about to do.

She looks away, swallowing the lump in her throat. Daniel stands and places his hands on the side of her face, forcing her to look at him.

"We can figure this out, baby." His breathing is ragged. "You don't need to do this."

Lynell reaches up and pulls his hands off her face. "I do. Because I love you. More than life itself." She turns and pulls out of his grasp, stepping into sight of Eric.

"Don't," Daniel says. This time his voice is hard and makes Lynell pause. "Lynell, don't leave me again."

Those words cut her open and she gasps, turning around.

"Not again," he says.

Guilt catches her. Is he right? Is she making yet another bad choice? Is she willing to surrender to Eric because she doesn't have the strength to fight? For the briefest moment, she feels strong enough to face anything as long as Daniel is by her side.

She nods. "Okay," she says, stepping toward him. Relief spreads across his face but is quickly replaced with fear. She turns around, and her heart sinks when she sees Eric looking back at them.

It's too late. He's seen them.

Lynell whirls back to Daniel to see him staring between her, Eric, and the guards walking toward them, eyes wide.

"Run, Daniel. Now. Find Anna."

He shakes his head.

"Run!" she screams. Daniel looks past her, and Lynell follows his gaze. The guards are running now, holding their guns out. "They'll shoot you. I'm sorry, Danny. Run, please!"

The first gunshot rings in the air and both Daniel and Lynell drop to the ground. Lynell covers her head. When she looks up next, the guards are only a couple hundred feet away, and Daniel is still standing behind her, refusing to run.

The man on the right raises his gun and points it right at Daniel. Lynell can see his finger on the trigger and knows he won't miss. She's about to scream, to turn and push Daniel or jump in front of him, when the shot echoes in the air, followed by a loud crash and a shriek.

Lynell reaches for Daniel, gaze fixed on the large black car that just crashed right into the guard.

Zachary Elysian is leaning out the window.

"Get in."

DAY 11 ————————————————————○

Anna didn't cry when she was born. Lynell was scared she was dead. Really, the umbilical cord was wrapped around her throat. When they untangled it, Anna let out a loud and beautiful scream. Lynell smiled, then passed out, dreaming about returning home to Daniel.

When she awoke, Mother Adella let her see Anna. Lynell cried when she held Anna, who slept soundly, wrapped in a soft gray blanket.

"I change my mind," Lynell had said, looking down at Anna's soft, perfect face. "I want to keep her."

"I'm so sorry," Mother Adella said, reaching down for Anna.

"No!" Lynell yelled. Anna stirred and whined but didn't wake up. "She's my baby. Mine. I want to keep her. I want to be a family. Please, let me be a family. Let me be a family."

But Mother Adella took Anna away.

———————

The clunky black clock on the nightstand flashes "1:42 a.m." in bright green numbers. Lynell turns to look at Daniel lying next to her. The sheets pull against her shoulder as she reaches up to hold a hand over his face, feeling each puff of hot breath. His eyes move under his lids, lost in a dream.

Satisfied that he's still alive, Lynell climbs off the bed, draping the covers back as she does. The floorboards creak under her feet, and she holds her breath, moving on her tiptoes until she's out of the room and the door is shut behind her.

"Can't sleep?" Zach asks from his seat at the kitchen table. He wraps his hands around a mug and lifts it to his lips.

She shrugs and sits next to him. "Don't know if I ever will again."

"Want some warm milk?" he asks, gesturing to the mug.

Lynell grimaces. "Sounds disgusting."

"It's supposed to help you sleep."

Lynell shakes her head and leans back in the chair. She stretches her legs and closes her eyes. She can still feel Daniel's blood on her hand as she held pressure on the injury in his shoulder where the bullet had grazed him. A superficial flesh wound, painful but not life threatening. Knowing that did nothing to ease the terror in Lynell's chest. His moans of pain as Zach sped through the streets still ring in her ears.

The silence stretches on, and Lynell opens her eyes. She quirks an eyebrow at Zach, watching the way his eyes take in every exposed bruise and bandaged part of her body. Her skin flushes and she clears her throat, wishing she hadn't left the small bedroom behind.

"Look, I—"

"Where are we?" she interrupts.

Zach closes his mouth and drops his head into his hands, letting out a deep breath. "Some old lady's apartment. A boarding school buddy's grandmother. Dad doesn't know about it. Doesn't even know we were friends, much less that I know about his dead grandma's empty apartment. We're safe here."

She scoffs. "And I'm supposed to blindly trust you after everything that's happened?" She grits her teeth, forcing down the memory and fear.

"Not blindly, but we don't have many other options." His voice is breathy, revealing his exhaustion. There are several cuts on his face, one on his eyebrow, one at the corner of his eyes, and another splitting his lip.

She stands, kicking the chair as she does. Despite her anger, Lynell remembers Zach's own fear. She hears him tell her to choose good and knows that he's finally following his own advice. "I want to hate you," she says, meeting his eyes. "I want to blame you. But I can't. And that pisses me off."

He stares at her for a moment before standing up and crossing the kitchen. He opens one of the cupboards and pulls out a plain black mug with a chipped handle.

"What are you doing?"

Zach ignores her and fills the mug with water before putting it in the microwave. He stands with his back to her, hands on the counter and head hanging forward. The sounds of the microwave whirring grates on Lynell's nerves and when the countdown reaches one, Zach opens it before it can ding. He sinks a tea bag in the steaming water and hands it to Lynell. Avoiding her eyes, Zach stretches his fingers before pulling up his shirt.

Lynell gasps.

There's a large bandage covering his torso beneath his ribs with blood seeping through. A bruise blossoms from beneath the bandage and wraps around as if creeping along his skin to his back.

"What . . ." She trails off when Zach lifts the shirt up more and turns so she can see his back. She counts seven long cuts crisscrossing his back before he lowers the shirt.

"What happened?"

He returns to his seat at the table. "I shot my dad. He didn't like that."

Lynell follows suit, sitting across from him. "I wasn't sure you'd escape."

"I didn't," Zach says, looking up with a small grin. "I was so close. Just made it to the side entrance. I was going to take you guys out that way. Some of the guards over there hate my dad and always let me do what I want. It's easy to get mistreated men on your side with a little kindness." He sighs, pulling a hand down his face. "Unfortunately, the loyal brutes caught me."

"And didn't kill you?"

"Dad told them not to. I have no idea why. He probably knew I'd be able to get in touch with you."

Lynell sits back, crossing her arms. "Which you did. You set us up."

He shakes his head and shifts in his seat, reaching out to grab his mug of warm milk. "I didn't. Or . . . I didn't mean to. I was in a cell in the dungeons until yesterday morning. Reggie was given freedom to punish me. He was in the middle of getting creative," he says, gesturing to his side where the large bandage was. Lynell flinches, trying not to envision Zach strapped to a table with a rat under a bowl above his hip. "He'd just started when . . ." Zach clears his throat and takes a long sip of his drink. "Then my father came down." He takes a deep breath and Lynell holds her mug close, so the steam dampens her skin. "He took me to his room, and we were in there when my watch started dinging and flashing."

Lynell grimaces and Zach nods.

"I knew it was Daniel and somehow, Dad did too. Maybe he caught on to how he and I communicated back in the day." He shrugs, tapping the side of his mug. "Anyway, he planned to use the watch to find you, whether I helped him or not."

"So, you just told him?"

"Lynell—"

"You did. You set us up!"

"No! I mean . . . Yes." Zach holds his hands up, as if submitting to her accusation. "I just told him the colors meant the location. I didn't tell him about the danger or mission success colors."

"Oh, thank you. That makes it so much better," Lynell says, voice dripping with sarcasm.

"I knew that Daniel would put the success and danger colors together and realize something was wrong. I was hoping he would get what I meant, that the success was dangerous. Dad's success is dangerous."

Lynell gapes at him. "What?"

"Well, he got it, didn't he? He didn't go all the way to the warehouse. He must've known."

Lynell shakes her head. "No, he just thought we should wait to watch for a while, to make sure it wasn't a trap."

"My point. You didn't get caught."

"We were about to."

"I know. I should have gotten there sooner, I meant to get there hours before you, but escaping was more difficult than I'd anticipated. Thankfully, I've gotten some of the guards on my side over the years. They practically drool over the opportunity to follow someone other than Dad." He takes another deep breath and runs his finger over the edge of his mug. "I really am sorry. I got there as soon as I could."

"Yeah, well . . . Daniel still got shot," Lynell says. Guilt washes through her, reminding her that she's the reason he was there and she's the reason the guards saw them. Not Zach.

"I know, and I'm so thankful it wasn't worse."

The moment stretches on, and Lynell drops her head next to the mug.

"How did we get here?" she asks, voice muffled.

Zach sighs. "Eric."

Lynell senses more in that one word and looks up, startled to see Zach's eyes now bright red. "Why do you obey him?"

He fingers the handle of his mug, looking into it while he speaks. "For a while, it was blind loyalty and faith in the Registration. I believe in the Registration, so I thought that meant I believed in my dad, too. After I was able to separate the two, I only obeyed him out of fear. Then, when I got older and showed signs of not caring what he did to me if I didn't obey, he threatened my mom."

"Your mom? I thought . . ."

"I didn't know her for most of my life," he says, returning his gaze to Lynell. "I found her about five years ago. I tried to keep our relationship a secret, but of course, Dad eventually found out. I wasn't allowed to see her anymore. I thought as long as I left her alone, she'd be safe." A new surge of empathy for her cousin fills Lynell's chest.

"I hadn't seen her in about a year. Until I couldn't take it anymore. I was done with my father. Done with the Elysian name." He pauses and takes a deep breath. "And Daniel started to make me question the Registration, too."

"Really?"

"You must know what he thinks. That the Registration is barbaric and no different from cold-blooded murder. I didn't know what to believe and needed some space to think. So, I left to find my mom again."

Lynell takes a swig of her tea, savoring the heat.

"But he found me," Zach continues. "I'd never seen him angrier. He threatened to have her Registered if I didn't come home and obey him. I didn't want to be the cause of another death. I didn't want my mom to die. And so I've been at his fucking service ever since. That is, until I—"

"Saved me," Lynell finishes.

He nods. "One night I told Danny all about the secret heir. I knew he was your ex. That's actually . . . originally, that's why I befriended him. It was an order. But I swear, it didn't stay that way. I care for him, deeply. I wanted to protect him. I thought if I could be certain he didn't love you anymore, it would be okay. I wouldn't have to feel any guilt about what happened to you. So, I asked him what I should do. Should I find you myself, or leave it up to the others?" Zach glances at the bedroom door, smiling. "He told me to do what I thought was good. To choose good."

Choose good.

The words that kept her going. The words that made her make up her mind. Those words were Daniel's. She should have known.

"It wasn't until the day before the Registration that I told him the entire truth. Why our friendship started. That it was you I was going to Register," Zach says. "I don't know why I did." He shakes his head. "That's a lie. I did it because I knew he cared, and I felt guilty. I didn't want to hurt him. I didn't want to hurt you. He begged me not to do it, and I realized that you were a danger to my best friend. If Dad knew Daniel still cared for you like that, Dad would have him taken to get all the information he could."

Zach wipes a hand under his nose. He clears his throat and stands to clean the mug in the sink. Lynell has to lean forward to hear him as he keeps talking, his words muffled against the running water. "I told him my plan was to get you here and get the code as quickly and painlessly as possible.

They'd never know your estranged ex still loved you." He turns and sets the mug on the counter, looking at Lynell with heavy eyes. "That obviously didn't work, and I couldn't stand watching what was happening to you. Dad said it was me or Reggie, and I didn't want to hurt you, I swear, Lynell. But Reggie would have been way worse. I know that's hard to understand, but you have to believe me. When I realized I'd made a mistake bringing you home at all, I snapped out of it. I decided it didn't matter what would happen, I needed to get you out. You can't give him the letter. You can't let him have the code."

Choose good.

Lynell believes him.

Trusts him.

Maybe trusting him will be the dumbest thing she's ever done. But she sees the truth in the way his voice shakes and the proof he took a stand against his father in the many wounds covering his body.

She doesn't think she and Daniel can do this alone. Survive, keep Anna safe, figure out the code, know what to do with it.

They need Zach.

More than that, she wants Zach on their side.

"Maybe he will screw up and end the Registration," Lynell says.

"I doubt it. But if he did, it would be in the worst way possible. I'm not sold that ending the Registration is the smartest thing to do but if that's what we decide, then we have to do it the right way. We have to prepare the country and work with the oligarchs to have new laws in place. It will take time to make sure there is as little fallout as possible," Zach says.

His words convince Lynell that they need him. She has no idea what she's doing. But her cousin has grown up in this world. He knows the intricate details of the Registration. He has connections and a voice. Zach has power.

Lynell sits up straighter, strength seeping into her bones at the prospect of finally making a decision and taking action. For better or worse. "So, how do we do this?"

Relief visibly washes over Zach. He returns the clean and dry mug to the cupboard. "First, we keep you alive for the next four days," he says, sitting next to Lynell. "You're the real heir. The only one left."

Lynell drags her nails along the back of her thumb. "Actually . . ."

He turns to look at her, eyebrows raised. "What?"

"Danny and I . . . we have a daughter."

Hours later, feeling hungover, Lynell wakes up next to Daniel. "Good morning," he says, kissing the side of her forehead.

The bandage on his shoulder is tinged red. She reaches over to touch the corner and Daniel grabs her wrist, pulling it to his lips so he can press a kiss to her palm. "I'm okay," he says. She knows he's right and it could have been much worse. Daniel leans down to kiss her slowly before climbing off the bed. "Actually, I'm great! You said you loved me yesterday," he says.

Lynell can hear the smile in his voice, and she rolls over to sit up. He gives her a self-satisfied smirk and a blush rises to her cheeks.

"Right before you tried to get us killed, but still."

"Hey, I told you to run," Lynell says, head jerking up. Daniel laughs.

"How you thought I was going to leave you after all this is beyond me."

She stands and steps closer so she's standing behind him. She wraps her hand around his uninjured shoulder and kisses his back. "How are you feeling?"

"Honestly?" He folds his hand over hers. "Sore and like I could use some more pain killers. But mostly just badass."

Lynell laughs and circles him so they're standing face to face. She gazes up at his lined and tanned face. "My brave badass."

"Who's only alive because Zach hit my would-be-murderer with a car just as he pulled the trigger."

She grabs the back of his neck and stands on her toes to give him a chaste kiss. "Thank you for staying alive."

"What's my other option? I can't leave you. I don't think you'd make it a single day, let alone four more."

"Hey!" Lynell hits his chest softly. "I can take care of myself."

"I know, I know," Daniel says, pulling her in for a hug.

"I can . . ." And quieter, she says, "But that doesn't mean I want to."

"Doesn't mean you have to," Daniel replies before letting her go and stepping back. "Now let's go get some breakfast, I'm starving."

Once again, Zach is awake and sitting at the table, nursing a mug of steaming coffee this time. "Hey," he says. "I made oatmeal. And there's coffee."

Daniel makes his way to the counter, dropping a generous amount of food into a bowl.

"It's a mark of how hungry I am that I'm willingly eating something you cooked," he says.

Zach rolls his eyes. "Don't pretend you don't like my cooking. If I remember correctly, almost all our pranks involved me making cookies or brownies for no apparent reason except you're a gluttonous pig."

Daniel turns and throws a raisin at Zach, who laughs and easily dodges it.

Daniel sets his bowl on the table before filling up another. "So, what's our plan?" he asks, giving Lynell the second plate.

"Lynell told me about Anna," Zach says. Lynell tenses as Daniel's fork clatters to the plate.

"Lyn, why would you—"

"I know I don't deserve your trust, but your secret is safe with me, Daniel," Zach says, hurt visible in his face. "I don't know how Dad doesn't know about Anna, but—"

"I never told anyone," Lynell interrupts. "And she doesn't exist in the system."

"Everyone exists in the system," Zach answers. "Her parentage may just say unknown."

"So, how do we find her?" Daniel asks, eyeing Zach with a tinge of suspicion while reaching over to lay a hand on Lynell's thigh.

Zach shakes his head. "We don't. It's too dangerous. Right now, as long as nobody knows about her, she's safe. If we make a move to find her, alarm bells will go off."

"Then what do we do?" Lynell asks, frustration and fear tingling under her skin. Daniel gives her thigh a little squeeze.

Zach blows out a determined breath before saying, "We plan for the worst."

"Which is?"

"Dad finds Anna and somehow gets the code," Zach says. "He figures out how to use the code just for himself and henceforth can literally do whatever he wants without consequence."

"Like he doesn't already," Daniel mutters under his breath.

Zach gives him a short look that Daniel ignores. Lynell can see the hours of friendship that built this easy rapport between the two men.

"It can get much worse, Danny," Zach says.

"Only if he actually has the code," Lynell says.

Daniel taps his fingers on the edge of the table, looking from Zach to Lynell. "Does someone want to explain the code to me?"

Lynell meets Zach's eyes. "You do it. I barely understand."

Zach agrees and starts explaining.

Daniel asks many of the same questions Lynell did, and she does her best to help Zach answer them. By the time they've finished, all their bowls are empty.

"If it can end the Registration, let's just figure it out now and do it before Eric finds us," Daniel says.

Zach narrows his eyes. "Just," he snaps his fingers, "end the very thing keeping our country together and fuck the consequences?"

"Zach, the Registration is not keeping our country together. It's slowly killing us." Daniel shakes his head, as if talking to an ignorant child.

"No, we were dying before this," Zach responds calmly, but he rubs his brow as if to ward off a headache. Lynell shifts in her seat, watching as her cousin and husband toe the dangerous line between disagreeing and fighting. "Remember the civil war? And before that, citizens having no semblance of power?"

"And a system that turns half of our citizens into murderers and the other half into victims?" Daniel says, bitter mockery filling each word.

"At least we don't have an immigrant problem anymore," Zach says.

Daniel scoffs. "Because no one wants to live here."

"Maybe we could make some changes to fix that. Maybe if people could get a Registration as an adult then—"

"Then people will move here just so they can kill whoever pisses them off," Daniel says. "There are other ways to resolve conflict. And better ways to attract foreigners to come live and work here."

"The majority of Registrations are not murder. They're ending pregnancies, finding justice when the system fails, helping someone in constant pain leave this world on their own terms or even Registering yourself so your family can get your life insurance."

"But what about the ones made for selfish, greedy, and vengeful reasons?" Daniel says, leaning forward.

"That's each person's right."

"So it was your right to Register my wife?" Daniel says, each word clipped.

Zach freezes. Lynell feels a cold chill pass over them.

Lynell grabs Daniel's good shoulder and pulls him back. "We're not debating the moral ambiguity of the Registration right now," she says. Daniel opens his mouth, but she cuts him off before he can say anything else. "We're not. We don't have to decide what to do with the code right now. All we have to decide is whether Eric should have it."

"Absolutely not," Daniel says without wasting a second.

Zach nods. "On that, we agree."

"Right now, no one has it," she says. "I know the letter by heart but have no idea what the code could be."

"We need to figure it out," Zach says. "We should be the ones to decipher it."

Daniel looks to Zach, as if trying to read what he's not saying in the set of his jaw and distance in his eyes. "I love you, Zach," Daniel says. "But you're still Eric's son. I'm not sure the code is safer in your hands than in his."

"Danny!" Lynell exclaims, head whipping in his direction. "Zach is not his father." She turns her attention back to her cousin and a sympathetic ache fills her chest at the look of betrayal in his eyes. "You're not your father."

Zach blinks and clears his throat. "He has a point. I am an Elysian."

"So am I."

"No you're not," Daniel says. His mouth is still pressed into an angry frown, and Lynell scowls at him.

"Yes, I am. Just because you don't like it, doesn't make it not true."

Daniel flicks his eyes away from Lynell. She sees the familiar war in his face. The one between kindness and anger. As always, kindness wins.

His shoulders relax and his face softens. "I'm sorry, Zach," Daniels says. "I know you're not your dad. But . . . the idea that anyone could control the Registration and make it even worse makes me want to scream."

"You may not believe me, but it makes me want to scream too," Zach says. "I don't want to help you decipher the code because I want to use it. I want to help because it's Lynell's to know. And because someone once told me to choose good."

His shoulders relax and his face softens.

Lynell wanted to get straight into code-breaking mode but Zach insisted that just in case they needed to run without warning, they should be prepared. So, he gave Daniel directions to a strip mall to get hair dye, clothing, food, and a burner phone.

"Why do we need a burner phone?" Lynell had asked.

"I have a buddy still working for my dad. We can trust him, I promise. I'll tell him to call if he hears anything suspicious."

"Suspicious?" Daniel asked.

"Say my father finds out about Anna. I'd just like him to be able to contact me if needed."

"In that case, I should call Mother Adella and ask her to tell us if anyone comes asking about me or Anna," Lynell said. At the men's confused looks, she adds, "Mother Adella was the head nun at the halfway house. I know I can trust her and if I ask her to, she'll call us to give us a heads-up."

So, they wrote a list of what to get, and Daniel, being the least recognizable of them, left to buy it all.

"Not too short!" Lynell says, dodging the scissors Zach extends as he cuts her hair. "I don't want to look like a little boy."

"If a haircut makes you look like a little boy, then you have more to worry about."

Lynell gives Zach a filthy look.

He chuckles and pulls her back into the chair. He makes quick work of snipping a few inches off her dark brown hair. When he's done, they switch places, and Lynell trims the sides of his hair as close to the scalp as she can get it without a razor.

"We'll have to shower after we dye our hair," Zach says, brushing pieces of hair off his shoulders. "Let's go raid the closet while we wait to see if we can find anything that will fit you."

Lynell follows Zach out of the bathroom and to the bedroom she and Daniel used the night before. "Wasn't this an old lady's home?"

"What? Scared you're going to look like a grandma *and* a little boy?" he teases. Lynell shoves him gently, aware of his many wounds.

"Was the woman married? Maybe you can find some nice old-man suspenders to go with that old-man scowl you love to wear."

"Ouch," Zach says, flipping on the bedroom light and turning to Lynell. He raises his eyebrows in delight. "Clever. You really do have the Elysian charm, don't you?"

"I don't think 'charm' is the right word." Lynell passes Zach and opens the door on the other side of the room. She's hit by the smell of mothballs and lingering perfumed detergent. A quick survey of the closet shows that either the old lady lived alone, or she lived with someone with the exact same clothing taste as her.

"Lynell, this is *so* your color!" Zach pulls a bright yellow dress from the far end of the closet, holding it against Lynell's body. She looks down, scowling at the putrid green design covering the top half of the dress.

"I think that fits your style more," she says, shoving the dress away. Zach laughs again and continues pulling out the ugliest clothes he can find. It doesn't take long for Lynell to break and start laughing, enjoying a fleeting moment of humor and joy with her cousin.

They find a pair of black slacks, a gray sundress, and several simple shirts that fit Lynell and make her go unnoticed in a crowd. The rest they shove back into the closet just as there's a knock at the front door.

Lynell rushes to open it, but before she can, Zach grabs her wrist.

"What are you—" she starts, but he holds a finger over his lips, and she falls silent.

There's another knock, followed by three quick ones, and then two more five seconds apart. Zach smiles and unlocks the door.

"Hey," Daniel says, walking through. He drops the bags and accepts Lynell's gentle hug with a muffled grunt of pain. "I was only gone an hour," he says, chuckling. Zach closes the door behind him and locks it before grabbing the bags.

"I know," Lynell mutters, letting him go. Daniel touches her hair, now shoulder-length, and she's about to ask if he likes it when Zach starts unloading the bags and calls them over.

He piles the clothes on a chair next to the table and fishes out the phone. "I'll call Jeremy first." He walks to the living room but is still close enough for them to listen while he speaks into the phone. Lynell notices Daniel staring at Zach, and she knows he's listening for any sign of Zach betraying their confidence.

Zach returns quickly and passes the phone to Lynell. "Do you have the number?" he asks.

Lynell nods. "The nuns made us memorize it." She'll never forget that number. She dials and holds the phone to her ear, biting her top lip as it rings three times before a woman answers.

"New Creations Home, Tammy Carranza speaking."

Lynell doesn't know a Tammy Carranza and assumes the woman must be new. "Hello. This is . . ." Lynell clears her throat and turns away from Zach and Daniel. "Rachel Doe. I was a resident two years ago. Is Mother Adella there? I need to speak with her."

There's a short pause before Tammy Carranza says, "Yes, of course. One moment, Miss Doe." Lynell hears some rustling and then the sound of someone walking. A door creaks open and everything becomes muffled, as if Tammy is holding her hand over the phone. Lynell thinks she hears voices, but she can't make out what is being said. Then, Tammy's voice becomes clear again. "Here's Mother Adella, Miss Doe."

"Hello?" Lynell instantly relaxes at the familiar voice. It's rough and low, as if from years of smoking, but simultaneously soft, like a grandmother speaking to a granddaughter.

"Mother Adella. It's Rachel Doe."

"Rachel, darling. How are you?"

Lynell shifts between her feet. "Uhm, okay." She shakes her head. "Actually, I'm not great."

"I'm sorry to hear that."

Lynell smiles softly. Anyone else may be saying that as a pleasantry, but Lynell knows Mother Adella is genuine. "I'll be okay. I'm calling because . . ." her voice cracks and a hand rests on her shoulder. Lynell looks up to see Daniel standing next to her, giving her a supportive nod. It's all she needs. "I have reason to believe someone is looking for Anna. I know you're not supposed to tell me anything about her, but I'm worried she's in danger."

"Honey, I would never give out confidential information."

"I know. But this person . . . he's dangerous. And he has ways of getting what he wants. I'm just asking that you'll call me at this number if anyone comes asking about Anna."

"Rachel . . ."

"Please, Mother Adella. I wouldn't ask if it wasn't important. I'm not asking you to tell me where she is. Just to let me know if anyone asks about her."

Silence answers her, and Lynell reaches up to grab Daniel's hand. Their fingers interlock, and Lynell closes her eyes while waiting for a response. When it finally comes, her entire body relaxes, and Daniel pulls her to him, kissing the side of her head.

"Of course. I'll call you."

"And can you do me one more favor?"

"What sort of favor?"

"Can you contact . . . Anna's parents?" She almost says *adopted* parents but swallows the words. Whoever they are, these people are Anna's parents. "And warn them that someone may be looking for her? Just tell them to be careful and not talk about where Anna came from."

"That's an odd request, Rachel. What's going on? Are you in some sort of danger?"

"Please just tell them."

"Honey, if you need some help—"

"This is all I need," Lynell says. "I just need to make sure she's safe."

"What sort of warning am I giving her parents? Who's looking for Anna? Her father?"

Daniel must hear Mother Adella. He squeezes Lynell's hand and she rubs his knuckles with her thumb. "No. Someone else. Someone dangerous." She wants to tell Mother Adella everything. She wants to explain how serious the situation is. But mentioning Eric Elysian may cause more harm than good. The nuns don't believe in the Registration and Lynell doesn't know what they would do if they knew Eric Elysian was interested in a past resident's child. And besides, the fewer people who know Lynell's true identity and her connection to the Elysians, the better.

"Tell them that Anna's birth mother has enemies and they may try to use Anna to get to her," Lynell says. She steps back into Daniel's chest, and he wraps his arm around her, holding her steady.

"Oh, darling. What have you gotten yourself into?" Mother Adella asks. "Are you sure we can't help?"

Lynell shakes her head even though Mother Adella can't see her. "You can help by warning them and calling me."

Mother Adella takes a deep breath, and Lynell imagines her leaning back in her chair, rubbing the back of her neck like she does when she's tired or stressed. "Okay, I will do that. But you have to promise me you'll take care of yourself."

"I promise," Lynell says.

"Be safe, Rachel."

"I will. Thank you again, Mother Adella," Lynell says. They exchange quick goodbyes, then she hangs up, setting the phone on the table.

"Everything good?" Zach asks.

Lynell nods and fishes through the bags Daniel brought back, finding the hair dye and bleach. By bleaching her hair first, the red will be a brighter, more noticeable change, rather than just giving her already dark hair a slight red tint. She sits at the table. Daniel wraps an old towel around her shoulders and doesn't even glance at the directions before pulling out the different instruments, clearly remembering the steps from when Lynell used to make him dye her hair years previously. He pulls the gloves on and gets to work, scratching her scalp periodically like he used to.

When Daniel is halfway through his work on Lynell, Zach emerges from the bathroom, showered and changed, with pitch-black hair.

Daniel whistles. "Looking good, Zach!"

"Shut up," he says, grinning as he rubs the towel over his hair. "I'm going to make some grilled cheese. Want some?"

Daniel nods and squirts bleach on a thick strand of Lynell's hair.

Twenty minutes later, Lynell washes her hair, cringing at the orange tint. Daniel is fast with the red dye and soon she's standing in the bathroom, dressed and staring at the mirror.

The mirror is cracked in the corners and has yellowed over the years, but Lynell's reflection still shows how the red hair brings out any blush under her skin and the tinge of pain and exhaustion in her eyes. She leans closer to the mirror, studying her face. The skin around her eye is still tinted from the bruise and tender when she prods the edges. There are small red dots that paint her nose and cheeks, pimples and blemishes from poor hygiene for over a week. Her eyebrows are overgrown, but at least the cuts on her face are healing, even the one on her lip. She touches it, remembering the multiple kisses she's shared with Daniel and how they simultaneously hurt and felt better than anything in almost three years.

She closes her eyes, braces herself against the small counter, pulls in a deep breath through her nose and turns away from the mirror to take another shower.

"If we can be sure they'll contact her if—oh," Zach says as Lynell emerges. Daniel turns and smiles at her, eyes wide.

"Wow," he breathes. "Never thought I'd see you with red hair."

"And?" she asks.

"Just that much more of a badass."

"You look ready to dip your head in the blood of your enemies," Zach says.

"Why would I want to dip my head in their blood?" Lynell asks as she sits down and grabs one of the grilled cheese sandwiches on the table.

Zach shrugs. "Maybe it's your victory ritual. Or maybe you're a vampire."

"If she was a vampire, she'd just drink the blood," Daniel says between bites.

"And if I had some sort of victory ritual it would be much more dignified than using my own head like a mop."

Zach laughs. "Good to know. Now maybe we should get started with decoding that damn letter."

The light atmosphere instantly fills with dread as if a cloud in blue skies soaked up all the water of a hurricane. Zach gathers a pen and paper and sets them on the table. Daniel clears his throat, kisses the side of Lynell's head, and gets up to clear the dishes into the sink. Lynell starts to stand, but Zach just points at the paper before her. She stares down at the blank page as she plops back down on the chair.

She didn't realize how hard writing it would be. The letter has been in her head so long that the idea of sharing it is disturbing. But she knows they have to do this. If for no other reason than to have a backup plan that will keep Anna safe.

<hr />

They spend hours reading the letter, rearranging words, asking Lynell questions to try and find a pattern.

"Maybe there is no code," Daniel says. Lynell and Zach both frown at him. "I mean, look at what he wrote. Love, joy, and forgiveness. Not very Registration-like, if you ask me."

"What about when people use the Registration out of love?" Lynell asks.

"And joy? forgiveness?" Daniel shakes his head in disagreement. "Maybe the code is simply refusing the Registration."

Lynell's eyebrows furrow together. "Except he also told me to use mine wisely."

"The Registration was Grandfather's greatest accomplishment," Zach says. "The code isn't refusing it. It was created to control it."

Daniel drops his idea, and they keep working. Lynell is on alert the whole time, expecting to hear their burner phone ring at any moment with bad news about Eric looking for or finding Anna. Three hours into working, Daniel sees Lynell pick up the phone, look at the screen, and put it down for the hundredth time.

"Baby," he says. "We don't want them to call, remember? That would mean she's in danger."

"She already is," Lynell says.

Zach sighs, handing out three fresh cups of tea. "He may never find her."

"May? Not exactly reassuring," Lynell says, accepting her herbal tea.

Sitting across from her, Zach rubs his face. "He's lived two decades in constant fear that someone would challenge his hold on the company. He's desperately tried to cover up his own illegitimacy while looking for possible children of Eli's."

"Which is how he found Lynell?" Daniel asks.

Zach nods. "He's found another child, too."

Lynell turns to him sharply, eyes wide and mouth open. "What?" Zach glances at her, guilt filling his face. "My father had another kid? Who?"

Zach sighs. "I think his name was Alexander. He was five years older than you. But he was illegitimate. We don't think Eli even knew about him."

"What do you mean 'was?'" Lynell prompts.

"One of the senior Researchers, the men my dad sends to find stuff out for him, kind of like his personal private investigators, found him two years ago and used his Registration. Alexander was questioned briefly, and when they realized that he knew nothing about Eli, they killed him."

Lynell looks down at her feet, but she can feel Daniel staring at her.

"Lyn?" he says, grabbing her hand. He ventures into the silence to pull her out of her thoughts. She closes her eyes and pictures him climbing into the pit she continually finds herself falling into. He's good at it now. Good at climbing down, pulling her into his arms, and carrying her out. God knows he's had to do it a million times before.

Zach glances between them, eyebrows low. "So . . ." Lynell says, "is Alexander the only other kid they've found?"

Zach nods. "But he has a whole team of Researchers looking for other possible children. And, unfortunately, that includes children of existing heirs. They dug into Alexander's past for an entire year before deciding there was nothing to find."

Daniel and Lynell exchange a look filled with fear.

"Have they looked into my past?" Lynell asks.

Zach nods. "That's why I was assigned to Danny. But last I heard, they didn't know you ever had a child."

Lynell drops her face into her hands. She can't help but picture her broken family tree.

The branches tainted by this world.

A cousin who Registered her, an uncle who wants her dead, a brother who died before she ever knew him, an abusive stepfather, a broken mother, and a father who was killed by his own brother.

"Stop," Daniel says, pulling her hand away from her face.

"What?" she asks.

He stands, pulling Lynell out of her chair and into his arms. "Thinking. You're going to spiral."

"I'm not." She lays her head against his chest and grips his shirt.

"It'll be okay," he says.

Lynell shakes her head. "Is it even possible to have a normal family?"

"Probably not," Daniel says. Lynell frowns and looks up at him. He smiles slightly and brushes his hand through her hair. "But it's possible to have a loving family. And it's okay to *want* a family." He quietly says, so Zach can't hear, "You're not only an Elysian, baby. Or a Mize. You're also a Carter."

She buries herself into Daniel Carter, wrapping both arms around his waist, holding onto him. When he lets her go, she returns to her seat and watches Zach read the letter for the millionth time, mouthing each word.

After a long moment of silence, he looks up. "Did you ever meet your father?"

She shakes her head. "Mom never told me much about him. She told me he was a foreign king who came into her life just to give her the greatest gift of all. But he couldn't stay because he had a kingdom to run. When I was older, I got some new stories. How they fell in love playing Scrabble and dreamed of running away together. But I never got more than 'a king who liked Scrabble.' A fat lot of help that was." Lynell sighs. She's about to keep talking when Daniel sits back down at the table and picks up the page.

"A king who liked Scrabble?" he repeats.

"Yeah."

"That's the only real story your mom ever told you about?" His eyes scan the words while he speaks. "That's random, don't you think?"

"Not really," Lynell says. "It's how they met and fell in love."

"No, wait, I think Danny is onto something," Zach says. He looks from Daniel to Lynell, his eyes going wide. "You were just a kid when your dad died. It makes sense that he may have told your mom something about the letter. Maybe he told her there was an important hidden message in it that you would need one day. Maybe he told her how to figure it out so she could help you."

Lynell frowns, picturing every moment her mom spoke about her father. It wasn't often and it always had to do with either him being a king or them playing Scrabble. And it was her mom who gave Lynell the idea to memorize the letter.

"Well, she was the one who urged me to memorize the letter," Lynell says. Is it possible? Could her mom have known there was a code in the letter? "I thought he would only leave the code to me, though. Would he want anyone else to know it was there?"

"He probably didn't tell her what it was," Zach says. "But he would need to make sure you'd look for it someday. Otherwise, you might never look at the letter as anything more than a letter."

Daniel sets the paper down and meets Zach's gaze. "Scrabble would be a perfect game for something like this. Think about it—every letter is associated with a number. That could be the key to decoding this."

"But no one else would consider using that if they didn't know it held personal significance to Eli," Zach says. They're leaning closer to each other now, excitement filling their voices.

"Wait, why wouldn't my mom try and figure out the code herself?" Lynell asks.

Zach shrugs. "Maybe she did. But I doubt she knew what she was looking for."

"Or maybe she knew it was just for you. Maybe she wanted to leave your dad's secret message to you."

"Feels like they were both leaving a lot up to chance here," Lynell says, frowning at the letter sitting in the middle of the table.

"Maybe he was okay with the code dying with him," Daniel says. "If your dad was questioning the Registration at all, or even if he was just worried the code would be used and make everything worse, he may not have cared if you ever found it."

"There's no way Eli would let the code die with him," Zach says. "He was the Elysian heir. Even if he was starting to question the Registration, he wouldn't just turn his back on it."

"You said yourself that using the code to end the Registration would cause chaos," Lynell argues. "Maybe he thought there would be a safer way to end it. People would riot and kill whoever they want in the confusion of the Registration being compromised. If the code either causes a free-for-all killing spree or gives the holder power to alter the Registration, it makes sense to try and get rid of it completely."

"Except he didn't. He left it for you," Zach says.

"So, either Lynell learns there's a hidden code in the letter and figures it out, in which case she has to decide what to do with it," Daniel says, holding up one finger. He lifts a second and adds, "Or she never discovers the code and it dies with him. Maybe he was okay with either of those options."

"If so, then he didn't really decide anything," Zach says. "He just left everything up to chance."

Lynell groans. "And put the responsibility on my shoulders."

"You're not alone," Daniel reminds her.

Lynell smiles at him. "I know."

"We're going to need the game to see if this Scrabble idea pans out," Zach says. "Unless one of you has the worth of each letter memorized."

Lynell throws her hands in the air, shaking her head. "Don't look at me. I had the letter memorized. One of you can figure out the letter values."

"Where can we get a copy of the game?" Daniel asks.

Before either Zach or Lynell can reply, a shrill ringing punctures the air. All three of them flinch, and Zach stands to grab the burner phone from the counter behind them.

He squints down at it with a deep frown.

"Mother Adella!" Lynell says, her heart dropping into her gut. She jumps up and grabs the phone from Zach's hand. He protests but she ignores him and flips the phone open, holding it to her ear. "Hello?"

Mother Adella answers on the other end. "Rachel?" she asks, using Lynell's fake name.

"Yes. Mother Adella, what is it?" Lynell looks back at Daniel, who circles the table to stand next to her. He leans in so he can hear Mother Adella as well.

"I wanted to let you know that there was a man who came today asking about Anna."

Lynell sways on her feet, and Daniel grabs her and takes the phone from her when she feels her body freeze and her heart turn to stone.

"What?" he asks, speaking into the phone. "Who?"

"He didn't give a name. But he was very unpleasant. He had a photo of you and called you Lynell." Lynell flinches. There goes her anonymity. "I told him there's never been a resident named Lynell here," Mother Adella continues. "He left when I didn't give him any further information."

Lynell's hands relax but the tension stays tight in her legs. "Thank you, Mother Adella," she says. Just because this man left doesn't mean he won't come back.

Clearly this means Eric knows about Anna and it's just a matter of time until they find her.

Zach follows Daniel and Lynell out of the apartment, yelling at them to slow down. "It could be a trap!" he shouts as Daniel rushes down the steps, taking them three at a time. "He probably forced her to make that call."

"No one makes Mother Adella do anything she doesn't want to do," Lynell says, circling the car to the passenger side. "If she called us, it was of her own volition."

"All the more reason to stop and think. If my father knows about Anna, he'll use this to lure you in."

Lynell turns to Zach, one hand still on the passenger's side door. "Stop and think? That's our daughter, Zach! I'm not going to let some mad man go after her without trying to save her first."

"How are you going to save her from one of his cells?" Zach says, holding the door open after Lynell climbs in the car.

"Close the door, Zach," Lynell says, glaring up at him.

"Please, I'm begging you. Think this through."

"Move, Zach!" Daniel shouts from behind the wheel.

"Danny!"

"Zach, I swear to whoever the hell is out there, if you don't move right now, I will run you over."

Zach blinks at Daniel and takes a step away from the car.

"Get in if you want, but we're going to find our daughter," Lynell says. He doesn't move but opens his mouth to argue. Lynell slams the door shut and looks at Daniel. "Drive."

Daniel doesn't even hesitate. The car flies into reverse and Lynell keeps her eyes locked with Zach's until Daniel shifts the car into drive and they turn. Lynell holds the handle of the door and focuses on pulling air in through her nose and blowing out through her mouth. The sun dips past the horizon, shielding itself with the curve of the earth as if sensing impending danger. Daniel flips on the headlights, two beams of light revealing the next three hundred feet.

Lynell feels blind. Even the moon seems dimmer than usual. She leans back and closes her eyes.

Lynell has to trust that Mother Adella won't give anyone information about Anna's whereabouts. *She'll be okay. She has to be. She just has to be,* Lynell tells herself over and over again.

"We'll find her first," Daniel says, reaching over to grab Lynell's wrist. He nods encouragement at her, but his complexion is growing paler, and his eyes are wild, betraying any calm he tries to force into his words.

She blinks and nods, skin starting to feel numb. "I'm sorry. If you'd married someone else—"

"Don't." He moves his hand to her face and looks between her and the road. "Don't you dare apologize." He rubs his thumb over her bottom lip and in her mind, she's dropped back into their hotel bed in Chicago. "I don't want someone else. I want you."

With a smile that's meant to reassure her, Daniel grabs the wheel tighter with both hands as he makes a quick exit.

Lynell pulls her knees up on the seat and wraps her arms around them. Daniel must see the sea of despair that threatens to engulf her and reaches over again, placing his hand on top of her knees.

"We'll find her."

She nods.

———

Lynell knocks loudly and only a few seconds pass before Mother Adella opens the door, looking at them without surprise. Her wrinkled face gives Lynell a sympathetic look and before anyone can speak, she pulls Lynell into a hug. The encompassing, soft embrace is instantly familiar. Despite being a few inches taller than Mother Adella, Lynell still feels smaller in the older woman's arms. She leans forward, closing her eyes. She could be three years younger, pregnant, scared, and hiding out in this halfway house while the nuns care for her without asking any questions.

When she's released, Lynell looks down at the nun. Her glasses are different, now so large they reach over her eyebrows and rest on her cheekbones. Mother Adella steps back, gesturing for Lynell and Daniel to walk inside. As they cross the threshold, Lynell says, "Mother Adella, you have to tell us where Anna is."

Mother Adella surveys them, holding her hands behind her back. She's probably noticing how pale they are or how their eyes, noses, and cheeks are bright red. Lynell realizes that Mother Adella has never met Daniel before and wonders what she must be thinking of him, especially with Lynell's exposed wounds.

The nun lifts her chin and frowns. "I did not give that man any of—"

"He'll get it," Lynell interrupts, reaching over to grip Daniel's hand. He looks up the stairs at a group of women and girls. A young girl, maybe twelve, is holding onto the banister. Behind her a bald woman, about twenty, stands with her arms crossed, glaring at Lynell and Daniel as if they had ruined a surprise. On the other side of the staircase is another girl and behind her is an older woman holding a sleeping baby. Two more nuns fill the room, and one steps forward, as if to intervene. She freezes when Mother Adella holds up her hand.

Lynell turns back to Mother Adella. The white wimple causes her neck to protrude slightly, giving her a softer look that has made many people underestimate her. Lynell knows Mother Adella can be the softest, kindest human on the planet. Or an unstoppable force.

But Eric won't underestimate her.

"Please, Mother Adella," she says, doing her best to ignore their audience. "Believe me when I say this man can get whatever he wants. I'm not trying to get Anna back or mess up her life, I promise. I'm trying to *save* her life."

Mother Adella nods and gestures for Lynell and Daniel to follow her. "We should speak in private," she says, turning and heading through the open doorway.

Lynell follows, Daniel close at her heels. The other nuns stay behind. Lynell lets out a large breath, her body melting into her shoes as she follows Mother Adella through the house she remembers well. Daniel grabs her hand as they pass through a large dining room that has two tables, each with ten chairs. He looks around, taking in the details of the room. Lynell watches him, knowing that he must be picturing what her life looked like in those months when he didn't hear from her at all.

"I believe you that this circumstance is dire," Mother Adella says, pushing open a door that leads to a massive kitchen that sports two fridges, a freezer, two pantries, and a large island. It's been refurbished since Lynell was here last, now with marble counters and black cabinets. "I know you, Rachel. Or Lynell, however you wish to be known. You are kind and would never willingly do anything to cause your child harm."

Lynell rubs her nose, noticing Mother Adella's choice of the word "willingly."

They cross the kitchen and into another seating area, this one small with a couch, two chairs, and a table with three bibles sitting on it. Lynell remembers waiting in here with other girls before having individual meetings with one of the sisters.

Mother Adella pulls a key ring from beneath her robe and opens the door on the other side of the room. She steps in and holds the door open for Daniel and Lynell. They both step through and look around. Lynell has never been inside Mother Adella's room.

There has never been a reason.

The room's only obvious decoration is a large cross hanging on the wall behind the door. A curtain splits the room in half. Lynell assumes Mother Adella's bed and sleeping quarters are on the other side of the curtain. On this side sits a long desk with a lamp, bible, cross, notebook, several pieces of paper, and a pencil sharpener. One wall is covered in filing cabinets, all closed and alphabetically labeled. The other wall has two bookshelves that are stacked full of books of all genres, religious, fiction, secular, and nonfiction. Mother Adella always stressed the importance of having a well-rounded knowledge and understanding of as many world views as possible.

Mother Adella walks around the desk and sits, folding her hands in her lap. Without being asked, Lynell and Daniel follow suit, sitting in the two chairs on the other side of the desk, facing the nun.

"The man looking for Anna will do whatever it takes," Lynell says. "I know the rules, and I don't want to break them, but he won't care. He is ruthless. If he doesn't get Anna's information from you, he'll get it from someone else. He'll threaten whoever he needs to and won't hesitate to follow through on his threats."

Mother Adella nods, listening carefully. After a pause, she says, her voice strong and steady, "Have you considered that he will find her through you? Perhaps this man is watching you and the moment you know where Anna is, so will he."

"We have considered that," Daniel says, speaking for the first time. "Which is why we didn't come until now."

"You're the child's father, I presume?" Mother Adella asks.

Daniel nods. Lynell says, "Daniel only wants what is best for Anna too. We don't want to take her away from the life and family she knows. We just want to protect her."

"You said you're the one with enemies, correct?" Mother Adella asks. "So what does he want with Anna?"

Lynell closes her eyes and swallows hard. They agreed not to share the details of their situation, but if anyone can keep it a secret, it's Mother Adella.

Lynell opens her eyes and looks at the nun. Her light, hazel eyes are surrounded by laugh lines from years of smiling. Lynell says in a whisper, "Eric Elysian is after me and any children I have."

Daniel sucks in a breath, and she can feel him staring at her. She keeps her gaze on Mother Adella, who doesn't show a sign of shock or fear. She doesn't reply immediately and with every second of silence, Lynell is worried she shouldn't have told her. But then Mother Adella leans back in her chair and gives a slight shake of her head.

"I never liked that man," she says. Lynell almost laughs. "Anyone who tries to play God will only create their own hell."

Lynell, knowing the phrase by heart, finishes it for Mother Adella. "And anyone who follows will think heaven is in a cell."

The nun nods. "I've always said our country is living in the hell Gideon Elysian created."

"I know," Lynell says. "I wish I'd listened."

"You did, darling. You just weren't ready to hear it yet."

"And now?" Lynell asks.

Mother Adella frowns as she studies Lynell. Then she stands and walks around the desk so she's standing next to Lynell. She reaches out and touches Lynell's still-bruised eye. "I believe you've seen firsthand what hell can do to a person. I also believe you're ready to escape."

"I just want Anna to escape. Please, Mother." Lynell's voice breaks; tears threaten to fill her throat. "I'd do anything for her. I've survived Eric Elysian once." She holds up her hand, still bandaged and rhythmically throbbing with pain. "And I'll do it again to keep Anna safe."

"Rachel, honey, I don't want to see you hurt anymore," Mother Adella says.

"I won't let that happen," Daniel says. "Not again."

"We can hide you both," Mother Adella says. "Let us help you."

"What about Anna?" Lynell asks

"I've called the number on file and left a message. We have to trust that they will be safe."

Lynell shakes her head. "I need to find them and make sure they know how serious this is. I promise as soon as I warn them, I'll do everything in my power to keep Eric away from Anna. But I have to do this. Not you."

Mother Adella doesn't look convinced. Lynell stands, anxiety filling her toes. She paces, keeping her eyes locked on the nun as she speaks. "You once told me that I have more power than I thought. That I'm allowed to demand my own safety and happiness. You also told me to accept the responsibilities given to me and stand taller than them. This is how I do that. What kind of woman am I if I abandon my child not once, but twice?"

"You did not abandon her. You gave her life," Mother Adella says.

"So let me make sure she gets to live that life," Lynell says, begging now.

Mother Adella's eyes are shining and after an agonizing moment of silence, she turns and heads for the filing cabinets. Lynell returns to her seat, watching Mother Adella open a drawer labeled "C-D" and thumb through the folders before pulling one of them out. She places the folder on the desk, sits back down, and flips it open to the first page, which brandishes a photo of Lynell from almost three years earlier, the name "Rachel Doe" beneath. Mother Adella flips through the pages quickly, stops toward the end, and, pulling her finger down the page, she reads slowly.

Lynell reaches over and grabs Daniel's hand. It's sweating but she doesn't care, she needs his touch to ground her.

"Ah," Mother Adella says. Lynell sits forward, trying to read the file upside down. Mother Adella closes it before she can, opens a drawer, pulls out a pen, and starts writing. The pen scratches against the paper, louder than an airhorn. Lynell knocks her knees together and counts her breaths.

Mother Adella finishes, rips out the paper, and folds it in half. She pulls an envelope from a drawer, tucks in the folded paper, and tapes it shut. She holds it up but before she hands it to Lynell, she says, "Come see me when this is all over and you're out of harm's way. Let me see you happy and safe and living a full life. You deserve it."

Lynell nods.

Mother Adella hands her the envelope. "Open that somewhere safe," she says, gesturing to the envelope in Lynell's hands.

"Yes, ma'am."

Mother Adella stands, and Lynell and Daniel follow suit. "Thank you," Daniel says. "For everything. Not just today but for all that you've done for Lynell."

Mother Adella gives Daniel a gentle smile. "Help keep her safe." Then she turns to Lynell and says, "Be with God, child."

Lynell nods and heads to the door, Daniel close by her side. He opens it and heads through but Lynell turns to face Mother Adella. "You may want to call in some reinforcements. Or send the girls somewhere else. Eric Elysian is not a kind man."

Mother Adella places her hand on Lynell's cheek. "Thank you for the warning. I believe we'll be fine." She drops her hand and looks up at the cross on the wall.

Lynell follows Mother Adella's gaze before looking back at her. "For the sake of everyone who lives here, I hope he will protect you."

DAY 12 ————————————————————

As soon as they get back to the car, Lynell rips open the envelope, and Daniel reads the note over her shoulder. Written in Mother Adella's elegant script are five lines that feel like a soothing balm on Lynell's anxious mind.

Mr. and Mrs. Raines
Last known address:
522 Byrd Street Weatherford, Oklahoma 73096
Last known phone number:
580-829-0094

Daniel immediately starts driving. They discuss going back to the apartment to pick up Zach but decide against it. And because they have the burner phone with them, and Zach lost his watch to his father, they have no way to contact him.

"Anna has to be our priority now," Daniel says, more to convince himself than Lynell. She agrees, sitting with her feet curled under her.

They drive for two hours as Lynell watches the clock steadily push to midnight and then spill over into the next day. She feels years older from when she stood in line at the Registration Office only twelve days ago, prepared to kill but not knowing she was about to be hunted.

"We need gas," Daniel says breaking a long silence.

"There should be a station at the next exit," Lynell says. "We could use some water and food too."

"We don't have any money."

Lynell curses at the realization and opens the glove box to dig through. She finds some napkins, a user manual, and the insurance card for the car, but no money.

"Check the console," Daniel says, tapping the compartment between their seats. Lynell opens it and pulls out a nearly empty bottle of lotion.

"No luck," she says, dropping the bottle back into the console. "We could just steal it." She hesitantly looks up at Daniel. "We have to get to Anna, and we can't do that without a working car."

Daniel flicks his eyes over to her and shrugs. "Desperate times, right?" He nods and scrunches his lips to the side as he thinks. "Okay. You go inside and try to snag some food and water. I'll get the gas."

"How are you going to do that?"

"I know how to siphon; I just need a tube and a gas can. Sometimes old cans are left out behind gas stations. If not, I'll figure something out."

"What?" She doesn't mean to challenge him, but she needs to know the plan. Otherwise, she'll freak out.

"I don't know, come in and steal one from the store?"

"Stealing a gas can will be more difficult than a few protein bars," Lynell points out.

"Duh!" Daniel seems exasperated, but then he winks and says, "I bet you could manage a distraction."

They quickly come up with a plan as Daniel follows the signs to the closest gas station. There are three pumps and only two cars parked outside. Daniel parks the car and disappears around the corner of the building while Lynell heads inside.

The station is small, with only four aisles and a single bathroom at the back. A young cashier with pimples covering his neck and chin is working the register. Next to him is the only other customer, an older guy with a wiry gray beard studying a shelf of tobacco. Lynell turns on her heel, carefully breathing in and out each breath through her nose to try and keep the anxiety at bay.

The wall of tools, car materials, and supplies, including tubes and gas cans, is at the end of the aisle directly in front of the register. Lynell picks up a small canister and a tube and sets it on the floor closer to the door. The back of her neck tingles and she looks over her shoulder to see the cashier watching her. There are some cameras, but there's no way to know if they're on. If they are, what will they do, track them down? By the time they're found, Lynell will probably be dead anyway.

Her heart stutters and she clears her throat, walking away from the tools and into the food aisle. When she can't see the cashier anymore, she slips a packet of crackers, a package of beef jerky, and a few protein bars off the shelf and slides them into her pockets.

Lynell hears the bell ringing as the front door opens. She walks to the end of the aisle and sees Daniel walk in. He gives her a barely noticeable nod before turning and walking away from her as if they were strangers.

Lynell's hands are cold with fear. She walks to the other side of the store, scanning the back wall. She finds what she's looking for in the corner. With a steadying breath, Lynell heads to the slushie machine and places a cup under the center lever. She glances over her shoulder once before pulling the lever as hard as she can. It only takes a few tries before she has it jammed so the lever doesn't go back and stop the pour.

"Oh crap!" she yells, stepping to the end of the aisle so she can see the cashier. "The slushie machine is broken! It's getting everywhere!"

The cashier runs over instantly, a scowl on his face. He curses when he sees slushie still falling from the machine and covering the cabinet and floor below it.

"I'm so sorry, I don't know what happened," Lynell says, pitching her voice up a few octaves to cover any sounds Daniel might make. "I was just trying to get a cup and then I couldn't get the lever back and it just kept pouring and I couldn't reach the plug to unplug it and—"

The young man cuts her off. "It's fine! I'll fix it."

Lynell mutters another apology before leaving the aisle. On her way out, she grabs two water bottles from the fridge and a handful of candy bars before slipping through the front door.

Rushing to the car, her heart still pounding wildly in her chest, she sees Daniel carrying the canister he'd taken from inside to their car.

"Nice diversion," he says. Lynell grins, turning to keep watch while Daniel pours the gas he'd siphoned into the tank.

"That was nerve-wracking," she says.

"You'd think you'd get used to tense situations at some point." Daniel drops the empty canister before climbing back into the car.

Lynell follows suit, locking the door behind her and unloading the food she's stolen into her lap. "I think the mundanity of that particular crime allowed me to feel the adrenaline."

Daniel reaches over and pulls a protein bar out of her lap. "That sounds like backward logic."

Lynell shrugs, ripping open a bag of Skittles. "I never claimed to think logically."

Daniel laughs and starts reversing out of the parking lot. "That is very true." He speeds up when they reach the highway and takes one of the bottles of water. "We make a good thieving team."

"I'm not sure that's something to be proud of."

"We also make a good surviving team," Daniel says.

Lynell lays her hand on his leg. Her voice is quiet as she says, "I think we make a good team. Period."

"Yeah," Daniel agrees. "We do."

They drive for another half hour, listening to pop music on the radio that sounds so upbeat it calms their fear. Lynell stares out the window, bouncing her leg. After another half hour, she pulls out the phone and the note Mother Adella wrote. She unfolds it for what feels like the hundredth time, tracing Mother Adella's flawless handwriting that spells her daughter's last name: Raines.

"How far away are we?" she asks, her voice shaking.

"Hour and a half. But once we get to Weatherford, I won't know where to go."

"Of course, we get the only car without a built-in navigational system," Lynell mutters. "And this phone is a burner without internet access. I'll just call them."

"It's almost two a.m.," Daniel says.

"I don't care, we—"

"No, I mean, just be prepared that they may not reply," Daniel says.

Lynell nods and types out the numbers.

Her hand shakes as she holds the phone to her ear. She leans forward and drops her head on the dashboard, fingers tight around the phone.

It rings, the sound scraping into her ears, leaving trails of burning flesh behind. The ringing climbs into her brain and ricochets off her skull, stinging everything it touches.

More ringing. Lynell sits back and clenches the phone tighter.

Daniel glances over at her and tilts his head forward in the smallest of nods. The call goes to voicemail, and she pulls the phone from her ear, muttering a nearly silent, "Shit," under her breath.

"Try again," Daniel says.

She does. The phone rings and rings and rings and rings and the grating voice of a recorded, mechanical woman speaks into Lynell's ear. She curses and ends the call.

"Maybe they shut off their phone," Daniel says.

"We can't afford for them to shut off their damn phones."

She calls six more times, shaking more with each unanswered call.

"Hey," he reaches over and pries the phone from Lynell's hand. "Take a break. They don't have to answer. We'll find them when we get there. It's not a big town."

Lynell nods and leans over the center console to rest her head against his shoulder. She closes her eyes, watching blinding white lights behind her eyelids. A headache forms behind her temple and causes sweat to gather at the back of her neck. She imagines the family they're about to meet. The happy couple and healthy child who have no idea what's coming their way. All she wants is for them to be safe.

"We're just ten minutes away," Daniel announces.

"Okay," Lynell says, sitting up and away from Daniel. "I'm going to try calling one more time." Without waiting for a response, she opens the phone and clicks redial.

No one answers. There's no bleary, annoyed male voice on the other end, demanding to know why he's being called over and over at two o'clock in the morning. There's no child crying in the background, distraught at being woken up. No mother shushing her to sleep. Nothing.

She drops the phone in her lap, staring through the front windshield without seeing.

The speed limit declines as more homes and businesses line the street. They pass several county roads and a closed gas station, now a mere graveyard for broken down trucks.

"That's creepy," Lynell says.

Daniel chuckles. "It looks like this town should be infected with zombies."

Lynell hits Daniel's arm in jest. "That is so not funny!"

They stop at a red light and a semi-truck passes in front of them. "On the contrary, I find your irrational fear of the undead quite humorous."

"It's hardly irrational. The zombie apocalypse could happen," Lynell says, crossing her arms.

"And if it does, I promise to shoot you before you have to witness it," Daniel replies. Lynell grins, remembering the night several years ago when she turned off the zombie movie they were watching ten minutes in before making Daniel promise to shoot her in the head in the event of a zombie apocalypse.

"Thank you," she says.

The light turns green. "Turn up here. Looks like this street is full of fast-food restaurants."

Daniel nods and takes the next right down Marshall Street. "What do you think it's like growing up here?" Daniel asks.

Watching an old apartment complex pass by, Lynell shrugs. "Quiet. Anna's graduating class probably won't have more than fifty kids."

"I bet they barely have any Registrations here," Daniel says.

"Or it's one of those towns where the majority of Registrations are gang or drug related."

Daniel shakes his head. "No, it's too peaceful."

"That's because it's the middle of the night." Lynell points down another street and Daniel turns. With each road they pass that isn't Byrd Street, Lynell's stomach grows more leaden.

Thankfully, only ten more minutes pass before Daniel sits forward, leaning over the wheel. "What does that say? Looks like Byrd to me."

Lynell follows his gaze, squinting at the little green sign. "Yes, it is!"

The car feels noticeably lighter as Daniel turns left on the street.

"These are nice houses," Daniel says, studying the two-story homes. Most have an attached garage and each one has a large brick mailbox at the end of their driveway with black numbers big enough to read without slowing down.

484. 486. 488.

"Do you think they have more kids?" Lynell asks when they pass a house with a swing set out front.

"I kind of hope they don't," Daniel says. Lynell doesn't reply but quietly agrees. She likes the idea of Anna being an only child and getting her parents' undivided attention. Plus, convincing the Raines to leave will be more difficult if they have more children.

They reach an intersection and Daniel rolls through the stop sign. The houses on this side of the intersection are slightly smaller and the numbers are in the 500s.

Lynell's stomach tightens and each breath feels like it's being dragged from her body and ripped from her mouth. As soon as 522 comes into view, she turns to Daniel with wide eyes. He returns her stare, slows down the car, and parks in front, behind a deep blue SUV. His lips are parted, and his face is filled with color.

She turns in her seat so she can grab Daniel's hand. "We're here to keep her safe," she says. "That's all."

He nods as if readying himself before they both climb out of the car. They head up the sidewalk, hand in hand, staring down the front door.

It's deep red and the paint is beginning to peel at the edges. A potted plant with bright green leaves sits next to the door, and the welcome mat says, "BEWARE OF DOG. HE LIKES LICKING." Lynell would chuckle if she wasn't riding on her last nerve.

She closes her eyes when they reach the door and takes a breath that pushes against her diaphragm. She knocks.

When nothing happens, Daniel steps forward and knocks louder. A light turns on in the house. It shines under the door and through the long, vertical windows on either side of the door. Lynell leans forward, listening.

There's a gentle thump as someone walks to the door. Then silence. Lynell looks up at the small peephole in the middle of the door.

"We have to talk to you," she says, trying to make her voice sound trustworthy and compelling. "It's urgent. It's about Anna."

The door flies open and Lynell jumps. Then she finds herself staring at the barrel of a rifle held by a tall, bald man. He's holding the gun against his shoulder, wearing a gray sweater and a pair of checkered sweatpants.

Daniel holds up his hands, palms out. Lynell does the same but takes a step forward so the gun is inches from her face.

The man pushes it forward. "Who are you and what do you want?" he demands, his voice not giving away a hint of exhaustion or fear. He has the same wild look in his eyes that Daniel has had for the last twelve days.

"I'm so sorry," she says, meeting the man's gaze. "I'm Lynell Mize, though you may know me as Rachel Doe."

His eyebrows furrow. "Why are you here?" he asks, the shotgun never wavering.

Lynell looks back at Daniel, who nods at her to continue. He seems unperturbed by the gun in their faces, probably used to guns after fighting with the rebels.

Lynell turns back to Mr. Raines. "I know it's the middle of the night, but this is an emergency. You need to leave. Leave town or something. You just have to take Anna away for a while." Hating how cryptic she sounds, she adds, "Anna's in danger."

Mr. Raines frowns, glaring at them with the gun still raised. "In danger?"

"Could you lower the gun, please, Mr. Raines?" Daniel asks, pulling Lynell back to step in front of her. "We'll explain everything." Raines looks between them, grip so tight on the gun that his knuckles are white.

Lynell looks down, notices his bare feet with long toenails and the tip of a tattoo that seems to be climbing out from under his sweatpants. "We only want to keep Anna safe. Please, Mr. Raines. You have to listen to us. For Anna's sake."

She holds his gaze for a few long seconds before he lowers the gun, still gripping it hard. "You're not staying. And you're not seeing Anna."

Lynell nods.

"Right. Then come in and start talking." He steps aside, allowing them to enter before closing the door.

They walk into a small living room that's littered with toys. There's a small, bright yellow tent filled with stuffed animals in front of the couch. A pile of large wooden blocks and Legos fills the entrance of a hallway. On the far wall sits a shelf displaying photos in front of a line of books.

Photos of Anna. She longs to go look at them but stays rooted, forcing her eyes away from the shelf. Those aren't her photos. This isn't her family.

But Mr. Raines must have followed her gaze. His jaw tenses before he exhales and says, "You can take a look." His voice, still stilted, now carries a trace of welcome.

Lynell doesn't move. "Are you sure?"

From the taut muscles in his face, she's worried he will change his mind. But Mr. Raines gives her a nod and gestures to the shelf of photos.

Lynell hesitates a moment longer before walking over. Her chest seems to push against her heart. It only takes one glance to confirm Anna is an only child. Lynell stares at the framed photo in the center of the shelf.

Anna has a head full of curly dark blonde hair. She's standing with her hands over her head, smiling at the camera. She's holding a small ball in one hand and a blue plastic bat in the other. Behind her is a small, blurry, black dog. Lynell itches to touch the photo, to hold this moment of Anna's life in her hands. But she keeps her arms at her side and looks at the photo to the right.

There, Anna is only a few months old. A light cloud of fuzzy hair is starting to grow, but she doesn't have any locks yet. She's laughing, and her chubby legs are covered in rolls, peeking out from her white onesie that says, "Wild Child." She's reaching out to the woman holding her, who has perfect, straight blonde hair and defined muscles in her arms. Her hands are wrapped around Anna's middle, holding her up so she can smile straight at her.

Lynell wipes away a tear and turns away from the bookshelf. Mr. Raines and Daniel are both watching her, the former still frowning and Daniel with glistening eyes.

"Okay. Now, start explaining," Mr. Raines says. He leans the rifle up against the wall next to the couch and sits on the arm. Lynell steps forward, opening her mouth, but is cut off when a woman enters from the hallway to the left of the couch.

"Josh?" she says. "Who was—" She stops short and freezes when she sees Lynell and Daniel standing in her living room. Mr. Raines—Josh—stands up and stops in front of his wife.

"Zoe, these are, um . . ." He clears his throat. "Anna's birth parents."

Zoe's eyes widen and she sidesteps Josh so she can peer at Lynell. Lynell fills with a surprising desire to hug the other woman. Zoe is wearing silk pajama bottoms and a light pink robe, and she stands with perfect posture like a dancer. She's got pointed, shiny, gold glasses held on the edge of her nose. Her face doesn't give away any thoughts, but somehow Lynell feels accepted in her presence. As if this woman would welcome anyone into her home.

"You're Rachel?" Zoe asks, scanning Lynell up and down.

"Lynell, actually. I gave a fake name. Mrs. Raines?"

"Zoe. How did you get our address?"

"They're saying Anna is in danger." Josh steps around Zoe so he's strategically placed between his wife and the strangers in his home. "They were just about to explain."

"Please do."

Zoe picks a stuffed bear off the couch and sits down, holding it against her chest. Lynell notices the left eye is missing and the ear seems chewed, the fake fur sticking together in weird ways. She guesses the dog in the photo is to blame.

Lynell turns to Daniel, who gestures for her to continue. Josh stands next to his wife, arms still crossed and the rifle resting behind him but within reach. He leans against the couch, glaring at them. Zoe seems to be absentmindedly petting the fur of the bear with one finger. She offers Lynell a soft smile, which causes tears to fill her eyes. She rubs them and pushes out a breath.

"Please know that I would never put Anna in danger. And that we wouldn't be here if it wasn't important. We just want Anna to be safe and happy."

"She is," Josh says.

"Let them finish," Zoe replies. She reaches up and touches Josh's shoulder. He looks back at her and they exchange a look before he visibly relaxes, arms uncrossing and shoulders falling.

"Right. Continue."

"Last Registration Day—" Instantly Zoe sits up and Josh turns to grab his rifle. Lynell cringes when she realizes they think Lynell and Daniel have Registered them, probably coming to take Anna back. Lynell quickly continues to put them at ease, even though she knows the truth is much worse than that. None of the tension leaves Zoe's body, but Josh lets go of the rifle, letting it rest against the wall again.

"Someone Registered me," she begins, and tells them in as few words as possible why Anna is at risk. "The problem is, they don't want anyone related to my father, or me, alive."

The silence stretches between them until it's snapped when Zoe gasps.

"I thought Anna's existence was a secret. Even Daniel didn't know about her for a while. But last night we learned that Eric is looking for her. I know none of this makes much sense, but you can't let Eric Elysian find her."

As Lynell speaks, Zoe's shoulders gradually hang forward, and she starts fidgeting with her hands, popping her knuckles and rolling her wrists until they crack.

Meanwhile, Josh grows eerily still, not even blinking as he glares at Lynell. His words are steady, carrying an anger that is more terrifying than if he shouted. "What do you think you're doing, coming to my house in the middle of the night and threatening my daughter?"

Lynell shakes her head and steps forward, freezing when Josh reaches for his gun.

"I'm not threatening her," Lynell says, aware that she sounds like she's begging.

"Of course, you're not," Zoe says. "I'm Anna's mother, yes. But so are you. It's not a simple thing to give birth to a child. You don't just forget them. You don't stop loving them." Her words are filled with tangible emotion. Lynell wonders if Zoe is speaking from experience. Perhaps she tried to have her own child before turning to adoption. Not for the first time, Lynell wishes she could direct all danger away from the couple in front of her.

Zoe turns to her husband. "Can't you see she's scared, Josh? She's warning us so we can protect Anna."

"Protect her against what? We're supposed to believe that some stranger is going to murder a two-year-old girl because of her bloodline?"

Lynell nods, feeling the urgency in the room climb, and the volume along with it. "Eric isn't just a stranger. He's the leader of the Registration. He's Anna's great-uncle."

Josh's nostrils flare. "That man is nothing to my daughter. He has no claim to Anna."

Lynell manages not to flinch. "I know. But Eric won't think that way. He won't even think of this as murder. He may even wait for the next quarter to make it a legal Registration, because a Registration, no matter who it is, isn't murder."

"It is when it's my daughter!"

"I agree!" Lynell says. "That's why you have to take Anna and leave, to keep her safe."

Everyone in the room falls silent. Lynell hears a dog outside barking and then . . . a child is crying.

Anna.

Lynell didn't expect it. Didn't prepare for it. And when it happens, when she hears it from down the hall, her heart leaps. A thrill of love and joy flows through her body, and she wants to find Anna and hold her close so she can chase away the nightmares and soothe her daughter back to sleep.

But once again, Lynell forces herself to stand still. She reaches out to Daniel and threads her fingers through his to help keep herself rooted.

Anna is crying. But it's not Lynell's job to comfort her. It's Zoe who stands and rushes down the hall.

Lynell watches her go and although she expected feelings of resentment, she feels gratitude.

Josh stares at them, still sitting on the couch armrest. The crying doesn't stop and after a few minutes, Zoe returns, Anna in her arms.

She's gorgeous. Big, sparkling blue eyes. Daniel's eyes. Her eyebrows are so light they're almost invisible and her hair, a bit darker now than in the photo, stands up at a dozen different odd angles, frizzy and tangled. She's holding a pink blanket with a small head at the top close to her face, one thumb pushed into her mouth. Zoe gently pulls it out of her mouth, but it only stays free for a few seconds. Anna holds onto Zoe with one arm and leans into her, staring at Lynell, confused and half asleep.

"Say hi, Anna," Zoe says.

Anna turns to look at her mom then buries her head into the crook between her neck and shoulder.

"Sorry, she's really tired."

Josh stands up and reaches out for Anna. She holds her chubby arms out and lets Josh pull her into his arms. "Of course, she is. It's 3 a.m.," he says, sitting on the couch with her.

Anna curls up next to his side, thumb still in her mouth and blanket clutched in her hand.

"Daddy . . ." Anna says, looking up at Josh. Her eyelashes are dark and long, just like Daniel's.

"Shh, it's okay, sweetheart," he says. He rubs his hand over her head, smoothing down some of the hair. She sticks out her bottom lip and falls into him, pulling up the blanket to cover more of her face.

"For her," Lynell says. The words fly from her throat easier than she expected. "Please leave for her."

Zoe looks between Lynell and Anna. She reaches out and grabs Josh's shoulder. He seems to concede, dropping his head and looking down at Anna, rubbing his thumb along her arm.

"I believe you," Zoe says. "I do."

Lynell relaxes and steps back, trying to keep herself from staring at Anna. "Good. Thank you."

"Tonight. You need to leave now," Daniel says.

Josh frowns and looks like he's going to argue, but Lynell holds up her bandaged hand. Anna's gaze darts between them, thumb returning to her mouth. "Please," she says. "Go tonight."

Daniel sits at the kitchen table, where he retreated after Josh refused his offer to help pack. The dog is inside now, a black lab named Tonks, and sits calmly next to Daniel, who hasn't stopped petting her since Zoe let her inside.

Anna sits on Zoe's hip with her head resting on her shoulder, thumb still firmly in her mouth, while they talk. She blinks slowly, staring at Lynell as Zoe bounces her.

"And what about you two?" Zoe finally asks. "Will you be safe? There are still a few days left on the Registration. People can still kill you and go scot-free."

Daniel scratches Tonks's ear and opens his mouth to reply, but Lynell beats him to it. "We don't know. But we'll figure it out."

Zoe nods and kisses Anna's forehead. "Do you want to hold her?" she asks.

"What?" Lynell says, eyebrows shooting up. She looks at Anna, who doesn't seem to react to the question.

"Can Lynell hold you, sweetheart?" Zoe asks.

Lynell watches with wide eyes and a racing heart as Anna looks between Zoe and Lynell. Her eyes are bright, glassy with sleep, but she stares at Lynell intently before nodding and holding out her hands.

"Really?" Lynell whispers. Her voice is rough, and she can feel her heartbeat in her hands. When Zoe nods with an encouraging smile, Lynell reaches out with one hand and Zoe helps transfer Anna to Lynell's hip. Anna rests one arm on Lynell's shoulder and keeps the other one holding her small blanket against her chest.

"I got Piggy," she says, looking up at Lynell and holding up the blanket.

"Oh?" Lynell answers. Her arm tightly wraps around Anna. "Is this Piggy?" she asks, touching the corner of the blanket.

Anna nods. "Aunt Jane gave me."

"Gave her to me," Zoe says.

Lynell smiles. "That was very nice of Aunt Jane."

"I love Aunt Jane," Anna says before returning her thumb to her mouth. Zoe rolls her eyes and gently pulls Anna's hand away.

"We've been trying to stop the thumb-sucking for a month now. So far, we haven't gotten anywhere. She hates pacifiers."

She says it all while watching Anna, her small fingers rubbing the back of Zoe's hand.

Lynell looks at her daughter, who calls someone else mom, and suddenly feels like her heart is going to explode.

"I'm sorry, I can't." She hands Anna back to Zoe, who seems surprised for a moment but accepts Anna in one fluid motion. "I'm sorry," Lynell croaks again.

"It's okay, I understand."

Josh returns to the main room, holding three bags. Tonks crosses the room to stand next to Josh, who says, "Ready?"

Zoe turns, surveys the other bags that are already sitting on the floor, and says, "All right, then let's get going." She turns to Lynell and Daniel, who are watching them with their hands firmly clasped together. "Where are you two heading?"

Daniel and Lynell exchange looks. He looks like he's about to fall asleep where he stands, eyes half-lidded and head nodding.

"Back to Dallas, I guess," Lynell answers, turning back to the Raines. "We don't have any money; lost it while running."

"Back to Dallas?" Zoe says. "That's a four-hour drive."

"We have to keep moving," Daniel says.

"Why don't we all go to a hotel tonight? We really shouldn't be traveling so late either," Zoe says.

Lynell shakes her head. "You should go farther. And go in the opposite direction than us. I think putting as much distance between us is smartest."

Zoe nods. "I won't be sleeping any time soon. We could go north, Josh. To Michigan." Her husband agrees and Zoe faces Lynell. "Let me give you some money, so you can stay somewhere tonight."

"Zoe," Josh says, but he stops talking when Zoe turns and glares at him.

"We really couldn't," Daniel says.

"Please," she says. She readjusts Anna on her hip and takes a step forward. "I'll forever be grateful for what you've done for our family. The least we can do is get you a hotel room for fifty bucks."

"We . . ." Lynell starts, looking up at Daniel.

"I insist."

Lynell nods. "Thank you."

"Josh." Zoe turns and holds out her hand. "Wallet." Josh digs through a large black purse and pulls out a wallet. He hands it to Zoe, who opens it with one hand and fishes out a hundred-dollar bill.

"We don't need—"

"I'm not sure how much the room will be, and you need food too. We aren't strapped for cash."

Daniel reaches out and takes it. "Thank you," he says. "So much."

"Of course. Thank you for warning us," Zoe says.

"All right," Josh says, picking up four of the bags, leaving two of them for Zoe to grab. Tonks jumps up, tail wagging. "Let's get out of here."

Lynell and Daniel watch the SUV drive away before they head in the opposite direction. They're quiet for the first thirty minutes of the drive, both feeling the loss of their daughter all over again.

"Let's stop soon," Lynell finally breaks the heavy silence.

Daniel just nods. He pulls into the parking lot of an old hotel twenty minutes later.

The lobby is yellow and blue, with a busy rug sitting in the middle of three yellow chairs, each sprouting a frizzy red pillow. Lynell curls the silver chain connecting a pen to the desk around itself while Daniel checks them in. He gives the receptionist a tired nod and smiles before pushing away from the counter. Lynell follows him to the elevator, already yearning for a soft bed to sink into.

"Room 314," Daniel says as the elevator doors close. "We should head back to the apartment in the morning to regroup."

Lynell just nods. She can still feel the weight of her daughter in her arms and can't pull her mind off Anna's soft face staring at her.

When they reach their room, both go straight for the bed. Lynell stares at the ceiling for a long while before Daniel reaches out and pulls her against his chest.

"They'll be okay," he whispers. "She's safe."

She falls asleep believing him.

It takes the front desk three calls before Lynell is awake enough to know it's not in her dream.

"Hello?" she mumbles into the phone.

"Hello, Mrs. Hunter. This is your wake-up call. Your checkout is in fifteen minutes."

"Thanks," Lynell says, setting the phone back and dropping onto the mattress again. Her head is muddled and filled with memories of the night before. Her skin is warm from lying close to Daniel all night, who's still fast asleep next to her, arm thrown over his eyes and shirt long discarded. She sees the stubble returning on his chin and knows it must be driving him mad.

"Almost noon?" Danny mutters.

She grunts in affirmation and they both lie still for a few more minutes before she groans and sits up. "We should get going."

The hotel is quiet while Lynell checks them out. When she's done, she walks over to Daniel, who's staring at the empty breakfast display with a frown.

"At least they still have coffee," she says, accepting the cup he hands her.

Rested, filled with cheap coffee, and munching on gas station breakfast bars, they start the drive back to Dallas. They only manage a few minutes of driving without bringing up Anna.

"She looks like you."

Lynell laughs. "Yeah, right. Her eyes are carbon copies of yours."

"But the rest of her, the hair and everything, is you. Remember that photo you showed me of your third Christmas? You could be twins."

"She's cuter." Lynell smiles.

"She's perfect," Daniel says. "The best of both of us."

"Yes, she is. Zoe and Josh are everything I wanted them to be."

Daniel nods, and instead of looking sad about seeing the daughter he never got to know, he mirrors Lynell's smile. "They seem like great parents. Exactly what Anna deserves."

Lynell picks at a hangnail on her thumb. Before she can overthink it, Lynell says, "They're a good family." She meets Daniel's eyes. "I want that."

She doesn't miss the almost imperceptible widening of his eyes. "You do?"

"I only have two more days to survive. And if we can figure out what to do about Eric, maybe I, and any other children I have, can be safe." The hangnail comes free and she holds her hand out, palm up in an invitation.

Daniel accepts it. He grabs her hand and his smile widens. "We already know that we make super cute babies."

Lynell laughs. "I wonder what our son would look like. Maybe we'll find out."

Daniel pulls Lynell's hand up and presses a kiss to it. "I would love that more than anything."

"You've been gone for twenty-four hours. I thought Dad got you!" Zach says after yanking Daniel and Lynell inside the apartment and locking the door behind them. He turns to Lynell, his eyebrows so low they're shadowing his eyes. "I've been trying to figure out how to sneak in and rescue you again now that Dad has surely told the guards to take me out on sight."

Lynell blinks at him. She'd been ready to say something sarcastic, but the sincere fear in his voice stops her short. "You would do that? Risk your life to save me *again*?"

Zach stops pacing and a genuine look of confusion flashes over his face. "Of course. You're family."

Somehow, those words etch themselves into Lynell's skull, hanging over all her other thoughts, and she knows they'll be there for the rest of her life, however long or short. The future she and Daniel allowed themselves to dream of now includes Uncle Zach, breaking the family cycle of abuse.

"Oh," is all she manages to say.

Thankfully, Danny saves her from any further awkwardness by dropping the bag of leftover gas station food in the middle of the table and saying, "Please tell me you have food that's not wrapped in plastic."

Zach does and busies himself with making dinner while Daniel updates him. Lynell, wanting to give him privacy with his best friend, takes a long shower. Pulling on puffy blue shorts, the only pair she finds in the wardrobe, and a soft polo, Lynell feels a renewed determination to live past the next two days. She craves the feeling of hope and joy she felt in the car with Daniel, imagining their future. She wants to be with Daniel. She wants to get to know Zach as her cousin, not as the person who Registered her or the person running from his father. She wants a family.

Resolved to not do anything else until they figure out the code and decide what to do next, Lynell returns to the kitchen.

"—the offensive," Zach is saying. "We've been playing defensive this whole time. We only have a small window where we can jump ahead of Eric and attack first."

"Attack?" Lynell says as an announcement that she's joining the conversation. "You mean the gimpy woman with only one working hand, the ex-rebel, and the disowned son? Yeah, we wouldn't be outnumbered at all." She plops onto the remaining chair and grabs the third bowl.

"Eric's attention is on Anna right now," Zach says. "It's the perfect time to make our move."

"What move?" Daniel asks.

"Lynell," Zach says.

Lynell raises an eyebrow, a bit of broth dripping down her chin.

"You make a claim. Take power from Eric before he can hurt anyone else."

"But what if he does anyway?" Lynell asks, dipping the spoon back into the soup. "What if he goes after Anna for revenge?"

"Take control and you'll have the power to keep them safe. You can assign them security detail or simply eliminate the threat."

"We need to figure out the code first," Lynell says, ignoring the implications of what 'eliminating the threat' would consist of.

"You can do that later. Right now, just challenge him."

"How? Make a statement to the press? Tweet it? 'Hey, internet. I'm an Elysian and have decided to make myself CEO of the Registration.'"

Daniel smirks, and Zach shakes his head, exasperation lining his forehead.

"Get into his home office. You'll need access to his contacts, those who work for him and the oligarchs. He has a computer in there with files, calendars, essential data, access to the small portion of the Regulation he can control without the code. You need to know the Regulators and their government counterparts, Sanitary Crew, Researchers, Registration office workers. He even has proof of your legitimacy and information on you and your family in there. If we can get you there, you'll have what you need to make your claim. Plus, you'll simply be more credible if you're in the Elysian house."

Zach watches Lynell and Daniel with expectant urgency.

Finally, Lynell gets her mouth to work, though her tongue is dry and seems to move slowly. "You want me to go back into that house just for a few phone numbers and informational lists?"

"When it comes to the Registration, information is power," Zach says.

"Do you remember how hard we worked to get her out of that house?" Daniel says, voice rising an octave.

"Yes. Just humor me by drawing up a plan, please. If we get nowhere, then I'll drop it and we can figure out something else."

Daniel and Lynell share a look, silently weighing the pros and cons of Zach's idea. The ticking of the clock on the wall behind her is the only sound in the room for a moment.

The fear of being back in that house begs her to say no.

But the idea that they could do something to end this outweighs her terror.

"Okay, fine. But I'm only agreeing to discuss it. Not do it."

Zach smiles. "Good enough."

Lynell leans against the wall, watching Daniel. His back is turned to her, and the thin blue shirt pulls against his shoulders, rippling as he moves. He and Zach do most of the planning, using Daniel's battle knowledge and their shared experience pulling pranks to craft a strategy. Two hours fly by before Zach requests a break and disappears outside for some air, despite Lynell's protests. There's an ulcer on the inside of her lip and she runs her tongue over it absentmindedly. Daniel lowers his hands and turns around. He grins at the sight of Lynell standing there, watching him.

"Stalk much?"

She shrugs. "Just admiring."

He crosses the room and she stands up straight, looking up at him as he brushes the hair out of her face. "This will all be over soon."

She nods and wants to smile, kiss him, hug him, anything to allow herself a moment of happiness. But worry eats at her and the only words she can muster are, "I need you on my side."

"I need you, too," he says. "Plus, being on your side has its benefits." There's a teasing note to his voice and a quiet, breathy laugh leaves her throat. She turns her head to rest against his chest and wraps her arms around his middle. He reciprocates the hug and presses a kiss to the top of her head.

They pull apart when the front door opens and closes. Zach locks it behind himself and starts toward them, his face pale and mouth parted. His eyes are glassy and lost as he looks from Lynell to Daniel and then down at the burner phone in his hand.

Lynell steps forward. Icicles form around her heart and a deep, empty feeling of dread slices its way into her gut. "Zach," she says. Her voice sounds foreign to her own ears. "What's going on?"

Zach blinks. His mouth closes, opens, closes again.

"Answer her, Zach," Daniel says.

"I called Jeremy to be sure he'll be covering the exit at the house when we go and—" His voice falls off as his gaze moves from Daniel to Lynell. "Eric answered."

Slices of dread make their way up to Lynell's chest. "And?" she asks in a louder voice than she meant.

"He—" Zach clears his throat and swallows before he continues, "Josh is dead and he has Zoe and Anna."

"What?" Daniel's voice booms in the small apartment.

Lynell staggers back and her legs go weak. She's about to fall when she finds a wall behind her to lean against. Zach's looking at her, talking to her directly, but his edges blur, and his words sound muffled as if she's hearing it all from inside a bubble.

"They went to Josh's brother's house apparently, but Dad had Regulators there already. Josh tried to fight, but they killed him and took Zoe and Anna to Dad's house. He said if we don't come, both of us, he's going to kill them. Lynell, it's a trap, we shouldn't—"

"Shut up, Zach!" Daniel yells, cutting him off. Zach steps back in shock, and Lynell looks between the men, a deafening buzz filling her ears.

"We have to be careful and think logically," Zach says.

"Haven't we been through this? That's our daughter!"

"I know! That's why we have to plan this."

"We can't just let him kill Anna!" Splotches of red fill Daniel's cheeks, and Lynell feels a distant desire to reach out and touch him, but she's frozen against the wall.

"He won't. She's a bargaining chip for him. He will leave her unharmed as long as Lynell is out here. But if we run in there in a panic, he will kill her! He'll kill us all."

"I swear, Zach. If I make it through this alive and my daughter doesn't, I will Register and kill you myself," Daniel says through his teeth.

Zach blanches and looks to Lynell, almost begging her for help, to talk sense into Daniel.

"Okay," Lynell whispers. Gathering any remaining energy, she pushes off the wall and steps between the men. "Okay, you're both right. We can't waste any time, but we also can't blindly run into a trap." Her words seem to deflate Daniel, and he lets out a breath. "Eric said he will kill them if we don't come?"

Zach nods.

"Who? All three of us?"

Zach's mouth opens and his eyes widen as he follows her thinking. "No," he says. "Just you and me. He didn't mention Danny at all."

Lynell sucks her lips in and nods, looking down so she doesn't have to meet Daniel's eyes. "So, we go. Just you and me."

She looks up at Zach and can tell he doesn't like it, but he still gives a slight nod. "It's not a bad idea."

"No, absolutely not!" Daniel says.

Finally, Lynell faces him. He's staring down at her with so much pain that she can physically feel it. And when he talks, his voice is so soft and broken that she thinks she'll never be able to get the sound out of her head. "You're not supposed to leave me again, remember?"

"No, we won't be leaving you," Zach says. Daniel finally rips his eyes from Lynell to look at Zach. "We're making you our secret weapon."

For the second time in less than two weeks, Lynell watches the world fly by as she heads to the Elysian house with Zach by her side. He's behind the wheel, silent, eyes focused straight ahead. He stops at the gate, the long driveway ahead of them.

"Remember, whatever he says—"

"Stick to the plan," she finishes for him.

Zach nods just as both his door and Lynell's are opened from the outside.

Lynell looks to the right and sees a guard standing there.

"Hey," she says. The guard frowns. "We have an invitation. Something about a family dinner party? I didn't bring a gift for the host. Do you think he'll be mad?"

Zach chuckles.

"We need to search the vehicle. You can ride to the house with Felix," the guard on Zach's side of the car says.

"I'm assuming you're Felix?" Lynell asks, looking back at the man who opened her door. He gives her a stiff nod. "I heard once that Felix means happy. But you don't seem very happy."

"Lynell," Zach says, a warning lilt to his voice.

She unbuckles her seatbelt. "Just trying to cut some tension," she mutters as she gets out of the car. Felix reaches for her arm, but she sidesteps out of his reach. "I can walk myself, thanks."

She and Zach follow Felix to a car waiting for them inside the gate and climb in the back. A woman with short hair and a thick neck sits in the passenger's seat. Felix gets behind the wheel.

As soon as they stop in front of the large house, Lynell's body tenses.

Two guards flank her and Zach when they step out of the car and walk up the white steps. A painful feeling of déjà vu hits her, though this time having Zach at her side is reassuring rather than terrifying.

The female guard passes them and opens the front door. Lynell steps closer to Zach, the heat of his body a talisman to keep her sane. Her hand curls into a fist, expecting to see Eric on the other side of the door. But instead, they're met with the empty corridor.

"This way," the female guard says. She leads them down a familiar hallway and into the only room of the house Lynell enjoys.

She steps into the parlor she explored all those days ago. Her eyes cover the room, the chairs, fireplace, and bookshelves. She remembers sitting in here for hours, wondering what it would be like to choose this family and live in a house like this.

She now knows the sacrifice wouldn't be worth it.

Next, her mind registers the people in the room.

Four guards, two at each door, including the two that lead Zach and Lynell in.

Eric, standing in front of the fireplace.

And sitting in the chair directly in front of Lynell is a terrified woman holding a small child in her lap. Her eyes are smudged with black and her nose is bright red, probably from weeping. Her pale blonde hair is up in a bun and her fingers are curled protectively around the girl she's holding. The child is gripping a pink blanket with a pig head and holds her thumb securely between her lips.

Anna. Zoe.

Lynell's face is hot and she steps forward, wanting to run to them.

Just as Lynell moves, the largest guard in the room steps forward and Zach grabs her arm. She looks back at him, and he gives a minuscule shake of his head.

"Welcome home, Lynell," Eric says, his smile splitting his face.

Her lips tremble with the desire to curl into a snarl.

"I'm so glad you could join us," Eric continues, stepping away from the fireplace. "I've had the pleasure of getting to know young Anna here and her adoptive mother, Zoe, is it?" he turns to Zoe, giving her a disgustingly sweet smile.

Zoe just chokes on a sob and looks away from him.

"Anna is a sweetheart," Eric says, moving closer to Lynell. Zach's hold on her arm instinctively tightens.

"She's very talkative, did you know? But, of course, you don't. You don't know her at all, do you?"

"Eric, I swear, if you hurt her—"

"She loves it at Uncle Eric's house," he says, interrupting her. Lynell steps back, causing Zach to move, too, his arm brushing against her own. "And I was kind enough to allow Zoe to come as well, to keep Anna happy." Eric turns, facing Zoe and clapping his hands together. "It's like a nice vacation for mother and daughter, isn't it, Mrs. Raines?"

Zoe tenses and drops her face, burying her nose in Anna's curly hair.

Eric chuckles, spinning back to Lynell. "Zoe here is from Oklahoma. That's where Anna has lived all this time." Lynell tries not to react to this information, afraid of tipping Eric off to the fact that she already knew.

"Unfortunately, the family wasn't home when we arrived. They were up north visiting relatives. So, they had a short flight back to Dallas earlier. It wiped poor Anna out."

Carefully, Eric turns and walks back to the chair with Zoe and Anna. Zoe shrinks away from him, her grip tightening on Anna, who frowns and looks up. "Are you tired, darling?"

Anna blinks. "No."

"Come here, let me hold you," Eric says, holding out his hands. Zoe shakes her head and curls a protective arm around Anna.

"Please, no," she mutters.

Eric shoots her a venomous look, and she flinches. She barely fights him when Eric grabs Anna and lifts her up to sit on his hip. "Smart choice," Eric says to Zoe before tapping Anna's nose lightly. "Do you like it here?" he asks her.

Anna nods. "Uncle Eric lives here," she says.

Eric beams. Lynell grits her teeth, and Zach whispers, "Careful."

"That's right!" Eric says, sounding genuinely proud. "You can trust Uncle Eric."

Anna turns to look back at her. "Mommy," she says, reaching out for Zoe.

"It's okay, darling. Mommy isn't feeling very well," Eric says. He bounces Anna on his hip and turns so she can't see Zoe anymore. The movement allows Lynell a glimpse of Anna's face. She's frowning, her bottom lip pushed out, probably signaling that she is about to erupt into tears.

"Please, Eric," Lynell says. "She's just a kid."

"I'm not going to hurt her. I'm not a monster."

She tugs at Zach's grip, but he keeps her back. "Could have fooled me. You already murdered her father!" She wants to shout it, to scream at Eric, but the presence of Zoe and Anna keeps her voice as a harsh whisper. The sight of tears welling up in Anna's eyes makes Lynell's own sting.

"Isn't her father Daniel Carter?"

This is it, she thinks. The lie she agreed to tell.

"Daniel?" She shakes her head. "No. She's not Daniel's." Without being able to stop herself, she glances past Eric at Zoe. The woman catches Lynell's gaze and seems to beg with her silently.

"Please," Zoe mouths.

Lynell looks back at Eric and quickly adds, "Let them go. She's not a threat to you. She's not a legitimate Elysian." Panic fills the entire cavity of her chest.

"Not according to my records," he says, moving Anna to his other side.

Guilt fills Lynell's stomach, mixing with the panic to create a toxic emotion that makes her feel dizzy. "I cheated on him. Anna isn't Daniel's. She's not legitimate. That's why I . . . I didn't want her. Please, she's not a threat to you."

Eric raises his eyebrows and looks down at Anna. "You look quite like your father," he says to her.

This breaks something in Anna, and she lets out a wailing cry. "Daddy!"

Eric flinches at the sound and turns to hand her off to Zoe. "Quiet her," he says.

Zoe takes Anna back, her relief evident. Every muscle in her body seems to relax with the return of her daughter. She starts smoothing Anna's hair, kissing the top of her head, and making promises she can't keep. "Everything's going to be okay, baby."

Lynell's knees lock, thighs tightening and toes digging into her shoes. She forces herself to look back at Eric. "She's not Daniel's," she says again, desperation filling her bones. "I'm telling the truth. Please, let them go."

"And how do I know this isn't a lie? A feeble attempt to get your daughter released?"

Lynell shakes her head. "It's not."

"You know there are ways to test your claim?"

"Go ahead." She swallows and focuses on Zach's grip on her arm to try and steady her voice. "You can ask Daniel if you want."

"He's aware?"

Lynell nods. "That's why he wanted me to use my Registration for her." She turns away, looking out the window. "When I found out, I couldn't . . . I couldn't keep it from him."

"Who's the girl's father?" Eric asks.

"His name is Oliver White," she says. "Look him up. I worked with him."

Oliver is a former colleague. His eyes are as blue as Daniel's. Lynell met his wife at a company Christmas party one year. She wonders briefly what Jennifer would say if she knew that Lynell is putting her husband on the radar of a psychotic murderer.

It's funny how there seems to be a limit to the amount of guilt a person can feel. Lynell's limit was pushed and reached and expanded years ago. Now she's numb to the feeling.

"I will do just that. Maybe pay him a visit to validate your claim."

"Let Anna go," Lynell says. "Talk to Oliver all you want, I don't care. But you promised to let Anna go if we came back."

"I don't remember that. Zachary?" he turns his gaze to Zach, who drops his hold from Lynell's arm. She feels the loss like a chord tethering her to earth being snapped. "Did I make that promise?"

Zach's voice is tight, controlled. "You said you would kill them if we didn't."

"Ah, yes. But I never said anything about what I would do if you obeyed."

Lynell glances back at Zach, eyes wide as he shakes his head slowly. She knew this, of course, but she still feels reduced to her bones, vulnerable to the harsh air of the world.

"Please, just . . . let them go," Lynell says, looking back at Eric.

Eric seems to consider that for a moment, the sound of Anna's wails filling the pause. "Okay, I'll release them," he says.

Lynell sways on her feet and notices movement on the other side of the room. Another guard has entered, standing with his own gun across his chest. Zach grabs her arm. She steps closer to him as Eric turns to face them again. He glares at Lynell, his white teeth glinting as he says, "As soon as you give me the letter."

The desire to agree, to give in, roils inside her like a hurricane. Only the slow movement of the new guard and Zach's squeeze on her arm keep her from agreeing.

"You give me the letter, and I let the bastard child go," Eric says, walking to Lynell. She looks up at him, drained and defeated. "You keep it from me, and I'll show Zoe the basement. Young Anna too."

"No!" Lynell yells.

Eric gives a dramatic sigh and shrugs, lifting his hands in the air. "The power to prevent it is in your hands."

Anna is still crying, though quieter now, and Zoe looks up. Her face is pale and her eyes seem to sink into her face.

Zach pulls Lynell back and steps forward so he's closer to his father. "And me? Why am I here?"

Eric nearly growls. "You're my son," he says, spit flying from his lips. "I will not have you betray me for a stranger."

"That stranger is my cousin. She's family."

"I'm your family!" Eric yells. Lynell barely notices the hurt and regret in his voice. "Not her!"

Zach looks quickly back at Lynell and gives her a nod. She catches her breath and straightens her back. "Okay!" she yells. Eric instantly looks at her. "I'll do it. I'll tell you what the letter said. Please, just let them go."

As soon as she's agreed, a guard steps forward and grabs Lynell, yanking her toward the free chair next to a coffee table. It's across the room from Zach and next to Zoe and Anna. Lynell can feel all their gazes on the back of her head as she sits and reaches out with a shaking hand to pick up the pen in front of her.

Lynell steals one last glance. Not at Anna, but at the extra guard in the room. His soft eyes return her gaze and before anyone can question it, she looks back to the paper and starts writing.

She's not even finished the "ell" at the end of "Little Lynell," when it happens.

Two gunshots ring.

Zoe screams. Anna cries.

Eric roars.

Lynell drops to the floor and rolls to push up to her elbows, looking around. Zach has taken down one of the guards and is holding up the gun he stole, training it on Eric's face. Daniel was able to surprise the man next to him with an attack and a shot to the chest, leaving two guards remaining. Daniel fights with one and the other has his own gun raised at Zach.

For a moment, there is no sound but Anna's sobs.

Then Eric laughs. "You think you can escape again? This place is surrounded by guards."

"I know you, Dad. I helped create your security measures. This is my home, too," Zach says. Lynell glances between her cousin and his father before checking on Daniel. He has the guard pinned to the floor and his gun raised, trained on Eric.

"This is not your home! You are no son of mine!" Eric bellows at his son.

Zach flinches at the word and for a terrifying moment, Lynell thinks he's going to lower the gun. Instead, he grips it tighter with both hands and says, "Then I have nothing to lose."

As if in slow motion, Lynell watches Zach's finger squeeze the trigger just as a deafening crack fills the room.

Lynell screams and scrambles to her feet. In a split second, Zach is on the floor, and Lynell drops to her knees next to him. She pushes a hand to the wound in his chest, blood bubbling up between her fingers.

Zach coughs and his eyes go unfocused. He doesn't even get a chance to have a last word. He's dead before Lynell can say his name.

Lynell hears Daniel yelling. There's another gunshot and her chest caves in on itself. She imagines Daniel falling too and knows she won't be able to handle it.

But a glance tells her it was Daniel who fired. His smoking gun is still raised, aimed at a spot past Lynell. Hair tickling her cheek, she turns her head to see the guard who killed Zach dropping to the floor with a bullet hole in the middle of his forehead. Lynell doesn't hear Daniel yelling at her to get up, to run. She doesn't even hear the next gunshot and the shatter of glass as the window explodes. Her eyes find Eric, who hasn't looked away from his son, lying dead in front of Lynell.

Eric's mouth forms a word she can't hear. Her mind is buzzing and her body thrums with panic and grief and anger.

In the corner of her eye, she sees movement. Daniel has crossed the room and is tugging Zoe out of the chair, saying something that makes her nod. She turns and runs to the shattered window, still holding Anna.

Daniel looks to Lynell and finally, sound returns.

"Lynell, get up!" he yells, taking a step toward her.

Eric turns, sees Daniel, then Zoe, who's made it out of the window.

She shakes her head, knowing what's going to happen before it does.

Eric pulls his own gun and barely aims before firing it.

Zoe falls.

Lynell screams again, struggling to stand. Zach's blood feels hot and slippery against her skin, and she feels torn as she starts for Daniel, who has already turned to the window. He makes it first and she's still too far away when strong arms circle her from behind.

The remaining guard holds her tight as she struggles. Daniel immediately turns from the window and raises his gun at the guard holding Lynell.

"Daniel!" She kicks and claws at the arms holding her, but the guard doesn't flinch. The doors behind them fly open and more guards fill the room. Outside, Anna is sitting on the ground next to Zoe's still body, crying.

"Danny!" Lynell yells. Daniel takes a step toward her, but she shakes her head as the guard drags her back. "Anna."

A war rages in Daniel's eyes. But with the arrival of new guards and the sound of Eric shouting orders to kill him and the child, he makes his decision.

The hot blanket of relief covers Lynell's shoulders when she sees Daniel jump through the window and scoop up Anna.

She goes limp for a second, and when the guard's grip loosens, she slips out of his arms and runs for Eric. "I'll kill you!" she yells, earning his attention.

She spits, and satisfaction fills her smile when the saliva hits his face. His top lip curls back and she freezes, body stuck between fight or flight. She spins, preparing to run for the window, when a guard punches her square in the middle of her face. Blackness oozes into the edges of her vision and she teeters. Before she can fall, a guard grabs her again, this time holding his arm around her neck.

Eric steps closer and whispers, "I will kill everyone you've ever known."

With a look over his shoulder, she sees Daniel is close to the open exit at the edge of the yard, thanks to her distraction. It was the only part of Zach's original plan that he'd been able to implement before learning that Eric had Anna. He got rid of the guards that were stationed at the exit by calling them, pretending to be a doctor, and telling them to head to the hospital because their wives were in an accident. He also made sure his friend, Jeremy, was conveniently there when they got the call so he could take over guard duty when they left. Then Jeremy unlocked the gate and left, turning it into the perfect unguarded escape route.

Lynell smiles, unconsciousness starting to claim her. "Danny . . ." she mutters.

The last thing she hears is another gunshot. The last thing she sees is Daniel jerking, then falling, just a foot from the exit.

Then darkness envelopes her.

She wakes in the middle of a panic attack. She sits up, screaming and sweating. She's on the skeletal spring bed in the basement of the Elysian house. She gasps and scrambles off the bed, falling as she does. Her vision spots when her left hand hits the ground, and she can't get enough breath to even scream. She crawls to the edge of the room, pushes her back against the wall, and squeezes her eyes shut.

Her heart is beating too fast. She can't be here.

"You're awake."

Her head snaps up, eyes flying open. Eric is standing in the doorway.

"Where's Danny?" Her fingers touch her cheek and she feels something wet, assuming it's tears. But when she pulls her hand away, she sees her hand is still covered in blood.

Zach's blood.

"Dead," Eric says. His voice is flat, lacking anger or sick enjoyment or anything at all.

Lynell shakes her head. "No, no he's not."

"He is."

She pulls her knees to her chest. "He can't be."

"Soon you will be, too. But first, I think you could use some time alone. Think about all you lost. All the death you've caused just by denying me a few simple words. You lost. I won. It's over." He turns and walks out of the room, leaving Lynell alone as the door shuts behind him.

She screams. The sound fills the room, shakes her bones, and echoes for years.

DAY 13 ————————————————°

The skin on her cheeks is tight from dried tears. The blood that poured from her nose is cracking. Her throat is sore, and her body feels like she was locked in a box and thrown from the top of a mountain. She can still hear her own wailing, though the room has been silent for hours. Her eyelids close slowly, as if it's taking all the strength in the world to accomplish a single blink.

Lynell is sitting with her back against the wall, knees to her chest, body swaying. Her butt hurts from not moving for hours but the pain doesn't feel like it belongs to her.

Every pain in her body—the broken fingers, cuts by her eye and on her lip, a broken nose and a fresh bruise on her cheekbone—every ache from running and hiding and fighting and falling and crying, every hurt is nothing, is even relief from the agonizing, shattering, tormenting pain that is waging a war in her chest.

Daniel Carter. The only man she's ever loved. The only man she thinks has ever loved her. The man who chases after what he wants, stands tall for what he believes in, loves fiercely, and forgives freely.

Lynell stares, unseeing, in the room she was deposited in hours earlier. Or minutes, she doesn't really know. Maybe days.

How long has Daniel been gone? Because he is.

Gone.

Must be.

That last gunshot found its mark in his back. Guards were filling the room. Eric said so himself. *He's dead.*

And Anna? She's just a kid. There's no way she escaped alone.

The thought makes Lynell drop her face to her knees.

Lynell, though still alive, is dead, too. Locked in the Elysian basement with no windows and only one heavily guarded door. Lynell only has two days left to live and decide whether or not to give Eric the letter. There's no reason to hold onto it. There's no reason to give it to him. There's no reason for anything anymore.

Daniel would disagree. He'd say there's always a reason to choose good. To do the right thing. But the right thing no longer seems like a clear path. It's been buried underneath all the pain and misery. She couldn't find the next step if she tried.

The air in the room is warm, but Lynell feels cold. As if death was standing in the doorway, just biding his time to claim her, too. Lynell blinks and forces her mouth to close.

She reaches up and wipes her hand across her face. It comes away with dried blood speckling her fingertips.

She should stand. Stretch her legs. Maybe relieve her bladder in the bucket still nailed to the floor.

But she doesn't. Instead, she closes her eyes again. Falling asleep is the sweetest escape ever gifted to her.

⸺

"Little Lyn . . . or maybe Little Lynell? You never did get the chance to finish it."

The words hit her from every angle. Her skull throbs. She flinches and shifts, tipping to the side. With a jolt, she remembers she fell asleep sitting up, and her eyes fly open, back straightening so she doesn't fall over.

Eric is standing above her, illuminated by yellow light and flanked by two guards. Lynell recognizes them, though she doesn't know their names.

The skinnier one seems tense, a muscle twitching in his cheek every time Eric moves without warning.

"I wonder if my dear brother called you 'Little Lynell.' What else did he write to you? I'd love to hear it."

It's a feeble attempt at taunting. She can hear something close to boredom in his voice, though his face is tired, eyes a noticeable pink. She desperately wants to continue sleeping. But Eric won't let that happen. Maybe he'll strap her to another machine that shocks her awake.

She can't say she'd mind it. Then she could let unconsciousness take her as often as it wants, just so she can feel that shot of electricity course through her body.

"Well?" Eric demands, snapping loudly in front of Lynell's face. The guard flinches. Lynell groans, the sound too sharp in her already clouded mind. "Oh, I'm sorry. Feeling a bit hungover?"

Lynell glares at him and rubs her eyes.

"I'm sorry to return you to this room. But I really had no other choice."

She pushes her hand down and leans on it to scoot back.

"Oh, come on. You can't be mad at me!" Eric says. He raises his hands to either side. "I mean, what do you expect when a stranger breaks into my house trying to steal my property?"

"Anna is not your property," Lynell says. Her voice is like claws dragging against her throat. She coughs and lets her head lull back against the headboard. "And neither am I."

"No, you're right. You're my guest," Eric says. The familiar tone of sick pleasure starts to make its way back into his voice, though with less energy. He steps forward and sits on the edge of the metal bed frame. "Would you like some breakfast? I had my cook make chicken and waffles."

Lynell sneers, her upper lip shaking with the effort. "Eat a dick, Eric."

Eric cocks his head, his mouth opening in feigned shock. "Language! I won't have my niece speak like that." Eric stands and turns to the guards, his hands folded behind his back. "I'll leave you alone," he says. He walks slowly, heel to toe, as if calculating each movement. "But if you start to become a problem, I'll station a few guards in here to keep you under control. If you behave, they'll stay right outside." He gestures to the door, and Lynell leans to the side, seeing two other men outside standing with their back to the wall, like statues. "If you begin to test my patience, I'll bring in some of my more creative men. Maybe you can have a reunion with Reggie." He steps out of the room and turns to look at her again. For a second, she sees a flash of Zach in his face, like a sick reminder that her cousin is dead, and Eric is still here. "I suggest ending it quickly and giving me the letter. It's what's best for us all."

With that, he leaves, the guards following, and the door closes behind them.

Sitting still in the quiet room disconnects her from her body. She floats above, still feeling the physical pain, but focusing more on the emotional loss. Faces fill her vision, and she hears the voices of her mom, Daniel, Zach, Zoe, Josh, and Anna as if they were in the room with her. She even imagines how her dad's voice might have sounded.

But as time goes by, those images become unbearable, and she has to move. Her body aches as she stands, legs shaking.

She walks to the door, knocking gently.

"Hey," she mutters, wondering if the guards outside can hear her. "I have to pee."

"Bucket," a man replies.

So, they can hear her. Makes sense. Someone will have to be there to listen when she finally hands over the letter.

She frowns and looks back to the bucket. With no worry for her dignity, she stumbles over and sits on it to relieve her bladder. For a moment, she wonders why she can't smell anything.

Then she realizes.

There's the silver lining to a broken nose.

"Hey," she says, walking back to the door. "Will that get emptied?" When there's no answer, she mumbles, "That's not very sanitary," and turns back to the room.

The light is built into the ceiling, too high for her to reach even if she stood on the bed frame. And even if she could reach it, the bulb is behind a metal frame that she has no hope of unscrewing. The same can be said for the air vent, which is in the corner of the ceiling.

The bed is the only accessible thing in the room.

She pulls on her earlobe in thought. She walks over to the bed and curls a hand around a metal spring. It's rusty and squeaks when she tugs on it. Kneeling, Lynell grabs a leg of the bed and lifts with all her strength. The bed rises a few inches off the ground and Lynell lets go so it drops again.

Heavier than she expected. Or she's weaker than she thought.

She tries to disconnect one of the wires from the rest of the bed. Success is within her grasp when the door opens and Eric stomps in, frowning at her.

She lets go, holds her hand up, and steps back. A dark orange stain covers the palm of her hand and exposed skin on her forearm from messing with the bed.

"What are you doing?" he asks.

Lynell doesn't answer.

"You're a pest and I can't wait to rid the world of you."

"That's not very nice," Lynell says with a hoarse voice.

"We could have avoided all of this," he says, raising his hands, gesturing to the room at large. "All the bloodshed and loss. If you'd only accepted my original offer."

"And give you the power to control everyone? To cause hundreds, maybe thousands, of deaths?"

He frowns and drops his arms. "My son, the bastard. He betrayed me. Giving secrets to our enemies and—"

"Saving the lives of his best friend and his cousin, *your* niece?"

"Getting himself killed," Eric spits.

"Your men killed him," Lynell counters, a surge of anger giving her the energy to step forward, closer to Eric. "It's your fault he's dead."

Rage burns bright in Eric's eyes, but Lynell doesn't have time to flinch before his hand is flying through the air. His fist connects with her jaw, and she feels the extra blossom of pain from his knuckles as she falls to the ground. A shriek falls from her lips involuntarily and white spots blot her vision.

"Maybe you'd like to see how it feels, to have a child taken from this world in front of your face," Eric says.

Lynell's stomach goes cold. So, Anna is still alive. *Where?*

"I think Anna will be glad to see her parents again."

Panic pulls Lynell up and she rises to her knees, eyes wide and heart beating madly as she looks up at Eric. "No!" she screams.

Eric's fierce scowl starts to turn into a grin. "You know my cost."

"And you know my price." Lynell's heart is thudding against her ribs. She can hear Daniel telling her not to do it, to choose good. But there's nothing left. All she can do before she dies is protect her daughter. Save one life.

"Promise you won't hurt her."

Eric raises an eyebrow. "If you give me the letter—the real letter—I won't hurt Anna. I'll let her live a life away from here, without ever knowing her true parentage."

Her thoughts feel like a bat beating against the inside of her skull. She hates herself when she opens her mouth and says, "Okay. I'll tell you."

Eric smiles wide. A guard comes forward and hands her a pen and paper.

"I knew you would see it my way," Eric says. Lynell's eyes burn but there are no more tears to fall. "This is good, Little Lyn. And I may still let you live. Someone will have to take over when I'm gone."

His words feel like dust in the air as Lynell writes. The words are shaky and look foreign to her. She grits her teeth as she writes, *"If I am killed in the attempt, do not be angry. Know that I left with a hope for the future."* She realizes now he said *killed* instead of *Registered* because he couldn't be Registered. Not as an Elysian.

What hope is there? What possible hope could Eli have had?

She has none. Eric won't let her live. Her claim is stronger than his. Even if he figures out the code. She will always be legitimate, and he never will be.

"Of course, you will live until I have the code. I can't take the chance that you're giving me a fake letter, can I?"

Her knuckles turn white when she grips the pen tighter, trying to ignore the guilt of what she's doing.

"Think twice about giving me a fake letter," Eric says. "Because you will regret it."

He's quiet until she's finished writing. Then he rips the page from her hands and scans it, frowning. Miraculously, he says nothing. Instead, he turns and leaves the room, taking all but two guards with him. This time, the guards stay inside the room, watching her closely.

Lynell's hands shake. She drops her face in them, pushing out a breath in the hopes of ridding her body of guilt.

It doesn't work.

It's been a few hours, and Lynell has seen no one but two sets of guards. Until Eric storms in, his face bright red and the letter crumpled in his fist. Lynell jumps, scrambling up from the floor as fear thunders under her skin.

"It's fake!" he yells.

She shakes her head. "No, it's—" Her words are cut off when he hits her. She manages to catch herself on the wall to keep from falling this time. Blood covers her tongue.

"What's the code? Tell me the code!"

She would if she could. But they never figured it out.

He grabs her hair and rips her head back, causing her to scream. His lips are so close that she can feel the breath of his next words against her ear.

"You'll regret this." Then he abruptly lets go and storms out of the room.

⌐─┬─┬─┐

She's not left alone for long. Reggie saunters in, wearing tight latex gloves and carrying a black bag. No Arnold, Lynell notices with a ghost of relief.

"Did you miss me?" Reggie asks. He drops the bag to the floor and zips it open. "How should we play today?"

Icy, numbing fear flushes through her system.

Reggie hums thoughtfully. Lynell hears him drop something back into the bag. "I say we start small."

Against her better judgment, she looks his way. He's grinning, holding a pair of pliers. "You're right-handed, correct?"

She tries to scramble away, and he easily hauls her onto the wire bed and begins strapping her down. Her left hand stays free, and the broken fingers throb in anticipation when Reggie grabs her forearm and positions the pliers in front of her fingers. "Anything you want to say? Anything about a letter or a code?"

Fear propels the words from her mouth. "It was real." She shakes when Reggie clamps the pliers down on her thumbnail. "I swear, I already told you, I—" Her stammering morphs into a scream when Reggie pulls.

⌐─┬─┬─┐

After Reggie grows bored with the pliers, he brings out a device that sends waves of shocks through Lynell's body. It doesn't take long for her to pass out. Her dreams carry her into the past and deposit her in a small room with her mother. She watches the memory play out like a movie.

Then she understands. Her mom tells her that words define and create them. That Scrabble, of everything in this world, is a game of connections. And that is the key. She wants to reach into whatever world comes next and hold her mother's face and tell her, *I get it now, Mom. Rest.* She's not sure how much time passes before she gains consciousness again, voices filling her head.

"I'll leave her for now. She may be out for a while. Probably for the next hour before Mr. Elysian returns."

She's still lying on the metal bed frame but is no longer tied down. A glove of grating pain covers her left hand and a headache throbs like a band around her forehead. The memory and Lynell's understanding pierces through it all. It's a light, a weapon, and hope for her to seize.

"She'll crack soon. There's no more fight left in her," someone says, and the straps holding Lynell down release.

Daniel once told her that she would never stop fighting, that it was built into the core of who she was.

"You're strong, resilient, and kind. You amaze me not because you're a product of your environment, but because you overcame it," he said.

Eli fell in love with Elizabeth because she could beat him at Scrabble.

Daniel fell in love with Lynell because she could beat life.

The door closes, and Lynell focuses on her breathing and listens to the guards shuffle and scratch their faces. One clears his throat and sighs, probably bored with his job of guarding an unarmed, unconscious girl.

A dozen locked doors. However many guards with guns, who aren't afraid to shoot. A wounded and exhausted body. No one to save her this time. Her options are limited. She has her life and the key to figuring out the code. That's it.

The code that unlocks a world of possibilities. The code that Eric so desperately wants. That Eli built a red-herring letter around just so he could pass it on to his child.

She needs time. Eric will do whatever it takes to figure out the code. He's probably playing a game with her. Giving her a countdown clock to her death. Letting her watch her breaths tick away before they're snuffed out completely. The last member of a family she finally let herself believe she could have.

Suddenly Zach's voice fills her memory. *"It's easy to get mistreated men on your side with a little kindness."*

Eric isn't invincible. His power comes from nothing more than a name and fear.

Well, Lynell has the same name.

Keeping her eyes closed, Lynell asks, "What if I ran at you?" She hears clothes ruffle, and one of the men takes a step. She lets out a deep breath, smirks and opens one eye to peek at the guards.

There are still only two. They've switched out since she was conscious. One is tall with wide shoulders that stretch the seams of his shirt. His face is square and smooth, nose flat, and he's frowning at Lynell. The other is shorter, and his muscles are smaller but still straining against his shirt. When she sees the scar on his face, recognition sparks. He was here last time. He was the first guard she spoke to before she was brought to this room the first time.

Lynell shakes her head, looking back to the shorter guard. His hair is still long and his beard patchy.

They're both wearing a uniform. A black button up suits that stretches for quick movements, black boots, and a belt that holds a gun and knife.

She closes her eye and hooks her thumbs over her stomach.

"If I just jumped up and ran, grabbed one of those shiny knives in your belt and tried to stab you in the neck." She focuses on making her voice sound nonchalant, as if discussing a movie with a friend. "What would you do?"

They don't answer, but she can hear one of them unclip the gun from his belt.

She chuckles. "Shoot me?" She shrugs, the bare metal underneath her scratching her skin. She manages to control the flinch and instead opens her eyes and sits up, cradling her injured arm. "Go ahead," she says, glaring at the men. The taller one points his gun to the ground, but seems ready to raise and shoot any moment. The other is standing in the exact same position he was earlier, arms crossed and weight resting on his back leg.

Lynell repositions so she's sitting on the edge of the bedframe, her legs dangling over the side. She raises an eyebrow and focuses her attention on the taller guard. "What do you think Mr. Elysian would do if he found out you killed his precious niece before she had a chance to give him the code he desperately desires?"

He doesn't answer, but she notices his finger twitch on the gun.

Lynell gives a dramatic sigh and shrugs. "Because I don't think he'd be very happy." She looks to the guard on the left. "What do you think?"

He squints at her, frowning. The silence stretches on, and she dips her head to prompt his answer.

"You said you don't know it," he says. The other guard jerks his head to stare at his coworker, eyes wide with shock that he replied.

Lynell laughs. "I lied." That's a gamble, she thinks. If these two tell Eric, he'll be even angrier and more dangerous. "But why tell Eric that when playing a scared, confused, naïve child is so fun?"

"Fun?" His eyes travel down her body, lingering on her hand and the bruises and cuts that litter any exposed skin. "You call this fun?"

Lynell bites a nail and shrugs again. "It's fun watching Eric squirm, don't you think? I mean, between you and me . . ." She lowers her voice and leans forward. "He knows he's a bastard and has no real claim to the Elysian name."

The shorter guard's eyes widen and the other one raises his gun. "How dare—"

"Why?" Lynell interrupts. "Because I'm wrong? I'm not . . . and you must know that. Why else would I be such a threat to him?"

"You are—"

"The only true, legitimate heir left," Lynell says. "The only person with the code."

The taller guard seems to be getting flustered. His gun is still trained on her, but his hands adjust their hold as he shifts his weight from foot to foot.

"Mr. Elysian is our boss. There are no real threats to him," he says.

"That's because he's taken what should have been a gift and turned it into a self-serving instrument meant to spread fear. He's a truly horrific man, and he isn't even legitimate. If you tell me right now, truthfully, that he's been good to you, I'll tell you the code."

They both gasp and the shorter one steps forward saying, "He's been good to us."

"Yeah? Where's that scar from?" she asks, jutting her chin out as a gesture to the scar on his face.

He doesn't answer.

"I did say truthfully, didn't I?" Lynell says.

The guards exchange a look, and Lynell feels her body beg her to lie down. She ignores it and stretches her back until she feels a satisfying pop.

"It's a shame because the code is pretty powerful," she says. The shorter man's eyes flick to the side before training back on her. Lynell opens her mouth and smiles "Oh, my god . . . you don't know what it does, do you?"

They don't answer.

"Of course, you don't. Why would Eric ever confide anything in two unimportant bodyguards?"

"We're not—"

"You're locked up in this shitty room with an unarmed, untrained, defenseless girl, who, in your opinion, has no real information. I'd call that unimportant."

"He said you're here because you have a code he needs," the taller guard says.

"That's how he put it?" Lynell asks. She sighs, lowers her right hand to the bed, and pushes, using the leverage to stand on shaking legs. She takes a moment to steady herself before turning back to the guards.

"Let me explain, Mr . . . what are your names?"

They both frown.

Lynell rolls her eyes. "If we're going to be talking, I'd love to get a name."

They exchange glances before the taller one shrugs and says, "Kenneth."

"Pleased to meet you, Kenneth. I'm Lynell Elysian." She places her right hand over her chest and nods to him before turning to the other. "And you?"

"Call me Smith."

Lynell pushes her lips together. "I take it that's not your real name?" Smith just smiles at her. "Seems a bit unfair. You get to know my full name, but I don't even get to know one of yours. Oh well. Pleased to meet you too, Smith." She holds out her hand to him and his fingers curl around his gun. She waves him off. "Calm down. I won't go for your knife. You're two grown men with multiple weapons. I'm not an idiot." She notices his grip lessen, but he keeps his hand on the holster.

Lynell turns to Kenneth. "And you can lower your gun, Kenny. It's not very welcoming when someone has a gun pointed at your face." He doesn't make a move, so Lynell takes a step forward. "Come on. You can continue holding it, but if you could just not have it trained on me, I'd really appreciate it."

He glances back at Smith, who nods. Kenneth lowers the gun, but keeps both hands wrapped around it.

"Thanks," Lynell says. She leans against the foot of the bed to take some weight off her feet. "Where was I?"

"The code," Smith says.

"Ah, yes. Thank you, Smith. The code. So, let me clear up anything Eric has told you. My name is Lynell Elizabeth Elysian. My mother, Elizabeth Crane, married my father, Eli Elysian." Kenneth and Smith exchange a quick look. "Yes, I thought you might recognize the name." She smiles.

"Eli was the only legitimate child of Gideon Elysian, the creator of the Registration."

"We don't need a history lesson," Kenneth says.

"You're right, I'm sorry," Lynell says, holding her left hand up in surrender. The motion puts the broken and marred fingers on display. Lynell tries to ignore the sight of dried blood caking her arm. "Just trying to explain my background. So, that makes me the only true heir."

"We heard you have a daughter," Smith says.

Lynell's heart clenches. It takes all her energy to keep her face from showing any emotion at the mention of Anna. "Yes, I do. Unfortunately, she was the result of an affair," she says. The lie makes her ache for Daniel. "So she, just like your beloved Eric, is a bastard and therefore not legitimate."

Smith and Kenneth exchange a quick look before turning back to Lynell. She pushes away from the bed and walks to the other side of the room, listening as both men turn and follow her movement.

"Eric is a big man with a lot of guns and a last name that means something in this world, but he's not the rightful heir," she says, looking at the far wall. "He's a ruthless, spiteful, and violent leader who doesn't care about anyone, including his employees." She turns to face the men, both of whom seem to be listening more intently now. "And he'll never have the code. He won't figure it out, and I'll suffer and die before I give something that powerful to a psychotic bastard."

They shuffle where they're standing. She ignores them and leans against the wall. "Why does he want the code so badly, though?" she asks. "What could it possibly do to warrant all of this?" She gestures to their surroundings. "He already has the Registration. You'd think that would be power enough, right?"

They don't reply, but Lynell sees a flicker of resentment in Smith's eyes.

"You're loyal to Mr. Elysian, right?" she asks. Kenneth nods. "Then I think you deserve to know what the code does. But first, you have to promise me you won't tell him what I'm about to tell you." She lowers her head and looks at them through her eyelashes.

Kenneth shakes his head, and Smith glances over his shoulder at the door.

Lynell frowns, pacing the room. "It's for your safety. If he knew you had information this important, you'd become a threat to him. He wants to be the only person alive who knows."

They exchange another look but say nothing.

Lynell sighs. "Fine, if you don't want to know . . ."

"Wait." Smith steps forward.

She smirks and sits on the edge of the bed. "So? Do we have a deal? You have the right to know what kind of man you're working for, after all.

Especially when there's another choice. You have to promise to keep this information to yourselves."

The silence stretches for a moment too long and Lynell starts to worry that Eric will walk in any moment now, cutting her time with these two guards short. Then Smith nods and says, "Okay, we promise."

"Both of you?" Lynell asks, looking at Kenneth, who grudgingly nods after studying Smith's expression. "Perfect," Lynell says. "Now, let me tell you a story of complete control."

— — —

Lynell explains what the code does, embellishing some to make up for her own lack of knowledge. She tells them it's a key to manipulating the Registration anonymously.

The person with this key could sell additional Registrations, take names off the list, or end it completely if they wished. She speaks until she hears movement outside the door and quickly lies back on the bed and closes her eyes. Both men exchange eager looks and turn to face the door as it opens.

"Wake up," Eric says. Lynell opens her eyes, wary of the light tone in Eric's voice, and stares at the ceiling. She takes measured breaths to keep fear at bay. "How's your day been so far?" he asks, standing at the head of the bed to look down at her. Lynell fights the urge to spit at him. "Mine hasn't been great, thanks for asking. Hours wasted trying to decode that letter since you refuse to be of assistance."

"What makes you think I can assist you?" she asks. The springs and metal creak below her as she sits up. Eric is standing tall, shoulders pulled back. "I've known this letter for most of my life and I've never noticed anything before."

"You didn't know to look."

"I've known to look for over a week and still don't see anything," she lies. "What if there's no code? What if you were wrong and all this was for nothing?"

Eric frowns, eyebrows furrowing together. The expression is so like Zach's that a pang of sadness slices through her.

"Then I have no reason to keep you alive any longer, do I?" Eric says.

Lynell shrugs. "You're going to kill me anyway. And now I have nothing else to lose."

"I could always kill Anna."

"You promised," Lynell says. She tenses, her blood heating.

Eric grabs his big belly with one hand and laughs without any humor.

"You think I care?" Eric says, letting out a long breath. "If I don't get what I want, I will use her."

Her chest caves in. "You already have everything," she whispers.

Eric frowns. "I *am* everything. I am the Registration. It will answer to me and so will you." His chest pushes out and his glare pierces Lynell.

She scowls. "And yet, you don't even have the key to unlock the door. You're not the Registration, Eric. You're its bastard."

She sees his hand coming and the next thing she knows, the world goes black again.

Elizabeth's arms were wrapped tight around Lynell as she sobbed into her mother's chest. Alan was getting worse, and Elizabeth was sick. Lynell didn't know that night would be the last time her mom could hold her. That the next morning she'd be left alone with Alan forever.

"He's never going to come save me, is he?"

Elizabeth didn't ask who because she knew.

Her father, the king who loved Elizabeth and Lynell but had to leave them behind. Her father, who loved Scrabble and told Lynell to cherish life and the privilege of choice. Her father, who left her with nothing but a broken family and a short letter.

In the early hours of the morning, lost in fear and longing for a life she wasn't given, Lynell barely heard her mom's answer.

"He will. But it won't be the way you expect. He'll come through your eyes, through your mind, through your heart. He'll come through you and you'll save yourself and it'll be that much sweeter."

———

When she comes to, there are different guards in her room. At first, she's disappointed, but then she takes it in stride and does her spiel all over again.

The more people she can convince to question Eric, the better.

These two take longer to persuade, and she's more exhausted than before. Her jaw aches from fresh pain, and she wishes she had a mirror so she could see the damage of the punch. Blood still fills her mouth and she swallows it, so she doesn't show weakness by spitting it out.

An hour later, she thinks she's got these two on her side, too. She told them what the code does, that she has it, and that Eric told her he was threatening to kill all his recruits as soon as he got the code.

She made up the last part, but she's getting impatient and antsy.

Eric returns and apologizes for hitting her. "You did say something incredibly offensive."

"The truth can be offensive sometimes," Lynell replies. She watches his jaw twitch as he bites back an angry response.

"Did you give me the real letter? What's the code?"

"Yes. And I don't know," she fires back.

"There has to be more. Some clue my renegade brother left you to figure it out."

Lynell pauses and pushes her tongue against a cut on the inside of her cheek to clear her mind with the pain. "Maybe it's impossible to decode it alone," she says, pulling on her own musings that she hasn't voiced. "Maybe someone else has a clue we need. Like Alexander or one of Eli's other children." Lynell shoots Eric an accusatory look, hoping to buy more time alone.

Eric's face purples and his hands curl into fists. "Is there anything my son didn't tell you?"

"I'm sure there's plenty he never got around to sharing. His life got cut short, after all."

Lynell watches Eric push his lips into a thin line before he leaves without another word.

It takes her a few minutes to gather her thoughts. When she does, she lets out a breath and looks up at the two guards, John and Lee.

"What was I saying?"

They listen closely and a few hours later, when Lee is switched out with another guard, she feels he is on her side.

The new guard wears a suit in a lighter shade and a badge with the Elysian seal. His dark curly hair sticks out from under a hat and he brings cold oatmeal and water with him.

"Thank you," Lynell says, accepting the food and smiling up at him. The guard frowns, pausing before walking to his position. "What's your name?" she asks. He doesn't answer. "Come on, John here told me his." John stiffens, gaze darting back to Lynell. "Don't worry about it. I'm going to die soon, so I might as well get to know the only company I have." She stops to take a bite of the oatmeal and tries not to frown at the bland taste. Chasing the swallow with water, she tilts the bowl to the new guard. "Want some?" He doesn't respond so she shrugs and takes another bite, talking around the food. "Eric doesn't want me to be comfortable or talk to you guys, but I say, to hell with that." She swallows and takes another sip of water. "You're prisoners in here as much as I am; we might as well get to know each other."

"I'm not a prisoner," the newcomer says.

"A prisoner is someone confined by an enemy and not allowed to leave," Lynell says. "I'm not saying you can't leave this house, but Eric is your enemy, and you can't leave his service."

The guard looks at John who shrugs before looking back at the door. "Mr. Elysian is not—"

"An enemy," Lynell says, "is someone who is actively hostile to someone else. Eric is an enemy to everyone but himself. That includes you. And I'm willing to bet my life, which I concede isn't worth a lot nowadays, that he wouldn't be too happy with you quitting and searching for new employment. You know too much, don't you? You're forced to be loyal. You're a prisoner."

He grips the butt of his gun and sniffs loudly, neck tightening with tension.

"I'm really sorry about that. But it's the situation we're in now and it's the situation he likes. I, on the other hand, am all for freedom." Lynell sets the bowl to one side and stands up. "So, prisoner to prisoner . . ." She holds out a hand. "I'm Lynell Elysian. You are?

He looks at her hand and lets the moment stretch before taking it.

DAY 14————————○

Before she sleeps, she talks to six more guards. They seem to switch out regularly. When Smith comes back, she gets his real name: Ramsey. Eric doesn't return.

She also meets a female guard who's the hardest one to talk to: Annemarie. She meets Phil, Anderson, Diaz, and Hayes. By the end of their watch, every one of them at least seems willing to listen to her. In the middle of her talk with Anderson and Diaz, she has to pee in the bucket again, which actually helps make her point that Eric is a monster.

It's a slow and difficult process, but it's all she has.

Soon, she can't keep her eyes open any longer and her mouth is so dry she can't keep talking, so she has no choice but to sleep. She dreams about playing Scrabble with her mom again. Though it's not as much of a dream or recollection of real events as it is a nightmare that crawled inside her mind, stole her fondest memories, and twisted them. She sees the words on the board as if they're written in blood, aiming to jump and lodge themselves in her throat and cut off her air until her face goes blue and her eyes pop out of her head. She sees "LOVE" first and smiles before seeing "ELYSIAN" made from the "E". Then there's "BLEEDING" and "GONE" and "ANNA" and "DANIEL" and "DEATH" and "REGISTRATION." She gasps for breath and looks up at her mother, whose face is shrunken and gray. Her mouth falls open, blood pours down her lips and stains the ground they sit on, and a shriek that sounds too much like Anna's cry escapes her mom's throat and—

Lynell sits up from her spot on the floor in the corner of the room, sweat covering her forehead, each breath raking her chest. Once her breaths level, she swallows and looks up.

Two new guards are looking at her with alarmed expressions.

"Well . . ." she gasps, wiping the back of her hand across her forehead. "That was dramatic." She blows out a breath and looks at the guards. They're skinnier and less muscular than the others, which makes her think that Eric leaves his less experienced guards with her in the middle of the night. One has bright red hair and a deep red beard. The other is bald, clean-shaven, with tan skin. They're about the same height and both wear expressions that scream, "I'm way out of my depth here."

She smirks. "You have the time?" They pull the classic look-at-each-other-not-knowing-how-to-respond dance and Lynell rolls her eyes. "Listen, telling me the time is not going to get you killed. I won't tell Eric that you talked to me."

The redhead clears his throat. "Quarter to six."

"Ooh, that's early." Lynell lies back down, and despite the cool, hard floor, she could pass out any moment. She flings her right arm over her face and asks, "How long have you two been here?"

They don't respond, and Lynell groans. She's too tired to ease into it, so she stands and takes three long strides to face the guards. The bald one goes for his phone and the redhead his gun. Lynell reaches out and touches the bald guard's arm to stop him from calling for backup.

"So trigger happy, the lot of you," she says. The guards pause, watching her with narrowed eyes. "I just want to talk. Help keep each other awake, yeah?" She raises her eyebrows and looks up at the guard, whose frown has melted away, but his hand still hovers over the phone. "Promise you won't call in my uncle?" Without waiting for an answer, she pulls her hand away and turns to the ginger. Upon seeing he's holding his gun out, she huffs, steps forward, and touches the barrel with her finger.

When she got so bold, she's not sure.

"Guns away, please? They make me nervous."

He complies. "Thanks. So, I'm Lynell. You two have names?"

"Steven," says the redhead.

"McFadden," the other says.

"You seem new. How long have you been working for Eric?" Lynell asks. Her eyes are heavy, and her face feels like it's clouded with spillover from her nightmare.

They don't answer.

"I'm going to guess not long. McFadden," she says, and he stiffens as if he's just been addressed by a superior officer. Lynell hides her smirk. "Who do you answer to?"

"The leader of the Registration. Mr. Elysian."

"Thought you'd say that," Lynell sighs. "Unfortunately, he's not the real thing."

McFadden and Steven are alarmingly easy to convince. Eric must be scraping for guards. They stay until seven a.m. and take every opportunity to ask Lynell questions. They don't seem to care about the code itself as much as the possibility of an end to the Registration.

It's not often you come across someone who wants the Registration to end and openly admits it. She never would've thought she'd find critics working for Eric.

As McFadden explained, many guards are descendants of Gideon's men, as if defending the Elysians is a family business as much as the Registration is. Steven's here because he fought with the rebels a few years ago and was given the option of serving Eric or being Registered. She also learns that Steven has a daughter of his own.

It's when she explains the death of her mother and the loss of Anna that Lynell thinks she's won him over completely.

"How'd you sleep?" Eric asks when he shows up just after a change of the guards.

Lynell is sitting cross-legged in the middle of the room, watching him pace. "Horribly, thanks for asking. You should really put mattresses on your beds."

Eric chuckles. "Your dad had a wry sense of humor too, you know." Lynell tilts her ear up as if it'll help her listen more closely. "He was always cracking jokes. Making fun of me. Making fun of our father. Making fun of the Registration. Our father hated it. Tried to beat it out of him." Eric laughs again, still pacing the small room. Lynell's hand curls into a fist and she hides it behind her left arm, trying to take deep breaths.

"Our father sent Eli to all kinds of reform schools. Up until he disappeared for almost a year. Father was furious. If my math adds up, that's when he met your mom and had you. They sure shacked up quick." He stops and looks up at Lynell.

"I think I only ever saw Eli cry twice," Eric continues. "Once when our father ordered him to never see his whore again." Eric smiles. "That's what he called your mom: whore. And the second time right before I killed him. I wonder if he was thinking about you in those last moments."

A spark of pain flashes in the palm of Lynell's hand. She opens the fist to find two tiny cuts where her nails had dug into her skin.

"You know, he never even told me he had a daughter. It took me years to find you. Then I learned of this letter, and you can imagine my disappointment now that I've read it and found nothing of use. He didn't explain how our father regretted the Registration in the end. Or that he begged me not to kill him. He said, and I quote, 'Please, don't kill me. Just let me go and I'll disappear. Please,'" Eric says, voice high and whiny. He lets out a bark of a laugh that makes Lynell jump. "Think he wanted to return to you and Mommy? Save you from mean old Alan? I bet your mom only stayed with that drunk shit to keep you invisible from us. Maybe that was my brother's idea. Well, it didn't work. Mom, dead. Dad, dead. Husband, dead. Child, we'll see. You?" Eric stops in front of one of the guards, who doesn't move an inch while Eric reaches into the guard's belt. Eric pulls a knife away and twirls it in his hand before pointing it in Lynell's direction. "As good as dead."

Lynell watches him with burning eyes and quivering lips, wanting to launch and scratch and bite and scream. She holds the anger down like trying to restrain a vicious dog.

"Tell me the code, Lynell, and I promise to kill you faster." She doesn't reply and Eric leans closer and she can feel his hot breath slam into her face. "Tell me the code and I'll make sure Anna is comfortable and happy before she goes."

Lynell spits in his face.

───

Lynell meets two new guards before Ramsey and Kenneth return. Ramsey is asking her how she found out she's an Elysian when the door opens. Steven's hand instantly goes to his gun, and Lynell would laugh if it weren't for their guest and her shiny array of knives she's carrying. She's a short woman with bright red hair and tattoos covering her hands.

"You're awake. Good." The woman grins. "Reggie has the day off, so I have the pleasure of persuading you to answer our questions. Want to get right to it, or are you ready to be helpful?"

"What, no foreplay?" Lynell says.

The woman frowns and pulls a small knife from her belt. The look in her eyes fills Lynell with fear. "Actually, I have a game to play." She twirls the knife in her hand and takes a step forward. "You win by telling me the code. I win if you beg me to cut your toe off."

"Sounds lame," Lynell says, though her voice gives a noticeable shake.

She glances behind her at Ramsey and Kenneth. She thinks she could stake her life on Ramsey being on her side, and she would gamble on Kenneth being sympathetic to her cause. Kenneth is standing with his back to her, but Ramsey is watching, lips pushed together and eyes following the woman's progress closely.

"You have a name?" Lynell asks the woman but keeps her eyes locked on Ramsey. He shifts uncomfortably.

"Not today I don't," the woman says. She steps closer to Lynell, knife still twirling between her fingers. "Now, shut up." She pushes Lynell back on the bed and it squeaks loudly. Lynell grimaces, teeth grinding together as the woman pulls Lynell's left hand up, tying it to a bar at the head of the bed with a zip tie.

"Wow, like it rou—" Lynell is cut off when the woman lunges forward and holds the edge of the blade against her throat.

"I said, shut up." Her voice is forceful, and she talks through her teeth, lips curling.

Lynell stays as still as possible. The blade is so sharp she can already feel it splitting her skin. Her gaze darts to Ramsey, who's watching with a deep frown. He reaches up to touch his scar, probably remembering the moment a knife was held to him. Kenneth has turned to watch, too, and Lynell glances at his hands, one of which is still curled around his gun.

"Good," the woman says, standing again. "You were annoying me."

As she goes for Lynell's feet, Ramsey steps forward. The woman turns to him and opens her mouth, but before she can say anything, Ramsey says, "And you're annoying me," and slams his fist against her head.

She goes limp, falling forward onto the bed. Lynell just moves her legs out of the way in time. She looks between the woman and Ramsey before smiling. Wasting no time, she reaches out, grabs the knife from her would-be torturer's hand, and cuts herself free before climbing off the bed.

"Thanks, Ramsey." He glances at her, mouth agape. "Help me get out of here and I'll give you the code. I'll put you in charge of everything. Or I'll set you free. Whatever you want, it's yours."

He doesn't respond. Kenneth is already strapping the woman's arms to the bed with her own zip ties. They seem to have reached an unspoken agreement: this all ends now, and Lynell is the way that happens.

The woman is still breathing. Lynell steps closer, pulling three more knives from her belt. With nowhere to put them, she hands two to Kenneth and keeps the other two gripped tight in her right hand. He tucks them in his own belt, gaze darting around the room.

He glances at his watch. "Guards change in two minutes. When they do, it'll be Hayes and Annemarie out there. They'll let you go."

"Are you sure?"

Kenneth nods. "Hayes hates it here. Annemarie wants more responsibility, and Eric will never give that to a woman. She'll bet on you."

Lynell nods. "Thank you, Kenneth." She reaches out and places her left arm, the hand still wrapped in bandages, on his shoulder. "Whatever you want."

He shrugs. "Just peace."

Lynell nods. "As soon as this is over," she promises. "As soon as I can." She turns to Ramsey. "You both need to leave as soon as you can. You need to—"

Ramsey shakes his head and steps forward. "I'm not leaving my post."

"Ramsey . . ."

"I'm a Registration kid. My parents worked for Gideon. I was born into this life. I was raised for this. I'm not leaving my post."

Lynell sighs, but nods.

"It's time," Kenneth says. "Guards should've just changed. I'll check."

Lynell holds the knives close to her chest as Kenneth pulls a key from his belt and unlocks the door. He opens it, leans out, and asks, "Just you two?"

"Yes," a woman, Annemarie, says.

Kenneth nods. "Take a break."

"What? Ken—"

"Let's take a break, Marie," Hayes says. Lynell is certain he's caught on and wants to take this opportunity to run. She can hear it in his voice.

There's a long pause before Annemarie says, "Fine."

Then Kenneth looks back at Lynell and opens the door to an empty hallway. "Take your castle, Ms. Elysian."

Was Daniel scared when he did this same thing almost a week ago? Did Zach lead him through these same dark hallways, heading to the dungeons rather than away? How many people did he have to kill? She wonders if her story will end the same way as Daniel's. But even if it did, no bullet can ever hurt as bad as the one that hit Daniel.

After they reach the top of the stairs, Ramsey motions for Lynell to go left down a small hallway. She pauses, holding the knives in her hand so tight that even the hilts seem to be cutting into her skin. Ramsey turns and raises an eyebrow, pointing behind him with his thumb.

"Is that the way out?" she whispers.

He nods.

She chews on the inside of her cheek, looking left, then right. Her chest feels tight, whether from anxiety or grief or the idea that freedom is so close, she doesn't know. The end of the hallway is dark and quiet. "How am I going to take the castle if I don't get rid of the king?" Lynell asks.

His eyes narrow, and he extends the gun slightly, seemingly prepared to follow her wherever she leads. "Are you ready for that? Look, I'll do what you think is best but our priority has to be safety."

"If we leave now, he'll come after me. I can't keep running. We have to stop it all."

Ramsey seems to internally argue with himself before relenting. "Okay. This way." He leads her in the opposite direction, holding his gun fully in front of him. She walks carefully so her bare feet don't make any sound on the wood floors.

They reach a door Ramsey unlocks with a key on his belt. Before going through, he turns to Lynell and holds his finger to his lips, gesturing to the wall next to the door with his eyes. She nods and presses her back against the wall as Ramsey sheathes his gun and knocks on the door.

"Williams. Martin," Ramsey says. The door opens toward them, covering Lynell from view. She turns her face to the side, holding her breath.

"Davenport. What are you doing?" a man says. His voice is so close it sends shivers down Lynell's spine.

"Been sent here."

"Really? You haven't been stationed at the boss's room in a few months."

"Volunteered. The girl was annoying," Ramsey says. "You two can head out, I've got Powell joining me. He's taking a piss but will be here soon."

"I thought we were supposed to leave at noon."

"You going to turn down an early relief?" Ramsey's voice is carefree, yet full of boldness. Lynell wonders if he has a higher ranking than most of the guards.

A moment of silence passes before one of the guys says, "Works for me."

The door stays open, and Lynell listens as two men walk away. Another door opens and closes, but she stays with her back pressed to the wall until Ramsey waves her forward. She lets out her breath and moves away from the wall.

He's smirking. "Gullible idiots," he says.

Lynell scoffs. "Annoying?"

Ramsey shrugs and gestures for her to follow. They step into what looks like a small foyer with two doors, one straight ahead and one to the left. There's another staircase on the right. The walls are deep red, darker than the rest of the house. In the free corner sits a brown armchair with an ornate mirror hanging on the wall above it. Ramsey stops and whispers, so quietly that Lynell has to lean close to hear him.

"His study is through there." He points to the left door. "He'll have a guard inside. I'm not sure who."

Lynell is in over her head and should just turn and escape. Find Anna and start a new life somewhere else. Then Ramsey interrupts her thoughts.

"I'll draw him out. Hide," he says, pointing to the armchair. Lynell obeys, squatting behind the armchair. "Ready?"

She gives him a thumbs up and pulls her hand back in, trying to make herself as small as possible.

Ramsey knocks rhythmically and there's a pause before a high male voice whispers, "Davenport?"

"Lucas," Ramsey says. "Where's the boss?"

Her willpower quickly breaks, and she peers around the corner. Ramsey is facing another, shorter man and the door is shut behind them.

"Study, on a call," Lucas says. He opens his mouth to say something else, but it turns into a muffled yelp when Ramsey pulls Lucas forward by the back of his neck. Ramsey covers Lucas's mouth with a hand and steps further from the door, dragging the struggling man along with him. Lynell sees the guard's eyes widen as they land on her, and he stops moving, as if stunned by her appearance. Before Lucas can make another sound or struggle more, Ramsey hits the back of his head with the handle of the knife. Lucas instantly goes limp, and Ramsey lowers him to the floor before turning to Lynell.

"You better make this quick. I say we have five minutes, max."

Lynell looks from Ramsey to the man on the floor, lips parted slightly. She stands and walks to the door on shaky legs. Ramsey takes hold of the doorknob, prepared to open it as soon as she's ready.

I love you, Danny, Lynell thinks as she grips the knives, tiptoeing through Eric's bedroom. On the other side of the bed is a large wardrobe, its doors open to expose a row of expensive suits. The bed is neatly made with black pillows that contrast the white comforter.

She looks up at the large clock hanging above the bed. 10:07 a.m.

Lynell grips the handle of the knives and gives Ramsey a nod. He turns the knob and the door silently opens. She tiptoes through onto a rug that's soft and gentle under her bare feet.

A desk sits in the middle of the room, facing the front door. Eric would have seen her as soon as she entered the room if he hadn't been standing at the window, looking out. The chair is turned as if Eric had spun it around toward the window before getting up.

The rest of the room is a blur. All of Lynell's attention is on her uncle. He's speaking loudly, saying something about useless legal roadblocks, gesturing. He's on the phone. He's barefoot and dressed in sweats and a T-shirt. He looks so ordinary that Lynell almost wonders if she's in the wrong office.

But no, this is Eric. Lynell bites down on her own teeth and raises the knives, prepared to step further into the room.

"I don't care what you have to do! Find the kid or I'll have you Registered!" he shouts and hangs up.

Lynell freezes, her heart jumping into her throat.

Find the kid. Is he talking about Anna? Does that mean he doesn't have her? She's gone? How?

Eric makes a move as if to turn but then just drops into his chair, his back still turned to her.

Each of Lynell's breaths feel jagged as she sidesteps the desk, coming up behind him silently, her every step swallowed by the rug. Her heart beats so fast that she's afraid she might have a heart attack. She can feel it between her ribs and behind her knees, which seem to be growing weaker with each passing second.

She reaches out, knives extended.

The chair turns.

And Eric sees her. First, his eyes open wide. Then his lips curl into a snarl. Before he can stand, Lynell leaps forward and presses the knives against his throat. Eric yells and as he goes to grab Lynell's wrist, she pivots so she's standing behind him, careful to keep the knives in place. She pushes harder, feeling his skin give in to the pressure.

"Good morning, Uncle Eric," Lynell says. She feels fear morph into anger and hatred, filling every fiber of her being, sharpening her mind.

"Lynell," Eric says, the word more like a rumble in his chest. "How did you get in here?"

Lynell ignores the question. "It's over now, Eric. We're done." Her legs tense, and she digs her toes into the floor.

"We don't have to be," Eric says, as if trying to sound sincere.

Lynell scoffs. "You killed my father. You kidnapped me, abused me, tortured me. You killed my cousin and my husband. You threatened my daughter's life." She holds the knives against him tightly, restraining him against the chair with her left elbow, bandaged hand resting on his head.

Eric begins reaching for the knives again. "Put the weapons away, and let's talk."

"Oh, sweet Uncle Eric," she says, imitating Eric's fake, breathy tone. "I believe you are misinterpreting your place. I have all the power, and you have nothing."

"I have the Elysian name. The Registration," Eric says, seething. "I have guards everywhere."

"You're a bastard, remember?" Lynell says. Her chin is pressed close to the side of Eric's head and her eyes are locked on the cracked door she just came through. "And you should really treat your guards better. A silver tongue and some kindness were enough to make them change sides. They're with me now."

Eric growls, his body shaking with rage.

"I'll have you killed for—"

"That'll be hard to do when I'm done here."

"You're not going to kill me." Eric's voice fills with confidence.

"But I can," Lynell says. "The riots have gotten worse and more people question your right to rule every day. Your loyal soldiers have turned against you. Your own son died fighting by the side of your enemy. You have *nothing*." She flexes her forearm, muscles twinging with the desire to slide the knife across his throat. "You *are* nothing."

Eric starts shaking, out of what Lynell first assumes is fear. But then laughter bubbles from his throat. "You have no idea how wrong you are, darling. It will take so much more than a knife to wipe Eric Elysian from this earth."

Lynell almost proves him wrong at that moment but remembers Daniel's words and Eli's letter.

Choose good. Be better.

"You think you own the world?" Lynell says. "You think a name and some money give you the right to gamble with people's lives?"

Eric pushes himself back, his thick neck rubbing against the knife. "You're playing a game and you don't even know the rules or the players," Eric says with a taunting lilt to his voice, as if he knows something Lynell doesn't. Something that will save him and damn her.

"It's nothing more than a cheap game of power," Lynell says, though the words don't sound convincing. "Because that's all you know. Power, and the thirst for more. I want you to know *that's* what ended you. Not me. Your own desperate desire for power." There's a tug in her gut that wants to spill Elysian blood. But something bigger keeps her frozen.

She can't do it.

Eric notices and his laugh starts again. "I knew you couldn't do it," he says. Then he throws his body back. The chair crashes into her chest, pushing her to the floor. One of the knives slides away. Air leaves her lungs and she gasps, pain pulsing as she tries to sit up.

Eric stands and turns to her. "You can't beat me." He bends over, grabs the knife she dropped, and steps toward her. "You can't beat the Registration." She's against the back wall, sitting on the floor, when he reaches her. "You can't Register me."

He squats in front of her and angles the knife over her heart. Lynell lifts her remaining weapon, but her body is weak and there's no way to kill him before he can kill her.

"You can't murder me," Eric continues. Maybe it's for the best, both of them meeting their ends in this office by each other's hand. "What can you do?"

"Show kindness." The words come from the doorway and both Lynell and Eric look up to Ramsey standing there, holding a gun. "Drop the knife, Mr. Elysian."

Eric's body radiates disbelief and fury colors his face. His neck turns red and a vein starts to pop. He lets out a roar, and Lynell thinks he's going to run for Ramsey, but instead, he turns to her.

It all happens in a flash.

Eric lunges at her with a knife.

Ramsey pulls the trigger, the sound deafening.

Lynell throws herself to the side and lifts the hand still holding a knife.

It sinks into flesh. Eric bellows and falls, half-landing on Lynell's legs. She rips her hand back, pulling the knife with it. Lynell feels the blade leaving her uncle's flesh more than she felt it sink in. The sensation is nauseating, and her stomach turns over, curling into itself.

She scrambles out from under him, not processing an ounce of pain. She can't tear her eyes away from Eric's face. He's staring at her, blood already bubbling to his lips. He groans and moves as if to lunge for Lynell again.

Another bang.

Lynell flinches, eyes slamming shut.

Something wet and warm sprays her face.

Each breath continues to bounce, ripping through her chest in quick succession, but no oxygen seems to reach her lungs. She feels dizzy.

"Ms. Elysian."

Her grip on the knife hilt tightens.

"We need to go."

She opens her eyes.

Red and black and fear and anger and relief splash across Lynell's vision. She's lying right next to Eric, his blood spreading with each second. She tries to push herself up but slips in the slick red fluid.

A hand closes around her arm and tugs, helping her to her feet. Her eyes don't move from Eric. She unsticks her fingers from the hilt of the knife and lets go.

It clatters to the floor, splashing in blood.

Her chest constricts, in desperate need of air. Lynell gasps.

And then she instantly gags. She stumbles away from Eric and out of Ramsey's grasp. She makes it two steps before vomiting all over her bare feet. She heaves two more times before sucking in a lungful of air. Black holes fill her vision and she sways.

Ramsey rushes to her side and wraps an arm around her middle, holding her up. She blinks at him. His jaw is set but he doesn't look concerned or upset or angry.

He doesn't even seem afraid, just determined.

"We have to go," he says.

Lynell looks down at her hands. They're red, Eric's blood mingling with her own. Her stomach turns over again when a few drops fall from her fingers, loosened from her shaking hands.

Instinctively, she looks back at Eric. He doesn't move.

"He's dead," Ramsey says.

Her heart slams against her chest with rising panic.

"Let's go," Ramsey says, pulling Lynell away from the carnage and toward the door. Prickling numbness starts at her scalp and washes down her body, making her legs feel disconnected and arms heavy.

Words fail her, but Lynell doesn't fight Ramsey as he leads her. Everything is a blur as they rush through the house and out a door that leads them outside. The bright late morning light slaps her in the face and makes her wince. The cool morning air brushes her arms, and goosebumps rise on her skin. Gravel crunches under their feet as they turn the corner. Every sound is simultaneously magnified and muffled and her head swims as she tries to make sense of everything. Her body tenses as she notices a car, but as soon as she can make out Hayes in the driver's seat, she relaxes. Ramsey helps her into the front seat and then climbs in the back before they take off.

Safely in the car, Lynell can speak at last. "But why are we running? I'm in charge now."

"They don't all know that yet," Ramsey says. "Some are blind, loyal brutes."

Lynell nods, staring out the front windshield. Her head feels foggy and her vision dark. She feels Eric's blood on her hands, infecting her every crevice. Any panic she had managed to control slips free again, and her breathing returns to shallow panting. Hayes reaches over and grabs her forearm. She feels the pain but doesn't pull away. Instead, she follows his arm with her eyes, until she meets his gaze.

"Hey, hey, Ms. Elysian, slow, deep breaths," he says.

"I killed him." The words are dry ice shoved down her throat, scorching everywhere it touches and filling her with frigid mist.

"You didn't," Ramsey says from the back seat.

"I stabbed him."

"Your stab wouldn't have killed him. I shot him. Twice. Once in the heart. All you did was defend yourself."

"He was a monster," Hayes says.

"He's dead." Despite running from her own demise for fourteen days, death has never felt so palpable.

The car is filled only with the sounds of Lynell's labored breathing and Ramsey's twitching leg in the back seat.

"Where are we going?" Lynell asks.

"The hospital," Hayes says.

Lynell doesn't recognize the relief that washes through her.

Her mom died at the hospital. Lynell woke up with Elizabeth struggling to breathe in her bed. Lynell screamed for Alan. He called the ambulance and Lynell rode along, holding her mom's frail hand the whole way. She sat next to her mom's bed, crying while smiling at the face that used to be so young and smooth and full of joy. Her mom placed her hand against Lynell's jaw, and Lynell covered it with her own, a silent tear falling onto the hospital bed.

"Don't leave me," Lynell had cried.

Elizabeth's voice was dry and quiet. "I love you, little Lynell. Do better than I did. Rule better than your father did. Love better than both of us, and you'll change the world."

There wasn't anything they could do, the doctors said. They were sorry, everyone at the funeral said. She was in a better place. So be it when life Registers you.

She wakes up but doesn't remember falling asleep. Pain fills her. In her face, in her body, everywhere. She tries to take a deep breath and open her eyes, but the world stays dark and the pain paralyzes her. Her body seems to be floating in a pool of thick blood. There is no up and no down. There is no light and no air.

She can hear voices. One deep and male, one feminine, and one familiar. Then she hears her own groan, and the voices cease.

Light streams in from every angle when she finally opens her eyes. Everything is white, the world comes into focus slowly, and Lynell begins to make out the faces around her.

There's a doctor with black hair and a gray beard, wearing a long white coat with a name tag that says, "Dr. Springers," an older woman with gray hair in deep blue scrubs, and Hayes.

"Good timing, boss," Hayes says. "Just got a call from Ramsey, he's got the team settled, ready to answer to you. And to ask some questions."

Lynell frowns and opens her mouth to respond, but her throat is a dry slope of rocks.

"As I said, sir," the nurse interrupts before Lynell can say anything, "she needs rest before receiving visitors." She pushes Hayes away from the bed.

"She's been resting for hours," Hayes says, almost pouting at the nurse.

"She was in surgery and recovery," Dr. Springers says. "That's not resting."

Lynell looks at the doctor and down at her hand, which is in a cast.

"You need to leave now, son. She can have visitors tomorrow," Dr. Springers says to Hayes.

"As I told you," Hayes replies, filling an amount of authority in his voice that surprises Lynell. "I'm staying. I won't talk to her if you insist, but she needs a guard in the room."

"We've already permitted two guards outside," the nurse replies. She looks severely annoyed. "I assure you this hospital is very secure."

"I don't think you understand who this is," Hayes starts.

"You've made it very clear who she is," Dr. Springers says. He looks ready to argue, lifting his shoulders, but then concedes and says, "No talking."

Hayes gives the doctor a curt nod and moves to the edge of the room, standing tall with his hands behind his back.

The nurse frowns, and Dr. Springers picks up a tablet, shaking his head. He taps on the screen a few times before beginning to check all the machines. Lynell looks back to the nurse, who gives her a forced smile.

"I'm sorry about that, darling. I'm Nurse Carolyn. How are you feeling?"

Lynell swallows, winces, and says, "Not great."

Carolyn grimaces in sympathy and nods. "I'll increase the morphine. Do you know what happened?"

Lynell starts to shake her head but then nods. "Hayes and—"

Carolyn cuts her off. "Yes. Your friend," she says and turns so her back is to Hayes, "and another one, bigger and meaner, brought you in this morning. You were in quite a shape, but they didn't seem to want to answer any questions. Darling, are you okay? Are you safe? They gave us your name, but we couldn't find a Lynell Elysian in the system." The last sentence is quiet, like she's terrified of questioning Lynell's identity or doubting she's one of *those* Elysians.

Of course, they're concerned.

"Mize," Lynell says. "I'm in the system as Lynell Mize."

Carolyn looks up at the doctor, and Lynell turns her head to watch him nod and start typing on his tablet. Not even a minute passes before he frowns, and his eyes widen. He looks up at the nurse, obviously at a loss for how to move forward with whatever information he just found out.

"I never figured it out," Lynell says, making both of them snap their attention to her. "How many people Registered me?"

The doctor clears his throat and shifts on his feet before saying, "Eleven."

Lynell's eyebrows raise and she chuckles, which causes her throat to burn. "What time is it?" she asks.

"Ten to five," she says.

"So, seven more hours?" Lynell whistles and straightens her neck, looking at the ceiling. "Never thought I'd make it."

The silence stretching between them is uncomfortable. Lynell can feel the nurse and Dr. Springers dying to ask if she's really who she says she is. And if so, how she could be Registered and how she managed to stay alive these past two weeks.

"No one is going to come for me," Lynell says, shattering the silence.

"I'm sorry, Ms. Mize," Carolyn starts.

"Actually," Lynell begins, looking at the nurse again, "please call me Mrs. Carter."

"Carter?" Carolyn says. Her eyebrows pull together, and she frowns, exchanging a glance with Dr. Springers. Lynell catches sight of Hayes shifting his weight behind them.

"Elysian by birth. Mize by law. Carter by choice," Lynell says, avoiding the nurse's gaze, instead training her eyes to her hand that plays with the soft cream blanket draped on top of her.

"By marriage?" Carolyn asks. Lynell nods.

"What's his name?"

"His name was Daniel," Lynell says. "Daniel Carter."

Lynell suddenly regrets her decision to ask them to call her Mrs. Carter. Thinking about Daniel, saying his name, feels like every part of her body is being slammed with a hammer.

"Um," Carolyn starts. Lynell looks up at her, ready to ask her to leave, when she stops at the nurse's expression. "Your husband is . . ."

"Dead, I know," Lynell bites. Her blood feels hot and tears start clawing at the back of her eyes.

"No. He's here. Came in yesterday with two bullet wounds. He was rushed into surgery. It went well. He's recovering. He's alive."

* * *

They give her more painkillers and make her rest a few minutes before agreeing to take her to Daniel's room. Her breaths feel cleaner than they ever have, and the drugs must have kicked in, because the pain feels dull and distant. Carolyn transfers her to a wheelchair. Three guards, including Hayes, who tries to ask a question but is instantly cut off by Carolyn, follow them down the hallway, into the elevator, and up two floors. The trip on the elevator lasts years. Lynell is aware of everyone's breaths, the hum of the elevator, and the rhythmic dinging of the transportable machine still attached to her.

They pass three other nurses, one of whom follows an old man who struggles to walk down the hallway, and two doctors, conversing in low tones, before they stop in front of Daniel's door. Hayes demands that he check it first before Carolyn wheels Lynell inside.

Daniel's face is sunken and pale. His lips look dry and all the light that Lynell is used to seeing in his eyes is absent. Until he looks up and sees her.

His mouth falls open. "Lynell."

Lynell smiles. Carolyn wheels her forward and as soon as she's close enough, Lynell reaches for Daniel and wraps her arm over his chest. She buries her face in his neck and lets the tears loose.

He grabs her with one hand, grips her shirt, and presses his lips to the top of her head.

"Please, be careful," Carolyn says. Lynell ignores her, holding onto Daniel even tighter, despite the awkward angle.

"I thought you were gone," he says.

Lynell leans back and looks into his eyes. "I thought you were gone, too."

"I promised I'd never leave you again, didn't I?"

Lynell nods. They press their lips together, and the world seems to straighten.

"How'd you do it? How'd you get out?" Daniel asks when they pull apart.

"Eric's an ass, and I'm a smooth talker," she says, suddenly aware of Hayes and the other two guards in the room. She turns around and says, "Would you please wait in the hallway, guys." Hayes looks ready to argue but at Lynell's expression, he nods, and they disappear. She turns back to Daniel who raises his eyebrows.

"It's mine. All of it. Eric is dead." The word causes her throat to freeze for a second. "Ramsey, one of the guards, shot him to save me."

"And . . ." Daniel says, eyes casting down. "Zach? Is he really gone?"

Lynell sucks her lips between her teeth and nods. "I didn't want him to die," she whispers.

"Without him, we would both be gone. Anna, too," Daniel says.

Her next breath tumbles from her lips with a wet cough. Heat radiates from her nose and eyes, and she asks, "Is Anna okay?"

Daniel nods.

Her body thrums with urgency. "Where is she?"

"With some cops in protective services. She's safe. She's alive and unharmed."

Lynell deflates slightly, her body at war with contradictory emotions. Grief, pain, relief, fear, anger, joy.

"We were almost out when I got shot," Daniel says. "It hit high but the force knocked me down. I was sure they'd shoot again. But I managed to get up and out with Anna. I couldn't even hold her, just grabbed her hand, and got her to run. We were just far enough away for me to call 911 before I passed out. I'm so sorry. I shouldn't have left you. I wish I didn't have to, but I had to save Anna."

"Shh," Lynell says, grabbing Daniel's face and pulling it to meet hers. She pushes his hair back and shakes her head, kissing him again. "You saved our daughter. Don't ever be sorry for that."

A shameless mention of her name convinces the hospital staff to move her into Daniel's room. She gets her own bed and they have to rest, but Lynell doesn't care as long as she can look at Daniel's face whenever she wants.

Ramsey returns with an update on the Elysian house. News spread among the guards that Eric is dead and Lynell is claiming her right to the Registration. Most are taking the change of bosses in stride. The few who showed opposition, Reggie included, were rounded up and fired. Hayes argued they should be put in the dungeons until the next quarter's Registration, but Lynell disagrees.

While she's in the hospital, Ramsey is in charge, which the guards seem to be taking well.

"I'm pretty sure I figured out the code," Lynell says when it's just them and Hayes in the room. Daniel looks at her, mid-bite of pudding. "'Know the worth of love, Lynell. Of joy. Of forgiveness. Know the worth and double it. Live it. Hope for more. Do not transpose your values,'" she recites. "The only thing my mom ever really told me about my dad was that he and Gideon loved Scrabble. My guess is we'll need to calculate the Scrabble value of the words 'love,' 'joy,' and 'forgiveness.' But that's not all. My dad couldn't make it easy. We've got to decipher it."

"How?"

"Double it. Transpose. I always thought that was a weird way of wording it. '*Do not transpose your values.*' Did you know there's a cipher called the double transposition cipher? That's it. Has to be. And the keywords are 'live' and 'hope.' Now, I just have to figure out how to actually decode it."

"You're sure?" Daniel asks.

Lynell shrugs and takes a bite of her own pudding. "No."

"What are you going to do?" Daniel asks, his forehead scrunched in thought.

"I don't know," Lynell says. "What do you think I should do?" She glances at Daniel, and he shakes his head.

"I can't tell you that."

"I know . . . I just . . . I want it all to end. But I don't know what that would look like. What's more human? Kinder? Releasing it, or letting it continue, unaffected? Or something else entirely? Eric wanted the code so he'd have more control and the ability to change how the Registration works. Maybe I can do that." Lynell pauses, remembering the words that sustained her. "'Don't settle for what has always been,' my dad said in the letter. 'Demand better. Be better.'" She shakes her head. "If only I knew how."

Daniel reaches over and grabs Lynell's hand. "I don't have an answer. But I know one thing: I know you'll make the right decision. I know you'll choose good."

"I'm not so sure," she says. "I screw up all the time. I mean, look at you. Two bullet wounds. If you'd fallen in love with someone else, you—"

"Let's get one thing straight," Daniel says, cutting her off. "I love you. All of you. I don't care who you are, where you're from, or what you've done. Lynell Elizabeth Carter, yesterday, today, tomorrow, and forever, I'll love you."

She stares at him before leaning into his bed and pulling him into a deep kiss.

"I love you, too. More than life itself."

They stay up and watch the clock tick to 12:01 a.m., hands clasped together. She's done it, she's outrun the Registration. Her life lies before her, an unwritten book full of blank pages waiting to be filled.

With good.

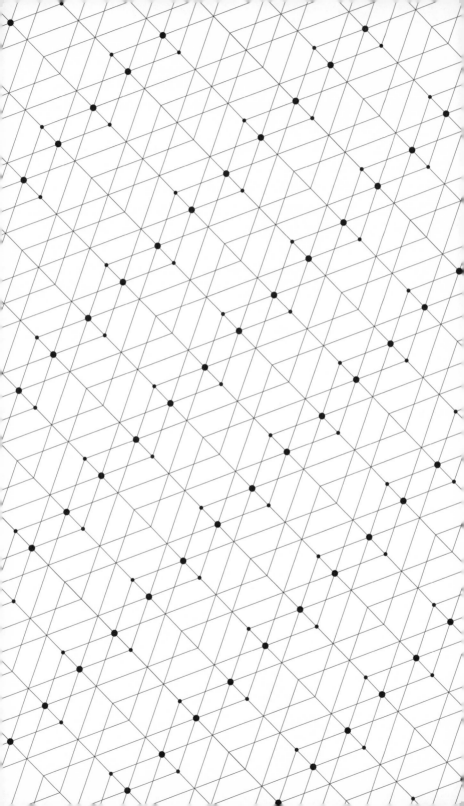

ACKNOWLEDGMENTS

I have loved writing stories since I was a child, but I truly believe I would not be here, witnessing my debut novel enter the world, if it wasn't for my incredible parents. My mom and dad have supported me and my dreams since the beginning and cultivated my love for writing, reading, and learning. Without their love and encouragement, I would have given up long ago. Mommy, you are my best friend and the best evidence that there is genuine love in the world. Daddy, you taught me every day how important joy and forgiveness are. You exemplified selfless love, loyalty, strength, bravery, humility, and wisdom every day. Thank you for guiding me through both the journey of life and the journey of writing a book. More than anything, I wish you could be here to see this book on the shelves. Thank you so much for going above and beyond to be fantastic parents, teachers, protectors, friends, and supporters. I could never thank you enough for all you've done for me.

I would be remiss to not thank my incredibly encouraging sisters, Meg and Haley. Despite being super busy running their own businesses, raising children, and traveling the world, Meg and Haley continually make time not only to read my manuscripts, but to discuss them with me and commend my hard work. Haley, thank you for always being there for me no matter what. You exemplify persistence and hope every day. Meg, you are one of the most honest, loyal, and talented people I know. Thank you for being my biggest fan. You're my spider sister for life.

As the amazing sister I am, I also want to thank CJ and Aaron, two supremely loving and patient husbands to my sisters. CJ, thank you for answering my calls at random hours of the day to answer bizarre medical questions with no context and for not assuming I'm a crazy serial killer. For the last decade, you have been the brother I always wished for and the brother I never wanted. Aaron, you might not have been in my life for as long, but you are just as important, and I'm so grateful to you for all you've done for my sister and our family.

I'm eternally grateful to my awe-inspiring grandparents, Nena and Gaga. Not many people are lucky enough to have grandparents as incredible as you two and very few have the chance to spend so much time with them. Nena, I will always cherish our Monday night dinners. I am *honored* to be your granddaughter. Gaga, you are my partner forever. You perhaps saw my potential and talent before anyone else, and you were my first reader, editor, and fan. I believe the day I realized I would never stop writing is when you handed me my first printed manuscript of the truly horrendous book, *Crystal Clear,* filled with annotations and told me never to stop imagining new worlds. I miss you every day.

Without the friendship, support, influence, and feedback from all my incredible friends, this book would not exist. There are far too many people to list, but I must individually thank a few. Zoe, you're my person. You will *always* be my person. I'm sorry I named those characters after you and Josh.

Cat, I'm so thankful for you. On one of the hardest days of my life you said, "Don't worry, this is just a chapter in your future autobiography," and I remember that every day.

Emily, Dakota, and Lea Nell, thank you for being this book's first readers. Mollee, LJ, Terri, and Madeline, you've kept me writing and reading and imagining in the hardest years of my life. Thank you. And never stop writing; the world needs all of your voices.

Some may laugh at this, but thank you to my dog, Teddy Lupin. You've not only kept me sane, but you saved my life, gave me purpose when life felt hopeless, and made me smile when I didn't think I had any reason to.

Having an idea and turning it into a decent novel is just as hard as it sounds, and the process would've been impossible without all of my incredible beta readers and editors. Specifically, Marni MacRae and Erin Healey, thank you for all your help and input. It means so much to me.

Dreams don't become realities in a vacuum. They take hard work, dedication, and teamwork. I would not be experiencing the reality of my dream to be a published author without the amazing team at CamCat Publishing. There are so many people behind a project like this and each and every member of this team has my eternal gratitude.

Helga Schier, I'll never be able to fully express how much you've done for me and this book and how thankful I am. You dedicated so much priceless time and energy to this project and the result is a better novel than I could have dreamed of. Thank you so much. Also, I must acknowledge Sue Arroyo for the work you've done at CamCat, in general, and with me and my writing specifically. Thank you for pursuing this book and singing its praises from day one. I'm so glad *The Registration* found its way to your hands.

Last, but CERTAINLY not least, thank you to my astonishing, hardworking, and compassionate agent, Julie Gwinn. One of the best days of my life was when you said you wanted to represent me. I can't think of anyone else I would want in my corner, believing in this book and fighting for it. I so look forward to all the projects yet to come, and I hope for many more years of working alongside you and the amazing team at Seymour.

ABOUT THE AUTHOR

Madison Lawson writes speculative fiction novels full of suspense, social commentary, and complex relationships. Her work is represented by Julie Gwinn at the Seymour Agency. *The Registration,* published by CamCat Books, is her debut novel. Madison has published several short stories in literary journals such as *Eckleburg* and *Water Soup.* In 2019, she won the Koresh Award for a flash creative nonfiction piece titled "Share," and in 2018 she won the Gordone Award for a creative nonfiction piece titled "Goats and Goodbyes." Madison received her BA in English with a focus on Creative Writing from Texas A&M University and is in the process of earning her MA in English Literature from North Carolina State University.

Growing up in a small Texas town, Madison began exploring the world through the page so much that she often lost sleep to finish a book, got detention for writing a story in class, and convinced herself it was okay to read *Harry Potter* one more time. As her curiosity expanded, she began writing, reading, and traveling to discover the world, make new ones, and understand her own a bit better.

Madison currently resides in North Carolina with her dog, Teddy Lupin, and her friend and co-author on their upcoming trilogy *Last Born,* Mollee Gressley. To learn more and stay updated, visit Madison's website madisonlawson.com and follow her on Instagram (@madisonlawson) or Twitter (@madisonlawson96).

If you enjoyed

Madison Lawson's *The Registration,*

you'll enjoy

David Oppegaard's *Claw Heart Mountain.*

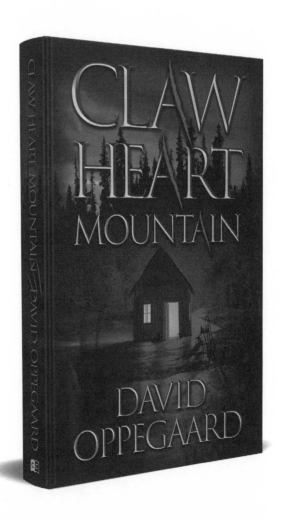

PART
1

1

WINDFALL

C law Heart Mountain sat apart from everything, like a forgotten god hunkered in thought. It looked both eternal and lonely, without a friend in sight, surrounded by rolling hills dotted in sagebrush and cheat grass, the summer sky a hazy blue above it. Nova watched the mountain through the SUV's windshield, hypnotized by its looming presence. She was driving while her friend Mackenna sat in the front passenger seat, playing a game on her phone. The three dudes—Landon, Isaac, and Wyatt— were all sprawled in the SUV's two-tiered backseat, either asleep or listening to music on their earbuds.

The SUV was quiet except for the soft roar of the air conditioning fans. Nova, who'd turned eighteen the month before, didn't like listening to music or talk radio when she drove; she preferred to focus on driving, which she took seriously. The SUV, a probably super expensive luxury Mercedes, belonged to Mackenna's wealthy family. Nova was worried she'd wreck the vehicle in a random accident, get everybody mad at her, and ruin her driving record before it had really started.

At a petite five-two, Nova felt slightly ridiculous piloting such a massive beast of a vehicle, like a toad telling a dragon what to do. Still, they'd made it this far. They'd left Greenwood Village, a suburb in south Denver, later than planned. They'd agreed Mackenna would pick them all up by ten in the morning, but she'd been late and they'd gotten a late start. Mackenna had driven for the first two hours, through the traffic of Denver and into the mountains, before claiming she was getting sleepy and asking Nova to drive. Nova protested, asking why Landon, Mackenna's boyfriend, couldn't drive, or one of the other guys, but it turned out all three of the dudes had eaten marijuana gummies before they'd even left Greenwood Village. She should have known. This was their big, end-of-summer road trip before returning to college, so why not get stoned before they even arrived at their destination?

They'd all gone to the same prep academy in the Denver suburbs and were now enrolled at Colorado College in Colorado Springs. Nova, who was a year younger than the others, was going to be a freshman, while everyone else would be a sophomore. Nova had told her parents she'd be spending the next three nights at Mackenna's cabin in Vale, with Mackenna's entire family. This was partially true—they were going to stay at *one* of the Wolcott's cabins—but it was her family's cabin on Claw Heart Mountain, across the state border in Wyoming, and nobody else in Mackenna's family would be there. The friends would be unsupervised, without a real grown-up in sight.

Nova didn't like lying to her sweet, trusting parents (and this trip was by far the largest lie Nova had ever told them) but she knew they would have otherwise said no. It was the end of a long summer for Nova—a summer that had started with getting dumped by her boyfriend—and she'd grown tired of hanging around her house and her lame suburban neighborhood, going for walks and eating her dad's overcooked barbeque while she waited for college to start. The memory of endless time on lockdown during the COVID-19 pandemic still fresh (sometimes it felt like being stuck at home, bored, had been her entire teenage life), by mid-August Nova had decided she'd finally reached the point that she might literally wither away and die if she didn't go *somewhere*.

So, basically, Nova had lied to her parents to save her own life.

Kind of.

Nova glanced at Mackenna, who was still absorbed in her phone. Mackenna was a tall, tan, volleyball-smashing Nordic beauty, with a mane of curly blonde hair that cascaded down her shoulders. Nova, on the other hand, with her pale skin, brown pixie-cut hair, dark eyebrows, hazel eyes, stubby nose, and short chin, thought she resembled a woodland elf more than anything an average person would consider "sexy." Which was fine with her. She'd seen all the attention Mackenna got, both in high school and the real world, from all kinds of people, and it seemed like a huge pain in the ass. Nova would much rather float along under the sexiness radar, free to live her life without everyone drooling over her all the time.

Mackenna looked up from her phone.

"What?"

Nova looked away and focused on the road.

"Nothing."

They weren't too far across the border into Wyoming, maybe thirty miles, but Claw Heart Mountain still seemed different than the mountains in Colorado. Its outline appeared indefinite, its edges somehow blurry. Which didn't really make sense, because like every mountain in Colorado, Claw Heart must have been a part of the Rocky Mountains, which stretched all the way from New Mexico into Canada.

Mackenna leaned forward against her seatbelt and peered through the windshield. She drummed her hands on the SUV's dashboard.

"Huh. Claw Heart looks even more badass than I remember."

"How long has it been since you've been here?"

Mackenna tilted her head, thinking. "Last summer, I guess."

"You haven't been to your own cabin for an entire year?"

"We used to come here more often, but that was before we got the second cabin in Vale. Now Dad mostly uses this one for hanging out with his business buddies and entertaining clients. Claw Heart Mountain's good for hunting. Dad pays a neighbor to look after it for most of the year."

"So why aren't we just going to Vale?"

Mackenna wrinkled her nose. "It's being fumigated. Mom saw a cockroach when she was there last weekend for her book club retreat."

"Huh. Vale cabin problems, huh?"

Mackenna sat back and sighed.

"I know, right?"

Nova glanced in the rearview mirror. The dudes were all oblivious, their eyes closed as their earbuds pumped noise into their ears. Nova felt like a mom driving her kids to summer camp. For the seventh or eighth time that day, she wondered why she was friends with Mackenna and the dudes. Or friends with Mackenna, anyway, since Nova hardly knew the dudes at all. Landon, with his good looks and blonde, fake bedhead hair, was hot but sort of dumb, the kind of guy she'd normally ignore and be ignored by, the average Great White Bro. Isaac was smart but mean, a handsome Jewish kid with piercing brown eyes. Wyatt was probably the nicest of the three dudes, a genuinely sweet Black guy with a big smile who talked to everyone. He'd moved to Colorado from Minneapolis three years earlier and didn't seem worried about being popular, which, of course, made him super popular.

Nova swerved to avoid a dead critter in the road. This particular buddy had exploded all over the place and was unrecognizable. Nova felt her heart go out to the creature, whatever it had been, and straightened in the driver's seat, determined to avoid any similar roadkill. The highway sloped sharply upward as they reached the base of the mountain and climbed the first length of a switchback highway, which appeared to zigzag all the way up the mountain.

Isaac removed his earbuds and leaned forward from the backseat. Nova could smell the cologne he was wearing, a subtle musk that made her think of a dim coatroom at an adult cocktail party. Isaac pointed at the windshield.

"What the hell is that?"

Nova frowned and examined the road. It took her a moment to see what Isaac was pointing at because it was light blue, almost the same color as the sky. It was a brick-shaped armored van, lying upside down on the road, its wheels in the air. The van's small side windows had shattered and its roof was crunched.

"Holy shit," Mackenna said, lowering her phone. "Looks like an accident."

Nova slowed and came to a stop twenty yards from the overturned van. She put the SUV in park, rolled down her window, and stuck her head out. A path of broken trees and torn earth went straight up, maybe a hundred yards, to the next switchback tract of highway. A haze of dirt hung in the air, still filtering down from above. Nova sat back and turned to Isaac and Mackenna. Landon and Wyatt were still sleeping in the backseat, oblivious.

"They fell," Nova said.

Mackenna blinked.

"What?"

"They fell down the mountain."

"Woah," Isaac said, sitting back and rolling down his window. The smell of gasoline drifted into the SUV and Nova pulled to the side of the road, in front of the overturned vehicle. She thought back to her excruciatingly dull driver's ed classes and activated the SUV's flashers. She wondered if they had a road kit. They could light some road flares and set up a warning lane. They needed to call 911 and report the accident. They had to check for survivors.

Nova turned off the SUV's engine, unbuckled her seatbelt and opened her door.

"What are you doing?" Mackenna stared at her like Nova had turned into a talking dog.

"We have to help. We might need to give them first aid."

"But it's dangerous. This road is so narrow. What if a semi-truck comes along and smashes us, too?"

"We'll be fast."

"We will?"

Nova nodded, feeling a surge of adrenalin kick in. This was finally it. A real-life important adult-type situation. A real adventure. Nova got out of the SUV and slid around on the loose rock that had sprayed across the highway. She peered up the mountainside, checking to see if anything else was poised to come crashing down to the highway, and noticed a disturbance high among the trees. Something enormous was moving through the shadows—something almost as tall as the trees themselves—but it appeared to be headed further up the mountain, not down, and within a few seconds its shape disappeared into the trees altogether and Nova was left wondering if she'd seen anything in the first place.

Shaking off the unsettling vision, Nova ran up to the front of the overturned van. The side of the van read STEEL CAGE ARMORED SERVICES. Gasoline was pooling around the van, its surface a hypnotic sheen of purple and blues. The smell was so strong it made her dizzy. Nova got down on her hands and knees and crawled closer, trying to get a better look inside the van. Both front seats were empty, as was the rest of the van's cab. A steel partition wall, still intact, blocked off the rear cargo area of the van.

Nova scrambled to her feet and brushed the road grit from her pants. She went around to the back of the van. Its rear doors had buckled and one thick steel door was wedged open about two feet. Nova pulled on the door to increase the gap, but it wouldn't budge. She shouted hello into the opening. No response. She turned on her cell phone's LED flashlight and shined it into the gap. She leaned into the darkness and stood motionless, gawking at what she'd discovered: a large green and white cube wrapped in clear, industrial strength packaging film. Through the film, Nova could make out stacks of paper bound into packets.

It was a cube of money.

So.

Much.

Money.

2

"Nova? What is it?"

Mackenna came up and stood behind Nova. Nova instinctively shielded the van's opening as best she could with her body, but Mackenna was taller and peered over the top of her head. Mackenna gasped and gripped Nova's shoulders.

"Holy fuck."

"It might be fake," Nova said, actually half-hoping this was true. This was too much. This was too much of a thing. She could already feel the energy caused by the sight of the money cube radiating from Mackenna's clawing fingertips into her shoulders. It was a wild, hungry energy. A crazy energy.

"It's not fake," Mackenna said, starting to bop up and down. "I know cash when I see it. That's real money, Nova. Fucking real money!"

Nova stepped through the two-foot gap between the van's jammed door and its frame, shining her phone's light in front of her. She noticed jagged shards of wood covering the cargo hold like confetti. It was the smashed remains of a pallet, which the cube must have been resting on before the van tumbled down the mountain and everything went topsy-turvy. Nova leaned down and picked up a shard of wood. It looked like a huge toothpick, or a knife.

"Where'd the driver go?"

Mackenna shrugged.

"Maybe they walked away to get help."

"I doubt it. Would you leave all this money behind?"

"Hell no."

"I wouldn't either. I'd wait for help to come along."

Mackenna turned and glanced over her shoulder. The highway was still quiet behind them. "It seems so deserted out here," Mackenna said, putting her hair back in a ponytail. "I still don't see anybody coming in either direction. Maybe they didn't want to wait for somebody to come along. Maybe they couldn't wait."

Nova heard Isaac's voice coming from outside the van, asking what was going on. His head popped into the doorway a second later. He looked at Nova crouched with the wooden shard in her hand and the cube of money behind her.

"Is that . . . ?"

Nova shrugged. She poked into the plastic with the shard, gouging a hole into its clear surface. A part of her hoped the money was fake and they could just go on without worrying about it. Once she'd made a hole in the plastic, Nova pulled at it with her fingers, widening it. She dug into the tightly packed paper and pulled out a single bundle. It was bundled, held together by a white paper band with yellow edging that had $10,000 printed on it. She ran her thumb against the edge of bundle, examining the bills just like they did in the movies.

"Are those all hundred-dollar bills?" Isaac asked.

"They feel real," Nova admitted, holding the bills up to her eye and focusing the light of her cell phone on them. "They look real."

Mackenna pushed her hand through the cargo hold doorway. She moved fast, like a snake striking its prey. She had those athletic fast twitch skills.

"Here. Let me see."

Nova looked at her friend, hesitating. The cold, uneasy feeling she'd gotten when she'd first peeked into the back of the van was growing. Mackenna saw the hesitation in Nova's eyes and darted forward, snatching the packet of money from Nova's hand before she could decide to hand it over or not.

"Hey!"

Mackenna thumbed through the money while Isaac stepped back from the doorway and shouted to the other dudes to come quick. Nova stood up and exited the upside-down cargo hold, returning to the world of wind and heat and fading sunlight. Even though they had barely started up the mountain yet, she could already see far across the plain below. Mackenna was right. No other vehicles were in sight for miles. Nova had never seen such a deserted stretch of highway. She peered up the mountainside and checked for traffic coming from higher up. Nothing moved and all she could hear was the wind, rustling the trees.

Landon and Wyatt came around to the back of the van. The two boys looked at Mackenna, who was grinning and slapping the bundle of cash against her palm, her eyes gleaming with manic joy.

"It's our lucky day, fuckers."

The boys stared at the cash, not understanding. Mackenna nodded at the van. "Check it out."

The dudes took turns grabbing a bundle of cash each and thumbing through it themselves. This looked surreal to Nova, everyone except her now holding their own ten thousand dollars in cash by the side of the road, in broad daylight. The van still smelled like gas, but at least it hadn't blown up yet. She wondered what it would be like to watch the cube burn. Millions of dollars igniting in a hot blaze. You'd be able to see smoke rising from the valley below, maybe all the way to the last town they'd passed through twenty miles ago.

What was that town called again? Some kind of insect?

Oh yeah.

Scorpion. Scorpion Creek.

"This isn't our money," Nova said, patting the side of the armored van. "We can't just take it."

Mackenna snorted and looked around, shielding her eyes with the flat of her hand. "Well, I don't see anybody around, do you? Haven't you ever heard of finders keepers?"

"This is a lot of money," Landon said. "This is so much money."

"Thanks, Captain Obvious," Isaac said, smirking. "Nobody else here noticed that."

"We'll never need to work again," Wyatt said, his eyes foggy at this idea. "Even after splitting it five ways. We could pay our student loans. We could all buy our own mansion and swimming pool."

"Shit," Landon said, "my family already has a swimming pool. I'm going to buy my own private plane and travel around the world."

"You mean, we'll travel around the world," Mackenna said, putting her arms Landon's neck and giving him a kiss. "We'll be a millionaire power couple. How fun will that be?"

Isaac poked his head into the back of the van again. "Nova's right, though," he said, his voice muffled. "This isn't our money. If we take it, somebody will come looking for it, sooner or later. The armored van company probably has its own detectives."

"How do you know that?" Mackenna said. "You don't know."

Isaac looked back at the group.

"Have you ever heard the expression nothing in life is free? This random van stuffed with cash probably is included in that."

"Shit, why are you fighting this, dude?" Landon asked, scratching the side of his head. "Is it because you're Jewish?"

Wyatt laughed.

"Oh fuck. Landon's racist. I knew it."

"I just meant are you worried about the stereotype," Landon said, looking sheepish. "About how Jews love money so much. Like, are you worried about reinforcing it?"

Wyatt laughed again and slapped Isaac on the back.

Isaac rolled his eyes. "No, dipshit. I'm not worried about reinforcing Jewish stereotypes. Also, fun fact, everyone loves money. Our stereotype is more about how good we are at handling it, fuckface."

"Oh. Right."

Mackenna clapped her hands together. It was a loud and demanded attention.

"Hey, I know! How about we stand around with our thumbs up our butts until another car comes along and sees us? How about we do that, huh?"

Everyone looked at each other. Wyatt cleared his throat and Nova knew what Wyatt was going to say before he said it. She'd known this suggestion would be inevitable since the moment she'd first argued the money wasn't theirs. It was how groups of people had been making huge mistakes since the beginning of time.

"Okay," Wyatt said, raising his arm in the air. "Let's take a vote."

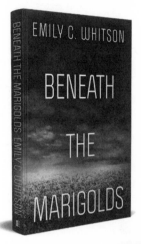
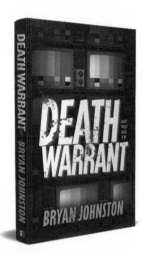
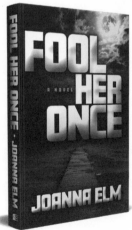

CamCat
Books